# ELVA BIRCH'S SERIES STARTER

ELVA BIRCH

# INTRODUCTION

Welcome reader!

This collection is a portal to worlds of whimsy and wonder, and I invite you to pull up a comfortable chair and a favorite drink and stay a while. This set of complete stories introduces four of my series: *The Royal Dragons of Alaska*, *A Day Care for Shifters (World of Instinct)*, *Suddenly Shifters*, and *Lawn Ornament Shifters*.

Most of my stories take place in different worlds with different shifting rules—some shifters take their clothing with them, some don't, some even have to learn to do it! Some of the settings will feel very familiar—Nickel City could be any small town in Montana, except for the secret shifters!—and some will have intriguing differences. From an alternate history version of Alaska ruled by dragons, to a city where flamingo shifters and gnomes and trolls live together, to a simple un-magical town where suddenly ordinary people are able to shift into animals, all of them have internal consistency and a dash of magic and enchantment.

In each tale, you'll find humor, heart, and a happy ending. I like capable heroines and non-toxic heroes, complicated and diverse characters with relatable quirks. Some of the series are more interconnected than others, but every book follows the emotional journey of a central pair of characters (or more!) to a satisfying end...even if there are some lingering questions about overall plots arcs. I promise to bring you all the answers by the end of a series, with a thrilling and captivating conclusion.

Ready for an escape? Buckle up for adventure, love, and magic and enjoy this introduction to my paranormal fantasy romance!

Love recklessly,
Elva Birch

Subscribe to Elva Birch's mailing list and join her in her Reader's Retreat at Facebook for sneak previews!

# The Dragon Prince
## of
# ALASKA

# ELVA BIRCH

# ROYAL DRAGONS OF ALASKA

This book is part of the Royal Dragons of Alaska series, a modern fantasy romance set in an alternate Alaska ruled by a secret dragon shifting monarchy. Reluctant royalty! Relentless enemies! These stories are steamy and full of adventure, with rich world building, humor, and romance.

All of my work stands alone (there's always a satisfying happy ever after for a featured couple and no cliffhangers!) but there is a strong story arc across this complete series, with a thrilling conclusion and a lot of surprises you may not want to spoil. This is the recommended reading order:

# CHAPTER 1

Carina Andresen surged to her feet, sweeping her camp chair out from under her as a make-shift weapon.

*Wolf!* her brain hammered at her. *Wolf!* She was going to become an Alaska tourist statistic and get eaten by a wolf on her second week in the kingdom.

Logic slowly caught up with her panic.

The animal across the campfire from her was smaller and *doggier* than a wolf, and it was only a moment before Carina could get her breath and heartbeat back under control and recognize that it was well-groomed, shyly eyeing her sizzling hot dog, and wagging its tail.

Alaska probably had stray dogs, too; she wasn't *that* far from civilization.

"Hi there, sweetie," Carina said, her voice still unnaturally high as she put her chair back on its legs. "Does that smell good? Want a bit of hot dog?" Carina turned the hot dog in the flame and waggled it suggestively.

The non-edible dog sped up his tail and when Carina broke off a piece of the meat and dropped it beside her, he crept around the fire and slurped it eagerly up off the ground.

The second bite he took gently from her fingers, and by the second hot dog she dared to pet him.

Within about thirty minutes and five hot dogs, he was leaning on her and letting her scratch his ears and neck as he wagged his tail and groaned in delight.

"Oh, you're just a dear," Carina said. "I bet someone's missing you." He was a husky mix, Carina guessed; he was tall and strong, with a long, thick coat of dark gray fur and white feet. His ears were upright, and his tail was long and feathered. He didn't have a collar, but he was clearly friendly. "You want some water?"

The dog licked his lips as if he had understood, and Carina carefully stood so she didn't frighten him.

But he seemed to be past any shyness now, and he followed Carina to her van trustingly, tail waving happily. He drank the offered water from a frying pan, and then tried to give Carina a kiss dripping with slobber.

"You probably already have a name," Carina said, laughingly trying to escape the wet tongue. "But I'm going to call you Shadow for now." She had a grubby towel hanging from her clothesline and used it to dry off his face. They played a gentle game of tug-of-war, testing each other's strength and manners.

Shadow seemed to approve of his new name and gave her a canine grin once she'd won the towel back from him.

"Alright, Shadow, let's go collect some more firewood."

The area was rich with downed wood to harvest, and with the assistance of a folding hand saw, Carina was able to find several heaping armloads of solid, dry wood, enough to keep a cheerful fire going for a few days if she was frugal. It was comforting to have Shadow around for the task; she wasn't quite as nervous about the noises she heard, and he was a happy distraction from her own brain.

He frolicked with her, and found a stick three times his own length to drag around possessively.

"So helpful!" Carina laughed at him, as he knocked over an empty pot and swiped her across the knees so that she nearly fell.

When she sat down beside the crackling fire in her low camp

chair, Shadow abandoned his prize stick and crowded close to lay his head on her knee. Carina petted him absently.

"Someone's looking for you, you big softy," she said regretfully. She would have to try to reunite the dog with his owner but, for now, it was nice having a companion around the camp.

Of all the things she expected when she went running for the wilderness, she had never guessed that the silence would be the worst. She had been camping plenty, but it was always *with* some-one. Since their parents had died, that someone was usually her sister, June, but sometimes it was a friend or a roommate. She was used to having someone to point out birds and animals to, someone to share chores with, stretch out tarps with. When it was just her, the spaces seemed vaster, the wind bit harder, and even the birds were less cheerful.

"You probably don't care about the birds that would make my life list," she told Shadow mournfully.

Shadow wagged his tail in a rustle of leaves.

She didn't have her life list anymore to add to anyway. Every-thing had been left behind: her phone, her computer, her identity. Her entire life was on hold. She had the van to live in, some supplies and a small nest egg to start from, so she ought to be able to stay out of sight long enough to regroup and…she didn't know what to do from here. Find a journalist willing to take her story and clear her name?

To fill the quiet, and to help ignore the ache in her chest, she read aloud from the brochure on Alaska that she had been given at the border station. She'd found it that evening while she was emptying the glovebox to take stock of supplies, and Shadow seemed as good a listener as any.

"Like many modern monarchies, Alaska has an elected council of officials who do most of the day to day rulings of this vast, rich land. The royal family is steeped in tradition and mystery, and holds many veto powers, as well as acting as ambassadors to other coun-tries. Known as the Dragon King, the Alaskan sovereign is a reserved figure who rarely appears in public. Margaret, the Queen of Alaska, died twelve years ago, leaving behind six sons." There was a photo, with boys ranging from about seven to maybe twenty-five. Two of the middle children were identical. One of the twins was wearing a hockey jersey and grinning, the other wore glasses and looked annoyed. The oldest—or at least the tallest—was frowning seriously at the others. The only blonde of the bunch was one of the middle boys, who was looking intently at the camera. The youngest looked painfully bored. They all had tongue-twisting names of more syllables than Carina wanted to try pronouncing.

Carina thought it was an interesting photo. The tension between the oldest two was palpable, and they were all dressed surprisingly casually. She didn't follow royal gossip much beyond scanning headlines at grocery store checkouts, but Alaska never seemed to make waves; they were rarely involved in dramas and scandals.

Shadow raised his head and cocked his head at some imagined noise in the forest.

"That's a lot of siblings," Carina observed, ruffling his ears. She felt so much safer having him beside her. "Just one sister was more than enough for me." She didn't want to admit how much she missed that sister right now.

Shadow returned his head to her knee. "Alaska is a member of the Small Kingdoms Alliance, an exclusive collective of independent monarchies scattered throughout the world. Although Alaska has large amounts of land, they qualify for membership because of their small population."

Carina turned the brochure over. "There are hot springs about fifty miles north of Fairbanks! I hope to make it there." *Before* she ran out of cash. It looked expensive. Maybe she could get work there...she'd heard that it wasn't hard to find under-the-table jobs in this country.

Shadow suddenly leapt to his feet, barking at something crashing through the woods behind them and Carina nearly tipped over backwards in her camp chair trying to stand up.

She expected to find a moose, or possibly a bear, and she was already picking up the chair to use as a flimsy defense against a charging wild animal.

But it was only a man stepping out of the woods, in an official dark blue uniform emblazoned with the eight gold stars of Alaska.

For a moment, terror every bit as keen as the panic that had gripped her at the first sight of Shadow washed over her. They'd found her.

"You're trespassing on royal land and I'm going to have to ask you to leave," he said.

She realized with relief that it wasn't a police officer. He was only a park ranger.

# CHAPTER 2

Toren could not understand his dragon's laser focus on their task. He was just rousting a squatter. They got a few colorful characters every year, usually in tents or old trucks, camping in the fringes of the royal forest. Once, one of the interlopers had managed to get a stolen train car hauled up an old logging road. Toren had helped Kenth carry the thing back to the rail yard, swearing the whole way.

He circled over the place—a break in the trees by a little stream with birch trees shaking down golden coins of leaves. There was a van pulled up to one side, one of the old style VW camper vans with the top that popped up. The squatter had obviously been there for some time; there was a blue tarp covering an area by the fire, and laundry was drying on lines strung between trees. There was a substantial pile of scavenged firewood, and an axe and handsaw lay nearby with a pair of gloves.

*There*, his dragon urged, as if Toren was incapable of noticing the figure sitting by a crackling fire with a gray dog.

*I see him*, Toren said.

*Her*, his dragon corrected avidly.

Toren looked for a place nearby to land and shift. If he could get the squatter to leave without revealing his dragon, he was supposed to do that, but he had some leeway; dragons—all shifters —were secret, but the type of person to trespass on royal lands was rarely the type to be taken seriously if they were raving about flying monsters.

It was a narrow clearing, mostly taken up by the dirty white van, so branches broke as Toren landed behind it, and he shifted swiftly, just as the dog barked in alarm and the woman—*Yes, her!*—rose from her fireside chair and turned.

Something washed over him—terror, he thought—and he realized that it was *her* terror. He felt like he'd just been drenched in cold water.

*Make her feel better! Fix this!* his dragon demanded.

Toren said the only words he could form, the ones he'd been practicing on his flight here: "You're trespassing on royal land and I'm going to have to ask you to leave."

For a moment, Toren had a bad feeling that she was going to fight him, her chair held in two grim hands and her dog growling at her side, then she laughed in giddy relief and lowered it.

"I know I'm not supposed to be here," she said sheepishly. "It was just such a nice place, and...um...the campground was full?" She was a terrible liar, blushing and full of hesitation, and Toren knew that tourist season was already ebbing. "If I promise to leave tomorrow, can I at least stay overnight and pack up in the morning?"

Toren would have agreed to anything she asked, would have handed over his entire hoard at the very hint of her desire for it. He felt like he was looking straight into her, straight at his own destiny, and he could feel all of her courage and all of her aching vulnerability. He had never been so swept away, like he was feeling too many emotions to fit in just this moment, like he was being flooded by a lifetime of them.

She was American, by her accent, and had been camping for some time by her smoky scent and messy braided hair. She was also, unwashed state or not, the most gorgeous woman that Toren had ever laid eyes on. Her face was red-cheeked and round, and the hopeful smile she was shining at him was utterly enchanting. Her sun-streaked blonde hair was escaping around her face like a golden halo, and her eyes were a hazel green that made Toren think of autumn moss and…kissing.

Everything about her made him think of kissing.

"You're on royal land," he repeated faintly.

"Do you really have to kick me out before dinner, though?" she asked winningly. He could somehow *feel* the almost hysterical relief off of her in waves. "I fed Shadow the rest of my hot dogs, but I have a can of chicken and a box of macaroni and cheese. The good kind of mac and cheese, with the squeeze cheese, and it makes way too much for me to eat by myself."

"You're inviting me to dinner?" Toren asked, dazzled.

*Accept her offer*, his dragon hissed at him. *Accept anything she offers us!*

"That's not something illegal here is it?" The woman's smile hesitated and Toren was sideswiped by her spike of fear. "I'm not trying to…er…bribe you or anything. Exactly. I just…" she looked down at her hands. "Never mind."

"No, nothing like that, nothing illegal," Toren assured her in a blind panic. "I'd… I'd like that!"

"I'm Carina," she said, setting her camp chair back down. "Have a, ah…" she looked around. "Let me get you a chair. Do you mind putting a log on the fire?"

*Carina.* It was the most beautiful name that Toren had ever heard. "Sure."

"I promise it's all deadwood, I didn't chop down any royal trees," she teased. "Or shoot any royal moose!"

She went around the back of the van and Toren picked up a few pieces of wood from the pile by the campfire and tossed them onto the flame.

The fire promptly went out.

"Oh, no," Toren said in a panic. "What have I done?" He poked at it futilely and all it did was smoke and sputter. The dog wagged his tail in clear amusement.

Just as Toren wondered if he had time to shift into his dragon form and light it on fire decisively, Carina returned with a second, mismatched camp chair, folded tight in a roll.

"What did you do to my fire?" she asked in horror.

"I, er, added wood?"

"You smothered the poor thing!" Carina said, shaking her head. She knelt and skillfully separated the logs, coaxing reluctant flame back to life. "You have to give it air, you know."

"I'm Toren," he managed to tell her, taking the chair as she stood back up. Her dog was sniffing his leg curiously and Toren cautiously patted his head before he tried to figure out which parts of the chair were which.

She watched him try unsuccessfully to set it up for a moment before she took the folded fabric and metal tubes back from him, unsnapped a strap, grasped two of the limbs, and magically set it down as an actual chair.

Toren sat gingerly into it. "Thanks." He almost tipped over backwards as the gray dog stuck its nose into his side. "I like your dog."

"He's not mine," she said swiftly, though she felt almost possessive to Toren's addled senses. "He just showed up a little while ago. He likes hot dogs, and I'm calling him Shadow."

"He seems friendly." Toren said, patting him absently. "No collar?" He was still having trouble thinking around the dazzling presence of Carina, who was busily fussing with the fire and balancing a grate over the flames between two piles of rocks.

"Nope," Carina said. "I should take him to Fairbanks and have him checked for a chip."

"Will you keep him?" Toren asked. "If he doesn't have an owner?"

"I'd like to," Carina said, kneeling beside him to rub Shadow's ears. "But I didn't really budget for dog food. And look how well cared for he is! Someone is bound to be looking for him."

Toren could hear the longing in her voice. She'd already lost her heart to the canine and Toren was unfairly jealous.

"Do you really live here?" he had to ask. "In that van?"

"Well, I did," Carina said plaintively. "But apparently I'm on royal land."

Toren wanted to drown in those eyes. How could he explain that he wanted her to stay with him…not just for a day or a week, but for a lifetime. *Why do I feel like I've been hit on the head?* he demanded of his dragon.

*Our mate,* his dragon sighed, and Toren really did fall out of his rickety camp chair then, startling so hard that he grabbed the arm and managed to half-fold it around himself as Shadow dashed back with a yelp of alarm before he toppled backwards.

Carina's laughter was like sunshine as she reached to help him up. "I should have warned you about the chair," she said kindly, and then her hand was in Toren's, and something inside him clicked.

He'd never expected true love, and it had honestly never occurred to him before that the Compact might tap *him* to be king. But now, nothing could be more right, or more perfect, because Carina *was* his mate, and he recognized her, who she was, and everything they could be together.

And then he remembered what else that meant.

# CHAPTER 3

*C*arina pulled Toren easily to his feet and then stood too close to him for a moment before she could get her raging hormones under control. He was the most gorgeous man she'd ever seen, and it seemed like it had been a long time since she'd been this close to one.

He was tall and strong, with a grin frozen on his face that showed straight, white teeth. He had dark hair and light eyes that were probably blue but looked almost silver in the evening light. He had a fresh, clean-shaven look that was either youth or really good personal grooming, and he smelled like night sky and stone, with a weird after-scent of sulfur. She kept thinking that his face must be really expressive, because she could read his confusion like a book, but really, he was mostly just grinning like some kind of sports model who'd just won a competition he hadn't entered.

"Thanks," he breathed.

"First time in a camp chair?" Carina teased, finally remembering to let go of him. "I'm guessing you haven't been a park ranger long."

"No," he said. "Not long. Brand new. To all of this."

His clothing certainly did look new, and Carina thought with appreciation that the flattering lines of the Alaska ranger garb was a lot better than either the American or the Canadian version. She'd always been a sucker for a guy in a uniform, but this was something more. The stars looked like real gold, and the detail in the stitching...made her realize that she was still standing entirely too close. She seemed to be swirling in emotions, and none of them really made sense. Some of them didn't even seem to be *hers*, and that was just crazy.

"Anyway, I'm sorry about the chair," Carina said apologetically, stepping back. "I don't use it and didn't realize what a piece of crap it is." She set it back up again, noting that one of the arms was considerably more bent than it had been.

"You live here *alone?*" Toren eyed the chair in challenge and once again lowered himself into it.

"It's the twenty-first century. Women do that all the time nowadays." Carina tamped down her flash of fear. He was just asking an innocent question. He probably wasn't thinking that it seemed *suspicious*.

He blushed. "I meant no offense, I only...ah..."

The wind chose that moment to shift, and they got faces full of thick smoke. Carina coughed and moved, only to have the smoke follow her. "It knows," she said, waving ineffectively in front of her face as her eyes stung from the irritation. "Oh, the water is ready!"

"Can I help?" Toren threatened to tip over his camp chair trying to stand up. The smoke didn't seem to bother *him* at all.

"No, sit! I got this. There's only room for one camp cook."

He subsided.

The pot she'd put over the fire was starting to boil, and she opened the macaroni and cheese box and dumped in the noodles. She popped the top off of the canned chicken and drained it into the hottest part of the fire, then set it to the side of the grate to warm.

"You...ah...seem really good at this." Toren seemed to have the hang of his camp chair at last and was at least no longer tipping one direction and then another.

Carina reminded herself that it was an innocent question, not an interrogation. "Yeah," she said cautiously. "I went camping a lot as a kid. Things sort of went sideways with my life and Alaska seemed like the kind of place I could...get away for awhile."

To her surprise, he didn't follow that with questions, and Carina was glad she didn't have to tell him any lies. She was terrible at lying.

"So what do you do? When you aren't being kind of hopeless at rangering?"

Toren grinned at her again, and Carina felt her heart give a dangerous skip.

"I play hockey, go hunting. I like...ah...flying?"

Carina laughed. "You really are the cliché of an Alaskan. Even if your campfire skills do leave a lot to be desired."

She was beginning to doubt he really was a ranger, even a brand spanking new one. There wasn't any other real reason for a strange guy in an official Alaska uniform to be wandering around in the forest, but Carina didn't want to pry. And as long as it wasn't an official Alaska *police officer* uniform, she didn't really care what he was; if he wasn't going to enforce his move-out orders, she was going to stay as long as she possibly could.

Mostly because she had no idea what to do next.

She stirred the noodles and tasted one, burning her fingertips as she spooned it out of the bubbling water. "Ouch, ouch. Needs another minute."

She took that time to go to the van and dig out a second bowl and spoon. Then she considered, and got a third bowl. On her way back, she paused to stare at her visitors.

Toren was sitting in a plume of smoke, completely oblivious to it, murmuring at Shadow as he stroked his ears. The canine was leaning his head into the man's lap, his fluffy tail thumping in the dirt.

In the space of about an hour, she had somehow acquired a guy and a dog...and Carina was disturbed by how comfortable it felt. She liked the idea of sharing her food, of having someone to make observations to, of having someone to warm her cold bed...

Carina shook her head firmly. She had problems to solve, problems that didn't involve roping anyone else into her mess, and if she stood here daydreaming like a schoolgirl, her next problem was going to be a mass of overcooked noodles she couldn't serve anyone. Even the dog would turn up his nose.

She drained the noodles and stirred in the cheese packet and canned chicken more vigorously than strictly necessary. "Dinner is served," she said, setting a small bowl in front of Shadow, who wolfed it down like she hadn't just fed him all her hot dogs. "A spoon for the park ranger with opposable thumbs," she said, handing Toren the utensil and a heaping bowl of food.

She settled into her own camp chair and tried not to watch Toren too obviously. He took the bowl with a polite murmur of thanks, but his look was clearly skeptical. It was a rather unattractive color and texture and Carina suspected that he was used to better fare by his careful manners and hesitant taste.

But campfire smoke had a near-magic way of making everything taste better than it otherwise should, and Toren's face lit up with delight. "This is great," he said, eating enthusiastically.

Carina was surprised to burn her tongue on her first bite, given the way both Shadow and Toren had downed theirs without hesitation. "One of my favorite meals," she said, sucking air into her mouth to cool it. "Not that classy, maybe, but always delicious."

It was crazy, how sexy he managed to look, eating fluorescent food from a chipped plastic bowl with a bent spoon. He had clearly mastered the camp chair, perched with his weight carefully balanced on the rickety structure. Carina couldn't stop watching the way his shoulders moved, and the way the evening light fell on his cheekbones. He was utterly gorgeous, and she had never been so immediately attracted to someone in her life.

She had to wrench her eyes away and focus on her food. She had bigger things to worry about.

He finished first, and Shadow came to beg at her feet as she polished off her last few bites. "You got yours," she scolded him. "*And* all my hot dogs."

He twitched his ears down and wagged his tail eagerly.

She let him lick out her bowl, and then the pot she'd stirred the food in, and she and Toren shared a giggle as he had to chase it around until he could corner it against the foot of Toren's chair, nearly unseating him again.

"Can I get you a drink?" she offered, when she stood to collect the dishes. "I've got water, I think there's a beer left, tea, instant coffee."

"Thank you, no. May I help you…in some fashion?" Park ranger or not, he had beautiful manners, Carina thought. Not the kind of kiss-up manners of someone who wanted something, just casual, well-bred polish. Maybe it was just how Alaskans were. Carina had been expecting more surliness and rough edges.

"Thanks, no. I've got a system." Carina rinsed the dishes in the stream and set the pot full of stream water on the grate. She wouldn't drink it, but it was fine for washing up.

The sun was just down behind the mountains, slowly sinking, and the sky overhead was purple and streaked with red and orange clouds. The falling birch leaves made a soothing whisper just audible above the babbling of the little stream, and it smelled like campfire smoke and moss.

"This is my favorite time of day, and my favorite time of year," Carina said contentedly, for the rare moment able just to enjoy it. "The falling leaves, the smell of the forest…"

"It's beautiful," Toren said, gazing around as if he'd never seen anything like it.

"The best part is that all the mosquitoes are dead," Carina said cheerfully. "A few weeks ago, they would have driven us into the van in about ten minutes." She had to try very hard not to think about him shut in her van with her, or what they might do on the fold-down bed.

Shadow came with her on the second trip to the stream with a collapsible bucket for rinse water, and put his front feet in.

"If you go swimming, you are not stepping one foot into the van tonight," Carina warned him.

For a moment, she actually thought he understood her and was going to stay dry. Then he plunged into the stream, frolicking out into the flowing water and splashing her. "Argh!! That's *cold!*"

# CHAPTER 4

*T*oren wished he'd accepted a drink. Something to do with his hands. Somewhere to look that wasn't *her*.

He nearly upended trying to get out of his camp chair again at Carina's cry of outrage, and he was standing before he realized that the stray dog had simply splashed her. It was easier to continue standing than to try to get back into the chair, so he came to help her up the bank from the stream.

"Can I...?"

"I've got it," she said firmly, but his hands were already outstretched to help her up the bank, and after the slightest hesitation, she put her free hand in his and let him haul her up, directly into his arms.

He hadn't meant to, but there she was, so close to him, and Toren wanted so badly to kiss her that he felt like his mouth was burning.

She was gazing up at him, her lips just parted, her hand still holding tight to his, her body against his, and Toren might have risked dipping his head to kiss her...if Shadow had not chosen that moment to come galloping up the bank to wedge his wet body between them.

They broke apart with exclamations of disgust, laughing as Shadow shook and sprayed them with cold creek water.

The moment of opportunity was gone and Toren desperately wanted that moment back. If he were suave like Fask, or smart like Rian, or funny like Tray, maybe he'd know what to do, how to get from this awkward place where they were to that place where he could tell her who he was...what *she* was.

Laughter died on his mouth.

She was his mate.

She was his *mate*.

And if he'd found his mate, he was first in line to be king. And not just the first *in line*, but they'd be jamming a crown on his head before *spring*.

Carina was kneeling by the fire, stirring the hot water in the cook pot with a few drops of camp soap and efficiently swiping out their bowls before rinsing them in the clear creek water.

"Want to help me dry?" she asked, and Toren startled from his thoughts. He wished he'd kissed her when he had the chance, because now he was alternating between cold terror and hot need in a wild seesaw, and there were emotions in his head that weren't his and he couldn't make sense of them.

"No!" he said, more firmly than he meant to. "I have to go."

Carina stood up, a towel in one hand and a chipped bowl in the other. "So soon?" she said, and Toren thought she was trying to say it humorously, but his ears were roaring.

"I'm sorry," he said, and he was, for the mess he was about to pull her into.

"Do I have to leave tonight?" Carina asked.

For a moment, Toren was confused, thinking she meant 'go back to the castle with him,' then he remembered that she thought he was just a ranger, evicting her from an illegal camping site.

"No," he said blindly. "No, stay here tonight. If anyone gives you trouble...tell them Toren said you could stay. But no one will. Give you trouble, I mean."

"Right," Carina said. Did she sound a little forlorn? Toren was having difficulty separating his own emotions from hers. "Thanks."

"Thanks for dinner," Toren said, reluctant to go, but at the same time desperate to escape.

Carina waved her towel at him. "My pleasure," she said flippantly.

Shadow looked from her to him, and back again, clearly picking up on the unexpected tension between them, and Toren bolted down the old road that Carina had driven the van up.

Toren had to walk quite a distance to find a space big enough to shift and take off in—landing was a little more contained, but lift-off required wingspan. It gave him far too much time to think about everything that was wrong with the whole situation...and everything that was right about Carina's smile, and her lithe body, and her sweet, brave laugh.

Then he was in the air, circling once above her and straining against his dragon's desire to return.

If she looked up, she would only see a shimmer in the air, a hint of the aurora against the deepening night sky.

He wanted nothing more than to dive into the clearing and scoop Carina up into his arms and tell her...what? That he was a dragon shifter? Oh, and not just any dragon shifter, supposing *that* revelation didn't send her running, but the youngest prince of Alaska? And then he'd have to explain that by meeting her, he'd just been selected to be king?

Would she want to be a queen? Toren wondered. Wasn't that the fantasy? Rags to riches? Van to castle?

But he pictured her, squatting next to the fire to stir noodles, remembered her simple, addictive delight in camp food and falling leaves. None of the riches he could offer her would ever cause so much uncomplicated joy.

And joy was all he wanted to give her.

He made himself fly back to the capital, over the wild forests and alpine swamps to Fairbanks, where the castle loomed in the hills west of the little city.

He didn't go straight to his own rooms, but landed on Rian's balcony, wings outspread to brake his flight. He shifted and knocked, then barged in, because the only thing Rian would have going on was a hot date with a book.

Rian looked up crossly from his computer. "Did you get rid of him?"

Toren stared blankly, then remembered his original duty. "No. I mean, it wasn't…Rian, I need your help."

# CHAPTER 5

"Sure," Carina said, pouring a fresh bucket of water over the smoldering ashes. "Toren, the 'brand new park ranger,' gave me *personal* permission to camp on royal land. That excuse will go over great."

She didn't know who Toren really was, beyond *gorgeous* and *funny* and perpetually looking a little stunned, but she knew what he wasn't: a ranger. His arrival was weird, his departure even weirder, and Carina had been burned by *weird* too recently to feel good about it.

She wasn't going to wait around for whoever was going to come hassle her next. She'd felt inexplicably safe in his presence, but now that he was gone, all of the gravity of her situation had come tumbling back. And feeling *his* feelings? That was the most ridiculous part of it all.

"I should have stuck to the campgrounds," she told Shadow fiercely as she untied the tarp and dragged it to the widest space that she could find in order to fold it. "I should have stayed strictly legit." Shadow tried to walk out on it as Carina dragged one edge of the tarp to the other. "Get off, mutt!"

Shadow scampered away, his nails making the plastic rustle like the leaves that were swirling down to cover it as she folded the tarp.

"I should never have gotten complacent." The wood tools were thrown into the back of the van with the folded tarp and the messily coiled ropes.

"Idiot," she scolded herself as she folded her laundry and wound up the line. "You let yourself get lazy."

Alaska had been so beautiful and peaceful, so far away from people and bustling cities. It was easy to think that she could stay hidden for a while.

Shadow followed her from task to task, clearly puzzled by her strange human behavior. He sniffed the cold fire, and finally lay in front of the side door to the van. His message was clear: if Carina was leaving, he was, too.

Carina stepped over him to secure the built-in camp stove and switch the propane refrigerator to travel mode. Then she stretched up on her toes and pulled the bar that lowered the tented pop-top. In moments, the van was dark and snug, the canvas top tucked in and buckled into place.

For a moment, Carina sat on the back bench and looked around out of the windows, trying to recapture some of the peace and safety she'd felt when Toren was there.

Shadow cautiously crept up into the vehicle and put his head on her knee. She petted him before she realized that he was still wet from splashing in the creek. "Ugh. Alright, let's pull up our tent stakes and get out of here."

She pulled the door shut and Shadow whined from inside as she circled the van, turning off the propane and giving the dark camp-site one last sweep with a flashlight; the shadows leaping away from her beam made Carina feel jumpy and nervous. Convinced that she wasn't leaving anything behind, she hopped into the driver's seat and started the van.

Shadow hopped into the passenger seat and sat, eagerly looking out of the windows.

"You are definitely not just a stray," Carina said, reaching over to scratch his ears as she adjusted the seat and turned on the head-lights. It was very comfortable to have a travel companion.

She let herself indulge in a moment of imagination, picturing Toren in the seat beside her, remembering that queer feeling of safety and wholeness. She took her hand back from Shadow and put it firmly on the steering wheel.

Then she pointed the headlights back down the road she'd driven in on and set off. Again.

# CHAPTER 6

"*P*romise you won't tell anyone," Toren begged. "Promise!"

Rian frowned at him. "Tor, you're being really weird."

That wasn't a promise; Rian had been extremely careful about making promises he didn't want to keep since the time his twin brother Tray had gotten him to agree to wear nothing but wool socks for an entire week. The rest of the palace had been scandalized by his nudity, and photographs of the prank had made it into an international gossip magazine and from there had spread to the Internet. Rian had very soberly declared that it served him right for being imprecise about the terms of the bet, and vowed never to let it happen again, but he wouldn't put clothing on until the week was up.

Because he had promised.

It was one reason Toren had come to him; if Rian promised to keep it quiet, he would.

"I'm not going to tell you until you swear not to tell anyone," Toren said fiercely.

Rian frowned. "If you're in trouble..."

"I am in so much trouble," Toren confessed, then he pressed his lips together firmly.

"What if it's something I feel obligated to report?" Rian asked.

Toren raised an eyebrow and narrowed his mouth further.

"What if I think that keeping it secret will make it worse?" Rian prodded.

Toren couldn't make his lips any thinner, but he tried.

"Fine," Rian conceded.

"Say it," Toren insisted, unwilling to get caught in any loopholes.

"I promise not to tell anyone unless…"

"Just promise not to tell!" Toren begged.

"I promise not to tell," Rian agreed reluctantly.

"Well, you know how father has been…indisposed for some time?"

It was an understatement. It wasn't unusual for older dragons to hibernate for periods of time, even as long as a year. But what had started as a lengthy nap had stretched into an unusual slumber, and then into a worrisome coma. They'd been trying to rouse him for several years now, without so much as a flicker of an eyelid.

"It has come to my attention," Rian said sarcastically.

To be fair, it hadn't been a problem at first; the king's position was largely for show and Fask had been able to step into his shoes with the barest public deflections about his father's health and travel.

"And you know how we need to have a king to send to the Compact Renewal before next summer?"

"Still with you, little brother."

"And you know how the next king is picked…"

Rian was starting to look more suspicious and less irritated. "If you listen to Fask, it's an outdated tradition. Supposedly, the Compact shows the next king his mate and there's some ridiculously vague double-speak about sparking recognition. The Compact is tricky, though; I've never been sure it wasn't just a roundabout way of saying the king must be married."

"It's not," Toren said with absolute certainty.

Rian's stunned silence was a weak salve for the ratcheting discomfort that Toren was feeling. "You *met* your mate?"

"Her name is Carina, and she was the squatter I was sent to evict, and I've never felt like this before, and she thinks I'm a *park ranger* and Rian, I don't want to be the king and I don't know if she wants to be a queen or not, but I don't even know how to tell her I'm a dragon and she's *American* and I think I'm going to be sick."

"Well," said Rian practically, "if you're going to hurl, do it outside and don't get it on the books. Some of these are first editions."

Toren sat heavily down in a chair, not noticing the books on the cushion until his weight was on them. "Ouch."

Rian made a noise of protest as Toren upended the books onto the floor and flopped back into the chair.

"Where is she now?" Rian asked, looking around as if Toren had somehow smuggled her into the room without his notice.

"I left her at her camping spot...she's got one of those antique VW pop-up vans with the tent tops. It's a really nice set up, actually."

"Is she here on a visa? How long has she been here? Do you know anything about her family?"

Toren could only shrug.

"What does she know about you?" Rian scowled.

"She knows I'm an idiot who can barely sit upright in a camp chair," Toren groaned, running fingers through his short hair.

"She's really your mate?"

Toren's dragon gave a sigh of longing. "Oh, yeah," Toren agreed dreamily. "I looked into her eyes and it was...this...thing. I could see right into her soul. It was like this beautiful, crazy...thing." Orator, he was not.

"So, are you going to bring her here?"

That would be the logical thing, Toren knew. It was also pretty much the last thing he wanted to do. He wanted to hoard her to himself, to steal her and run away from all the complications finding her had added to his life.

Rian frowned, perhaps guessing his train of thought. "Okay,

then...have you considered asking her on a date and asking her the kinds of questions you would ask a date?"

"A date?"

Rian gave a long-suffering sigh. "I don't know why you came to me for romantic advice," he said, shaking his head. "Wouldn't Tray have been better at this? Or *anyone*? But sure, a date. Take her to that Thai place downtown."

That was as good a plan as any. But, "What am I supposed to do about the...*king*...thing."

Rian frowned at that. "Well, I guess you'll be king."

Toren moaned. "No one wants that. Least of all me. Fask is the oldest, and he's the best at this."

Rian's frown softened. "It's not like we'd all leave you to do it alone, or anything. I mean, I guess it would pretty much just be a formality, no one would expect you to write contracts or anything."

"But only the king can attend the Compact Renewal. And I'd be expected to...do all those diplomatic dragon things..." Toren had only the vaguest idea what those things were; he'd always been happy that Fask enjoyed that kind of thing and that, as the youngest, Toren was generally expected to stay out of the way.

But even *he* knew that if the Compact wasn't renewed by an Alaskan king, they'd be a target for take-over by the other kingdoms; their father's absence was becoming problematic, and many of their enemies were getting restless.

The Compact was the official document that laid out the alliance of the Small Kingdoms and protected the human countries...and the public copy of that document was a heavy tome of thick legal restrictions and trade agreements.

The *private* version of the Compact was a closely-guarded secret, shared only with the member royalty, and it was even longer, more involved, and steeped in structured magic. It was incredibly specific about successions and the power structure of the affiliated kingdoms. And one of the things that was laid out explicitly was that every king had a *mate*, chosen and confirmed by the Compact itself.

The document was periodically renewed, but never altered, and it enforced itself, *absolutely*. If Alaska couldn't send a king to the

Renewal, they would be dropped from the alliance and lose the protections it offered.

"We'll teach you what to say and write your speeches," Rian assured him.

Toren tried to find the words for what was warring in his chest. He'd never loved the spotlight, but even more than that, he didn't want to let his brothers down. He didn't want to let the whole *country* down. They deserved a real king. The kind of king that could actually...rule. The kind of king their father had been.

If he had to wear a crown, he wanted to *earn* it, not just luck into it by finding his mate.

And his mate...

Toren couldn't stop *thinking* about Carina. He kept remembering the graceful way she moved, how brisk and efficient she was, how capable and funny and kind. She took in stray dogs and stray park rangers with equal aplomb, and served boxed macaroni and cheese like it had been specially catered for them.

He wanted desperately to do a date like Rian suggested...but just a date. No photographers, no uniforms, no crowns, no pressure. He wanted to find out what music she liked, where she'd grown up, and what she did for fun. Did she like hockey? Why was she so afraid? How could he protect her? He wanted to see if she tasted the way he imagined, hear what kind of noise she would make when he found all the places that made her blood run hot. He wanted to know if her lips were as soft as they looked, and whether she would...

Rian cleared his throat noisily and Toren realized that he'd been speaking for some time and Toren hadn't heard a word.

"Daydreaming?"

"I think you've got the right idea," Toren said apologetically. "I'll go ask her on a date. We can tell the others later, after I've had a chance to get to know her a little." He started to the balcony, but Rian stopped him.

"It's the middle of the night," he reminded Toren. "Maybe you should ask her in the morning, rather than barging into her campsite while she's sleeping."

Toren nodded and turned around, already trying to formulate his request. *Want to get a cup of coffee?* No, he wanted something better than that. *Will you accompany me to Fairbanks for dinner?* Way too formal.

Toren tripped over the books he'd left on the floor and side-tracked to put them back on the chair. "Thanks, Rian," he said absently, going to the door into the castle.

"Tor," Rian said warningly.

Toren paused in the doorway.

"Secrets are trouble," Rian said. "Secrets will only give you problems."

For a moment, Toren thought he meant keeping the secret of his mate from his brothers, but Rian continued. "Tell her who you are. Especially who you are *now*. All of it."

Toren nodded slowly. "I will," he promised. "I will."

And then Rian did the most unnerving thing of all and bowed his head in unexpected respect.

Toren fled in terror.

# CHAPTER 7

*C*arina pulled into Angel Hot Springs Resort at dawn and parked at the far end of the parking lot. "I'm going to have to get you a collar and a leash at some point," she told Shadow, who eagerly bounded out of the van to sniff for other dogs and stretch his legs.

Her van smelled like damp dog and Carina was surprised to find that she didn't really mind. She yawned. She'd taken a brief nap in a roadside pullout, but was still tired.

"I'm going to have to leave you in here for a little while," she apologized, when she shut Shadow back into the vehicle, and she spent a little time finger-combing the thick hair around his neck first. "You're such a good dog."

Shadow snuffled at her happily, his tail thumping against the back of the passenger seat. He seemed entirely content to stay behind in the van.

Carina took a duffel bag from the back of the van, stuffed a change of clothing, a bathing suit and toiletries into it, and slung it over her shoulder. She made sure the windows were all cracked for Shadow, who was already steaming them up with his hot breath in the crisp morning air.

She stood at the door to the pool house, frowning at her wavery reflection in the glass door. It was an hour until they opened, though she could see people moving around inside as they set up for the day.

"You left your camping spot."

Carina gave a startled yelp and swung around with her duffel bag slipping off her shoulder. She tried to catch it, and between her flailing snatch and the momentum of her turn, managed to slam it into Toren, who was suddenly, alarmingly, standing behind her.

He barely moved at the impact.

"Where did you come from?!" Carina demanded, her heart hammering in her chest. She tried to convince herself that it was only alarm, not the fact that he was even more handsome than she remembered, and standing distractingly close.

"I went back to find you this morning and you weren't there," Toren said, as if that explained anything.

"I was trespassing on royal grounds, remember? I didn't want to get in trouble. Did you *follow* me?" Carina couldn't make sense out of how he would have been able to track her.

"No," Toren said swiftly. "I waited until morning. I didn't want to wake you up, or scare you...though I have apparently done a poor job of not scaring you. And then...I just found you."

Carina wondered if he'd frightened her into shock. Her brain could not figure out how he had checked on her campsite that morning...and still managed to drive this far to find her. The sun was just barely rising over the hills around them now, so how did those logistics even work? Her brain really couldn't think of anything beyond the great, beautiful presence of him, and the way he filled up the shoulders of his uniform. His eyes didn't look any more blue in the early morning light than they had the night before; they were a shimmering silver-gray with crazy amounts of gemstone depth.

"Oh," Carina managed, when she realized that she'd been gazing into them for entirely too long. She grasped desperately for a topic of conversation. "Well, we're here too early. The pools don't open for another hour."

Toren scowled in through the glass doors. "They know me. They'll let us in," he said confidently, and sure enough, when he waved at the little gray-haired man who was busy behind the desk, he came to the door as soon as he saw Toren and unlocked it, starting to bob his head politely.

"You're..."

"We're early," blurted Toren firmly, cutting him off rather rudely. "But I was hoping that we could get in for a soak before breakfast. If it's not any *trouble*."

The man looked a little as if Toren had asked him to hold a snake. "I...er..."

"Not if it will get you into trouble," Carina said with a winning smile. "We can come back later."

The man looked at her, eyes wide, then back at Toren, then back at her, a slow, cautious smile pulling up his mouth that turned knowing. "No, my...er...ma'am. It's no trouble at all. Let me fetch you towels." He bowed them into the pool lobby so respectfully that for a moment, Carina wondered if he was mocking them.

"Being a park ranger has privileges," Carina remarked to Toren in a stage whisper.

She was looking at him, because she couldn't help it, and she caught a blush that betrayed him and made him look even cuter and more confused than ever, and she felt a wave of guilt from him.

"I'm...er...not..."

The man brought them three giant fluffy towels each, and showed them where the dressing rooms were. "Don't I need to buy a swim pass?" Carina asked quietly, eyeing the price chart above the desk. Towels were listed at five Alaskan dollars apiece, and access to the pools started at fifteen.

"I have a pass," Toren assured her, after he had exchanged a significant look with the towel-bearing man.

Carina wasn't going to look a gift towel in the mouth, and every dollar mattered, so she shrugged. "I'll...see you out at the pools, then."

The dressing room was absolutely magnificent, tiled in what looked like marble and jade, and trimmed in gleaming chrome.

Framed mirrors were hung over a short row of sinks, and even the toilets looked like they were marble.

There weren't very many lockers, compared to the number of people that Carina's guidebook had led her to believe visited the springs, and each one was practically an individual closet. She picked one at random and stashed her belongings, hanging her towels on the hooks.

She shimmied into the bathing suit. It was her sister June's, and it was a practical plain-colored one-piece that she suddenly wished was something sexier. She wished *she* were a little sexier. Less skinny. Bigger breasts. Hair that didn't look like birds were nesting in it. She wished a lot of things were different about her life until she firmly lifted her chin and reminded herself that now was *now* and she was going to enjoy it, because things could definitely get worse.

Toren was already out in the room with the pools by the time she found the second entrance to the dressing room.

He hadn't gotten into one of the tubs yet, and Carina had to suck in her breath at the sight of him.

He was tall, and stood with an easy confidence that she had suspected was due to the park ranger uniform but clearly was *not*. His short, dark hair was standing up in spikes that indicated he had obeyed the signs mandating a shower before soaking. He had magnificently muscled arms, and shoulders, and legs, and...

Carina wasn't sure where he'd gotten his blue and gold shorts, as he hadn't been carrying a bag, but they left nothing to the imagination.

And he was looking at her like she was something edible, something that he was starving for, his silvery eyes shining in the low resort lighting. It even seemed like she could *feel* his desire.

He cleared his throat uncomfortably and Carina had to try very hard not to notice that his patriotic shorts were betraying his unmistakable interest. He moved the towel he was holding as subtly as he could manage to preserve his dignity.

"So, which pools do you recommend?" she asked, gazing around at the options. There were a number of small pools like hot tubs with various temperatures marked on electronic read-outs, and a large pool that might even be suitable for swimming, if it wasn't too warm. The whole room was steamy and finished to look like natural rock and landscaping, with tropical potted plants everywhere.

"None of these," Toren said swiftly. "Come see the outdoor pools."

The door to the outdoors was heavy and wooden, with a caribou antler handle. Toren opened it for Carina and stood aside while she stepped out into the bracing cold. "Oh, brrr!" Signs to a rock pool led her down a covered walkway, stepping lightly and quickly over the damp, steaming mats.

The walkway turned a corner and led down into a pool with a long, low ramp. The first step in was shocking, then it was utterly delicious and Carina waded eagerly out into it until she could duck down and put her whole body in, Toren splashing at her heels.

She had to wonder if the chilly walk had tamed his rising desire, but she didn't turn around soon enough to check.

It was just over waist-deep on her, sandy-bottomed, and pleasantly hot. It would be perfect to stand up and cool off just a little, and it was simple to crouch, or use one of the tiered underwater benches to sit with just her shoulders out of the water.

"This is amazing," Carina crowed, letting herself lean back into the water.

It had a slight mineral smell, but it wasn't as overwhelmingly sulfur-smelling as other hot springs she had visited. The pool was landscaped much as the interior pools had been, with rocks that looked mostly natural but were just a little too perfect. Instead of potted plants, there were small spruce trees planted all around so that the pool was shrouded and private from anyone who might be coming from any direction but inside the resort. It was just a little below freezing and the trees were sprinkled with shimmering ice crystals.

Fog wafted from the water, swirling thickly enough to obscure the far end of the pool, where Carina could hear running water.

"Carina…"

Toren wasn't appreciating the talent of the resort's landscaper or the beauty of the frosted trees.

He had followed her into the pool and was gazing at *her*, strange silver eyes gleaming. She couldn't tell what was his desire, or what was hers.

Impulsively, Carina floated towards him, and he put out his arms to catch her.

It was the most natural thing in the world to tip her head up for his kiss.

# CHAPTER 8

She was the most beautiful woman that Toren had ever seen, her body absolutely intoxicating even in the practical, sport-style swimsuit she was wearing. The planes of her face, the modest swell of her breasts, the subtle curve of her hips…Toren had never seen anything he wanted more.

He remembered Rian's words. He didn't *want* to keep secrets from her. He wanted to tell her everything he was, give her everything he had, follow her anywhere, be anything.

"Carina," he started, ready to explain everything.

And then she swam into his arms and lifted her face to his, and he could do nothing but lean down to kiss her the way he'd been dying to since he first saw her brandishing a camp chair at him.

She was every single thing that he'd imagined the entire sleepless night before, her lips like electricity on his, her arms soft and strong and perfect. He could not stop kissing her to breathe, so desperate for her mouth, for the strangely intoxicating feel of her teeth against his tongue.

He could not get enough of how her arms around him felt, her fingers clawing at his shoulders as she drew him closer and wrapped a leg around him, pressing against the erection that he hadn't been able to hide or control.

He nearly drowned them both, trying desperately to hold her closer, to feel more of her, and kiss her more deeply, and they finally dragged apart from each other, panting and hot-eyed.

"Hot," said Carina, dazedly, and Toren realized that their frantic love-making had taken them into the hotter area of the pool. "So! Hot!"

"Mix the water," he advised. "The hot water sits on top, mix up from the bottom and it will be less painful." He glanced around, half-expecting to see a familiar figure materialize from the steam, but they were still alone in the pool.

She followed his advice, and the relief in her eyes was immediate. "Good trick," she said breathlessly.

There was a waterfall at this end of the pool, and they drifted towards it, kissing, floating, nearly falling over. They passed a set of stairs that were chained off, with a sign: "Upper pools reserved for the royal family of Alaska."

Carina gave the sign a curious look, and Toren wondered if this was his opportunity to bring up who he really was.

But Carina was dragging him past it to the waterfall before he could figure out how to explain; it wasn't like he could invite her to the upper pools anyway. It wasn't just a reserved luxury for royalty, those pools were usually many degrees hotter than human flesh could tolerate, and not even the royal family went there without an *invitation.*

Carina ducked into the waterfall, gasping at the cool, driving rush. "Oh," she said in pleasure, closing her eyes and letting it pound down over her head and shoulders. "It's as good as a massage," she said as she stepped away from it shaking her wet head.

Toren, unable to resist, gathered her into his arms and dragged her back into it, and they kissed deeply, the cooler water cloaking them.

When they broke apart at last, they ducked back into the water to warm up again, drifting back to the hotter areas. "You should come here when the weather is colder," Toren told her.

"Colder than this?" Carina protested. "I almost had a heart attack getting out here."

"It's brisker at thirty below," Toren teased. "But the pools feel even better. Everyone freezes their hair and beards into frosty shapes."

"Don't you get frostbite?" Carina said in wonder.

"The water keeps your core so hot, you can't get frostbite. And if your nose or ears feel cold, you can just duck them into the water."

"It's *magical*," Carina said, but she wasn't looking at the pools.

Toren pulled her back into his arms, turning her backwards so that he could simply hold her against him, burying his face into the side of her neck and wrapping her up tightly against him, as much of her against him as they could manage as they half-floated in the steam. It was like licking an ice cube in the face of terrible thirst—a tease of possible satisfaction, but so little compared to what he really wanted.

*Patience,* he told his dragon, and he had to laugh at the turn of events that had *him* cautioning patience. *She is ours.*

*She is ours,* his dragon agreed avidly.

"Toren," she said, twisting in his arms as she put her feet on the sandy bottom of the pool and stood. "Headrush..."

Then her eyes rolled back into her head, and Toren was catching her limp form.

They were back in the hottest part of the pool, Toren realized, and they'd been in the pools for most of the hour, making out avidly. He wasn't bothered by the heat, but she was only human, wasn't used to it, and on an empty stomach, probably dehydrated...

Toren gathered her into his arms and swept her up out of the pool.

# CHAPTER 9

arina came to as Toren waded up the ramp and the cold morning air touched her wet skin. She'd been so hot…and now she was so cold. She shivered and wrapped her arms around Toren. He was bare out of the pool in a way that he hadn't seemed to be when they were submerged together, and his skin was warm and safe.

The resort had opened to the public for the day, and there were tourists and local users starting to come in; they stared at Carina, being carried out of the pool by this tall, gorgeous guy like she was a feather.

"You can put me down," she said, embarrassed. The dizziness had passed.

Toren refused to do so, until they'd gotten through the antler-handled door into the pool room, where he laid her down on a padded lounge chair. "I'm such an idiot," Carina murmured.

"Someone get her a bottle of water," Toren commanded, not taking his eyes off of her, and several people scattered away.

"I'm fine," Carina insisted, but when she tried to sit up, Toren put a gentle, immovable hand on her shoulder.

"Rest," he said. "I shouldn't have let you stay out there so long."

"You're not the boss of me," Carina reminded him. Then, more quietly, she added, "Anyway, we were having fun…"

Toren's face split into a boyish grin. "Yeah," he said, his face coloring.

Someone brought a towel, which Toren insisted on putting under her head, and he let her sit up to gulp down most of a bottle of lukewarm water.

"Better?" he asked.

"Yeah," Carina said. "I was stupid. They have signs all over the place about drinking water and not staying in too long."

"It happens," Toren said comfortingly, twining his fingers in hers possessively.

The little crowd that had gathered slowly dispersed as it became clear that Carina was not (to their disappointment, she was sure) going to die dramatically. They wandered away to their own soaking, whispering and speculating.

"We should get some breakfast in you," Toren said decisively, and for one wicked moment, that was not at *all* what Carina wanted in her.

But eating some food was probably much smarter than dragging Toren back into the water for more hot not-a-ranger make-out time. "There's a really great restaurant at the resort," Toren told her.

"That sounds like a good idea," Carina agreed. "Right now, I'd eat my hiking boots and my dirty socks sound delicious."

They walked back to the dressing rooms they'd come in through together and Toren reluctantly let her go into the ladies room alone. "If you aren't out in ten minutes, I'm sending someone in to get you," he warned her.

"Make it fifteen," Carina said. "I want to wash my hair."

Toren frowned, but agreed, and to her surprise, bent to give her a quick, possessive promise of a kiss that somehow didn't strike Carina as presumptuous. "Fifteen," he agreed.

Not for a moment doubting that Toren would indeed send someone in after her, Carina rushed through untangling her braid, washing, and conditioning it. To her surprise, the shower stalls were stocked with product that was far higher quality than what she'd brought...and no one else was in the dressing room whatsoever. There weren't even any swim bags lying about, or any towels but her own, untouched.

She showered swiftly, found some spray in conditioner for her hair, brushed it fiercely, and blew it halfway dry before she realized she hadn't looked at the time when she came in. She dressed in her last clean change of clothes, left the towels in an empty wicker hamper, and was out in the lobby...by herself. A few tourists were looking over the postcard display on the counter, but Toren was nowhere in sight.

The tourists were directed to completely different dressing rooms than Carina had just come out of, their swim passes firmly in hand and towels of a much lesser grade than she and Toren had gotten over their arms.

*Toren must have a helluva pool pass,* Carina thought suspiciously. She came to look over the postcards on the counter. Maybe she'd send one to her sister, she thought. Then she remembered that she couldn't and put the one she'd picked up back in the rack, tamping down her worry with resolve.

Then she caught sight of the postcard behind it and she felt a rush of dizziness not unlike the one that had sent her swooning into Toren's arms.

It was a portrait postcard, with a caption that said, "The royal family frequently enjoys visiting Angel Springs Resort." It was dated four years ago.

It featured a silver-haired, bearded man who was clearly the king, looking absolutely, undeniably kingly in a *very* familiar uniform indeed, standing near the rock entrance to the resort. Ranged beside him were six young men that Carina recognized from the brochure in her van. The oldest two still looked like they didn't care to be standing next to one another, one of the twins still looked bookish and the other looked like a jock, the only blond of the bunch looked like he was in a staring contest with the camera...and the youngest one was very definitely not a child any more.

Toren's silver eyes and grin were unmistakable. He was not the shortest one any longer, though he wasn't the tallest, but he was by far the most irreverent-looking.

He was also, Carina thought furiously, the best-looking of them, and her kiss-swollen lips burned.

# CHAPTER 10

"$\mathcal{I}$ have to go," Toren said shortly into the phone, glancing at his watch. He wasn't sure if fifteen minutes had actually passed or not, since he'd failed to take note of the time he'd left Carina at the dressing room door, but he knew that every moment he spent away from her company left him feeling bereft.

"Fask wants to know if you got rid of the squatter," Tray said from the phone. "Just give me something to tell him, baby brother."

"The squatter has moved on," Toren said, ignoring the subtle slight. "No problem." It was the literal truth.

"So you'll have time to help me coordinate the visit of the King and Queen of Mo'orea," Tray said brightly. "Great! I think that Fask is interested in their daughter—"

"No!" Toren said in alarm. Sitting down with the press secretary to plan a formal dinner and entertainment did not fit in with his plans to find somewhere nice and lay Carina down in a pile of rose petals.

"Look, I know you want to go hunting, or playing hockey, or whatever it is you do when you're shirking your family duties, but Fask isn't wrong about us doing…"

"Later," Toren promised vaguely. For a moment anger and frustration slashed through him. He wished he could just be *normal*.

Bad enough that he came with a giant nosy family. Bad enough that he was going to have to explain to Carina that he was a dragon shifter. But on top of that, that he'd have to be *king*?

And that meant she *would* be queen.

It wasn't a suggestion, it was a mandate. They would bring her to the coronation in irons if that's what it took to save Alaska.

And Toren already guessed that Carina didn't particularly like to be told what to do.

Whatever Tray said, something about *duty* and *responsibility*, was swept away when he came out of the dressing room and found Carina standing in the lobby.

If she had been beautiful with her unkempt braid and soot-smudged cheeks, she was now a goddess. Long, loose blonde hair fell in damp waves nearly to her waist, and she was wearing a jumper over thick striped tights showing off her long, strong legs, an insulated plaid flannel shirt several sizes too big over that. She had the duffel bag she had tried to accost him with at the door over one shoulder and she was standing at the counter looking fixedly at something in her hands.

Her nose was straight in profile, her kiss-hungry mouth pulled into a tight, thoughtful pout.

Then she turned and saw him. Her hazel eyes flashed gorgeously and Toren recognized the heightened level of beauty in her face as fury even as he *felt* it.

"Gotta go," he said frantically, trying to thumb off his phone without looking at it.

She was holding a postcard, one that Toren had signed a hundred copies of at least, and he could not hope that she hadn't recognized him.

Not the way she was glaring at him now.

"Should I curtsy?" she asked in frigid tones.

"You don't have to curtsy," Toren said with a sigh.

"I suppose 'you were going to tell me,'" she scoffed.

Toren had been meaning to, but he suspected that saying as

much wouldn't help him much now. He tried a charming smile. "Want to go have breakfast with me?"

"If I decline Your Majesty, will your guards have me arrested?"

Toren actually glanced around to see if his honor guard had shown up, then realized she was only joking. Angry-joking.

"You don't have to," he said. "I just want you to. I've got...wow, I've got a lot to tell you. Anyway, it's Your Highness, not Your Majesty." *For now.*

She seemed to be expecting more resistance, or maybe guilt, but Toren was only glad. This had saved him having to explain one thing, even if he had a bucket of other incredible explanations to try to make. Rian was right, he thought, keeping secrets was only trouble, and he was looking forward to coming clean about everything.

"Want me to sign your postcard?" he offered with a grin.

She stared at him in astonishment. "I'm still mad at you," she said, putting the postcard back. "And I have to let Shadow out."

"Can I come with you?"

She swept an exaggerated bow. "Yes, Your Majesty, please come to my humble van so that my noble hound can go *pee.*"

"Thank you, My Lady," Toren replied with perfect courtesy, giving her an equal bow with a hand flourish.

He dashed ahead of her to open the door, and she followed him bemusedly.

"I knew you weren't a ranger," she grumbled, but the corners of her mouth were twitching.

"I never said I was," Toren reminded her.

She came to a complete stop. "You don't think that's the same as honesty, do you?" she asked narrowly, every trace of her humor gone.

Toren soberly came to a stop with her. "It isn't," he said firmly. "And I should have figured out how to tell you sooner. I'm sorry."

She blinked at him. "You are full of surprises," she said, frowning.

"Some of them are good, I hope," Toren said, giving his most charming smile.

"I haven't decided yet," she said, but Toren caught the reluctant smile on her face before she stalked ahead of him to her van.

But when they got there, Shadow was gone.

# CHAPTER 11

*C*arina wandered around the van, poking into the underbrush. "Shadow, here Shadow!" She had left one of the side windows open and the ajar screen suggested how he had escaped.

Toren, in very unprincely fashion, joined her, calling and whistling, and they walked the length of the parking lot.

"He's not even my dog," she reminded herself unhappily.

"I'll help look for him more after breakfast," Toren suggested. "And we'll report him missing at the front desk of the resort.

"Don't you have more important princely things to do?" Carina asked, and Toren winced and felt guilty, as if she had struck a nerve.

"They can wait," he said firmly. "None of them are more important than this."

"I *am* really hungry," Carina admitted. She also really didn't want to faint in front of Toren again. As unexpectedly lovely as it had been to gain consciousness in his careful embrace, she didn't care to repeat the spectacle.

"Your Highness," they were greeted at the door to the restaurant, and Carina abruptly realized that man who had let them into the pools that morning had not been starting to say 'You're early...' or 'You're not allowed...' but 'Your.' As in Your *Highness*.

Feeling stupid made her scowl, and the server quickly added, "My Lady," and raked her with a gaze as if he was desperately trying to find some symbol of her rank on her insulated flannel.

"A private table," Toren said confidently.

"Yes, Your Highness."

They were led through a small, quaint restaurant to not only a private table, but an entire private room, with a large central table and a few smaller satellite tables. None of them were set, but there were rather suddenly three servers frantically putting out candles and cloth napkins at one of the small tables.

"We sometimes come here for holiday parties," Toren explained.

"Well sure," Carina said casually, keenly aware of her ten dollar dress and striped tights. "And when the president of the United States visits."

Toren was quiet so long that Carina realized that he probably *had* entertained the president in this room.

"Never mind," she choked. Their seats were ready and the servers stepped aside to let Toren slip her chair back and tuck her into place. He was then seated by one of them, and heavy cloth napkins were spread into their laps.

Everyone moved in easy, practiced patterns, and Carina felt like she was in one of the OCD memes on the Internet, the one tile that didn't match.

There was a full spread of cutlery, and wine glasses full of ice cubes and water and Carina wasn't sure what to use. Then, to her amazement, she was being handed a hot towel with a pair of tongs.

She mimicked Toren, who wiped his hands and put the towel back on the tray being held for him.

"I bet this isn't the service they get in the main room," she joked.

Then she was handed a menu that she was very certain they did not offer to anyone in the rest of the restaurant. The choices included king salmon and king crab and bacon-wrapped moose tenderloins and truffles and some things in French that Carina didn't even recognize. There were no prices listed.

If you have to ask...

She *did* have to ask. "You were going to *tell* me, right?"

Toren put down the menu he'd been studying and looked earnestly into her eyes. "I was going to tell you. I want to tell you everything."

The server's approach kept them from continuing that train of thought.

"Can I get you something to drink?" she asked courteously.

"Coffee," Carina said. "Nothing fancy. In fact, the worst coffee you have, please. Instant, if you've got it. I don't want to ruin my tastebuds for camp coffee."

Toren grinned at her. "Coffee," he agreed. "Something a step above that, please."

"Do you know what you'd like for breakfast?" the server asked, smothering a smile.

Carina glanced over the menu again. "Can I just get an ordinary omelet with lots of veggies and cheese and some toast?"

"Sourdough, white, wheat, or bagel?" the server prompted, her face serene again.

"Sourdough seems appropriate," Carina deadpanned in return.

Toren ordered crab eggs Benedict.

And then they were alone in the fanciest restaurant that Carina had ever seen from the inside. The servers had lit the candles, which seemed a little inappropriate for breakfast, but she had to admit that it was atmospheric. There were a few windows letting in midmorning light, filtered through lace curtains.

"So... why me?"

Toren's eyes really were silvery, barely blue at all. "Why what?"

"After you evicted me from royal grounds...why'd you follow me? And for that matter, *how*? I never saw a car, yesterday, and it took me hours to drive here. But mostly...why?"

He took a bracing breath. "Because you are my mate."

"Ow ya goin', mate?" Carina replied in a dead perfect Australian accent.

# CHAPTER 12

*W*hatever Toren had grimly expected a mate to be, it was not whooping laughter over lace tablecloths, or Carina's straight-faced humor, or the way her eyes would crinkle at the corner whenever something amused her. He had never found a face like hers, so interesting and expressive that he simply wanted to watch it, and never let it out of his sight because it was possible he'd miss something there, and that thought broke his heart.

He wanted her, like he thought he would be attracted to a mate, but he never expected *wanting* to be like this, a strange mix of physical need and emotional longing and deep contentment in her presence. He was starting to realize that a lot of what he was feeling wasn't entirely his own, either; he could feel her reactions to things. Even weirder, there were moments when he felt like he'd known her for years, with all the attendant comfort of familiarity, not just a few awkward hours.

Almost like he was feeling what he *would* feel for her after they'd been together for a very long time.

"So, no," she insisted, once they had both gotten their laughter under control and she'd used a corner of her linen napkin to wipe her eyes. "Why'd you follow me?"

"I'm serious," Toren said, but then their breakfasts were served.

"That was fast," Carina said in surprise. "And that is not an ordinary omelet."

It was a beautiful omelet, fluffy and folded full of fresh chopped vegetables. When she cut into it, it oozed three colors of cheese, and there were perfect circles of green onion scattered over it. There was a side of berries—tiny wild strawberries and blueberries. Carina looked at them dubiously, undoubtedly comparing them to their much larger and grander—and far blander—commercial varieties, then tasted one.

Her eyes widened. "Good things come in little packages," she observed. She ate all of hers, and then all of his, when he offered them, then tucked away her omelet with earnest good will.

"You're my mate," Toren tried again, after a few false starts around his own fine food. "It's not Australian, and it's not crazy. Well, it's all going to sound a little crazy, so hear me out, okay?"

"I'm sitting here eating with royalty after kissing you in a hot springs pool and fainting in your arms," Carina reminded him. "Crazy appears to be the theme of the day. Hell, it's the theme of my life lately." She mopped up some stray cheese with her toast and Toren felt a wave of frustration and fear that wasn't his own.

"Well... you know how they call my dad the Dragon King of Alaska?" Toren attempted to act casual.

"Crazy," Carina muttered under her breath, but she gestured Toren to continue as she picked up her water glass.

"We're actually dragons."

Carina's eyes met his over the rim of her glass, and to her credit, she continued drinking without spilling it on herself. "You don't look like a dragon."

"We're dragon shifters, we can take either form at will. But there's something else..." Toren sucked in a breath.

"Something more than *being a dragon*."

"A king is chosen by...well, it's magic. Dragons chosen to lead don't do so alone; there is always a ruling *pair*. They have to find their true mate in order to be a true king; they won't be accepted by the Compact if they don't have their queen at their side."

"A true *mate?*" Toren could see her reconsidering her Australian joke.

"For me, that's you, and I recognized you as soon as I saw you, and I don't ever want to be without you again."

Though her hand was shaking just a little, Carina managed to get the glass down to the table. It thumped down harder than she probably intended.

"Like love at first sight?" she said thinly.

"Not always. It can be people who've known each other. No one exactly knows how or when or why a mate bond gets activated, just that it always happens when one of the kingdoms needs a ruler. It's all written out in the secret version of the Compact, something about *fertile ground* and *great need.*"

"Anything else?" she asked dryly.

"Because I'm the only one of my brothers to *have* a mate, I am now the *crown* prince, and they'll need me to marry and be crowned king before summer so that I can sign the Compact Renewal and save our country..."

Her face lit up and her eyes narrowed into laughter for a moment until she realized that Toren wasn't laughing with her, and she immediately sobered. "You can't be serious. I mean...you warned me about crazy, but that takes the cake."

Toren was full of relief. Rian had absolutely been right: secrets were nothing but trouble and he felt like there was a great weight off of his shoulders.

Even if she really didn't look like she actually believed him and he could feel her waves of doubt.

"I'm not really queen material," Carina said slowly.

"I beg to differ," Toren said. "But honestly, I'm not really king material. Any of my brothers would be better at it. I haven't told anyone but Rian yet and I'm absolutely dreading it."

"We just met," Carina protested. "This is..."

"I know," Toren said, knowing that he was smiling foolishly at her.

"What do you think happens now?" Carina asked with deep skepticism.

"Come to Fairbanks with me," Toren said thoughtfully. "Meet the family." That was the right thing to do, no matter how much he didn't want to do it. No secrets.

Carina put her forehead in her hand and gave a tired sigh. "Just *supposing* that this isn't some kind of heat-induced hallucination, did you consider that your family won't want me for a queen?"

At the last moment, Toren kept himself from blurting that they didn't have a choice. Maybe he *was* getting better at diplomacy. "They'll love you," he assured her. "Like I do."

Carina's eyes shot to his, wide and alarmed. "We *just* met," she repeated. "You don't even know me."

Toren reached across the table and took her un-resisting hands in his own. "Carina…"

"Even if I was willing to marry you after one hot make-out session in a pool, you should know…" She paused, her hazel gaze skidding away from his and Toren could sense her fear.

"It doesn't matter."

"It kind of does," Carina said, looking up through her eyelashes at him. "Since Alaska undoubtedly has an extradition agreement with the United States and I'm pretty sure I'm wanted for murder."

# CHAPTER 13

Carina took a certain amount of pleasure in the disbelief in Toren's face. It was about time that she was able to dish a little of that back, after his outrageous revelations about being royalty and a dragon, by the way.

It was all completely implausible and Carina could feel her brain trying to accept the information, circling around the facts, and the evidence, and all the beautiful, crazy possibilities.

"You are not a murderer," Toren said with comforting conviction. His belief in her innocence unwound something tight in Carina's chest that she hadn't realized was there.

They both fell awkwardly silent as one of the servers came into the room to take their plates.

Once the server had refilled their waters and left them alone again, Carina looked speculatively at Toren and tried to figure out where to go from there.

She believed that he was the prince of Alaska; it was a little insane, but service like this, his face on a postcard, everything about his bearing...it was undeniable.

The revelation of dragon-people, that was a little more of a stretch.

And being his soulmate was a *ridiculous* idea.

Except...

Carina closed her eyes.

She had never reacted to anyone the way she responded to him. It wasn't just the way he set her body on fire. And it wasn't just the way he was so good looking it almost made her ache to look at him.

It was the way she felt safe with him, the way nothing had felt safe in such a long time. It was the way that she wanted to tell him everything, to unlock the secrets that were thick on her tongue.

It was like magic.

Because it *was* magic. That's *all* it was. It was actually comforting, having a reason for her crazy-intense emotions, for the way she could imagine she was feeling his emotions and staring into his very soul.

He was still holding onto her, making lazy circles on the backs of her hands with his thumbs.

"Hey, hey, you want to go for a walk and tell me about it?"

She desperately wanted to tell him everything. Did he have any idea what a turmoil she was inside? Did he guess how desperately she was clutching at humor to keep from breaking down? Was he feeling her emotions the way she seemed to feel his?

"Yeah," she said quietly. "Let's go for a walk."

They shed their heavy napkins. Toren made no motion to pay or leave a tip. Carina idly wondered if they paid a monthly fee, or if the royal family would be billed later. Maybe they actually owned the place. She swallowed back the hysterical laughter that bubbled up in her throat.

Carina went for the door they'd come in, but Toren caught her hand. "Let's go out the back," he suggested. "Our pictures are probably already online."

"Our...pictures?" Carina had a stab of terror. She was supposed to be keeping a low profile until she could figure out her next steps, not letting photographs of herself out on the Internet where they might be seen by all the wrong people.

"I think some people noticed when I carried you out of the pool.

I bet that the Prince Toren Fan Page is already wild with speculation."

Carina could not quite keep her unladylike snort to herself. "There's a Prince Toren Fan Page? On Facebook?"

Toren blushed. "Ah…yeah."

"Is it popular?"

He blushed further, confirming Carina's suspicion that it was.

"I'm tempted to join," she teased him. "And post about how hopeless you are at making campfires or sitting upright in a basic chair."

"Don't do it," Toren begged. "Some of the admins are really catty and I wouldn't be able to resist posting in your defense, and then they'd ban me, and that would be really embarrassing on my own fan page." His silver eyes were dancing.

Carina laughed. "I won't do it. I'm staying off of Facebook anyway. Wanted for murder, remember? I threw out my phone before I drove into Canada."

"You have a hell of a story to tell me," Toren said, frowning at her.

"It's not as good a story as being a dragon shifter and in line for the throne because of a magic spell," Carina told him, not sure if she was joking or not.

They passed one of the servers as they snuck out the back. "Thanks," Carina told her, waving. "It was delicious!"

The afternoon was glorious, a perfect Alaskan autumn day. A slight breeze rustled the leaves that remained on the trees, and the light over the hills around them was golden and warm.

And Toren's hand in hers, mate nonsense or not, was the most wonderful feeling Carina could remember.

They stopped briefly at the gift shop and Carina, in a moment of hopefulness, bought a souvenir leash and dog collar in dark blue with gold stars all over it. They stopped again at the van and called hopefully around for Shadow with no luck.

Twice, she tried to start telling her story to Toren, but they ran into people and were driven to silence.

"This way," Toren said, taking her by the hand.

There was a marked trail to the ridge of one of the nearby hills, which gave them a wide view of the valley through the trees as they climbed the boardwalk. They passed another couple, and the woman grasped her partner's hand and stared at Toren with recognition and unabashed curiosity.

It was quite unnerving.

And just a little bit fun.

Then Carina remembered that Toren thought she was going to be an honest-to-God *queen* and it seemed a lot less fun.

"This way," Toren said unexpectedly, as they walked through a stand of dark spruces. He tugged her off the trail behind a frame of rock outcroppings and a sign that explicitly warned hikers not to leave the trail and they scrambled together up a trackless slope and over a short ridge.

"Where are we going?" Carina asked breathlessly, letting him pull her up over a rock about the size of her van.

"There's a place I want to show you..." he said, leading her along a barely visible trail.

Then they burst out of a narrow crevice onto a meadow, dressed in russet seasonal colors.

"It's beautiful," Carina said, gazing over the rustling grasses. The far end was fringed in dark evergreens, and she could see the distant glimmer of a pond. There was something about the land that made her feel like she was exactly where she was meant to be.

"I found this place when I was trying to get away from my brothers," Toren told her. "We used to come here a lot...when my father was awake."

His father. His father the *king*.

Carina shivered and folded her arms around herself. She buttoned the collar button of the oversized flannel she was wearing, and sat down on a mossy boulder. "Well, you've told me your crazy story, let me tell you mine."

# CHAPTER 14

*C*arina's unrest was like sitting on a porcupine, Toren thought. She felt like prickles of doubt and fear and despair. He wished he could protect her from all of it.

"I was an accountant, for a big company in Portland," Carina started, as she settled down onto a moss-cushioned rock. "I was fairly new, but there were some job promotions that were coming open and I really wanted a chance at them. So I was taking all the overtime projects, working late and trying to convince my bosses that I was lower middle management material by showing initiative."

Toren, suspecting a lengthy tale, took a seat next to Carina and put his arm around her. Her unrest felt prickly but after a moment, she leaned into him and all the sharp edges smoothed.

"I was working late one night. You know the drill: creepy music, empty hallways, the sound of that one janitor down the hall that you never see. And we have a client, a big client. It's a bank I guarantee you've heard of. We were doing some routine independent review of their financials, and we had access to necessary non-sensitive customer data. Like, we got the bank account numbers and the dates the account were created, and the financial transaction lists, but not their name or contact information."

"You found something," Toren guessed.

Carina gave a hiccup that he thought was meant to be a laugh but didn't quite make it.

"Mostly, we use this interface that crunches the data, but I like seeing things in charts, so I pulled up the raw database. And, I'm skimming through some accounts, looking for the ones that were flagged for review, and I noticed...a whole bunch of accounts were exactly the same. Not their balances, but their account creation dates. The interface just shows you a month and year of creation, so you'd never notice anything weird from there, plenty of accounts are created every month. But the database saves a time-date stamp, and these were all created within about twenty seconds of each other. Not just a few accounts, but spontaneously this bank had like three hundred new accounts and all of them had money in them. None of them individually had enough to raise any flags, none of them more than a hundred thousand. Some of them were even really small. But I added balances up and there was over five million US dollars sitting in these fabricated accounts."

"Money laundering?" Toren barely knew what money laundering was, but he knew enough to recognize that something was very wrong with what Carina was describing.

"Well, at first, I thought it might just be a spontaneous buyout... like maybe they'd acquired a smaller bank or something? So I started looking further. We had about eighteen months of data, from just one of their geographic locations, and I found three clusters of these accounts. And that made me think, how long had this been going on? I was looking at almost fifteen million in imaginary money in a relatively short window of time for just their Pacific coast branches. So I called the bank and told them we were missing some of the data we needed for analysis and I asked..." Carina caught her breath and Toren could feel guilt threaten to swamp her. He tightened his embrace, and after a moment she could go on.

"I asked the secretary I got on the phone to send me the files going back further, and I took a chance and asked for the information from other districts, too. And she hemmed and hawed about policy and privacy and...I told her what I'd found, and what I was actually looking for. She was scared. She didn't want to get involved, and I didn't think she was going to, but a few days later, she called me back."

"She gave me her direct number, and sent me the files I needed on a flash drive by courier. She said that she'd started looking deeper from her end, and that she could confirm that there hadn't been any buyouts at the times these accounts were created."

"And I was right, there were more of these account clusters, going back years, all over the world. *Billions* of dollars. Sitting there, invisible, in these perfectly legit looking accounts that had been created by someone at the very top of the company. I was holding a bomb, and I knew it." Carina was shivering now.

Not sure what else to do, Toren took off his uniform coat and wrapped it around her, even though he knew it wasn't because of the cold.

She cuddled into the blue coat. "Well, *they* knew it now, too. When I got the flash drive, I called to thank her, and tell her what else I'd found, but she wasn't the one who answered. It was a man's voice, and he started asking questions. I hung up in a blind panic."

Carina's voice was growing raw. "I said I had a headache and went home early, but instead of going home, I went to my sister's place and told her everything. She gave me lunch and put me in a shower, and when I came out, there were men in suits at the door asking about me. I hid in the hall, listening, while they told her that the secretary at the bank had been found dead and they wanted me for questioning."

"I knew my sister was good on her feet, way better than me, but I didn't realize how good she was until I saw her deflect those guys. They wouldn't show badges, and didn't have a warrant, and my sister brushed them right off. The flash drive, with the Amco Bank logo, was sitting right out on the table behind her, too."

"Wait," Toren stopped her. "*Amco Bank?*"

"I told you you'd heard of them," Carina said wryly.

"That's one of the largest banks in the world," Toren said in horror, beginning to glimpse the scope of her problem.

"Exactly. June, that's my sister, she gave me her passport, because we look enough alike to pass, and her van, which she'd packed to go camping with her boyfriend that weekend, whatever cash she had, and I threw out my phone and drove north. I haven't...I haven't been able to contact her since then. I figured it was safer for her if I didn't."

"And you came to Alaska."

"I needed to stay low for a while, find someone who could help me out," Carina said. "I thought maybe I could find a journalist who would take the story and blow it wide open. And Alaska is where you go to get lost."

"You came here to be *found*," Toren said with utter conviction. "I'll make some calls when we get back to the resort, and we'll check on your sister. We'll see if there even *is* a warrant out for you, and Rian will know how to get you diplomatic immunity if there is. We've got an international lawyer who can represent you, if it comes to a trial."

She looked into his face, and Toren didn't even need to feel the emotions to see the tangled up fear and relief in her eyes. "I feel so stupid for getting mixed up in this."

"It wasn't stupid," Toren told her. "It was brilliant. You're smart and you're ethical. We'll make everything right. You don't have to be strong by yourself anymore."

Carina turned to bury her face in his shoulder, shaking. "I feel like this is all so surreal. Like I'm stuck in a dream that can't decide if it's a horror or a fantasy. Wanted for murder, magically in love with a prince...make up your mind!"

"I can only promise it has a happy ending," Toren said, pushing her hair behind her ear and kissing her temple. He desperately wanted to do more than just kiss, but then he thought of something that might cheer her up even more.

"Do you want to go for a quick flight?"

# CHAPTER 15

arina was puzzled at the offer, then abruptly remembered that Toren was a *dragon*. It still seemed utterly unreal. But the weirdest part was that she could *feel* his confidence in the idea. He didn't think he was lying. He wasn't deceiving her. She wasn't sure he *could* deceive her.

And she didn't think she could deceive him, either.

"I'd...like that?" she agreed cautiously.

He stepped back carefully, gave a curious ripple and then suddenly expanded into space, spreading wings like giant sails into the air over Carina's head. He was bejeweled, with scales that shimmered with a thousand different dark rainbow hues at every subtle shiver of his hide, and his long, graceful neck was arched so that he could regard Carina from giant, dark eyes that seemed to glimmer with very distant coals. His nose was long, and when his mouth opened in a way that was somehow similar to Toren's human grin, there was a row of teeth, each one the size of Carina's hand.

His wings moved with flexible precision, and he sat up on hind legs the height of Carina herself to extend a... paw? claw? There were three digits facing forward and one opposable that suggested a thumb, and all of them were tipped in curved claws the size of Carina's head. She cautiously touched one; it looked like gemstone and was warm under her fingers.

Toren crouched then, turning his side to her and folding his wings back.

Carina hesitated.

His nearest wingtip swept out, gesturing toward his shoulder.

Carina buttoned the toggles on Toren's big uniform jacket, then stepped close. She put her hand up on his elbow, and scrambled ungracefully up to throw her leg over him and straddle the ridge of his back. The position keenly reminded her of their kissing adventure in the pool earlier, and the fact that they'd never done anything about the tension they'd ratcheted up.

Toren gave a little shake that reminded Carina exactly how far above the ground she was and she settled herself more firmly against him, leaning forwards. This close, she realized that the scales were actually very knobby and textured, and that there were very natural handholds all over his hide. She found two good grips, pressed close to Toren's neck.

Toren gave an experimental bounce that took Carina's breath away, then sprang into the air with a whoosh of broad, leathery wings.

She was glad she had been lying almost prone at take-off, because the press of the air as they rose up would have flattened her. At first, it was all she could do to catch her breath, to keep her balance, and not lose her grip on scales.

Then, slowly, she dared to open her eyes and lift first her head and then her torso.

The land below her was brilliant folds of yellow-gold birch and dark evergreen, spun through with ribbons of rivers and set with precious gems of lakes and ponds. They were high enough now to see snow-capped mountains. Carina tried to remember what they must be from her vague understanding of Alaskan geography. The White Mountains?

The wind was making her eyes tear; she would have to get aviator's goggles if she was going to make a habit of this, she thought, giggling.

Toren tipped then, banking into a slow, gentle curve that felt anything but slow or gentle to Carina. She clung for dear life and pressed her head back down to Toren's neck. Her thighs ached from squeezing, and she was glad to recognize the meadow they'd taken off from through her streaming tears.

Toren landed so gently that it was almost anticlimactic, and Carina carefully released her cramping hands and half-fell down his side.

Riding a dragon wasn't exactly the Never Ending Story sequence with arm raised in victory, and Carina found that she'd broken two of her nails and scraped herself in several places. Her hair was sticking out in every direction, tangled impossibly, and her ears were bitterly cold.

Still, "That was amazing!" she crowed, swaying in place as her stressed thighs remembered how to hold her upright again. *"Amazing!"*

There was an odd, sudden suction of air, and then Toren was standing beside her, looking entirely self-satisfied.

"Won't people see you when you do that?" Carina asked, trying to tame her hair with her fingers.

"They'll only see a little shimmer in the sky if they look up during the *day*," Toren explained, closing the distance between them.

*Cloaking magic. Sure, why not,* Carina thought. There were dragons and mates, after all.

"What would they see at night?" she asked, suddenly hearing the specifics in Toren's explanation.

"Can't you guess?" he teased.

"Northern lights," Carina said, laughing. "Of course. I saw them the evening you came to evict me."

"There are real ones, too," Toren said modestly.

Carina wasn't making much progress with her hair. She managed to tangle her fingers into it and had to wiggle them out. "You know what people are going to assume if I come back looking like this, don't you," she scolded Toren.

"That you went riding on a dragon?" he teased.

"I think they'll guess something a little more mundane first," Carina told him shyly, toying with the toggles on his uniform coat.

Toren's grin went wider. "It would be a shame to raise those kinds of expectations with no basis in reality," he suggested, and to Carina's delight, he bent to kiss her.

# CHAPTER 16

*T*oren's dragon was a constant presence in his head, a subtle undercurrent to his thoughts, with his own emotions and the occasional dry comment. Usually, that entity was Toren's anchor; when he was feeling angry or anxious, his dragon was a voice of reason and serenity.

Now, it felt like *he* was the steadiness to his dragon's eagerness and yearning.

*I'm not going to rush this,* he said firmly, and his dragon's impatience and desire nearly swamped him.

Not that his own desire was any less.

And hers wasn't either.

Flushed from their flight, her lips parted, her eyes bright, Toren had never seen anything more beautiful than his mate. He was standing close enough to see her pulse, pounding at her throat, and he wondered if he imagined the sizzle in the air between them.

He didn't imagine Carina's hands, sliding down his chest, down over his hips, and up at last, more centrally located.

The pressure of her fingers gliding over his cock, even through the fabric of his pants, was almost enough to send Toren over the edge.

*Ours, she is ours,* his dragon sang joyfully.

"Mine," Carina was saying with equal possessiveness. "You are all mine…"

Toren had to concentrate very hard to make his fingers do something as intricate as unbutton the jacket that Carina was wearing, but then he could slip it off and lay it down on a mossy slope with Carina, who was trying and failing to kiss him and undress him at the same time.

Every part of her that was revealed was a new treasure, a place to kiss and worship, as she wriggled out of her dress and slipped off her tights and pulled helplessly at Toren's shirt as he licked her bare skin and kissed and nibbled.

"Toren…"

"Carina…"

After that the conversation was basically composed of *yeses*, with the occasional **oh** *yes*, and punctuated with hisses and moans of pleasure.

Toren got his shirt off and only lost two of the buttons from the cuffs. Carina's bra was unclipped and tossed aside so that he could put his hands around her perfect breasts and lick her nipples and drag his teeth across her skin as she arched up to him.

He kissed down her tummy to circle around via her thigh and slipped a finger slowly between her folds, releasing the juice that waited there. His tongue followed, lapping carefully as he stroked into her.

Her fingers dug into the moss as she cried out in release of her pleasure and no dragon could have kept Toren back. He tore off his pants, barely not literally, and didn't even bother to remove one of the legs off of his ankle.

Then he was pressing at her entrance, his every plan to go slow and prolong things vanishing in the heat of his desire. Driven exquisitely by her sounds and the way she rose beneath him, he was reduced to instinct and reaction, following the needs of his nature, and the response of her own.

When she came again, clenching around him, Toren was lost… tumbling off a cliff of pleasure and catching an updraft.

# CHAPTER 17

$\mathcal{C}$arina wasn't sure what made her feel more limp, the exhilaration of flying on an honest-to-God *dragon*, the utterly melting after-effects of making love to a gorgeous man who knew exactly how to touch her, or the relief that someone finally knew her whole story and believed her...someone who actually had the power to protect her.

She felt absolutely safe with him.

*Illogically* safe, she told herself, as they dressed and she despaired of fixing her hair. It was probably part of that *spell*.

They hiked back to the boardwalk, and Carina reminded herself that Amco Bank was powerful. Arguably as powerful as the kingdom of Alaska. Her problems weren't magically over because an Alaskan prince had apparently tripped in a puddle of *true love dust*.

"Let's have lunch at the resort and head back to Fairbanks," Toren suggested, walking hand-in-hand back to the trail with her. "I'll call Rian and get him started on figuring out how to protect you. We can be there for dinner."

Dinner. At the *palace*.

None of it seemed real.

They ate in the main room of the restaurant, at Carina's request. "The private room is so fancy," she said plaintively. "Have some pity on the poor van-dwelling hippy fugitive before you drag her to the palace and make her wear heels and a tiara!"

"A tiara? No, no, it will be a full crown," Toren cautioned her with a wink. "Probably fifty pounds of gold and gems. You'll barely be able to lift your head."

Carina elbowed him, recognizing his teasing.

Toren bought a resort logo sweatshirt to wear instead of his uniform coat, and they only got a few curious stares and second glances; most people looked right past them when they were led to their table.

"Maybe we could run away," he muttered.

Carina was inspecting the menu. "What's that? I'm thinking I need a burger. Are we going to go back out to the pools again before we leave? I'm trying to balance enough food to keep me from fainting again with not so much food that I sink to the bottom."

"Maybe we could run away," Toren repeated, wistfully.

Carina forgot about her menu and gazed up at him. "Really?" she said breathlessly. Then she shook her head. "I doubt you'd be comfortable in my van," she said lightly, as if that was the least of their problems.

"Why not?" Toren asked, looking a little offended.

"Look at you," Carina teased him. "You're looking around for your hot towel right now."

Toren blushed. Their water glasses had been filled twice in the few moments they'd been seated, and the servers were clearly nervous about his foray into the main dining room, but they were doing their best to treat them like any other couple. "I could rough it," he said, adorably defensive and secretly doubtful.

Carina patted him lovingly on the hand. "Of course you could," she said, like she might say to Shadow. She frowned then, recognizing the cadence in her voice. Shadow had not been near the van when they checked it again, and no one they talked to had seen him.

"Carina..." Toren looked at her anxiously. "You haven't said much about what you left behind. I mean, I'd understand if being queen of Alaska didn't fit your life plans. I honestly don't know what to do about that, but...I'm sorry."

Carina stared at him. "You're apologizing. Because you want me to be a *queen*." She laughed and shook her head helplessly. "I admit that it wasn't even *adjacent* to my original plans. But it definitely beats my own ambitions to make enough at a boring job to afford a house in the suburbs and maybe buy a nice car...and get a dog."

She'd meant it flippantly, but the reminder of Shadow stung.

Toren turned his own hand over and caught hers, stroking her comfortingly.

"I'd put up lost dog posters," Carina said, trying to stuff down her feeling of loss, "but really, he's only been my dog for less than a day. I don't have any real claim on him."

"You loved him," Toren said. "Isn't that a claim?"

His gaze was intense and direct, and Carina had to rein in the irrational joy that bloomed in her.

"*This* isn't love, is it," she said reluctantly. "I mean, you said yourself, it's one of those *magic* things. It's just..." she flapped her free hand helplessly. "Not that you aren't hot, but I usually move a lot slower than this."

"It's not like a *love* spell, exactly," Toren tried to explain. "I mean, magic can't make you *feel* anything. It's just...well, it can *show* you feelings." He looked like he had a mouthful of needles he needed to spit out, then, inconveniently, the server at his elbow cleared his throat.

Carina took her hand back.

Subdued, the two gave their orders.

"I don't know how it is for human mates," Toren said quietly when the server had gone. "I don't even know how it is for dragons, because I never once considered it would happen to me. But I know that you are mine, forever, and that I would never be whole without you."

Carina couldn't answer that, she was such a tangle of longing and it was almost like she was feeling her *own* emotions from a very great distance.

Toren frowned fiercely and for a moment Carina worried that

she had inadvertently hurt him. Then she realized with relief that he was frowning past her and she was glad to have something else to say. "Is anything wrong?" she asked.

"Just someone staring at us. Probably nothing." He grinned. "You think I'd be used to it by now."

~

*a*fter lunch, Shadow was waiting by the van, and he greeted them enthusiastically, whining and jumping and wagging his fringed tail. He even threw himself over in the frost-crunchy leaves, wriggling on his back in absolute canine ecstasy.

"Oh, who's a good dog?" Carina asked, scratching at him and kneeling in the leaves to wrestle enthusiastically with him. "Who's the best dog? Who's my *best* Shadow?" It was everything she could do not to cry in happy relief.

Toren greeted him with only a little more decorum, bending to grab him from behind the ears and ruffle his face.

The dog didn't appear to be any worse for the wear after his mysterious adventures.

The van, however…

"Oh my god!" Carina said, sliding the side door open.

The vehicle had been completely tossed. All of her toiletries had been dumped out on the floor, every food box was out of the cabinet. Even the contents of the fridge had been taken out and left on the bench seat, which had been slashed.

Carina went to the back cabinet, where her tools and clothing were in complete disorder. "They didn't take my money," she said, relief and confusion in her voice.

"They weren't looking for money," Toren said thoughtfully, fingering the cuts in the cushions.

Carina went cold with terror. "The flash drive. They were looking for the flash drive."

"Did you bring it with you?" Toren asked.

She slowly nodded. "I didn't want to leave it with my sister. I made her promise to say that I'd stolen the passport and van once I was gone. I…don't know if she did, but I didn't want to drag her into this. I didn't want to drag *anyone* into this."

"Is it gone?"

Carina drew in a deep breath and glanced around. There were a few people at the far end of the parking lot, exclaiming loudly about a dog mushing display and snapping photos. "Let's find out," she said softly. She took a screwdriver from the tool box and went around to the front of the van.

The driver side headlight cover popped off, revealing a small hollow space beneath the bulb. Carina reached into this and fished out a plastic-wrapped, duct tape-sealed package. She didn't unwrap it, but she did bounce it in her hand thoughtfully before she returned it to its hiding place and replaced the headlight cover.

Carina felt pale with nerves and Toren pulled her into his arms. "They can't hurt you now," he said fiercely. "I won't let them."

She remained stiff and unconsoled. "I should have switched vehicles in Canada," she said plaintively. "Or…found someone to counterfeit me a new passport or license plates or…I don't know anything about this. I thought I'd gotten far enough away. I thought I'd be safe…"

Toren tipped her chin up to gaze into her eyes. "You *are* safe. They will have to get through me to get you now. Me and the entire kingdom of Alaska, because you are ours now. I don't care how big and powerful and rich the bank is, they don't stand a chance against my brothers and I. We have resources they can't even imagine."

Carina slowly relaxed, and her smile was crooked. "And dragons. Don't forget, you're dragons."

Toren kissed her forehead. "We'll protect you," he said confidently. "*I'll* protect you."

She took a shaky breath. "This is really not what I thought my life would look like a few weeks ago. The most exciting thing in my future was the possibility of a promotion."

"Me neither," Toren confessed. "Last week, I was hunting caribou on the North Slope, no thoughts about the future beyond the vague idea that things would be freezing up for hockey soon. This week, I'm staring at a throne. It's…"

"...crazy?" Carina finished for him.

"Crazy," Toren agreed. "And a little terrifying. But Carina... Carina, my love, I wouldn't trade it for anything if it meant not having you. I could face anything with you at my side."

She sighed into him, not wanting to admit how completely and foolishly she trusted him. "What now?" she asked plaintively.

"Fairbanks," Toren said. "Let's get your van tidied up and go to Fairbanks. We can talk to my brothers. They'll know what to do."

They straightened up the van and Carina patched the cushions with duct tape.

Shadow remained underfoot for the entire process; he clearly had no intention of being lost again. Carina put his new collar on him, and he immediately sat down and tried to scratch beneath it.

When Toren went to sit in the passenger seat, he found that the dog had already claimed the seat. "Move over," he told the grinning hound.

Shadow reluctantly gave up the chair and sat between them until Carina started the vehicle. Then he climbed into Toren's lap to watch out the window. Toren laughingly let him stay there as they drove away from the resort.

# CHAPTER 18

*C*arina's van was under-powered and drove like a box of nails, rattling loudly over potholes and frost-heaves. But Toren had to admit that there was something freeing and *fun* about hitting the open road with a large dog monopolizing his lap and Carina sitting so close that he could reach out and touch her any time he wanted to.

He could feel some of the tension leaching from her as they left the resort gates behind them. The road was a safe place, for her, and he wondered if his presence gave her any of the same irresistible contentment that hers gave him.

"I have questions," she said, after a few miles.

"I will answer anything I can," he replied, scratching Shadow's ears.

"I hardly know where to start," Carina admitted, setting the cruise control. "So, there's dragons and magic in Alaska, which doesn't somehow surprise me as much as it should. Are there other dragons? Is everyone in the whole kingdom a dragon shifter?"

"Only the royal family," Toren answered. "Er, all the royal families in the Small Kingdoms."

Carina chewed on that in silence for a moment, while Toren

tried to decide if he should elaborate at all. They came around a curve in the road where bright sunlight was suddenly sharp in their faces because of the low angle of the sun. Carina winced and put the visor down.

"Who knows?" she asked. "Is it a big secret, or am I just especially oblivious?"

"I don't know how it works in every kingdom, but it's a pretty close secret here. Immediate castle staff knows, and some members of the elected council. Some of them are other kinds of shifters themselves."

"Other kinds? There are other kinds of shifters?" Carina glanced at him in alarm. "Like unicorns and firebirds?"

"I've never met a unicorn or a firebird," Toren said, adjusting Shadow on his lap so that the dog's elbows weren't digging into his leg. "But there are *normal* animal shifters. The captain of our guard is a polar bear shifter. One of our regular housekeepers is an otter shifter."

"And is *that* a secret?"

"In most places, yes. I mean, except on a few of the more isolated islands, people aren't out there just shifting around in public. It's something your family usually knows, because it's usually passed to children, and maybe a close friend or two."

"But just in the Small Kingdoms?"

Toren shook his head. "All over the world. In the United States, too. They just keep their heads down and stay in the shadows."

"Werewolves," Carina said wonderingly.

"Misdirection may be used on occasion," Toren warned. "Most of the big media outlets are run by shifters, so they have reason to keep the movies splashy and the real news quiet."

"Makes sense," Carina agreed, though Toren could feel the rumbling disquiet of her worldview resettling.

After a moment, she asked, "So...magic. Can all shifters do magic?"

Toren hesitated, then explained, "All shifters *are* magic. But not all shifters *do* magic. And some non-shifters can do magic, too."

"So you don't *do* magic to change shape?"

Toren had never had to describe the rules of magic before, and it was harder than he'd guessed. "My brother, Raval, he'd be able to clarify this better than I can, but there's natural magic, and there's *structured* magic. Natural magic is what shifters have. We can move between two forms, and there's the cloaking to keep people from noticing us. It's all very innate and informal; you just think about it, and there you go."

"So, what about the other kind?" Carina asked.

"The other kind?"

"You said there were two kinds, natural and...*not* natural?"

"Structured." Toren laughed despite himself. "Okay, so some people—I'm not one of them—can basically use natural magic to do...er, things. They have to write the words out, very specifically."

"Like, a spell? There are *wizards*?"

"Except that it's not a poem or Latin or whatever. They have to write down what the magic is supposed to do, and it does it. The kingdoms have this...pact."

"Even I've heard of the Compact," Carina said. The road had turned again, and she put up the visor.

"You've heard of the *public* version of the Compact," Toren clarified. "That one lays out trade agreements and stuff." Toren was keenly aware that he was out of his depth for this explanation, as well. Fask generally kept tabs on that kind of thing. "But the private version is a lot longer, and stickier, and has a lot of rules about magic and succession. For example, it doesn't just *say* that we can't use magic against one another, it actually *stops us* from using magic against one another; spells we cast against each other would backfire terribly. The Compact itself is generally accepted to be the most complicated spell in existence. It protects the kingdoms from using magic against each other, and it...picks the succession of each kingdom."

"By magic," Carina said flatly. "This *mate* thing."

"Right," Toren said, gazing at her profile. His mate. His destined partner. "It makes sure that we meet, and that we know each other when we do."

She was silent, frowning forward at the road, then cast a sideways glance at him. "Destiny," she said softly. She didn't feel entirely happy about it.

Shadow was getting restless in his lap and Toren snapped his fingers to draw him off. The big dog walked to the back bench of the van, then returned to sit between them and finally lie down.

Carina mused, "It's kind of hard to wrap my head around this spell idea. You just write it down? Like in a notebook?"

"Spells on paper only work once; there's too much power and it burns up. You can also anchor the structured magic into an object. Like a rock. Or a jewel. Or the Compact itself, I guess. Or a piece of metal. But of course, it's harder to write on those things."

"Like a magic sword?"

"Sort of. It wouldn't be like a sentient weapon that talks to you or anything, but it could have special properties. There's an obsidian dagger in my father's hoard that is spelled to kill any dragon with just a scratch. Moose!"

"It will kill a moose?" Carina asked in confusion.

Toren pointed. "No, there's a moose!"

# CHAPTER 19

*C*arina stomped on the brakes. The moose at the edge of the road, his broad antlers dripping with strips of velvet, chose that moment to cross.

He was a magnificent animal, nearly as tall as her van, and he gave Carina a baleful glance from one beady eye as he sauntered in front of her.

Shadow whined, dancing between the seats and bouncing in place to see out of the front window. His tail wagged furiously.

"Wow," Carina said, watching the moose pause at the side of the road to strip the tips off a stand of willow. "What a beast."

Shadow tried to climb into her lap for a better view out the side window and Carina pushed him off. "He doesn't want to play, Shadow."

Something occurred to her. "If there are people running around in animal form, how do you know if you're looking at a regular animal or a shifter?"

"A shifter is smart enough not to run around in animal form during hunting season, usually," Toren pointed out. "And knows better than to cross the road in front of traffic."

"They don't have...like a secret handshake or something?"

Carina eased off the brakes again as the moose wandered back into the forest and disappeared. For such a large creature, he was invisible almost at once.

Toren chuckled. "Not to my knowledge."

Carina put the van in motion again. Shadow gave a suffering sigh and sat down, putting his head in her lap. They drove in silence for a while, Carina trying to sort out all the things that Toren had told her. Magic. Shifters. Succession. *Queen of Alaska.* She caught herself slowing the van down as her brain swirled reluctantly. She reset the cruise control so that she wouldn't slow to a crawl.

"Your family…"

"They're going to love you," Toren said, as if he could guess at the nervous spiral of her thoughts.

Carina wasn't convinced. She had no illusions that the quality of her character in any way balanced the baggage of her recent past.

She had to take the van out of cruise control as they got closer to Fairbanks and there was suddenly traffic again. From lots of nothing, there were suddenly houses again: first lone dwellings barely visible down long driveways, then more and more of them until they were abruptly in Fairbanks.

Fairbanks was barely large enough to call a city. Even the so-called downtown had only a few buildings more than three or four stories, and the tallest looked smaller than fifteen stories. Compared to Portland, it was downright puny. But it was a pretty city. The buildings, as Carina skirted the city, were a mix of dated architecture and newer structures. Many of them had colorful murals. Toren directed her along the bank of the river, which was traced with a wide recreation path and edged by a wrought iron fence.

There were trees everywhere, even right downtown: big, dark spruce trees and birch trees in autumn colors, plus shorter ornamental trees hung with red leaves and dark berries.

The palace was nestled into the side of a hill, several sprawling wings of it just visible over the forest it was settled into. It grew larger every time Carina saw it through the trees. Houses and business fell away behind them and the final approach was through a gate—they were waved through—down a long, private driveway through wild-looking forest that opened onto a huge yard. She pulled to the bottom of wide steps leading up to massive front doors with big glass panels. *Did they build the entire castle to dragon scale?* Carina wondered in awe.

Then those great doors were opening, and Carina was sorely tempted to slam on the gas and follow the driveway around and back out the way they'd come in.

# CHAPTER 20

oren hadn't been particularly detailed on the phone when he called Fask to let his brothers know that he was bringing a mate home. He'd given them the barest skeleton version of Carina's troubles, and her full name, so that Fask and Rian could begin investigating...and very little else.

He knew they must be wild with curiosity, not sure what to expect. He could feel Carina's nervousness, fluttering like a panicked bird in her stomach. His new world and his old were about to collide.

Shadow was getting agitated in the stopped van, sure that this meant he could get out and confused about why he wasn't. He climbed into Toren's lap and put his nose on the window, panting in excitement. Carina reached back and found his leash, clipping it firmly onto the collar. Toren took the lead.

The door to the van squeaked open as a casually-dressed member of the castle staff came forward to assist. At the slightest gap, Shadow was bolting out, and only dragon strength kept him back as Toren scrambled out after him. "You'd be a good wheel dog," Toren chuckled. "You're stronger than you look."

Carina came around and hesitantly gave her van keys to the

man with a glance for confirmation at Toren. "I don't think this old thing has once in its life been parked by a valet," she observed. She took Shadow's leash from Toren, and Shadow, his ears swiveling and his tail wagging low, immediately attempted to circle around them both.

Toren wasn't quite fast enough to step out of the leash before it had wrapped around his legs, and Carina's, and they had to cling to each other for balance as Carina desperately said, "Shadow, no! Don't! Wrong way!" and tried to untangle them.

Shadow whined in mad, trapped panic and tried to lunge away, until Carina bodily tackled him, dragging Toren with her.

"It's okay, boy. It's okay." Carina had a solid hold on the big dog. Toren was able to unclip the leash, unwind it from around them, and clip it back on.

Carina brushed off her knees and straightened her flannel over-shirt. "That was not the first impression I was going for," she admitted in a stage whisper.

Shadow leaned against her legs and panted, but stepped forward when they went forward to meet the three men who were coming down the steps. The big dog gave a belated impression of a well-behaved dog…until they arrived at the bottom of the stairs, where he lifted his leg and peed briefly on a statue of an important-looking man.

If Carina had looked embarrassed before, it was mortification on her face now. "I'm so sorry," she managed weakly. To her credit, she kept her chin up as she faced down Toren's brothers. Toren slipped his hand into hers and she squeezed it.

"Nice dog," Tray said.

"Welcome," Fask said.

Rian didn't say anything, but his nod was polite.

"This is Carina," Toren said, wishing he'd practiced this part. "She's…she's my mate."

He wasn't sure if Carina's squeeze was out of new terror or if she was trying to give him courage. Either way, he held on so tightly he was surprised either of them had feeling in their fingers.

There was a moment of quiet as everyone present was reminded of the significance of the statement, then Fask stepped forward and extended his hand. "We're happy to have you here," he said sincerely. "Please make yourself at home."

"I'm afraid that Mrs. James isn't going to want the dog inside," Rian pointed out, after taking his turn at shaking Carina's hand.

"He can go hang out in the kennel, can't he," Tray suggested, coming forward to greet Shadow as enthusiastically as he greeted Carina. "Who's a good dog? I've always hated that statue, too." He stood up and offered his hand for the leash. "I'll take him if you want. I promise he'll be well cared for."

Carina hesitated, then quipped, "I never did ask what dragons eat," and everyone froze again.

After a breath of surprise, Tray gave an un-princely snort of humor, Fask grinned, and even Rian cracked a smile.

"Burgers, mostly," Tray assured her. "Thai food. I'm Tray. I'm the good-looking twin."

"I like wild caribou," Fask said. Then he smiled and added, "But I like it grilled, or cooked into sausage best. Fask. I'm the oldest."

"Bossiest," coughed Tray with a wink at Carina.

"The only dogs I eat are hot dogs," Rian said, straight-faced. "Call me Rian."

They parted to lead Carina into the castle as Toren gave Tray the leash for Shadow and she petted him and said goodbye.

Some of Toren's nervousness evaporated. They were going to accept Carina; they knew that she'd be a perfect queen, just like he did.

Then he remembered that this meant he was going to be king, and all the nervousness came rushing back and he wished he'd pushed harder for running away. Maybe they could have gotten lost in Canada.

Carina's awe when they walked in made Toren take an appraising look at the castle. Past a big arctic entryway, sweeping stairs went up to the second floor.

A chandelier four times the size of her van glittered from the high ceiling over the foyer. Everything was done in Art Nouveau style, with long, sweeping lines everywhere. His grandfather, lacking anything resembling subtlety, had commissioned the returns of the stair railings to be dragons, leaping to the ground, their wings tucked to their backs. The downstairs foyer was practically an art gallery, with choice pieces of art hanging on the walls, mostly Impressionist and Renaissance paintings, but also a selection of Sydney Laurence's most famous Alaskan landscapes and a wide array of Native Alaskan masks.

"We do most of our entertaining at the hot springs," Fask explained as he led them further in. "The palace is set up much more as a home then a hotel. But we've got plenty of extra rooms, and I hope you'll be comfortable here."

"Some home," Carina observed breathlessly, craning her head to see the great beams of the ceiling above.

Most of the central structure was stone, but the floors were polished wood, and there were natural log columns at each side, leading the way to the wings. The architect had apparently thought that Alaska meant log cabins, and the wings were all rich, warm log wood on the interior. The natural wood grain made up most of the visual interest, and lace curtains framed big windows that looked out on birch and spruce forest. The upper floors had views of the mountains to the south.

The Art Nouveau theme followed them into the log wings, and there were wrought iron handles in graceful shapes on everything. A large, glass-fronted fireplace insert gave a wide view of the flickering fire within.

Across the top of the fireplace, stylized metal salmon were leaping, and the metal art continued around the room, stark black against the sunny wood; there were moose browsing at waving willows, with wolves howling in the distance. The furniture in the study was all comfortable, wood and leather, with more black iron accents. Thick, plush rugs covered the wood floor here.

Toren had never really appreciated any of it; it had always struck him as tacky, over-the-top, Alaskan-to-the-max. But Carina, as they ushered her into the study, gazed around like she'd never seen anything like it, and she clearly loved it.

"May I take your coat?" Rian asked. He kept trying to meet

Toren's eyes over Carina's, but Toren was too busy watching Carina drink in all the new sights, reveling in the delight and awe she was feeling.

"We've had a room made up for you," Fask said kindly, taking her insulated flannel shirt from Rian as if it were the finest fur coat. "I hope you'll be very comfortable here. Let me have Mrs. James make us some refreshment."

He vanished, while Rian settled into one of the leather chairs. Toren drew Carina down beside him on the loveseat. She sat very primly, smoothing her jumper over her knees, and he could feel the nervousness rippling through her.

"So, Carina," Rian started. "I understand you're wanted for murder?"

# CHAPTER 21

*C*arina was saved having to answer by the return of Tray, who flopped into a chair opposite from them. "Shadow has been fed and given a lovely house full of straw and I promise that no one has eaten him," he said, laughing. He was wearing a bright blue hockey jersey for the Alaska team and Carina found him an odd foil to Rian; the two were identical and yet very definitely distinct. Rian looked like a gruff librarian, Tray looked like someone who got caught hamming it up on the sports audience camera frequently.

"Thank you," Carina murmured. She reminded herself that Shadow was not actually her dog and that she should take him to Fairbanks to get checked for a chip and compared against lost dog reports. Toren squeezed her hand as if he'd felt her sudden grief at the thought of giving him up. Probably he had. The idea was both deeply unsettling and somehow comforting.

Fask returned with a tall woman in a sharp uniform carrying a sheaf of papers. "Captain Luke has been checking into the accusations," he said, as they both took seats across from Toren and Carina.

Captain Luke was a beautiful, ageless Native Alaskan woman

with a round, warm-skinned face who looked like she could twist
Carina into a pretzel without trying. Dark hair was pulled back in a
neat bun, and she had three dark lines tattooed down her chin.

Carina tried not to stare at them.

"We've confirmed that there is a warrant out for your arrest,"
the captain said smoothly. "For murder in the first degree, automo-
bile theft, identity theft, and corporate espionage."

"I never did any corporate espionage!" Carina protested. Then
she heard her own words and had to laugh dryly. "Or the murder,
of course."

"Of course," Fask said, without a trace of humor. Carina
supposed she should be glad that he seemed to believe her.

"My sister?" She was almost afraid to ask.

"Your sister appears to be unharmed," the captain said reassuringly. "We haven't tried to make contact yet, in case she's being
observed."

"We'd like to hear your account of the events," Fask said.

His voice wasn't unkind, Carina thought, and she could feel the
supportive warmth of Toren at her side as she drew in a breath. "I
was working for an accounting firm in Portland," she began. She
told them the story as dispassionately as she could manage, from the
discovery of the data to her flight out of the country.

They all listened grimly, nodding and asking questions, and no
one implied that she'd been an idiot for not trusting the police to
protect her or trying to go public without more support.

"I didn't really know what I'd do when I got here," she
confessed. "I guess I hoped that I could just stay low, regroup, and
find someone who was willing to help me find justice."

"What made you choose Alaska?" Captain Luke asked shortly.

Carina tried to convince herself it didn't sound accusing. "I
could drive here," she said. "And, no offense, but Alaska still has this
reputation of being the kind of place you could go to a bar and
throw darts at your own wanted poster."

That earned her a ripple of laughter, and the captain seemed to
relax a fraction.

Someone cleared their voice from the doorway and Carina look around to find a figure who must clearly be Mrs. James. She was a stout-looking woman of indeterminate age with brunette hair in a practical bob.

She circled the room, handing each of them a drink. Carina smelled coffee and chocolate, but her own cup was a tea of a gorgeous pink color in a clear mug.

"Wild rosehip, rose petals, lowbush cranberry, dried lemon peel, hibiscus, and a little honey. Some of these fools drink coffee this late, but I thought you could use something a little easier on the nerves after the day you've had." Her dark eyes were kind and gentle and Carina gave her a cautious smile as she took the hot cup.

Carina took a careful sip, and it was as bright and delicious as it looked. "I didn't realize it was so late," she admitted. It had taken some time to drive to Fairbanks from Angel Hot Springs, and their lunch had been ages ago. Outside the windows, the forest had turned twilight blue, though it was still plenty bright enough to see by.

"Some of the questions can surely wait until morning," Mrs. James said, with a meaningful look at Fask and at the captain.

"Of course, Mrs. James," Fask acquiesced immediately.

Captain Luke stood and bowed crisply. "I will check the security of the van and see to the attachment of a guard to Ms. Andresen." She left at Fask's nod, not even glancing at Toren.

Mrs. James cheerfully said, "I've had Felix prepare a light meal to be served in forty-five minutes. Miss Andresen, your room has been made up and if you'd like to bring your cup, I can show you where you'll be staying and give you a chance to freshen up."

Carina scrambled to her feet, nearly spilling her tea in her haste, and everyone else stood politely. Was Mrs. James implying that she *should* freshen up? The castle was magnificent, but everyone was dressed reassuringly casually.

She took a hasty gulp of her drink so it wasn't so full, and shot Toren a longing look; he was her anchor in this whole crazy, upside down world. His look in return was just as desperate, but he let her fingers slip from his without protest.

*A queen,* she reminded herself, feeling dizzy. She should at least try to act like one.

So she drew in a deep breath and followed Mrs. James, concentrating on keeping her chin high and her tea *inside* the cup.

# CHAPTER 22

Once Carina was gone, Toren felt everyone's attention shift as they settled back into their seats.

His cup, full of hot chocolate because Mrs. James still insisted on treating him like a wayward child (and also because he continued to request it), was suddenly very interesting.

The whole dynamic in the room was new and different.

It wasn't just that everyone was looking at him; that frequently happened when he said something dumb, or when he was in trouble for shirking tutors or duties.

It was that everyone was looking at him *thoughtfully.*

All of sudden, he'd gone from the *screw-up youngest brother* to *going-to-be-king,* whether any of them liked it or not.

"So," Tray said archly. "*Car-ee-na.*"

Toren made the mistake of looking up from his foamy cocoa.

Tray was leering suggestively, and Toren had a sudden primal urge to punch him.

*Our mate's honor,* his dragon rumbled.

"She seems clever enough," Fask said peacefully, giving Tray a quelling look. "And she's lovely. I think she'll appeal to the people, and we'll be able to come out on top of this little drama."

"I didn't mean to," Toren said, feeling very young and stupid.

"Mean to what?" Fask asked sharply.

"Find my mate. I mean, everyone wants you to be king. I didn't want this. Not that I don't want *her*, I..." Toren put his cocoa down on an end table more firmly than he meant to and a little splashed over the side.

"I can't be sorry for it," he said softly, meeting Fask's gaze. "I feel like I ought to apologize, and I'd give this to you if I could. Not her, I could never give her up. I'm... oh, lights," he groaned, slumping back in his seat. "I'm not saying any of this right. I'm going to be the stupidest king in the history of the Small Kingdoms and Alaska will be the laughingstock of the Compact."

Kind laughter answered him.

"Poor kid," Tray drawled, reaching over to ruffle Toren's head.

Toren batted him away in irritation. "I have a real problem here," Toren protested. "The Compact has clearly made a terrible mistake," Something occurred to him. "Can I give the crown to someone else after the Renewal?"

Fask frowned. "Leave him alone, Tray," he said. "You can't really take away the crown once it's in place. Not without another king to pass it to."

"Maybe father will wake up," Rian suggested. "I mean, it's still possible that he's just going to come around."

"We can all hope so," Tray muttered.

"I'm still studying the Compact for a way around this," Rian said. "Interestingly, there's a woman at the University of Florida who was doing a thesis on the Compact. It looks like the library there had an unaltered copy of the Compact."

That took all the attention away from Toren at least.

"Unaltered?" Fask repeated in alarm.

Copies of the uncensored Compact were kept under strict lock and key. That someone in a human nation had a copy of such a thing was alarming to say the least.

"*Had*," Rian repeated. "Small Kingdom agents replaced it last year. The thesis hasn't been finished. But the public prospectus had some *very* interesting theories and fresh insights. I'm going to be getting in contact with the student, see if I can pick her brain about some of the things she must have seen."

Fask frowned. "Tread carefully," he advised. "The last thing we need is an exposé to cover up."

"I've got a good feeling about this," Rian said.

Toren looked at him dubiously. Rian didn't usually run on feelings. He was always the logical one, looking for proof, reasons, and hard data.

Fask still looked concerned. "If she's got too much information, she may need to be silenced," he cautioned.

Everyone looked at him.

"Not like that," Fask protested. "Geez, you guys. I meant that we might have to hire someone to hack in and delete the thesis prospectus from the university database and pay her off."

Toren wondered if these were the kinds of decisions that he was going to be expected to make. It wouldn't have occurred to him that someone's *thesis* might endanger their greatest secrets. Shouldn't a king have thought of that?

"In the meantime," Fask said impatiently, "we've got a name to clear and a wedding to plan."

Toren looked at him blankly until he realized that Fask meant *his* wedding. His wedding to Carina. They were all looking at *him* again.

"I suppose a quiet courthouse wedding is going to be out of the question?" Toren attempted a laugh.

"Do you really think that the people are going to let the first royal wedding in sixty years happen at a courthouse?" Fask asked. "No, we're going to have to go all out."

"We'll have to invite royalty from the other Small Kingdoms," Rian said thoughtfully.

"And diplomats from the United States, probably," Kenth suggested. "Does she have a big family?"

"I have no idea," Toren whispered, suddenly as horrified by the prospect of a giant wedding as he was of being king. "I haven't technically asked her to marry me yet." Panic washed over him. "What if she says no?"

Everyone laughed, which did nothing to soothe Toren's ruffled nerves.

"I'll get working with the guard and our lawyers to figure out how we're going to clear Carina and I'll hire an event coordinator," Fask said, because Fask knew how to get things done. "Your job, your *only* job right now, is to get your mate to marry you."

"Even Toren ought to be able to handle that," Tray said, standing. "I smell food, and I want to wash up before dinner."

Everyone else rose as well, and Toren drifted along behind them in a daze.

Everything was happening so fast that he had no idea what to do or how to do it.

And the further in he got, the more Toren wished that he and Carina really had run away.

# CHAPTER 23

$\mathcal{M}$rs. James was not even slightly subtle as she showed Carina where Toren's rooms were, just down the hallway and around a corner from the third story apartment that had been prepared for her.

"There's not a lot of traffic in these halls after bedtime," Mrs. James assured her, face serene. "But there are sometimes spirits. They won't hurt you."

Carina had no idea if she was teasing or not and glanced sideways to see if there were clues on her face.

That was when she noticed the two guards following discreetly behind them.

Then Mrs. James opened the doors into her room, and any suspicion that she was being mocked vanished into astonishment.

The walls here were polished log, and the big, triple-paned windows were hung with lacy curtains. There was just enough light left in the sky to see the range, huge and distant and blue, edging the horizon over the tops of dark evergreens.

"Wow," she said. But the view was the least of the room's features.

A giant four-poster bed was against one wall, an entire sitting room with couches and a desk against the other, and an open door suggested a giant private bathroom. Tall, ornate wardrobes were bolted to the walls.

There were clothes laid out at the foot of the bed.

"I'm... ah... thank you," she said.

"The clothing won't fit terribly well, I'm afraid," Mrs. James said apologetically. "We have an excess of men's clothing in all sizes, but for women's sizes, it's just my closet and the housekeeper's." She didn't suggest raiding Captain Luke's closet, but Carina privately wondered if the captain had any clothing that wasn't a uniform.

The clothing was not the fancy ballgowns that Carina had been half-hoping for and half-dreading. There were two knee-length skirts, a few blouses, a white sweater, and a pair of stretchy leggings. There was no underwear, and there was one package of black men's socks. "I do have some clothes at the van," she said. "But this looks great. Thank you so much, Mrs...ah..."

"You may call me Julia," the woman said kindly. "But the boys may not." She gave Carina a wink. "They won't take me seriously if I don't maintain boundaries."

"You're the...housekeeper?" Carina guessed, not wanting to assume.

"Close enough," Julia said. "I've been with the family since Fask was young, and when they didn't need a nanny any longer, I stayed to make sure they didn't get into trouble. The boys are good about doing their own chores, so we don't have a lot of full time staff. I'll be sure to introduce you around tomorrow."

She smiled at Carina kindly. "We'll have some formalwear made for you, but this is Alaska. No one will blink if you want to wear jeans and flannel most of the time. We can sit down together and put together an on-line order, or I can send you with a driver to do some shopping downtown, whichever you'd prefer. Or, if you'd like a road trip, Anchorage has a wider selection. We can arrange a flight or a drive if you'd like to see the sights. There isn't snow in the forecast yet, so it would be a scenic trip."

"That would be amazing, thank you," Carina squeaked.

She led Carina into the bathroom. "All the standard amenities.

If there are any brands you prefer, please leave a note and I'll have it stocked. Extra towels are here; there's a bathrobe behind the door."

They returned to the main room. "If there's anything you need, please don't hesitate to ask. Dinner will be in about thirty-five minutes, down one flight and to the right for the informal dining hall."

"Thank you," Carina murmured, because she ought to say something, even if she'd already said *thank you* so many times it was starting to lose meaning.

Julia paused in the doorway. "We're all glad to have you here," she said warmly. "If those boys give you any trouble, just threaten to tell Mrs. James. Toren's a sweet lad, and I'm happy for both of you."

Then, with a twinkling smile, she was shutting the door and Carina was alone.

Not wanting to squander her time before dinner, Carina took a brief, luxurious shower. She gave the bathtub a wistful look, but that would wait.

She dried off briskly, and put on the leggings under one of the skirts. They were a little bit short, but at least they covered her legs. She picked a maroon blouse that mostly matched the skirt, and put the sweater over it. Men's socks and her worn hiking boots completed the image.

It was definitely…not royal looking. But it was clean, comfortable, and warm, which was more than Carina had been able to say for a while.

She towel-dried her hair and combed through it, then drew in her breath, gathered her courage, and left the room.

She was not surprised to find the two guards waiting there.

"I'm just…ah…going to dinner," she said shyly to them.

"Yes, my lady," one of them said, just as the other said, "Yes, ma'am." They gave each other startled looks.

They didn't know what to call her, either, Carina realized.

For some reason that was a great comfort. She mentally named them Grim and Amused for their original expressions.

She walked down the hall and drew up at Toren's door. Was he even there? Should they arrive together, or was she expected to make an entrance by herself?

As she was still considering whether to knock, keenly aware of the guards watching her with their bland faces, the door burst open.

"Oh, Carina," Toren said, and then he was sweeping her into his arms and everything was as it should be again. She had to remind herself that this was just a magic spell because it felt so safe and wonderful in his embrace.

"We should have run away when you first suggested it," Carina whispered. "I bet we could be in Canada by now."

"Everyone is being nice to you, aren't they?" Toren demanded, putting her down and giving the guards a fierce look over her shoulder.

"Yes, everyone is wonderful, I shouldn't complain," Carina said quietly, hoping she didn't sound ungrateful. She could feel all the tension, trembling inside of her.

Toren gave her one chaste kiss on the cheek and whispered in her ear, "We should grab Shadow and make a break for it now…"

Carina's stomach growled audibly. "Maybe after dinner?" she suggested with a giggle. She could do this. She could keep it together a little longer. That was how she'd gotten this far, just taking it moment by moment, step by step.

The whole castle smelled amazing, and it only got stronger as Toren took her arm and led her down one flight of stairs.

Clinging to one another, they sailed into a dining room that Carina would never in a million years have called informal, and were led to side-by-side seats near the head of the table. The chair at the end was empty, though a place was set.

"You're moving up, little brother," Tray said, elbowing him in the side.

"You're not going to be able to call me that when I'm king," Toren hissed back.

"You will always be our little brother," Tray teased.

Everyone sat at once when Fask, across the table from them, gestured, and Carina followed suit.

The meal itself was surprisingly casual; everyone passed dishes around and served themselves. There were no extra forks to wonder about. There were chicken legs, noodles tossed in pesto sauce, small red potatoes and gravy, green beans, sliced tomatoes, and hot biscuits. Carina wasn't sure what she'd been expecting, but it felt surprisingly homey and comfortable.

"Your timing is good," Fask told her from across the table. "This is all local produce, including the basil in the pesto. A few months from now, all of our fresh vegetables will have to be shipped in, and the quality declines sharply."

"There are downsides to being at the ass end of the supply chain," Tray said. "Ouch! I can say ass." He glared at Rian, who had apparently kicked him.

Rian muttered something Carina couldn't quite hear about *being* an ass.

She was introduced to Raval, the blond brother that she remembered was the one who worked in structured magic. He didn't seem much like a wizard, but he was quiet among the chaos of his brothers.

Gradually, Carina began to relax.

This wasn't the state meal she had expected, or the snooty air. These were brothers, teasing each other and tossing biscuits down the table, and they were kindly trying to include her and put her at ease. They asked about her life in careful ways, skirting the topic of murder accusations and corporate espionage.

To her surprise, they whole-heartedly approved of her living in her van.

"Those old VWs are really cool," Fask said enthusiastically. "They can go places a lot of modern RVs wouldn't fit."

"Like logging trails and royal land," Rian said, with a friendly wink at Carina.

"Did you really think you could stay all winter there?" Tray asked around a very un-princely mouthful of food.

"I hoped I wouldn't have to," Carina said. "It has a propane heater, and I have two sleeping bags and long underwear. But to be honest, I'm just as happy I don't have to test the theory that I *could*."

"It'll definitely be warmer in Toren's bed," Tray said, nodding wisely.

Toren blushed, adorably, and Carina had to giggle.

Her laughter died on her lips as she remembered that it was just a magic spell, it wasn't really love.

# CHAPTER 24

*a*fter dinner, their dishes were quietly removed and their water glasses were refilled. Toren found himself the unwelcome center of attention again. At least this time Carina was at his side. He could feel her unease, but he wasn't sure what was causing it. There was a lot to choose from.

"Let's talk about timing," Fask said mildly. "We need to host an engagement party, then there's the actual marriage, and a coronation. We don't want to stack these all up on top of each other."

"People might think we hurried the wedding to cover the pregnancy," Tray said slyly and Carina choked on the water she was drinking.

"I'm not—!" She seemed to realize that Tray was teasing her and glowered at him.

If he had been in reach, Toren would have punched his brother.

"On that topic..." Fask started gravely, and Toren sputtered in protest.

"I have an IUD," Carina said firmly. Her cheeks were scarlet, but her chin was high. "And I have no plans to remove it soon. Can we please tackle one crazy life-changing event at a time?"

"You don't have to get that personal," Toren growled. He

wondered if it would be too obvious if he took her hand. It had been easier—or at least less complicated—to save her from drowning than to save her from his siblings.

"We actually do, little brother," Tray said. "The whole point of a king having a mate is that the line continues."

"We don't know that," Rian argued. "The Compact never mentions children."

"At any rate, it can wait," Fask said quellingly. "I apologize for making you uncomfortable, Carina. What can't wait is the engagement party. If we want this to look like a natural progression, that should be soon."

"And the murder accusation?" Rian reminded them.

"That makes everything quite tricky," Fask confirmed. "It's going to take time to clear charges like that. I'll arrange a meeting with the bank's executives and see if I can't start a negotiation. We should try to have the engagement party immediately; we want to make sure that our claim on Carina is established. I think we should time it for the diplomatic visit from the Mo'orea king and queen next weekend."

*Our claim,* Toren's dragon snarled. *Not his.*

Toren wrestled him back. "What are you going to negotiate?"

"We can offer to destroy the flash drive if they make the charges disappear."

"You want to just let them get away with it?" Carina cried in outrage, cutting across their conversation. "They laundered billions of dollars and murdered some poor woman! That's *bullshit* and I won't be a part of it!"

"Proving any of that will be exceedingly difficult," Fask said warningly. "They have resources beyond even ours, the best lawyers, and they clearly aren't afraid to dirty their hands to cover their own tracks. They've killed once and they've probably done an admirable job of scrubbing the evidence from their own systems by this point. The only thing we have is one flash drive that may or may not prove something that it's going to be hard to pin on any one person. Justice would be the hard road, and it would take time we don't have. Years, probably. Years you could spend in prison, I should point out."

"Then it takes years," Carina snarled. "It takes years and it's done right, or I'll walk now. I'm not going to let her die in vain, and I'm not going to take a *crown* in return for my silence."

Toren, familiar with his brother's expressions, watched him wrestle with several emotions and settle on grudging respect.

"Spoken like a true queen of Alaska," Fask said at last.

"Can we keep her?" Tray asked lightly.

Carina's knuckles were white on the arms of her chair. Toren ached to take her into his arms, but didn't want to undermine her show of strength.

Fask was shaking his head. "I respect your decision to take the high road, my lady, but we still need a way to protect you if America requests extradition."

"Can't we just give her asylum?" Tray asked.

"Framed for murder isn't one of the protected grounds for persecution," Rian said.

Everyone looked at him blankly.

Patiently, Rian explained, "She can appeal for asylum, but we have policies that we have to apply and Alaska can only grant asylum if the applicant can prove that they would be unfairly persecuted by their *government* for reasons of race, political opinion, religion, or nationality. If she committed a crime—is suspected of a crime—then she has to stand trial for that crime." He gave Carina an apologetic shrug. "Even if we believe you didn't commit it."

"Give her a new identity?" Tray suggested.

Carina made a noise of protest.

Rian shook his head. "I don't think we'd be capable of giving her a new identity that would defeat the celebrity columns and Internet busybodies."

"Or the deep pockets of Amco Bank," Fask said thoughtfully. "They clearly already know that she's here."

"A fake identity could also negate some terms in the Compact," Rian cautioned. "There are a lot of specifics in there regarding falsehood and deceit."

"No new identity," Fask said firmly. "Rian, talk to our lawyer and see if you can find any loopholes in the asylum rules."

"Maybe they just won't ask for extradition?" Toren hazarded.

Tray snorted. "I'm guessing Fask wasn't thinking about a secret engagement party. She's going to be spread out across every glossy gossip magazine and all across the Internet. It won't take any sleuthing at all to know she's here."

Toren gathered his courage. He didn't usually make suggestions during these meetings, but he wasn't going to sit things out with Carina at stake. "Yeah, but will they really *ask us* to extradite the crown princess of Alaska? With all the negative publicity and political tensions it would cause? Let's go as big as possible. They're going to dig up her warrant, that information is public record, right? So come out in front of it, tell the truth. Say she's here in fear of her life, that she was framed, that she's afraid to leave...that we fell in love. People will eat it up with a spoon. The US won't *want* to ask for her. Not without a fair, public trial. And Amco Bank doesn't want that if Carina's got evidence, so *they're* going to stall, and we can take the time we need to figure out how to bring them down."

They all stared at him with various expressions of concern, doubt, and surprise.

Carina reached over and took his hand, smiling at him, and that was the only look that mattered.

"Are you seriously suggesting that we try to bluff the United States out of asking us to hand over a wanted criminal?" Tray asked.

"For a little while, at least," Toren said faintly.

"Ballsy," Raval said approvingly.

Fask looked darkly worried. "I'd want the details kept quiet," he said. "Say it's classified. Don't call Amco Bank out by name until you're actually prepared to fight them. Alaska doesn't have that kind of power."

"We should put the flash drive somewhere safe," Rian said.

"Nothing could get into our vault," Fask said grimly.

"Tonight?" Carina asked plaintively. "It's been a very long day."

They all seemed to realize at the same time that it was getting quite late. The windows showed more reflection than anything, implying darkness beyond.

"Tomorrow is early enough," Fask said. "The van is safe within our gates. You should get some rest."

They all stood up from the table and each of them filed by Toren and Carina and shook their hands.

"Welcome to the madness," Raval told Carina with sympathy.

Tray took her into a full embrace, declaring, "I always wanted a sister!" Then he let go of her and added, "Besides Toren, I mean."

Toren almost hit him in the shoulder, but before he could, Carina had fixed Tray with an icy stare. "I presume that isn't some kind of sexist dig because you think a sister is somehow lesser than a brother."

Raval nearly fell over choking on his laughter and Tray, after a moment of surprise, gave a stumbling apology and looked entirely abashed.

Fask very gravely shook her hand. "I wish that we had had a chance to get to know each other under different circumstances, but know that you are very welcome in our family, and we all wish you every happiness."

See, that was kingly.

# CHAPTER 25

Carina felt like everything was just a little surreal, like if she hadn't been wearing heavy hiking boots, she might have just floated away into space. Here she was, the honored guest of the royal family of Alaska, eating dinner with them while they planned her uncertain future.

"Can I see Shadow? Just to say goodnight?" she asked Toren as the last of the brothers shook her hand and gave her a formal welcome.

"Toren, if I could have a moment…" Fask said at the same time.

"I can show you the kennels, Carina," Tray volunteered.

Carina was loath to leave Toren's side, but she reminded herself that if they wanted to throw her to the proverbial wolves, they probably wouldn't string her along like this. She would be safe with Tray.

Toren kissed her goodbye, both of them embarrassed by the scrutiny of the others, and seemed as unwilling to let her go as she was to go.

*Magic*, Carina reminded herself.

Then she was walking with Tray down the stairs and out the

back. Tray, she recognized, was the ham of the family. She knew his type because she'd *been* his type, always looking for the joke.

"We only have one team left," Tray told her. "Dad used to race, but none of the rest of us took it up, and he let them age out and become housepets. A lot of people have adopted retired royal dogs."

"Dog racing?" Carina for a moment pictured greyhound racing and was confused.

"Dogsled racing," Tray explained. "We have enough to pull a sled, but I prefer to take out just one or two at a time and go skijor-ing. You can go almost as fast, but it's a lot freer. Just you, your dogs, and your skis."

The dog yard didn't look like much, just some boxes and loose straw over packed ground, scattered with gnawed rawhide and water dishes, but the tied up dogs were certainly happy and healthy looking. They all bounded to their feet when Tray and Carina appeared, barking and twisting around in delighted greeting.

"Mukluk, Anya, Jeebers, Angie, Thomas the Engine—he's our wheel dog." Tray introduced her to a dozen dogs, smaller than she had expected, all of whom wanted to lick her and lunge at the end of their runs and put their paws on her legs. "Dusty, Tanana, Sheba, Tricksy—she's slipped her collar more times than it should be possi-ble. Dana, Shayla, and Phoebe. She's expecting a litter of puppies in a few weeks!"

Shadow was sulking on a lead near the back, but he rose to his feet at their approach and whined hopefully.

Carina sank down beside him in a pile of sweet, fresh straw, and buried her face in his ruff. Life had been so much simpler when it was just the two of them at her campsite. For the whole twenty minutes before Toren burst into her life and made it more compli-cated than *ever*.

Her chest ached.

She wanted to go back to being a nobody who knew *nothing*. Then she thought about *missing* meeting Toren, and the moment of loss was so sharp and deep that she was staggered.

She muttered nonsense into Shadow's fur about *good dogs* and *who's the best* until she was sure she wasn't going to cry in front of

Tray, who, when she finally looked up, was abashedly trying to pretend like he wasn't feeling as awkward as she was.

"We can take you dog sledding once there's snow," he offered. "It's a lot different than snowmachining. No engine noise, just the swish of the sled and crunch of the snow. They go a lot faster than you might guess."

"Snow*machin*ing?" Carina was grateful for the neutral topic.

Tray smiled. "I think Americans call it snowmobiling."

"Oh, sure," Carina said, standing. Shadow pressed against her legs. "That would be fun." She gave him one last ruffle. "I'll give you a nice long walk tomorrow," she promised.

"It's really brave of you, what you've done," Tray said as she reluctantly drew away from Shadow.

"It's mostly stupid luck," Carina said. "And desperation."

# CHAPTER 26

*W*atching Carina walk away from him with Tray was torture for Toren. Having to have *a talk* with Fask was worse.

"Let's sit," Fask suggested, leading Toren to the front of the second floor.

This was the big room, open to below, where they held diplomatic functions and seasonal parties. At one end was a low dais with chairs. They didn't look like thrones, exactly, being rather more plain and in the wood and iron motif of most of the castle, but they conveyed the power of the crown and were just enough higher than the rest of the room to look out over it.

There were seven chairs. Fask chose the throne to the right of their father's central perch and Toren could feel the choice he was being given: sit in the king's chair, or take the seat to Fask's right.

It was a test, and Toren had no idea what the right answer was. That was what his life was going to be from here on out, he realized with despair. One big series of tests.

Well, he wasn't king yet. Toren took the chair to Fask's right.

"You don't have to worry about anything," Fask told him warmly as they looked out over the empty room. The windows were like dark holes in the walls. "You know that I'll...that we'll have your back. We'll keep on keeping on just like we have, and we'll all make sure that you know what to say. It won't be so bad."

"It's going to be awful," Toren said. "No one wants me being the public face of anything."

Fask laughed, and Toren thought it sounded kind. "You're going to do fine," he assured Toren. "Just keep your chin up and step out strong."

Toren grinned crookedly. That had been Fask's advice when he was first starting to learn to skate. Step out strong. Timid steps inevitably meant falling.

"I'll try," he promised. Too bad this didn't come with hockey pads.

"And don't let Carina take all of the spotlight," Fask warned then.

Toren felt a shiver of defensiveness; he wasn't sure if it was his own feelings or his dragon's. "What do you mean?"

"She's strong-willed and smart," Fask said, sounding admiring. "The people will love her. But if you let her run away with all of the attention, it's going to look like a circus instead of a succession. Her story is exciting and dramatic. We need to downplay that as much as possible. I think you were right," he hastened to add. "It's best to come out in front of the information, take control of it instead of letting other parties twist it first. But this can't be all about her. This is about you. You becoming king. It has to be Alaska first, Carina second. People need to know where your priorities are."

Toren nodded slowly. That made sense.

"We should also fudge the timing a little. People might think a two-day romance is a little unreasonable."

"Happens in movies all the time," Toren said with a shrug. He disliked the idea of lying.

"Just...don't say how long you've known each other explicitly. You met while she was living in her van. There's no need to say that the spectacle at the hot springs was the very next day. The last thing we want to do is try to explain the real power of the Compact. Right now, people just believe we have peculiar traditions."

Secrets. So many secrets.

Toren was quiet, then nodded.

"Was it really love at first sight?" Fask asked curiously.

Toren remembered his first glimpse of Carina's hazel eyes. "It was more than that," he said with a sigh. "It was this...possibility. This brilliant certainty that I could be happier with this woman than I could ever imagine. It was knowing what she was, knowing how we could be...like I would never be complete without her. Like I never *had* been complete."

"How exactly did it happen?" Fask prodded. "Did you see her from the air and know?"

Toren considered. Had he known when he circled the clearing, when his dragon was weirdly focused on their task? Or even before that, when he had first gotten his assignment to encourage the squatter to move on? His dragon had insisted that they needed to go.

"I didn't really understand until I looked into her eyes," he explained thoughtfully. "But I felt a kind of pull before that. Like I was supposed to go there. Like I was supposed to go meet her."

Fask nodded thoughtfully. "Raval thought it might feel like a tug or a compulsion. He's suggested that a *potential* mate bond could be *activated*, without violating the Compact. He's been investigating how to possibly awaken it, and use something like a dowsing rod."

"I can just see you, staggering around in the tundra with a forked stick," Toren teased. "Just to hit the ocean and realize she's on another continent."

Fask laughed with him. "Magic is generally impractical," he said agreeably. "But I'm going to have Raval continue on this track."

Toren felt a moment of hope. "Do you think one of you guys could find a mate? And I wouldn't have to be king?"

"We'll try," Fask promised. "But I don't know if we'll succeed. The Compact chooses, and it chose you, and usually, that's the end of it. You might as well get used to that chair." He hitched a shoulder towards the empty chair of their father.

"Kenth still thinks we should be trying to wake him up," Toren said thoughtfully. Kenth and Fask were oil and water, and Kenth spent most of his time outside of the capital city, avoiding inevitable conflict.

Grief passed over Fask's face. "I think we're beyond that," he said regretfully. "This can be how dragons pass, slow and silent. It's been so long…I think that father isn't really *in* there anymore."

"I never knew him very well," Toren said quietly. He had so many questions he wished he could ask.

"It's a pity," Fask said mournfully. "He taught me so many important things."

He shook himself, as if trying to shed grief off like a dog with a wet coat, and stood. "I'm going to call our lawyer, make sure he's here first thing tomorrow to start looking into the asylum angle. We'll protect Carina, Toren. Whatever it takes."

"War with America?" Toren didn't even want to think about it, rising to his feet beside Fask.

"I don't think it would come to that," Fask said firmly. "Let's hope it's all nothing more than a minor diplomatic strain." He stepped down off the dais.

Toren remained behind as his brother left, staring at the reflections in the dark windows, wondering what path his life was going to take from here. After a moment he turned and walked to his father's throne, sitting down into it gingerly.

It wasn't such a different view than he was used to, just a slightly different angle, a slightly larger chair.

And a huge responsibility.

# CHAPTER 27

*T*ray walked Carina to the beginning of the third floor wing.

"I'm just down here, thanks," she said, hoping that her dismissal was the right combination of subtle and unmistakable. Her guards had fallen in a few paces behind them when they came in from the kennel, and they paused discreetly a little distance back.

"Have a good night," Tray said kindly. "And welcome to the family." He bowed over her hand and walked away merrily.

Carina was just wondering if she could somehow get rid of the guards as well, slowly walking down the hall to where she would pass Toren's door to get to her own, when she heard laughter and a wolf whistle around the corner where Tray had disappeared.

*Toren,* she thought in relief, just as she heard his voice saying, "Suck an egg, Tray!"

"Not very kingly, little brother," Tray teased him back.

Then Toren was stalking around the corner looking exasperated and her heart leaped in her chest.

The smile that bloomed on his scowling face when he saw her was so wonderful that Carina didn't even care if it was a magical compulsion, because she felt exactly the same, like the sun had just risen over her, or beautiful music had started playing somewhere.

"Carina," he said longingly, and they were both closing the distance between them and she was in his arms again at last.

"Oh, Toren," she said, feeling all undone and helpless and confused and *safe*.

For a moment, he just held her, and she sobbed into his shoulder as the day came crashing down around her. "I'm just an accountant," she cried. "I'm just a stupid person in the wrong place at the wrong time, with the wrong information. I can't possibly be a queen, I don't understand how all of this could happen, I'm so afraid..."

Tighter and tighter his arms got, and he was kissing her forehead and neck, and then he was picking her up and taking her into his rooms as if she weighed absolutely nothing.

His rooms were, if anything, larger than hers, but full of personal items, obviously not just guest quarters. He took her at once to his wide bed and laid her down and crawled in beside her and simply held her until the panic had ebbed away.

Faces close together, nose to nose, Carina took comfort from his breath, from his embrace, from the simple primal presence of him.

After a while, her sobs turned into whimpers and their touches turned from comfort to something more carnal.

She couldn't be close enough, couldn't feel enough of his skin under her fingers. Every touch was intense, every kiss was deep and desperate. She couldn't have said how they got out of their clothing, only knew that the feel of his skin was a panacea to all the ills of her life.

He was so strong, so sweet and kind, and when he filled her with his hard cock, Carina felt like the rest of the world simply went away, pleasure and gratification swelling inside of her like a musical phrase.

At first, they were side by side, slow and careful, but it grew more intense, and he rolled her onto her back, his weight protective and perfect as she fell from the heights of pleasure. He grew frantic, desperate, and Carina cried out in a second wave of bliss as he came deep inside of her and made noises of need and release.

They remained coupled long after they had finished, kissing and murmuring to each other. Carina wasn't sure what she said, or what he said, except that she was safe with him, and that...he loved her.

Afterwards, they washed together in a shower that could have fit five of them. They explored each other gently: the slopes of his shoulders, the small of his back, the framing of his hipbones. Her collarbones, the length of her neck, the place where ass became leg. He lifted her up against the cool tile wall of the shower and kissed her deeply as she wrapped her legs around him.

Everything felt perfect, when it was just the two of them, safe and private and bare, each to the other.

"I don't want to be king," he told her as they dried each other's backs.

She took a decadent second towel for just her hair, and replied sympathetically, "I don't want to be queen. I don't want to be a martyr. I don't want to be a crusader for justice."

"But here we are. King, queen, martyr, crusader." Toren took the towel from her and dried her hair more gently than she had been.

"It sounds like a book title."

"A terrible book they'd make you read in high school."

"And they'd want us to write a report on it exploring the underlying themes of *futility*."

"Speaking of futility," Toren said wryly, "I'm sorry for my family. They're a lot to take, and I think they embarrassed you."

Did he sometimes feel waves of emotion from her, the way she felt them from him? Carina wondered. Was that part of the spell? "They were fine," she assured him. "They had to ask the things they asked."

She could definitely feel the discomfort then, a confused, mixed-up hesitation. "And kids...?"

"Someday," she said thoughtfully. "I mean, I always figured I would, just not any time *soon*."

Relief, like a cool shower after a hot day, flowed from him. "Me, too."

"They're going to nag us ceaselessly, aren't they?" Carina said with dread...but not as much dread as she expected.

"It will definitely be a topic of discussion on my fan page," Toren groaned. "If it isn't already. Oh!" he said. "You're already internet famous."

Carina felt her stomach drop. "Hot topic on your fan page?"

"Front page of Yahoo and TMZ." Toren handed her his phone and Carina put a hand over her face. Sure enough, there she was, dripping wet in Toren's arms wearing her sister's plain bathing suit. There was another shot of her drinking water and looking wan while Toren gazed at her adoringly. The headline was: *Alaskan Prince Rescues Unknown Woman From Drowning At Angel Hot Springs*. A subtitle asked, *Wedding Bells for the Alaska Royal Family at Last?*

"I wasn't drowning," Carina protested feebly. "I was fainting."

"Tom-ay-toes, tom-ah-toes," Toren scoffed. He was looking at her photo with the same besotted gaze he'd given her *in* the picture and Carina had a sudden stab of dismay that she hoped she stuffed down before it could escape her.

This mate thing really was like a magic spell. He clearly couldn't help himself, and there wasn't anything more to it than a random forced compulsion. It seemed like a poor way to pick a new queen, to Carina. Alaska itself couldn't possibly want her for their ruler, no matter how 'in name only' the title was.

Carina took the phone and scrolled through the articles, bemusedly reading speculation about who she was and shaking her head at some of the guesses. An island princess? Deposed Russian nobility? A European trust fund bunny? A server at the hot springs was quoted as saying she was some kind of sports celebrity.

Carina snorted.

It wouldn't be long before they uncovered her real identity.

Besides being American, and besides being wanted by the law because she'd stumbled across corruption in one of the largest banks in the world, who was she really? Nobody, that's who.

She was the most junior accountant in a big, completely anonymous financial firm. She didn't come from money. The closest she'd gotten to fame, before this, was a picture in the paper for winning a scholarship. There had been seven other people in the same photo. And none of them had been a prince.

It occurred to Carina that she was holding a phone. "Do you think I could call my sister?" she asked plaintively.

Toren hesitated. "We should check with Fask," he said cautiously. "Sorry."

Mrs. James, undoubtedly guessing that Carina would not be returning to her own room, had dropped off a pile of clothing for Carina that included a pair of pajamas and undergarments still in packaging that she gratefully wiggled into. Toren put on refreshingly pedestrian sweatpants and a t-shirt for a band called Gangly Moose.

It didn't feel like being royalty. It felt like sneaking into the honeymoon suite of a fancy hotel with a boy she'd just met. They curled up on his giant bed and talked about growing up and their favorite books and music. He liked old pulp novels like Doc Savage and modern action thrillers. She devoured historical romance. He liked an eclectic selection of bluegrass and jazz and rock, she had to giggle into a pillow as she admitted she liked pop music and boy bands.

"I'm not proud," she apologized as Toren made gagging noises.

"That's it," he said. "The wedding is off! Irreconcilable differences! It's doomed before it started!"

She had to tickle him for that, and they wrestled and kissed and finally slept, curled together under a thick down comforter, with moonlight spilling in through the open curtains.

# CHAPTER 28

*T*oren woke blissfully, but even before his eyes were open, he remembered the week he was facing and his groan woke Carina.

"Sorry," he said, kissing her forehead.

"If I screw my eyes shut can I just keep sleeping and pretend that none of this is happening?" Carina asked plaintively.

"None of it?" Toren couldn't resist asking.

"Maybe some of it," Carina said, tipping her head to intercept his next kiss with her lips.

A knock on the door interrupted anything else that might have happened next and Carina gave a groan of her own.

"Your Highness," a loud voice called. "Breakfast is served."

Carina put her head under a pillow.

"Thank you," Toren called in return.

"We've got a helluva day ahead of us," Carina said, muffled.

"Let's get it started," Toren said with more confidence than he felt.

After a quick shower, Carina picked an outfit from the pile of clothing that had been left for her and put her hair into a tidy, utilitarian braid. "I'll want to take Shadow for a walk after breakfast, if that's alright."

Toren started to say that they could ask Fask about the schedule, then remembered that he was going to have to make those kinds of decisions himself as king. "That sounds fine," he said. "Let's plan on eating lunch in Fairbanks. It's equinox, there's a festival downtown! I can show you around, and you can pick up anything you need in town."

"It sounds like my timing was good for once," Carina said wryly. "Do you have a spare toothbrush?"

"Under the sink!"

How had they fallen into such easy domesticity? Toren wondered. He liked to be alone, to have his space to himself whenever five brothers allowed such a thing. But now he couldn't imagine waking up without this woman, didn't want to picture his rooms without her.

*Ours,* his dragon reminded him, deeply satisfied. *As it should be. As it always will be.*

Breakfast was filled with dragging details about the engagement party, which Fask thought they should host the following weekend to coincide with the visiting royalty that had already been arranged. "That should give the most important people time to get here. I've got a press release written, and we can do questions with journalists later this morning."

He turned to Carina, who was nursing a cup of coffee and stabbing a sunny-side-up egg on her plate. "We'd like to get that flash drive into the vault as soon as possible for safekeeping."

Carina cast a desperate look at Toren, who remembered that he'd promised to take her into town.

"After we do that, we were going to head in to Fairbanks to catch part of the festival," Toren said, as casually as he could manage. "We can do the press release later this afternoon." To his surprise, no one countered him, just accepted his amendment without question.

"I'll let you know where we'll do the press conference when I have the details," Fask agreed.

Carina gave a grateful smile to both of them and finished her coffee. The conversation centered around who would be invited to both the engagement party and the wedding itself.

"My sister?" Carina suggested tentatively, when they'd gotten down to second cousins and minor nobility from island nations.

"Certainly," Fask said. "Any family you wish. Give Mrs. James the details and she'll arrange the flights."

As the other brothers finished their meals and stood to go, Fask said across the table to Toren, "I want to talk to you about what you'll say to people."

"I was planning to go walk Shadow and assure him that I haven't abandoned him," Carina said. "Do you need me?"

Fask frowned. "I only want to caution you not to say too much yet. We'll coach you in specifics before the engagement party, but in the meantime, stick to 'it's classified,' and 'I can't say much.'"

Carina nodded solemnly. "I can do that." She gave Fask a wry smile. "I didn't get across two international borders by being gabby about my problems. I'm good at vague answers, don't worry."

Fask laughed. "I shouldn't underestimate you, my lady."

"Is it my lady now?" Toren wanted to know.

"Close enough," Fask said. "She'll officially be the fiancée of the crown prince of Alaska by next week, so let's get people used to it. *Your Highness* won't be appropriate until you are married, and *Your Majesty* will be after the coronation, of course."

Toren filed the information and Carina gave him a brief kiss on the cheek before heading out to walk Shadow. Two of the guards at the door peeled away to follow her at a slight distance.

"Is she in *danger?*" Toren asked Fask quietly after she'd left.

"We'll have guards trailing her any time she isn't with one of us," Fask said confidently. "I've already got the local police quietly on alert; there will be extra patrols downtown at the festival as well."

Toren wasn't sure that really answered the question, but it did make him feel better.

"Make sure your phone is on," Fask reminded him. "And no ignoring it."

Toren grinned. He was notorious for not answering messages.

He glanced back as he heard swift footsteps at the door, and was stepping to meet Carina almost before he registered the expression on her face. "What's wrong?" he asked.

"Shadow," Carina said miserably. "He's gone."

Behind her, Tray was holding Shadow's blue and gold collar in his hands and looking almost as distressed as she was.

"He slipped his collar sometime last night. I went out to feed them this morning and he was gone."

Toren folded Carina into a comforting embrace, but she remained stiff and distant, inconsolable in the loss he could sense from her. "That's twice now that I've lost him, you'd think I'd be used to this by now," she sniffed.

"I checked the fit of his collar yesterday," Tray protested, looking guilty. "It was properly sized. I don't know how it happened."

"He's a bit of an escape artist," Toren said to his brother. Then, to Carina, "We can check at the animal shelter while we're downtown, maybe put up fliers."

Carina wiped her face on her sleeves, clearly trying to regain her composure. Toren was keenly aware of Fask watching them and he was irritated that they were always going to be under that kind of scrutiny. "Maybe he's just off exploring and he'll come back for supper," he said optimistically, guiding Carina away. "Let's go check around the garage and get the flash drive."

# CHAPTER 29

oren's concept of a garage was much different than Carina's. It was more like a giant *Batcave*, and was *full* of cars. There were vintage cars, muscle cars, race cars, two limos, a Jeep, several pick-up trucks, and a handful of motorcycles. There were a few four-wheelers and several snowmobiles. No, wait, Tray had called them snow*machines*. It was a hodgepodge of styles and tastes, well-lit, and much cleaner than Carina expected from a garage; it still had that tangy smell of oil and metal, but the concrete was spotless and the workbenches were tidy.

Her sister's van looked terribly out of place near the end where they came in, with its dents and rust. It looked as though they had washed it, but nothing short of an overhaul and a paint job would make it fit in with the royal fleet.

Kind of like Carina herself, she thought miserably.

Shadow was nowhere to be found, though she'd yelled herself hoarse in a circuit around the large building. Maybe he didn't recognize his name, she thought. After all, she'd just assigned it to him randomly two nights before. She had no claim over him. Not even the kind of tenuous magical claim that she had on Toren.

Raval was there, tinkering with one of cars. He nodded at Toren and Carina as they came in, and even asked, "Did you find the dog?"

Carina shook her head, not trusting herself to talk, and Toren squeezed her hand. "We'll keep looking," he said to both of them. "He's come back before."

Carina squeezed him back, wishing he felt hopeful, and they walked around the far side of the van...where they drew to a halt.

There was broken glass on the cement.

In this immaculate garage, there were fragments of broken glass scattered on the clean, white cement.

Broken headlight glass.

Toren figured out what it meant before Carina could put the pieces together in her head.

"Raval, has anyone been in here this morning? Call the guards! I want security here immediately. Maybe the police...we need to look for evidence. We need photos. Get Fask! Oh, I'll call him."

His voice was just nonsense in Carina's head as she walked forward, her hiking boots crunching over the shards.

The headlight was completely broken out, and when she reached her hand into the cavity, she knew what she would find.

"It's gone," she whispered. "It's *gone*."

The only proof that she had of the crime she'd found, the only evidence that would carry any weight in the fight for justice and her own freedom...it had been stolen.

"Who knew?" Toren asked her. "Who knew where the drive was?"

The rest of the van was untouched. It was a surgical extraction, someone had known exactly where it had been hidden.

"No one," Carina said, hearing the note of hysteria in her voice. "We never told your brothers or the captain where in the van it was, only that it was there. You and I were the only ones who knew where I hid it."

Toren frowned. "Your sister?"

"I didn't tell her," Carina said, choking down her fear. "I figured out the hiding place myself, right before the Canadian border. I felt pretty clever for it, too." She tried to laugh and failed.

"Could someone have seen you at the hot springs when you showed me where it was?" Toren said, brows furrowed. "Maybe someone was watching with binoculars? There was that man in the restaurant who kept staring at us, and we know that *someone* tracked you *to* the resort."

Carina shrugged one shoulder, feeling like her whole body was somehow numb and on fire at the same time. This wasn't at all how things were supposed to be going.

The garage door opened and the whole place felt suddenly smaller as a dozen guards swarmed in with a blast of cold air and began taking photos and asking questions and poking around in the small space between the van and the next vehicle.

The captain frowned fiercely at Carina as if it was her fault personally, and then crisply sent several people to check the perimeter and draw up logs and camera footage. Fask quizzed Raval, who hadn't seen anyone since he'd come in after breakfast.

"It must have happened last night," Fask said, frowning. "Are you alright, Carina?"

Carina could only stare at him. No, she wasn't alright. She was a fugitive. The last tenuous hope for clearing her name had just been *stolen*. She felt like she'd been punched in the gut and was gasping for air.

She felt *delirious*.

"What can I do?" Toren asked Fask. "How can I help?"

"You can't," Fask said dismissively.

"Does this change our plans?" Toren asked, and for a moment Carina thought he was talking to her.

"No," Fask said. "But we're sending guards with you into town."

"Do you still want to go?"

That was for her, this time, and Carina turned away from the people sweeping up the glass and nodded numbly. "Sure." Pretend it was normal. Pretend any of this was normal.

The security footage outside the garage showed Shadow, to Carina's grief. There wasn't a camera on the dog yard, or inside the garage, but he loped into the frame for a few moments, sniffing around the building, then vanished. Shortly after, the cameras had gone down, presumably when the person after the flash drive broke in.

"The wires were cut. Someone knew exactly where to clip them." The captain was furious, and everyone else ranged from agitated to angry.

Carina was glad when she could finally escape with Toren in a car with Grim and Amused, who looked far less amused than he had when she had named him in her head.

"Carina…"

"I can't," she said fiercely, voice low. "It's too raw to talk about it all now, and I'm not going to. We're going to a festival and I'm going to forget about all of it for a little while and we're going to figure it all out later, okay?"

Comfort. He felt like comfort and safety, even now, when Carina was starting not to believe in either of those things.

"I'm here whenever you're ready," he told her. "Let's have a fun time, eat some food, pretend we're not involved in breaking up big corporate cons, not royalty, not missing Shadow. No, wait, we'll stop at the shelter first and file a report. Then we'll pretend we're not any of those things for a few hours and I'll show you a little of the city."

"I'd like that," Carina said, and she thought, with Toren at her side, that she could actually enjoy it.

# CHAPTER 30

S hadow wasn't at the animal shelter, and none of the missing dog posters matched his description. Toren left his details and the woman at the counter solemnly promised to call if the dog was turned in.

Carina seemed to take it well. Toren could feel the stress, leaking out around her like a poorly sealed beach ball, but she *trusted* him, trusted that he—that his family—could protect her.

He would do anything not to betray that trust, he thought, giving her a sidelong look as they climbed from the car.

She looked absolutely determined to enjoy herself, as if she could will herself into happiness.

Downtown Fairbanks was decked out for autumn equinox, with Alaska flags flying from every building. The bridge across the Chena River had been decorated in fall garlands, and there was a brass band playing at the memorial park by the river. Open booths were set up lining First and Second Avenue, both closed to motorized traffic. They were filled with vendors selling crafts and furs and food.

They heard the festival, then smelled it, and then rounded the corner into happy chaos. A dance troupe was keeping warm with a stomping Russian dance, the audience cheering happily as they squatted and flung their feet out in classic form. A trio of spangled belly dancers were waiting at the side of the stage, huddled in coats as they anticipated their turn.

"I'm starving," Carina said, nose in the air. Breakfast had been hours ago.

"Got a preference?" Toren asked. There was an international selection: American pizza, Thai food, Greek pitas and gyros, sandwiches of many varieties, hot dogs, and more.

"What's Alaskan?" Carina asked. "Pretend I'm a tourist. I mean, I basically *am*."

"Ah," Toren said knowingly. "I know just the booth."

He led her down the street and around the corner as the belly-dancers gave a loud *zhagaroot* to announce the start of their routine.

A busy booth boasted caribou sausages in buns and salmon burgers, with chips and local-made pickles.

Carina, after agonizing a few moments, chose a salmon burger, and they went to the riverside park to sit and eat.

Carina was shivering. "I'm going to have to find a second hand store and buy a warmer coat," she said. Although it was sunny and the sky was brilliant blue, it wasn't terribly warm; there was a biting breeze that promised the coming winter. "How are my clothes going to work out?" she asked. "I was half-expecting ball gowns to be laid out on my bed in the morning, and I don't know how queenly my hiking boots are."

"It doesn't matter how you dress most of the time," Toren assured her. "There are some formal affairs, but even at those, you'll find that one guy in overalls stained with chainsaw oil. Tray practically lives in hockey jerseys. It's Alaska; we're practical and independent, and we rarely dress to impress each other."

"How refreshing," Carina said, taking the last bite of her food.

"Admit it," he teased her. "You were hoping for the frilly dresses and tiaras."

To his delight, Carina laughed. "Well, come on, if I'm going to be a princess, I want to do it *right*." She considered, then added, "I have to admit, I'm *glad* I don't have to wear heels."

Toren wiped his hands on napkins and stood. A couple of girls sitting nearby were eyeing them curiously, whispering together. "It's not him," one of them said clearly.

"I have an idea," he said. "She's usually down this way." He took Carina's hand decisively and they went down First Avenue to the end. They didn't make very fast progress; the booths along their way were filled with arts and crafts and Carina dawdled, admiring the carvings and dolls and masks. She didn't offer to buy anything, but she did compliment the vendors, who smiled at her and grinned at Toren. He recognized a good number of them from previous festivals and was *sure* they recognized him.

The crowd swirled around them, cheerful and full of celebration. Children went bolting around them, some of them with dogs on leashes.

When they arrived at the crafters at the end of the aisle, Carina's mouth made a very satisfying O.

"Pick something out," Toren said. "Hi, Anna."

A large, smiling Native Alaskan woman was sitting in a booth filled with parkas and hats and mittens, all in luxurious fur and colorful fabric patterns. She was beading on a pair of fur slippers, a wild rose pattern in bright pink. "Toren, you scamp. If you knock over a display, you're paying for the whole thing."

"I haven't knocked over one of your racks since I was eleven," Toren protested, bending close to kiss her on the cheek. "I'm a little less clumsy than I was then, and you are no less lovely."

"No less of a suck-up than you ever were, either," Anna scolded him. She looked appraisingly at Carina. "You're with this one, then?"

Carina scrambled forward in the narrow space and offered her hand. "Hi," she said shyly, ducking around the coats. "I'm Carina."

Anna's handshake was firm and calloused. "Nice to meet you," she said briefly. "Can I help you find something?"

"Oh no," Carina said quickly, though she shivered. "I don't have this kind of money..."

"It's my treat," Toren said swiftly. "Don't worry."

Carina gave him a hesitant glance.

"He owes me a sale, for all the ones he's lost me over the years," Anna said shrewdly. "Always running through with his rowdy brothers like he owns the place, putting dirty fingerprints on the wares, scaring the customers. Pull down that teal parka, Toren, see how it suits her."

"We *do* own the place, Anna," Toren teased her. He picked out a pull-over parka in a flowered teal-green pattern that matched her hazel eyes, trimmed in mink.

Anna snorted. "You own the *land*. You *earn* the people. Now hold that up for her. Yes, try it on."

Carina took off her light jacket and wriggled into it, pulling the generous hood up over her head to test the fit. "I would never in a million years get cold in this," she said in wonder. Toren wisely decided not to mention that this was only a medium-weight parka, and she'd need something warmer to be out in the bitterest cold of winter.

The crafter laughed and pulled out a full-length mirror. Carina twisted to see the back. It covered her sweet ass, which Toren thought was a shame but he accepted the concession as important to warmth.

"That's mink on the hood," Anna pointed out. "My son traps them out on the flats. Won't frost when you're out in the cold."

There was beautiful embroidery tape all along the cuffs and hem, twining forget-me-nots and wild roses. Toren unwound the price tag from one of the buttons before Carina could see it. "We'll take it," he told Anna.

"I should think so," Anna snorted. She took the credit card Toren offered. "You need a bag?"

"Can I wear it?" Carina asked wistfully.

Anna looked pleased. "If you have any problems with it, you come see me. All of my work is guaranteed for craftsmanship."

"It's so beautiful," Carina told her, eyes gleaming suspiciously as she hugged herself. "Thank you so much."

Anna waved them off. "You're blocking the way for other paying customers," she scolded them.

"This is an amazing festival for a town this size," Carina said, as they continued to wander among the booths and enjoy the entertainment; there was a woman juggling knives and a man in drag doing fortunes.

"This is one of our smaller ones," Toren said offhandedly, though he was pleased by Carina's happiness. "The summer solstice festival is our biggest event—it goes two blocks further and runs until midnight."

"With fireworks?" Carina teased.

"No fireworks," Toren said. "You can't see them in the summer because it doesn't get dark. We save those for New Year's."

Carina blinked. "I hadn't thought of that." She laughed. "The queen of Alaska ought to know that," she said sheepishly, shaking her head. Then, "Do you know everyone?"

Toren, caught in the act of waving at one of the other vendors, chuckled. "Not everyone," he protested. "But the city isn't that big, and you see a lot of familiar faces at these things. We...used to make more regular appearances at festivals when I was younger, but we don't do it so much now."

"Now that your dad is...sick. Sleeping."

"He loved this kind of thing, walking among the crowds, being one of them, listening to their problems firsthand," Toren said thoughtfully. "He never acted like being a king made him better than anyone else." He heard the longing in his voice before he recognized it in his chest. People had stopped asking about his father, he'd been absent so long. The gregarious man he remembered had been replaced by an impression of isolation.

They paused to listen to a bluegrass band. "They aren't *bad*," Carina conceded. A loose dog bolted around them, chased by a swearing owner, and Toren watched sorrow wash over her face.

"Do you think Shadow came back to the castle?" she asked wistfully.

At that moment, the phone in Toren's pocket buzzed. Hope swirled between them as he pulled it out. "Fask wants us back at the palace for the press release," he said, disappointed, but not nearly as disappointed as Carina was. "Was there anything else you wanted to see?"

Carina shook her head. "No, I'm ready to go back."

"They're going to love you," Toren promised. Then, hesitantly, "Will you quiz me on my speech on the way back? Fask sent notes for both of us."

"I'd love to," Carina said. "I was in a high school production of My Fair Lady, so I know all about *e-nun-ci-A-tion*."

He took her hand and nodded back at the guards who were trailing them discreetly.

Just for just a moment, the crowd parted and he saw the same man he'd seen at Angel Hot Springs, standing with his arms crossed, avidly watching Carina.

Then a group of laughing tourists walked between them, and when Toren tried to spot the man again, he was gone, lost in the crowd.

# CHAPTER 31

The drive to the palace was as beautiful as their first trip was, but Carina watched very little of it. Their practice of the speech was very silly, Toren trying at first to very solemnly read his cards, but swiftly descending into a mockingly officious voice. "We have gathered," he said, twirling an imaginary mustache, "to make an announcement of the gravest urgency," he improvised.

Then he switched to a panicked voice. "You guys have to help me! They're making me get married! Tell the press! Get me out of here! It's a train! Oh, noooooo!"

Carina mimed a frying pan, and they collapsed together in the seat of the car, laughing and glancing forward at Grim and Amused in the front seats. The two guards were trying very hard to keep straight faces.

She was still smiling, even when they arrived at the castle and found the press set up on the front steps. She was with Toren, and she was *safe* with Toren.

"I suppose we have to do this," Carina said, as the car pulled up into the drive and she got a glimpse of the press vehicles crowding the circle. "No going back."

They both sighed at the same time, and then the guards were opening the door to the car and helping Carina out.

Cameras turned to them as they came walking down the sweeping sidewalk to the castle, hand in hand, and they were greeted with a chaos of questions. Fask had set up a podium on the steps, and Toren drew Carina close as the microphone crackled and the noise died down.

Toren was quiet, staring out at them, for so long that Carina wondered if he'd gotten stage fright. She clung tight to his hand and tried to project every scrap of confidence she could at him.

He turned to her as if he'd felt it, and gave her a slow smile so sexy and adoring that Carina couldn't help but grin back at him.

"Thanks for being here," he said, finding the correct distance from the microphone after a false start. That was not at all how Fask's speech had started. "I'm really delighted to introduce you to Carina Andresen, and announce that she's agreed to marry me. I understand that you've probably heard a lot of crazy stuff and we can't really answer questions about that right now, so please don't be jerks about it, but if you want to know about how great she is or how happy we are, I have plenty to say about that."

Everyone laughed, like they were supposed to, and no one wanted to look like a jerk on record after that, so the questions were all very simple and Toren answered what he could while Carina smiled and blushed and waved. At the very end, she leaned forward to the microphone and said "Thank you," and everyone applauded.

"That wasn't as bad as I'd feared," she said with a sigh of relief as they walked up the steps to the castle and the press started to disband behind them.

"You got creative with the speech," Fask said with a frown, meeting them halfway up the stairs, but he didn't really seem bothered.

"Your speech was boring," Toren said merrily. "And I didn't say anything I shouldn't have."

"You did fine," Fask said grudgingly.

They were almost to the great doors when the big glass panel very suddenly shattered before her eyes and Toren was diving on top of her, driving her to the ground. She heard stitches rip.

"There's a shooter!" someone cried. "Get down!"

"Where is it coming from?"

"What's going on?"

"It must have come from over there…"

"Tell me you got that on tape!"

Beneath Toren's arm, Carina had a glimpse of Fask, snarling and shouting.

"Inside, Your Highnesses," Captain Luke said, very close by, and then Carina and Toren were being hauled up and hurried inside. She had just enough time to see a shadow in the air, and a vague ripple of light. None of the press members seemed to notice it, but Carina suspected one of the brothers had taken off to try to hunt down the shooter.

The *shooter*.

Someone had *shot* at her.

Carina felt like she was boiling inside.

Someone had stolen her evidence and tried to shoot her and her new parka had probably been torn in the fall, and her dog was lost, and she felt like a feral cat trapped in a corner. She might go down, but she was going to take someone's face off when she went.

Then they were inside, being rushed to the back of the lobby, while Captain Luke muttered furiously about the defensibility of giant glass panels in doors and the idiocy of architects.

"How'd the press release go?"

Tray, oblivious to the drama, was coming from the back entrance, but Carina wasn't looking at him whatsoever; all of her attention was on the shape beside him.

"Shadow!" She shook off Toren's hand and bolted across the hall to slide on her knees the last few steps as the big dog capered to meet her, tongue happily lolling from the side of his mouth. His tail was wagging furiously, and he wriggled and tried to lick Carina as she threw her arms around him.

Gray fur flew everywhere as she wrestled and scratched him, and he fell on his side in happiness.

"Where did you find him?" Carina asked, looking up at Tray as she wiped tears from her eyes.

Tray, looking pleased and relieved, shrugged. "He just came back," he said helplessly. "He showed up just a few moments ago looking hungry and tired. He's got a bit of a limp, careful with that front leg. He probably had a grand time *somewhere*. What's going on? What happened to the door?"

"We just got shot at!" Toren said, outraged, hovering just behind Carina.

"What?!"

"I didn't hear a shot," Carina said, still confused and feeling shocky with relief. She had Shadow back.

"It was too far away," Fask snapped. "The shooter might have been a half a mile away with good optics. You'd only hear the impact, not the explosion."

Carina thought he sounded more irritated than scared. Here she was, being more of a problem than *ever*.

# CHAPTER 32

*T*oren reminded himself that he didn't need to be jealous of a dog. Carina's joy at Shadow's return was strong and pure and washed away all of the terror of being shot at; if it weren't for the tense swirl of the guards and the missing glass panel in the door, he might have thought he'd imagined the assassination attempt.

Then he remembered that *someone had shot at Carina*, and he felt rage blaze through his veins until he wasn't sure how much of it was his and how much of it was his simmering dragon's. Possibly, some of it was Carina's.

He gave Shadow a suspicious look, but if the dog was a shifter, he was a master method actor, acting in every way like a common dog. Besides, Tray already had him in hand when the shooting had occurred. Which reminded Toren again that *someone had shot at Carina*.

Fask was quietly talking to Captain Luke, and Toren left Carina's side to uncharacteristically insert himself into their private conversation. "I want to know what we're doing to increase security," he said quietly, as firmly as he could.

Fask and Luke both looked at him in surprise.

"Luke and I can handle this," Fask told him. "You worry about—"

"About how I'm keeping my *mate* safe?" Toren suggested. "Because that's a big part of what I intend to worry about."

"You don't need to know the details," Fask said impatiently. "It would take too much time to bring you up to speed. You don't understand how anything here is run."

Toren felt stung. "Well, maybe I should."

Fask and Luke stared at him. Fask looked irritated, but Luke had an approving smile on her usually inscrutable face.

"I'm going to be the king of Alaska," Toren reminded them both. "I *should* know how everything is run. I should be part of...refining our defenses...or...whatever."

Fask gentled. "You don't need to know all the gritty details to be king," he said.

"You do," Toren pointed out. "You know how everything works, and everyone agrees that makes you the best candidate for the job. So how come when I want to learn all of that, you just brush me off? I don't want to just be a king, I want to be a *good* king." They both looked at him with deeply complicated expressions and Toren scrambled to add, "I mean, I don't *want* to be king...but if I'm going to be..."

Fask frowned thoughtfully. "Alright—"

Raval returned then, in a blaze of light, and shifted back to human on the front steps. The press had been herded away to write their shocking headlines and the castle staff had already taped clear plastic over the door and swept up the glass.

"I found the gun and the place the shooter must have been," Raval reported, handing over the weapon and an empty cartridge. "But they were already gone. It's a bluff with no foot access, nearly impossible for human access. It was a shifter, at least, almost certainly something that can fly, if I couldn't find them."

Fask gave a hiss of dismay and Luke actually growled.

"Does Amco Bank hire *shifters*?" Toren blurted, still thinking about Shadow.

"This isn't Amco Bank's work," Fask snarled.

Toren looked at him blankly, then the rest of the pieces fell into place. "One of our enemies under the Compact?"

"If you...or Carina...come to an unfortunate end before the Compact is renewed, Alaska is out, and open for takeover."

The idea that the shooter might have been shooting at him was almost a relief. It meant Carina was that tiniest bit safer.

But of course, it was the same outcome, no matter which of them was eliminated, until the actual coronation, so they were both still in terrible danger.

Something occurred to him. "Someone was watching Carina," he said. "Or maybe both of us. At the hot springs, and again at the festival."

He had everyone's attention. "It was a big man, taller than me, dark hair, olive skin."

Luke took as detailed a description as Toren could give, which wasn't very, and he was frustrated by his inability to be more helpful as the discussion turned to the involvement of the police to spread out their efforts to find the culprit.

He looked over to find Carina still sitting on the floor with Shadow, arms wrapped around him as his tail beat out an irregular rhythm on the warm wooden planks. Guards were around her in a loose semi-circle. She looked very small and lost.

"Go on," Fask said quietly to him, as Luke quizzed Raval for more details about the site of the assassination attempt.

Toren startled, looking at him. "I was serious about doing more, about learning everything. I don't want to be a paper king."

"It can wait," Fask said sympathetically. "You can't do everything at once, and your mate needs you right now."

Fask didn't have to tell him twice. He barely had to say it once. Everything in Toren yearned to be with Carina, to hold her in his arms and shield her from harm. Knowing how close she'd come to being shot...If he lost her...

The guards melted back as he knelt next to Carina and gathered both her and Shadow in for an embrace.

"Oh, Toren," she said, leaning her head against him. "I'm tired of being a *target*."

"If it makes you feel any better, they might have been shooting at *me*."

"That doesn't make me feel the slightest bit better," Carina said, but she laughed and squeezed Toren back.

"Come on, let's go get Shadow set up with a water dish and a rug in our room."

Carina dragged a hand over her face, dashing away tears that she seemed surprised to find there. "Won't Mrs. James have objections to that?" she asked with a hiccup as she rose to her feet with Toren. Shadow stood and leaned against her knees.

"Let her," Toren said boldly. "I'm going to be the king of Alaska. It's got to come with *some* perks."

# CHAPTER 33

"You said you'd be keeping a low profile!" June said furiously when Carina finally got her to pick up her phone. "And instead, you're all over the covers of the checkout stand magazines. In *my swimsuit*. That is not a low profile, Carina. That is the opposite of a low profile!"

Carina could hear the tears in her sister's voice. "Nothing has gone exactly like I planned," she confessed. "I'm sorry I couldn't call sooner."

"I know you probably couldn't," June sobbed. "But oh, wow, Carina, I've been so worried. They've been asking and asking and asking…and there are people constantly watching…"

Carina was crying now, too. "I'm so sorry. I never wanted to drag you into this."

"You're a princess!" June yelled. "I want to be dragged into that part!"

"I'm not a princess yet," Carina laughed tearfully. "But I want you to come up here for that. For a while. To be…safe."

"Is…there danger? Do they still think…?"

"We probably shouldn't talk much about it over the phone,"

Carina said reluctantly. "But John can come. They'll cover every-thing, travel, places to stay here, jobs, even."

"My job can kiss my ass," June agreed, sobbing again. "Cari, I'm so happy for you and so scared!"

They talked for a while about trivial things: the weather in Alaska, Carina's travels. They didn't mention the shooting. "You'd better not have put a single scratch on my van," June threatened.

Carina thought about the slashed seats and the broken head-light. "It's *pristine*," she lied, knowing that her sister would hear the fib. They laughed hysterically. "I'll pay you back," Carina promised. "I love you, Juney."

"I love you, too, Princess Cari," June wept.

Carina washed her face and cuddled with Shadow, who didn't particularly want to be cuddled, then went to find Toren.

He was in the so-called informal dining room with Rian, who nodded and invited her in.

"There was a case in Finland where they held a ninety-six day religious ceremony for a refugee while they negotiated with her government, so I've got a few ideas for things we can do with you if things get touchy about extradition," he said reassuringly.

"That's a relief," Carina said. Shadow lay down on the floor at her feet as she sat next to Toren and she let his leash rest on the arm of her chair. Even in the castle, she was making a practice of keeping him leashed, because he'd demonstrated a habit of bolting, and because she wanted to give Mrs. James as little grief as possible.

"I've also been in touch with the woman who was writing that thesis on the unaltered copy of the Compact," Rian continued. Carina noticed that color rose in his cheeks. "We've had some really interesting exchanges, and she has some theories I'm going to be looking into more carefully about mates. We might be able to *make* one happen for Fask. It's...kind of an awkward conversation at times because she doesn't know what mates are, and she thinks the dragon and magic references are code for something. I...might need to go see her in person."

Toren gave Rian a distinctly skeptical look. "You hate traveling."

"I could fly," Rian said.

"You could fly to Florida and talk to some stranger about a Compact she probably thinks she imagined," Toren proposed sarcastically.

Rian nodded in full seriousness. "It's not really fair to her. I mean, we basically destroyed her thesis by replacing the Compact. She probably thought she was going crazy."

"You've got to be careful about what you tell her," Toren cautioned. Then he smiled and laughed. "Have *I* ever said 'be careful' to *you*? Isn't this supposed to be the other way around?"

Rian grinned back at him. "Yeah, well, things are changing, Your Crown Highness."

"Never call me that again," Toren groaned.

When Toren rose to go, Rian stopped him. "Toren, when you first felt the mate bond...it was *before* you met Carina, wasn't it?"

Toren stopped and Carina watched his face curiously, aching a little. She was already standing, and Shadow was swirling at her feet, bored and restless.

"Yes," he said slowly, staring into space. "It was when you first told me what my job was, to evict the squatter. I mean, that's usually the last thing in the world I would want to do, and I was already trying to find an excuse to get out of it. But my dragon insisted that we needed to go, that it was really important, and I knew he was *right*. And that only got stronger, the closer we got."

He seemed to jolt back into himself, and the look he gave Rian was shrewd. "Why do you ask?"

Carina was sure she saw Rian blush then.

"Nothing," Rian said swiftly. "No reason."

A terrible thought occurred to Carina as they parted ways.

If one of the other brothers found their mates, they wouldn't have any reason to protect her. They'd made it clear that Toren was the least likely and least desirable brother to make king. And if they didn't need her to ensure that he *became* king...

She was nothing but trouble to them, a political problem of epic proportions. An embarrassment. A complication.

If another brother found a nice mate with half as much

baggage, they'd have no reason to fight her extradition. And without any evidence...

"Are you alright?" Toren asked, and Carina gave him a wan smile. She couldn't seem to feel what he was feeling—maybe because her own emotions were feeling so raw—but she could see the concern in his eyes and she'd learned to read his face. She hesitated a moment, wanting to tell him all of her doubts about *them*, and share the confusion she had about all of her feelings and fears. But he was already carrying arguably more load on his shoulders than she was, and he seemed blissfully content to believe that their love was magically undeniable and unshakable. She didn't want to take even a moment of that happiness from him.

"I'm fine," Carina said. "Just...it's all a lot sometimes."

Toren put his arm around her shoulders warmly. "Believe me, I know. Fask and Mrs. James have us booked non-stop for the next few days. You've got deportment lessons, and dancing instructors, and I get to learn how to apply royal seals, and there are going to be hours with the lawyers, and it's all going to be just fine, because we've got each other, and we'll get through this."

Shadow gave a canine cough like he was going to throw up.

"For now," Toren proposed, "let's take Shadow for a walk and I'll show you the pond and the ridge trail and we'll pretend we're going to run away."

# CHAPTER 34

The days to the engagement party passed like runaway trains, sweeping Toren along while he hung on for dear life and tried to pack as much into his head as he possibly could.

"You want a book on...what?"

Rian's surprise was understandable as he put the lid to his laptop down.

Toren moved into Rian's library, eyeing the shelf-lined walls speculatively. "Tax structures and capital expenses. Did you know that it cost more than five million Alaskan dollars to repair the North Haul Road after that big flood two years ago? I had no idea how much *dirt* costs."

"You know, Toren, you don't have to learn *everything* in order to be king," Rian reminded him. "You'll *have* advisors."

"I want to know when my advisors are full of crap," Toren said flatly. "Already this week, I've had people coming after me with...the craziest stuff. People clearly sucking up, people with all these genuine-looking problems and complaints, people who want favors, people who want to yell at me for screwing things up when I'm not even technically engaged yet, let alone making decisions."

"Isn't that all supposed to go through the press secretary?" Rian said. "Doesn't he screen everything?"

"I told him I wanted to see it all," Toren sighed. "That might have been a mistake. Oh, I also want to look at the Compact."

"I'll get something on the taxes," Rian said. "And you can chat with the PS about throttling back on what he sends through. But why do you want to see the Compact?"

"It's a big part of why we're doing everything we're doing, and I want to understand it."

Rian laughed dryly. "No one understands the Compact!" he scoffed. "It took all of the Small Kingdoms casters and a five-hundred year old dragon to make it, and no one is alive who wrote it, and it is seven hundred pages of complex spell that is supposed to save the world. Better men than you have tried to make sense of it. No offense."

Toren wasn't offended. "I'd still like to look at it," he said. "I should do that much before I'm bound by it. Especially if I'm going to sign the Renewal. I don't think that should be the first time I tried to read it."

Rian smiled at him kindly. "You've been working really hard this week," he observed. "Everyone is impressed."

"I don't want to let anyone down," Toren confessed. "I didn't ask for this, and I don't want it, but I want to do it right if I'm going to."

"Well, you're not going to do it right if you have a mental break-down," Rian advised. "Why don't you take the rest of the day off. We can check out the Compact in the vault after your big engagement party this weekend. Go take Shadow for a walk with Carina, play some video hockey or whatever you usually do. You can't do for everyone else before you do for you."

"Dad used to say that," Toren remembered abruptly.

"He wasn't wrong," Rian insisted. "Go spend some of your last free time with your mate."

Toren sighed, but he knew that Rian was right.

He found Carina in her van, still parked in the garage. The sliding door was open and Shadow was on a leash sulking at her feet. The big gray dog had been caught trying to escape twice, and seemed to resent being kept under close surveillance.

Carina herself was sitting on the back bench, a well-folded brochure about Alaska in her hands. Toren recognized it; he hated that one because it had a photo of himself as a kid, and he remembered how agonizing posing for that picture had been. Kenth and Fask had been arguing. Tray had been teasing Rian. Their father had been more patient than Toren thought they deserved.

Toren sat down beside her and she leaned into him as he put an arm around her shoulders. As always, he felt that bubble of peace and rightness that he always felt with her. Was it hers? His dragon's? He seemed to feel her emotions less than he had at first.

*It is right*, his dragon murmured. *It was meant to be.*

No matter how crazy things got, no matter how full with information his head felt, or how full of frustration he was with *how things actually worked* versus *how things ought to work*, every time that he found Carina and held her, everything was *better*.

This was what having a mate could be, he thought with contentment. For all of the weight and duty that had come with finding her, he couldn't once regret it.

She tipped her head up and kissed him, twining her fingers into his, and he could feel her relaxing, all through her body.

"Planning our big escape?" Toren asked. "Are we going to drive to Mexico? Do you have something picked out in South America?"

"I haven't quite worked out passports," Carina chuckled. She still hadn't been issued identification, and the United States hadn't officially pressed for extradition or acknowledged that they would. She was in a terrible, stressful limbo, and Toren was awed by how well she had held up under the strain.

Some nights, she confessed her fears and cried in his arms, and Toren told her all the ways he dreaded failing, and they comforted each other in every way that they could.

But publicly, she showed a brave face, smiling and laughing and picking her way through all of the new complications and dangers that had been thrust at her with her chin high and her eyes dancing. She was funny and kind, and Alaska already loved her. She was a better princess than any of them had any reason to expect, and she would be a better queen than they deserved, Toren thought.

"Hey, you want to play a round of hockey?" he asked abruptly.

"I know it's cold, but it hasn't been *that* cold," Carina chuckled. "And I can't skate anyway…"

"We can play field hockey," Toren said, tugging at her arm with enthusiasm. "Come on, I'll show you."

Shadow, suspecting excitement, surged to his feet and tried to bolt.

Carina grabbed his leash before it could spool away from her.

"Tray was talking about taking a dog for a run, he can take Shadow with him," Toren said, half-dragging her from the van. "You'll love it, come on! I'll get the gear."

"Will I need my coat?" she asked. She was wearing one of the old, insulated plaid flannel shirts that had been packed for her sister's van.

"You'll want gloves and a hat," Toren advised. "But I'll work you hard enough that you won't need more of a coat."

"Oo," Carina said with a grin. "I love it when you talk dirty to me."

Toren found a spare hat and gloves with the hockey sticks and soccer ball in the back of the garage and he pulled the wool hat down over Carina's eyes before he rolled it up to display the Alaska hockey league logo.

"I'm really living the princess life here," she scoffed, straightening it with a laugh. She pulled on the gloves, shouldered one of the sticks, and they went to the dog yard.

Tray, fortunately, was game for taking Shadow. "I promise I won't let him out of my sight," he swore to Carina. "I'll wear our new escape artist out on the upper trail with Dana."

Shadow looked distinctly unhappy about this arrangement, but Carina ruffled his fur and sent him away, gamely following Toren to the field behind the castle where there were already goals set up.

Toren couldn't remember the last time he'd played a simple game of one-on-one.

The rules were simple: try to get the ball in the opponent's goal, no hands, keep the stick low.

Carina played hard and cheated her heart out, swinging her hockey stick like a bat and using both hands to wrestle the ball from him directly at one point. They laughed and ran and she shed even her light flannel.

"What's the score?" she asked when they finally stopped, gasping for breath and feeling lighter-hearted than Toren thought possible. Their breath steamed in the air as they panted.

"About a hundred to one," he told her. "You're terrible at this."

"I scored twice!" she protested. Her ears and cheeks were bright red from the cold. "Don't you take that from me!"

"You cheated!"

"You let me!"

"Are you hungry?" Toren asked, and he didn't mean food.

"So hungry," Carina replied, and she didn't mean food either.

"Grim and Amused are going to have the best stories to tell the rest of the guard tonight," Carina said, as they abandoned their equipment and ran for the castle hand-in-hand.

Toren realized he'd completely forgotten the guards were there. This was the new normal.

# CHAPTER 35

The royal garage was the place that Carina felt the most comfortable. It was warm compared to the chilly outdoors, but cool compared to the castle, which was already being transformed for the impending engagement party. She could close the door and let Shadow off the leash inside; everyone knew to enter and exit carefully so he wouldn't escape. And the van was there, a promise of freedom that she couldn't quite reach.

Raval was often there, tinkering with one of the motorcycles, or rebuilding something on one of the workbenches. He was one of the middle brothers, Carina knew, and the one who could work magic. He was the only blond, and sometimes his gaze was unsettlingly direct. He didn't invite conversation, and she didn't pursue it.

"Do you have a screwdriver I could use?" she asked him cautiously, a few days after her field hockey game with Toren. "There's a cabinet door in the van that's a little loose."

Raval gave her one of those sharp looks, and nodded. "Second drawer in the tool chest."

Carina followed his gesture to a tall stack of drawers and found a neat row of screwdrivers in dozens of sizes. "Thank you," she said. She nearly tripped over Shadow, who had followed her hopefully, and gave his ears a ruffle.

She tightened every screw she could find in the van, even the ones that didn't need it, and went to return the tool to the drawer she'd found it in.

"Thanks," she told Raval shyly. Then she screwed up her courage. "Toren said that you...work magic."

She wondered if Raval's eyes were so unsettling because they were so much like Toren's: silvery-blue, with depth like gemstones, but not nearly as *warm*.

"Yeah," Raval said unhelpfully. Then he seemed to thaw a little. "You probably have questions."

Carina chuckled. "You could say that." There was an empty stool down the workbench from him, and she perched on it. "I feel like there are things that the queen of Alaska should know."

Raval nodded solemnly. "I'm happy to explain anything I can."

"Toren told me a little," Carina said, trying to figure out where to start. The stool was on a swivel and she had to resist her urge to spin herself. That was definitely not *royal*. "He said that you have to write it down. And that it burns paper."

Raval's face was guarded, and Carina realized abruptly how much she had come to recognize Toren's expressions over the past week.

"Let me start somewhere else," he said cautiously. "When I concentrate on something really hard, I feel like I'm pushing against something, like I'm trying to squeeze something that really doesn't want to go."

"Like you're squeezing that last bit of toothpaste out of a tube?" Carina guessed. Then she realized that Raval had probably never had to squeeze out the last bit of toothpaste in his life.

To her relief, Raval laughed. "Yes, exactly like that. And if you don't have a place for that toothpaste to go, there's a terrible mess. So I have to channel it all into words, broken down into letters, and the act of writing it down sort of locks it into place and keeps the intention sort of poised there until it needs to be used."

"So...you could just write down 'burn', and then you have a piece of paper you can use as a lighter?"

Raval looked horrified. "Not even a little."

Carina made herself not twist on the stool again.

He sighed. "Okay, so you've got this intention in your head, like..." he sighed "*burn*. But if you just set loose something like that, it doesn't know what, or where, or how long, though that will depend a lot on the strength of the person setting the spell, and you end up with basically that idiot holding onto fireworks in a viral video where the best possible outcome is terrible burns and humiliation. Have you ever read a really long legal contract? The kind of thing where seventeen lawyers were consulted and there's a clause for everything, even stuff that would never, ever happen? That's what you have to do with spells. If they can go wrong, they will, because magic is wild."

"Like genies," Carina said thoughtfully.

"Like...genies?"

"When you make wishes, you have to word it really carefully, or you end up buried in a pile of gold or married to a horse or a hundred years old."

Raval's mouth quirked into a reluctant smile. "Like genies. Or dealing with the fae."

The fae were real? Carina shook her head, trying not to get distracted.

"Okay, so you write out a legal document for magic. But not on paper."

"It can be on paper, if you only want it to work once. But it takes a long time to write out a good spell, so you kind of do want it to be on something that will last. I know a couple of casters who will spend a good month on one basic lock spell. It takes a lot of concentration, a lot of time, there are no shortcuts like copy machines. You have to write every single letter with intention, which takes intense concentration, and you may as well be carving it into something. The slower you go, the more power you can infuse it with. It will still *fade* with every use, but at least you get to use it more than once.

Anyway, it's almost always the case that you might as well just buy a lighter, or a deadbolt, or whatever. There are almost no cases where a spell is an improvement over something mundane."

Carina absorbed that, wondering if Raval didn't sound a little sad. It occurred to her that feeling Toren's emotions had given her a tremendous edge in getting to know him. "So, how do you activate a spell?"

"That has to be defined in it somewhere. Sometimes you give it a spoken keyword, something you say to make it happen. Sometimes you can put in parameters of some kind, like when it gets wet, or when it reaches a certain temperature. When I was a kid, I used to write spells for warmth and put them in my boots. They would activate when my toes got cold." Raval looked abashed, like he'd said more than he meant to, and he turned back to what he was working on: tiny, perfect writing, scratched all over what looked like an engine part.

"What's this you're working on?" Carina asked.

"It's an experiment," Raval growled, sounding uninviting.

Carina caught herself twisting on the stool when he didn't go on and she wasn't sure how to prod him.

"So, the fae are real?" she finally asked.

Raval nodded. "Some of the stories anyway. There are elemental spirits. Did you meet Angel?"

"Angel?" Carina had met a hundred people at least, since she'd come to the palace. "No, I don't think so."

"Out at the hot springs, you might have seen a beautiful woman in the mist?"

"Oh," Carina said. "I was kind of busy at the hot springs. Fainting, and all." She blushed.

Raval chuckled. "Oh, well Angel met *you*, at least. She's a naiad, a kind of water spirit. She controls the temperature of the water. She's a kind of natural magic, like shifters."

"Are there a lot of these spirits?" Mrs. James had mentioned spirits in the castle. Carina hadn't seen one, but she wouldn't have been surprised by one at this point.

"They're rare," Raval said. "And shy. We've got one here in the palace, but we go years without seeing her."

That must be the spirit Mrs. James had mentioned. "Are there a lot of shifters?" Carina asked.

"Maybe one in a thousand people," Raval said with a shrug. "It's hard to know, because they are secretive for obvious reasons."

"Are there a lot of magic...er...casters?"

"Maybe one in ten thousand? One in a hundred thousand? Less? I only know a few, and it's more secret than shifting."

Carina found a question close to the one she really wanted to ask, hovering on her tongue. "And the Compact..."

That earned her another one of Raval's sharp looks. "The Compact is older than Alaska," he said. "It's from a time so long ago that nothing is left but mythology. We don't understand most of it, and no caster is alive now who could do anything even similar."

"You said spells fade," Carina said. "If the Compact is so old, how is it still working?" And how did it work on *her*? she didn't quite dare ask.

"It is renewed," Raval explained. "The kings come together every hundred years with their parts of the compact and the spell is worked again."

"Their *parts*? I thought the Compact was like a contract. But I guess it can't be on paper if it's actually a spell..."

"The original Compact is on dragonskin," Raval said. "Every member of the Small Kingdoms has a part of the original, as well as a mundane paper copy."

Carina shuddered. "Dragon...skin?"

"The dragon founder of the kingdoms sacrificed himself to set it in place, according to the stories."

"That's a little creepy," Carina said.

"It's our history," Raval said, and Carina felt like she'd just had her hand smacked.

Shadow, who was lying on the concrete floor, gave a groan, and then bolted to his feet as a door opened with a swirl of cold air at the far end of the garage.

Carina rose, leaving the stool spinning free behind her, when she

recognized Mrs. James. She was undoubtedly needed for deport-
ment lessons, or dance practice, or to check the fit of something.
"Thank you," she told Raval, who was bending back to his work.
He gave the barest of nods.

Her head felt so full of new information that Carina walked
slowly across the floor, like it might jostle loose if she stepped
carelessly.

# CHAPTER 36

"*D*id you have fun at school today?" Carina asked, as she curtsied to Toren under the watchful eyes of the dance instructor. She was wearing heels, because she needed the practice not only walking, but especially dancing in them. She was wearing her striped tights, though, and a large sweater with holes in the elbows.

Toren bowed to her and offered his hand. "I got an A plus in applying royal seals and repeating my lines. You?"

"A minus in keeping my mouth shut and C plus in keeping my eye rolls to a minimum. I completely flunked the 'don't yawn during the droning speeches' practice, but I learned some tricks for not *looking* like I'm yawning."

Toren chuckled and pulled her into a dance position. Carina had been cramming on all the ballroom techniques, as well as a crash course on curtsies and polite small talk.

While she had been covering those things, Toren had been studying, non-stop, until his head felt like it would explode from all the history and civics he was shoving in. Rian had provided him with the tax codes and public works financial records, but that had required a simpler book on what all the words even meant. Carina had helped him understand the accounts, marveling with him over how much went into keeping a country solvent.

"Wait until you see the dress they're lacing me into," Carina said, keeping her chin up as the music started and she stepped into the dance with him. "You won't even recognize me."

"I would recognize you in anything," Toren assured her. "Even if you wore a mask."

"Oh, a masked ball!" Carina exclaimed. "I always dreamed of one of those. Is it too late to change the theme of the engagement party?" She started to step the wrong way, then corrected herself and gracefully regained her balance.

"Do you really think that Captain Luke would let anyone in wearing a *mask*?" Toren scoffed. "We're lucky she's letting the actual guests in here, and you'd better believe she's going to insist on being able to see everyone. At all times."

He regretted his flippancy at once, because Carina's face fell at the reminder of the danger they were in, and the next few steps were done grimly. He turned her, danced a few steps away and then back, and said softly, "I'm so sorry, Carina."

Her eyes were too bright when she looked back at him. "For what?"

"For all of this. For trapping you into being a queen. For putting your life in danger. For forcing you into this position. You ought to have choices, to have control of your own life and destiny, not be a pawn in old political magic."

Her whole face softened. "Are you apologizing because I have to be a princess? Isn't that every little girl's dream?" Her voice was light and carefully teasing.

Toren braved the wrath of the dancing instructor and drew her to a stop. "You deserve your own dreams," he said firmly. "You should choose your own future."

For a moment, Carina stared at him without speaking, then she smiled, crooked and sincere. "I sometimes think that this is where I'm supposed to be. Maybe this *is* how I meet my goals. God knows I couldn't face down Amco Bank by myself." She shot a sideways glance to the toe-tapping instructor and pulled Toren back into the steps.

"I've always been powerless," she murmured. "And it's kind of exciting to think that now I could actually do good things. That I can make life better for other people. That I can fix broken systems."

"Yes," Toren agreed. "*Yes*. We can do that."

"I just have to get through curtsy lessons and finish memorizing titles and diplomats," Carina teased.

They were still smiling into each other's eyes, making a good show of dancing the approved steps, when Rian cleared his throat from the door.

"Sorry to interrupt, but I need the crown prince."

Toren laid a kiss on Carina's cheek with a sigh. "Duty calls."

"You could let it go to voicemail," she whispered back. "The van is all tuned up and full of gas..."

Toren laughed and gave her a swift embrace, then abandoned her to the sour-faced dance teacher.

Rian led him to the informal dining room. "Fask needed you to sign some things. I also wanted to let you know that Kenth sent his congratulations and an engagement gift, but regrets that he won't be attending the party. He said he'd come to the wedding."

"Does Fask already know?"

"Oh yeah. Got the *united front as a family* speech already."

"He wouldn't care if it was Raval begging off," Toren observed thoughtfully.

Rian shrugged. "You know those two," he said carelessly.

"We should fix that," Toren said.

Rian gave him a surprised glance. "You think you *can*?"

Toren gave him a crooked grin. "I'm going to be the king of Alaska. What can't I do?"

# CHAPTER 37

*U*nlike other mornings, the castle wasn't quiet when Carina, staring sleeplessly at the ceiling, finally sat up on the morning of the engagement party. There were vehicles outside, and voices down the halls. None of it was loud enough to wake her; the thick log walls were far more soundproof than she had expected. But it was a constant undertone of sound to the murmur of anxiety in her head.

"Did you sleep?" Toren asked, sitting up with her.

"Barely," Carina admitted. "You?"

"Some."

They clung to each other for a desperate moment, then took an efficient shower that was *almost* distracting.

The original plan had been to host the engagement event at the hot springs. But the assassination attempt made Captain Luke put her foot down and insist that they have it at the castle itself, where she could monitor all the security arrangements. The wedding, she conceded, could be scheduled at the resort, once she'd had time to evaluate how best to protect the family.

Breakfast was in the informal dining room, which was already undergoing a transformation for the engagement party. Everything was hung in gold stars and sheer blue cloth. The other rooms on the second floor were even more underway, and golden lanterns were being hung by an army of workers.

"Your make-up artist and stylist will be here at one," Mrs. James greeted her, laying a style portfolio next to her as Carina sat at the table. "We'll walk through the ceremony at three, we'll do photographs directly after, and the event itself officially starts at five."

Was the make-up artist the same person as the stylist? Carina wondered, but she didn't ask, just took the cup of coffee at her seat and sipped it carefully.

Before she could eat, Fask put a small box near her elbow. "We just have time to resize this, if it doesn't fit."

"What's that?" Toren asked.

"Mother's engagement ring."

All the brothers stopped eating.

"I didn't even think about a ring," Toren admitted.

For a moment, Carina was cross. Everything was so hurried, she'd never even gotten an official proposal, just an assumption that she'd go along with this like she was going along with everything else and she hadn't ever pressed the issue. It seemed a minor complaint against the tapestry of the chaos her life had descended into, but what if the ring was hideous?

With trembling hands, she put down her coffee and picked up the box, opening it like it might contain a snake.

To her relief, it was a simple diamond ring, with a small, sparkling jewel in a plain gold band. She slipped it on, aware of all the eyes on her.

It fit remarkably well, and was ridiculously heavy. She started to slip it off again, but Fask told her, "Leave it on, you might as well get used to wearing it."

Breakfast, as good as it was, was hard to eat and Carina was keenly aware of the weight on her finger and sparkle of it at the corner of her eye.

After breakfast, she picked hairstyles and make-up from a catalog, and chose from a selection of family jewels laid out on velvet trays. Toren disappeared with Fask, and strange people came in and out at random to measure her and fuss with decorations and frown at her hair.

When Carina finally thought she might escape, Fask came back, and spread photographs across the table before her, pointing out all the visiting royalty that she would be expected to meet. "Green and gold are the New Siberian Islands, north of Russian. They're only sending a non-noble dignitary, which is a reflection of our opinions of each other. Purple and silver are Mo'orea, tiny island near French Polynesia, the king and queen will be here. Great friends of my father."

Toren came back while she was attempting to memorize titles and looked over her shoulder. He startled, and picked up one of the photographs.

"Teal and silver," Carina recited, practicing her smile at him. "Island of Majorca in the Mediterranean Sea. They're sending... um..."

"This is the man who was staring at you at the hot springs," Toren said, and everyone around them froze. "The man I saw again at the festival."

"Are you *sure?*" Fask asked.

"Positive."

Carina gazed at the photograph as a murmur of speculation rose around them. She groped for Toren's hand and held it so hard that the unfamiliar ring cut into her finger.

"He would certainly know how badly Alaska needs a succession to happen before the Renewal," Toren suggested.

Fask nodded grimly. "Drayger is one of six bastard sons and the king of Majorca has three legitimate children before you even get to those. He's got some kind of paper title—baronet, maybe?—but his chances of inheriting land are nothing on that postage stamp. If Alaska is carved into colonies, he'd have a shot at something worth having. Our enemies would be very generous with the man responsible for the conquest of Alaska." He frowned at Carina. "If either one of you dies before the coronation, we're screwed."

"No pressure," Toren muttered as the rest of the room exploded into speculation and suggestions.

"Never mind one of us *dying*," Carina murmured in reply.

But Fask was already walking away, speaking into an earpiece. He was undoubtedly ordering more guards and security. Captain Luke was going to have *kittens*.

Her breakfast like a brick in the bottom of her stomach, Carina finished committing the most important of the visiting dignitaries to memory.

# CHAPTER 38

oren had weathered many parties like this one, but they had always been parties with other people in focus. This was the first event where he was the headliner, the one in the spotlight, and he distinctly didn't enjoy it.

Carina, he noticed at once, was a natural.

She was a shining star in the blue dress that had been tailored to match Toren's uniform. The huge skirt was shimmering blue material in a dozen filmy layers. The bodice was solid blue with blue embroidery all over it. Gold stars were subtly tucked into the swirls. It had little cap sleeves, and a modest neckline that showed just a tease of Carina's cleavage. She had complained bitterly about having to wear heels, but agreed that her hiking boots didn't exactly complete the image.

She smiled and nodded and was shy and bold in exactly the right measures. She remembered everyone's titles and her simple charm and sweet smile set everyone around her at ease.

Her sister, June, and her big, quiet boyfriend didn't exactly fit in with the rest of the royal and royal-adjacent crowd, but they had good manners and followed their coaching with enthusiastic good will, bowing or curtseying only a little too much.

"Are they going to live with us here?" Toren asked, when conversation drew him a little away with Carina.

"You can't put June and I in the same house," Carina warned. "Not even one this big. I talked to Mrs. James about putting them up in town somewhere. I guess you have some nice properties? June's even talking about Anchorage. She wants to see a little more before settling down. Are you sure that's not an... imposition? To put them up?"

"It's no trouble," Toren promised. "Family of yours is family of mine."

"She'll probably go nuts without some work after a few months, she's like me that way. She's talking about volunteering somewhere. Maybe something with kids."

They were interrupted by the king and queen of Mo'orea then, and made idle conversation about trade agreements and family. "Our daughter wanted to come," the king said off-handedly. "She's always wanted to visit Alaska."

"Our house is always open for her," Carina said, before Toren could.

Toren added, "I think Carina would appreciate company that wasn't six loud brothers."

"She can be loud," the queen laughed. "I think she would like you," she said to Carina. "You've been very brave and we're all pulling for you right now."

It was as close as they came to talking about Carina's charges and criminal troubles. Not all the guests were that polite about the topic, casting curious looks at Carina, and asking questions that she neatly sidestepped.

Dinner was a lengthy affair, complete with stage entertainment.

Fask gave a heartfelt speech that managed to be completely *factual* and not address any of the driving questions that all the guests clearly had.

Toren stood, with Carina, at the end of the speech and they smiled at each other. Toren thanked everyone with a few brief words, and then dessert was served in the other room, where people could circulate and network. He wondered if he should have insisted on making the main speech, but was happy just to be grateful for one less thing to do.

Toren could see Carina flagging as the night went on, her smile growing more forced and her glances at Toren more desperate. He found himself playing interference more and more often, and he was not the slightest bit surprised when he looked up from a conversation with the dignitary from the New Siberian Islands about obscure hockey regulations to find that she was gone.

# CHAPTER 39

*C*arina knew that the guards weren't far behind, and she felt bad for leaving Toren to deal with their festivities by himself, but her mind was too busy for more idle chit-chat, more vacant smiles and more repeats of 'It's classified,' and 'I'm afraid I'm not supposed to talk about that.'

The ring was heavy on her finger, and she twisted it anxiously on her finger as she crept out. She'd gotten turned around in the halls, and where she'd meant to come out at the dog kennels where Shadow was under lock and key, she was on the side of the castle now, overlooking the wide lawn where she and Toren had played field hockey.

She didn't actually try to run away, though the temptation was strong. She just leaned against one of the massive log porch columns, and then slid to a seat as she realized that there wasn't enough strength in her legs to hold her up.

The fabric of her skirt crinkled as it folded around her in a nest of shimmery blue.

Grim and Amused burst out of the door, spotted her, and sedately retreated into an out of the way position at the far end of the porch as if she had never been out of their sight. One of them touched their ear and murmured something.

She should find June, Carina thought. Make sure that she and her boyfriend were settling in, *safe*.

But right now, it was quiet outside compared to the noisy, bright din of the party, and quite dark. The sky above was deep blue, with glittering stars barely visible against the interference of the light from the porch. Most of the leaves had already fallen from the bare birches, and the evergreens were dark sentinels of the forest around. There was a wide yard between the castle and the edge of the woods; Carina had first thought it was just for show, but considering it now, she realized that it was also a very convenient place to land visiting dragons, as well as an excellent lawn for field hockey.

There was an arc of color in the sky, a smudge of green and purple, and Carina's first thought was that she was seeing a faint aurora. Then it resolved itself into exactly one of the dragons she'd been considering, circling dark over the velvety sky, blotting out the stars as it grew near.

It didn't escape the notice of the guards, who stopped even trying to be in the background and came to flank her. One of them was talking into their earpiece as the dragon back-winged to a landing that whipped Carina's skirts into a flurry as the other took her arm and helped her to her feet without leaving it an option.

But before they could get her back into the castle, the dragon was shifting and calling out, "Carina Andresen, I have something you need!"

Carina recognized him at once; this was, without doubt, Drayger, the bastard son from Majorca.

Both her guards had guns out now, trained on the intruder. She could hear shouts from inside the castle, and there were more guards running from around the sides of the castle.

But Carina was staring at what Drayger was holding aloft.

It was a flash drive, the colors of Amco Bank clear even in the muted light from the porch.

"Wait," she said, a hand on the arm of the nearest guard.

"I'll treat with the princess," Drayger shouted. "Or this gets destroyed!" He held it between his fingers, and no one could doubt that he was capable of crushing it in his fist.

"I'm not a princess yet," Carina shouted back, not offering to close the distance between them. "Where did you get that?"

He remained where he was, not testing the resolve of the several dozen men and women who now had him dead to sights.

Did bullets kill dragons? Carina suddenly wondered. He was certainly doing his best to keep his hands up and look unthreatening.

Except that her evidence, her *freedom*, was on that flash drive.

"I'm not here to hurt you!" he called firmly.

"Then why the hell *are* you here?" Carina demanded. "And where did you get that flash drive?"

That was when Toren dropped from the second story porch, pouncing in dragon shape and seizing Drayger in wicked claws.

"He's got my flash drive!" Carina cried, and Toren froze with his claws flexed against Drayger's flesh. A thin trickle of blood stained his white shirt; he looked like he was dressed for a party.

*Their* party.

Drayger, to everyone's surprise, did not shift into a dragon to battle Toren, only hung limply in his claws with his arms raised in truce.

"I'm not here to hurt you!" he repeated.

Toren shifted, stepped forward, and swiftly punched him in the face. "You shot my mate!" he snarled.

Drayger's hands were still up, spread except for his grip on the drive. He took Toren's blow and staggered back to balance. "I didn't shoot your mate," he snarled back just as fiercely.

"Me, then?" Toren hissed.

Drayger shook his head, lowering his hands slowly. "I didn't shoot either one of you. I didn't even shoot *at* you. I'm a crack shot and if I'd wanted either one of you dead, you *would* be. I put that bullet right in the window where I wanted it."

No one knew what to do. The guards by Carina had drawn up their weapons when Toren entered the fray, not willing to accidentally shoot the crown prince.

Slowly, carefully, Drayger wound up and tossed the drive at Carina, who stepped forward in her swishing skirts to catch it, the guards still flanking her.

If it wasn't her drive, it was a perfect replica, with the same scratched corner.

"Is the data still on this?" she challenged.

"I didn't touch it," Drayger promised.

"Can you check?" Toren asked, looking rather like he wanted to deck Drayger again just for the fun of it.

"Not without Amco Bank's proprietary decryption software," Carina said apologetically, holding the drive tight in her fist. "Which is part of how it's good proof. How did you get this?"

Drayger smiled rakishly. "To be honest, I was casing the castle, flying overhead, and I saw an intruder cutting the camera wires. I was curious, followed him into the garage, and caught him lifting it from your van. I figured it was important, stashed in the headlight like that."

"Who could have known where it was?" Carina wondered out loud.

"I'm not done with the shooting at us part," Toren protested. "Why did you do it? Why were you following us? Because the reasons I can think of don't include 'saving us from theft out of the goodness of your heart'. You stand to gain a lot from a broken Alaska."

Drayger's smile cooled. "That's why they approached me."

"They?" Carina and Toren spoke together.

"We should speak privately," Drayger suggested, his gaze raking the audience that was starting to gather.

# CHAPTER 40

Toren still wanted to punch Drayger. He wasn't done with wanting justice for being shot at and terrified for Carina this last week.

"Majorca wants Alaska to fall." Fask had taken control of the meeting, of course.

"Who doesn't want Alaska to fall?" Drayger countered. "By pure dumb luck, you six have your claws on some of the richest lands in the world, and while the Compact protects you, no one can do anything about that." He didn't seem bothered by the scrutiny of five brothers and Carina, or the handful of guards flanking him. Captain Luke looked like she was a wrong word away from personally wringing his neck.

"I don't know who *these* specific players are," he admitted. "My contact is just a middleman. He said he represented a coalition of interested parties and...he made me a very tempting offer."

He continued confidently, "You aren't the only ones who've studied the Compact and figured out how to get you out of it. Plenty of people know your father is in a coma and unlikely to survive. And plenty of those same people know that if one of you finds a mate, you can take his throne. It doesn't take a high degree of intelligence to figure out that if you take out the mates, you take out Alaskan sovereignty."

"Are they responsible for our father's state?" Rian demanded.

"I don't know that," Drayger replied to Rian.

"You shot at Carina," Toren could not help saying.

"I gave a good show of shooting at Carina," Drayger corrected. "I was hired to kill her, but I...couldn't. I'm a soldier, not a murderer, and I'm not going to sell my soul. Not for land, not for anything."

"Did you change your mind *while* you were shooting at us?" Carina demanded.

"I shot near you," Drayger scoffed. "Just close enough to cause a scene. Get into the papers, thank you for having the press on hand, by the way. I made it look like I was trying, and gave myself an excuse to stay low. If I'd really wanted to kill you, I could have poisoned you at the hot springs in a hot minute." For the first time, he looked abashed and uncertain. "On this topic...I'd like to apply for asylum."

The room silenced.

"I'd have to check our treaty with Majorca, but that's probably the kind of asylum we *could* actually grant," Rian said thoughtfully. "It fits the usual restrictions."

"You want us to grant you asylum because you were hired to kill our crown prince's mate and you've had a crisis of conscience?" Fask's dry voice was perfect for the moment and Toren made a mental note to learn how to use it.

"Why didn't you come forward sooner?" Tray asked suspiciously.

"Would you have listened?" Drayger retorted. "I waited until I had some leverage."

Everyone looked at the flash drive sitting on the table between them.

"But you didn't use it as leverage," Carina said softly. "You just gave it to me."

"A gesture of goodwill," Drayger said carelessly. Toren thought that his easy pose was just that: a pretense to cover his anxiousness.

"Who was stealing it from the van?" Toren asked. "How would *they* know it was there?"

"It was a red-headed man with a kind of a weasel-y look to him," Drayger said. "No one I knew, no convenient name tag or business card. I asked him some questions he refused to answer, and when I started to insist, we had a...struggle. I hurt his wrist, he dropped the flash drive, and we heard guards coming. He fled on foot, I went on wing. I lost sight of him in the trees."

No one could identify the mysterious thief from that description.

"We'll circle back to him," Fask said. "Let's deal with one criminal at a time."

"I've read the stories about Miss Andresen's problems with the law, and given the hiding place of the drive, I guessed that the flash drive was an important part of her defense." Drayger gave Carina a long look. "Amco Bank is not a small enemy, my lady."

Carina gave a dry laugh.

"I don't trust this guy," Rian said flatly.

"Does it count as asylum if we put him in prison?" Tray suggested dryly.

"This isn't a lot to build a relationship..." Fask started.

"Wait."

Toren didn't realize that he'd spoken until he heard the words, and everyone's attention was on him. "Those guys still think you're working for them."

Drayger shrugged. "You're still alive, so I must not be very serious about it."

"But they don't know that. Your contacts...all they know is that there was an attempt, someone that matches your description in the news. You've gone to ground, for all they know. It would be smart to lay low for a little while after something that public. They don't know you've changed loyalties."

"Not wanting to kill a few innocent people isn't the same as changing loyalties," Rian cautioned.

But Drayger knew where Toren was going. "You want me to be a double agent," he said shrewdly.

Fask scowled, considering. "The guards all knew we had identified him, they had his photo to screen guests."

"All the more reason to excuse the fact that he hasn't made another attempt," Toren said. "If they still think he's working for them, we can get more information, and we can feed them information we want them to have."

"Like…?"

Toren's spy movie knowledge failed him. "Like…um…"

Carina swept to his rescue. "Rian is researching a way to selectively activate a mate bond. Tell them that you've already figured out a way to do this for each of the brothers. Trying to stage the death of one prince is not at all the same thing as having to kill off the entire line."

Toren took a certain amount of satisfaction in the dumbfounded looks over his brothers' faces.

"The Compact usually only taps one mate per kingdom," Drayger said patiently.

"I thought no one actually understood how the Compact worked," Carina replied evenly. "And usually isn't always."

Drayger actually laughed. "You are truly becoming a savvy politician, princess."

"I'm not technically a princess yet," Carina reminded him. "This is just an engagement party."

"There is more to royalty than empty titles," Drayger told her.

"There is more to loyalty than empty words," Carina countered.

"I will pass on any information you request me to," Drayger agreed with an admiring nod at Carina. "And I will bend my knee to the crown of Alaska." He kept his gaze on Carina, to Toren's mixed annoyance and pride. He appreciated that Drayger recognized Carina's power and cleverness, but was jealous of his obvious interest in her.

"We'll discuss what information we'll choose to pass along," Fask said sharply. "I'm sure you will understand if we keep you under guard."

Luke gave a growl.

"Perfectly understandable," Drayger agreed, with a glance at the

Captain. "But I will require the return of my phone in order to make contact with my handlers."

"Under supervision," Fask conceded. "For now, we will treat you as an honored guest. We'll even give you one of the third floor guest rooms with a view of the mountains. Nothing but our best."

"Testing my loyalty?" Drayger guessed. "I assure you, I very much look forward to a quiet time enjoying the *view*."

"Oh, I assure you, we have other protections in place. We aren't trusting your loyalty *that* far." Fask turned to his brothers. "I'll get the flash drive into our vault. The continued absence of half the royal family is going to be noticed at the engagement party." He gave Carina an unexpected half-smile. "If you mussed your hair and went back with Toren, the reason for *your* disappearance would be obvious."

Everyone chuckled, except the guards, and Tray and Rian slipped out of the room. Toren took Carina's hand into his elbow and walked out with her into the hallway. She sagged against him as soon as the door closed behind them.

"We've got your flash drive again," Toren told her, slipping his arm up around her shoulder to pull her close. "We've got all the cards. We know who shot at us, and why, and it won't happen again. It's all going to be alright. You're safe."

"I know," she murmured into his shoulder. "I know."

"I think Fask had the right idea," Toren suggested. Her lithe body up close against him made him forget the tangled problems of politics and trust. She was all he needed in the world.

"About keeping Drayger under guard?" Carina asked, pulling away to eye him quizzically.

"About mussing your hair," Toren said, and it was the first time since their hockey game that his grin felt truly natural.

# CHAPTER 41

There was no point in messing up her hair with her own hands, so Carina let Toren thread his fingers into her updo and pull her into a kiss full of hope and promise. Relief and happiness flooded through her.

Carina hadn't ever spent a lot of time imagining her perfect wedding or designing her wedding gown or mooning over cute boys. She had pictured a long, single life as a boring accountant, married only to her work. Maybe she'd get a dog.

And when her life had toppled upside down, marriage was the last thing on her mind. Even when she was forced into the arrangement, it seemed like a formality, just a title, just a name for a business transaction that was in everyone's best interests.

But something had changed, over the last week. Underneath her magical attraction, underneath her need for his protection, underneath all the pressure from every angle, Carina found herself more and more fond of Toren. He was her best friend, always in her corner, constantly picking her up and reminding her of her own strengths.

She would have agreed to marry Toren even if he hadn't been a dragon shifter and a prince. She would have married him if he'd been a pauper, or one of the crazy Alaskan sourdoughs with a beard to his knees.

She would have married him even without the mate magic, Carina realized, kissing him until she was breathless and dizzy.

It wasn't *just* that she felt irresistibly drawn to him anymore. If that compulsion were suddenly to go away, she would still love him.

The thought drew her up short and her lips froze.

She *loved* this man, this sweet, funny, clever prince of Alaska.

"Are you okay?" Toren asked, because of course he would. Carina stared into his silver eyes and wanted his infatuation with her to be real more than anything else in the whole world.

Tears flooded her own eyes. "Yes," she said faintly. "Yes, of course. Everything is working out at last."

"You've been so amazing and strong," Toren said, stroking his fingers along her cheek. She could feel that some of her hair had come loose and was tickling at her neckline.

"*You've* been amazing," she echoed.

"Yes, yes, you're both amazing," Fask said, coming up silently behind them. "That is very appropriately mussed hair, now let's get back to your party, lovebirds."

His smile as he passed them was tolerant and fond and Toren and Carina both beamed at each other foolishly.

Toren tucked a stray lock back in and declared her perfect.

Carina took his hand and felt strong enough to return to the sea of nobility and diplomats, with their prying eyes and all the questions she couldn't answer.

The floor had been cleared for dancing when they returned, and no one seemed to wonder where they had been or why Carina would prefer to float around in the strong arms of her fiancé prince to socializing.

They spent the rest of the evening with each other, dancing and deflecting questions in duet, until the guests gradually left and Fask finally dismissed them with a nod to trudge wearily back to their rooms, Carina's hated shoes in her hands.

"Carina…" Toren said at the door as they left the guards behind.

"I'm trying to decide if I'm too tired for a shower before bed," Carina admitted. Her scalp felt stiff with unfamiliar product, and she ought to at least scrub off the layers of make-up or it would be all over the pillow in the morning. She'd probably break out, too, and that would be very un-princess-y of her.

When she looked longingly at the bed, Toren took her hand and led her past, to the bathroom, where he turned on the hot water and slowly undressed her.

She had not expected to have the energy to want him that night, but every touch set her skin on fire. He tenderly pulled every jewel from her upswept hair, gem by gem, and combed through it with his fingers until it was soft and loose again, letting his hands just linger on her bare shoulders and arms as he did.

Steam rose from the shower, giving the bathroom a surreal feel on the tail of a very surreal day indeed. Then he opened the door and drew her into the hot water and she tipped her face up and let it spill over her.

In a few moments, he joined her, and they soaped each other gently, finding all the places that made each other hiss and moan. His cock was firm and focused, and it filled her hand as she soaped his balls. He washed her back and kissed her soapy neck and even carefully washed the make-up from her face, smiling at her tenderly as she trustingly opened her eyes at the end.

They made slow love in the bathroom, in a nest of towels, before moving to the bed, where Toren lay her down and drove into her, urgent and patient all at once.

He was perfect and princely and Carina didn't want to sleep afterwards, because it all felt like a dream that would vanish when she woke.

# CHAPTER 42

*C*arina was gone when Toren finally opened his eyes. The night's events flooded back as he sat up. The flash drive. Drayger's change of allegiance. The party, and the sea of dignitaries who might be involved in hiring to kill them. Carina.

He sat up with a sigh.

It was late in the morning, and low fall sunlight spilled in through open curtains.

"Oh good, you're up."

Mrs. James came bustling out of the bathroom with an armful of the towels that Toren was pretty sure they'd left on the floor the night before. She didn't scold him for leaving them there, or flicker an eyelid at the nudity he quickly hid under his blankets. "Fask wants you in his office as soon as you've eaten. You've missed breakfast, so you can feed yourself in the kitchen because no one is going to wait on you hand and foot *today*."

"Thank you, Mrs. James."

"Thank yourself," she said tartly in return on her way out.

Toren dressed quickly and wandered out into the common area. Carina was sitting with Fask at the dais. Shadow, who had been allowed back into the house now that the party was over, was sitting

next to her, leaning his big head on her knee while she scratched his
ears. Carina had also selected the chair to Fask's right, Toren noted,
not their father's throne. There had already been considerable
discussion about the size and position of Carina's chair.

"Fask was going to show me the vault," Carina said. "To put my
mind at ease."

Shadow's ears swiveled forward and his head lifted.

Carina told him, "Vault, Shadow, not w-a-l-k."

Shadow seemed unconvinced, his thick tail swishing on the floor,
and when Carina and Fask rose to their feet, he bounded to four
paws and seemed ready to lead the way.

"Want me to take him out while you do that?" Toren offered.

Shadow's ears lay back and he went to Carina's other side.

"It's like he understood that," Carina laughed, patting his head.
She reached for Toren's hand. "Come with me, and we'll all go for a
walk afterwards."

Shadow's ears perked back up at the word 'walk.'

Fask led the way down the wide back stairs, dismissing the
guards. There was clearance for a dragon, if it folded its wings in
and was careful of the railings.

It wound down into the caverns beneath the castle, and Carina
walked closer to Toren the further they went, Shadow at her other
side.

The walls turned to solid stone, beautiful granite catching the
intermittent lights.

"I've heard of dragon hoards," Carina said nervously as the
floor leveled and the sound of their steps echoed back at them.
Shadow's claws on the floor were particularly loud. "But to be
honest, I didn't think of you guys actually having one. When you
said vault, I assumed...a big wall safe or something."

"It is much more secure than that," Fask assured her.

They stopped at a door to the side of the hall, approximately ten
feet tall and unassumingly made of wood. It was covered from top
to bottom in words, and sizzled with structured magic. No battering
ram could break this door, no army could breach it.

Fask put his hand flat against it and spoke his full name before Toren could. "Faskritranum."

The door cracked open, and when Fask pushed, it swung soundlessly in.

"Oh," Carina said on an inhale. "Oh, I see."

Beyond the door was the hoard.

Toren honestly found it a little tacky and preferred the austere wealth of the public floors. This hoard was classic dragon treasure —piles of coins and collections of golden goblets and crowns and strings of pearls and exquisite necklaces and stacks of silver bracelets and copper trunks of rings. Each of the brothers had their own alcove of treasure—partly inherited and partly gathered. Fask's was rather impressive, but most of the other brothers had followed other pursuits. Rian's was mostly rare books and antique bottles. Raval had shelves of rare, sealed action figures mixed in with structured magic items. Toren found that he was a weird combination of reluctant and eager to show Carina his own modest collection of art and gold treasures. Would she care that he had one of Wayne Gretzky's Stanley Cup winning hockey sticks?

All of them together paled with their father's central hoard, heaped high with priceless treasures.

Carina nodded, walking into the room slowly with Shadow at her side. "Thank you," she said, and her voice was rich in meaning.

"Once these doors are closed, no one can get in but one of us," Toren explained. Carina's hand in his squeezed.

"Here," Fask said, leading them in through a maze of treasure. The flash drive looked out of place on the display table near the center. "There is no place in the world that is safer for this." He pointed out some of the other items on the table.

There were fine antique watches, some of the earliest ever made, a bracelet carved from a single emerald, a black ceremonial dagger in a stand etched all over with magic writing, crystal goblets, a fragile antique vase. The Compact was under glass, the paper copy next to the thick, dragonskin original pages that were in their care.

Carina picked up the dagger curiously. Fask and Toren both drew back. "Careful with that," Toren said.

"This is that knife you told me about," Carina guessed, putting it down swiftly. "The one that's spelled to kill dragons. Sorry."

Toren was so busy watching her face, embarrassment that he couldn't sense, but still recognized, flashing over her features, that he didn't notice Shadow at first.

Fask was standing at the far end of the display table. Carina stood before the table, Toren on one side, Shadow on the other, and by the time he fully realized that Shadow was changing, it was too late.

In one smooth, slithering motion, Shadow was standing as a red-haired man dressed in black at Carina's side. The blue and gold collar hung loosely around his neck, the leash still in Carina's hands.

Everyone was still startling as he dived forward and snatched the flash drive in one hand and the dagger in the other. In one fluid move, he had looped the arm with the dagger over Carina's neck, holding the blade to her throat.

"No closer, dragon brothers," he hissed. "Or she loses her lifeblood right here and now."

Toren froze and was distantly aware of Fask doing the same.

"Shadow?" Carina cried. "I don't understand."

He dropped the flash drive into a pocket and grinned at Toren. "Women can't resist a cute dog, can they?"

Carina struggled, then stopped, whimpering, as Shadow drew a line of blood at her throat with the razor sharp dagger. Even if it wasn't spelled to poison a human, it was sharp enough to slit her throat.

"You're my ticket out of here," he told her, his mouth entirely too close to Carina's ear for Toren's taste. "I don't want to have to hurt you. Yet."

"Who are you?" Toren demanded. His heart hammered in his chest and he watched the blood well along the cut on Carina's skin in horror. "What do you want with the flash drive?"

"I like the name Shadow," the man said, baring his teeth in a smile. "You can call me that. Amco Bank hired me to take care of their little problem. Follow her, find out what she knows, tear her throat out in her sleep once the flash drive is disposed of and I've verified there is no copy. It would have all been much easier if you hadn't been dragged out into the spotlight." That last was to Carina, his lips almost touching the side of her face.

She gave a keen of terror.

Toren's dragon raged in his chest.

"Don't you hurt her," Toren snarled desperately. "Not one hair on her head."

"That's a possibility," Shadow said smoothly. "If I leave in one piece with the flash drive, no one else has to get hurt. This can be a perfectly civilized negotiation. We get the drive, my employer doesn't have to worry about further problems. Carina's complications go away. You get your precious queen of Alaska."

"It's a reasonable arrangement," Fask said slowly. "We're reasonable people."

"We made a copy," Carina gasped, and Toren could hear the undertone of anger to her voice. She had no intention of letting them get away with this. "When we got the drive back, we made a copy."

Fask hissed at her, but Carina bluffed boldly on. "We made a copy and we've already sent it to the newspaper with a full reveal. That was our plan the whole time. We mailed it to the Alaska Times. The whole story will be spread across Alaska by tomorrow."

Toren almost choked. The Alaska Times had a circulation of approximately four hundred and was only published monthly, but Carina wouldn't know that. Fortunately, neither did Shadow.

The assassin growled in displeasure. "That was stupid," he said, in a low cold voice. "Because now I have no reason to keep you alive at the end of this."

# CHAPTER 43

*C*arina felt like her blood was boiling in her veins, like she was filled with helpless rage and betrayal. She'd trusted Shadow, taken him in and *loved* him. But he'd been sent to kill her, to finish destroying the life that Amco Bank had stolen from her, to cover up their terrible deeds and epic theft.

The fine line he'd cut on her throat itched as the blood there slowly dried, and she cast desperately for something to do. She met Toren's eyes and could see the fury there. *Don't do anything rash,* she thought at him with all her might. The knife at her throat might hurt her, but it would *kill* him, and she couldn't face that future.

"You need me alive to get out of here in one piece," she said in a trembling voice. "If I'm dead, there's nothing to keep them from toasting you alive on your way out." It suddenly occurred to her that she didn't know if dragons actually breathed fire. Probably, if she didn't know, Shadow didn't either.

"Apparently, though only a dragon prince can open the door, anyone can close it, and I've got just the magic to lock it against you from the outside." Shadow said darkly to Fask and Toren. "Her Highness and I are going to walk right out of here."

"I'm not a princess yet," Carina muttered automatically. She was still holding Shadow's leash in her hands; he didn't seem to even notice the blue and gold collar hanging loose at his neck. She kept her grip on it loose and her hands at her side and tried not to bring attention to it, hoping she'd have an opportunity to use it later. He was also handling the dagger gingerly. As a dog, he'd been limping slightly on one of his front legs. He'd let the vet do very embarrassing things to him, she realized; he'd been very thorough about embracing his role.

Drayger had scuffled with him and he'd dropped the drive, she remembered. He'd hurt Shadow's wrist in the conflict. Carina felt like she was on the edge of an idea.

Shadow shifted his grip on her. "You're close enough to a princess to get me past any guards we might meet," he said.

Carina saw Toren shifting on his feet, growling helplessly as Shadow pressed the blade against her neck a little harder.

They backed away together. Carina briefly considered going limp, or yanking on the leash, but she could only see that ending badly if Toren decided that was a cue to be heroic. She didn't want him to be killed trying to save her.

No, she wasn't willing to risk Toren, not with Shadow's hands on the deadly knife. She could get Shadow out of the room, save Toren from doing something stupid and suicidal and...

Then she was in the cool, dark hallway and Shadow was drawing the door shut. He had what looked like a shipping label covered in tiny writing that he peeled off and stuck to the door. It sizzled, and started to blacken around the edges.

She heard a muffled cry of rage from the other side of the door, and then flame flickered around the frame. Something impacted the other side with a tremendous thump, but the door didn't even shudder.

"That won't hold them long," Shadow said, and he took Carina's arm and dragged her at a half-run down the stone hall.

There were no guards in the stone hallway, to Carina's chagrin, and none at the top of the stairs. Of course not. What could possibly be safer than being with both Fask *and* Toren in their great castle basement?

For the first time, she was resentful of the fact that the castle wasn't bustling with people the way she'd always imagined a castle would be. Last night, it had been impossible to round a corner without running into a guest, or the help, but they were almost all temporary hires, and the guests had been put up in hotels and resorts nearby. Where were Grim and Amused when she could actually use them? But they were rarely shadowing her when she was with Toren within the castle, only when she was alone, or they were outside.

They walked through empty halls, their footsteps loud as they crossed the grand foyer.

"My van," Carina said desperately. "It's out front, at the end of the drive. It's really nondescript. You'll get further with it than you will stealing one of their fancy cars."

"You seem like a smart girl," Shadow observed, pulling her towards the front of the house. "Why'd you get go and get yourself mixed up in something like this? You must have known that you'd never have a chance against something like Amco Bank and the important people who own it."

"I thought I was doing the right thing," Carina said quietly. "Just because they are big or important doesn't mean they should get away with *murder*. Why would you get involved in something so unethical?"

"I've got a pack to think of," Shadow growled.

They paused just inside the front doors while Shadow frowned at the guards standing on the porch through the repaired glass panels. They were looking away, and after a moment of considering, Shadow simply snarled and dragged Carina with him through the doors, the dagger pressed threateningly at her neck.

"Stay back and keep your hands up and she won't be hurt!" he shouted, and the guards fell back dutifully and put their hands up.

"Where's the van?" he asked Carina through clenched teeth.

The van was actually around the back of the castle in a garage. "It's down past that delivery truck," Carina lied. "You have to get out further to see it."

They maneuvered slowly down the stairs, Shadow keeping the guards in his field of view as he hauled her down each step.

Carina closed her eyes, hoped that the slim chance she was grasping at would pay off, and screamed as loud as she could.

For a long moment, nothing happened, and she was sure that she had misjudged everything. Shadow started to relax.

The sound of shattering glass was her cue, and at that moment, she tightened her grip on the leash in her hand, yanking down as hard as she could. "Bad dog!" she shouted, and a black dragon dropped out of the sky onto them.

# CHAPTER 44

*T*oren battered himself against the locked door until Fask's yelling finally penetrated his fog of rage.

"You can't open it from in here," his brother snarled, as Toren shifted back and curled fists at his side. "He's put a one-way lock spell on it. We'll have to wait until someone opens it from the outside."

Toren couldn't resist giving the door one final kick and then he paced, tripping over the heaps of the hoard that he'd knocked over when he had shifted and charged the door. "If he hurts her…"

"He's going to keep her safe until he's sure she's not any use to him," Fask said coldly. "And that was a dumbass move, trying to bluff her way out of this mess instead of taking a perfectly logical compromise."

Of course she wouldn't compromise, Toren thought, his chest tight with worry and fear even while he felt overwhelming pride for her. Even with her life in danger, she was determined to do the right thing. She was better than any of them deserved.

*Our mate!* his dragon wailed in his head. *She's in danger! We must save her!*

*I don't know how,* Toren agonized.

"Toren, little brother, it's not your fault."

"It *is* all my fault," Toren raged. "Everything is my fault. I'm supposed to be a *king*, and I can't even keep my mate safe. I'm terrible at *everything*."

To his surprise, Fask caught his arm and pulled him into swift, heartfelt hug. "You're doing *fine*, little brother."

Surprise chased away Toren's worries for a moment.

Fask released him, and continued, "You stepped up, and it's impressed everyone. You've taken it seriously, worked hard, and been smart and diplomatic. You would have been a king that Alaska could be proud of. That I'm proud of."

Toren had craved his biggest brother's approval since he was a child. But now that he had it, it didn't matter to him. Nothing mattered but Carina, in the clutches of Shadow, being used as a hostage.

He returned to the door, prepared to batter through it with human fists if he had to, when he heard something on the other side, a crackling sound and the most wonderful thing he'd ever heard, Rian saying his own name.

"Prianriakist!"

The lock spell cracked beneath the stronger magic of the door and before Rian could even move aside, Toren was shifting and shoving his way past his brothers, surging down the hall after his mate.

He couldn't fly in the confines of the castle, but he could run, in the fast, humping gait of his dragon form, claws cutting into the wooden floor as he desperately made a beeline out the open front door for Carina, praying it wasn't too late.

He arrived in time to see a hail of broken glass fall from above as Carina yanked down on the leash that was still around Shadow's neck.

He glance up to see Drayger in his dragon form, struggling and suspended above them in a net of shining thread, a spell activated by the breaking glass; the third floor guest room had always been intended for diplomatic visitors of uncertain loyalty.

Shadow, surprised by the hail of shards and Carina's sudden

struggle, quickly recovered, but Carina was already fighting hard. She had dropped the leash to concentrate on the hand holding the deadly dagger. "Stay back!" she cried to Toren. "It's too dangerous!"

Toren had no intention of hanging back, and charged down the stairs with a roar of challenge.

Carina fought harder for the dagger, hanging on his injured wrist, but Shadow was larger and stronger, and every bit as determined. He roared in pain, but dragged Carina in an arc and Toren had to leap back as the assassin lashed out with the obsidian blade, snarling and circling. Carina stomped on his foot and elbowed him as she tried to pull down on his arm. The leash snapped loose around them.

"Don't let it touch you!" Carina begged Toren.

She and Shadow tangled together and he abruptly stopped trying to wrest free of her and drove the blade back at her with a furious slash.

Her scream of pain spurred Toren carelessly forward, and she twisted Shadow's injured wrist as she fell backwards, forcing him to drop the blade at last.

Then Shadow was standing alone, triumphant only for the moment that it took to occur to him that he no longer had a hostage *or* a magical dagger. Toren bore down on him, and the assassin shifted and tried to flee on four feet. He got no further than the drive before he was pinned beneath Toren's claws.

Toren's urge to simply shred the man was tempered only by not wishing for Carina to see him lose control, and he satisfied himself by merely throwing the man up against the statue of his grandfather, stunning him into unconsciousness and back into human form.

At the top of the steps, Fask cried out his full name and Drayger fell from the dissolved magical net, landed next to Fask, and shifted into his human shape.

Carina was sitting in a protective circle of guards with drawn guns, and there was blood staining her shirt.

"I'm okay!" she called, voice shaking. "I'm okay..."

Toren shifted, running to her.

"It's just a scratch," Carina sobbed, but she winced when Toren unbuttoned her blouse to draw the fabric back from the wound at her collarbone. It was bleeding, but didn't seem to be deep. "At least it was me and not you," she said, and she smiled bravely at Toren.

Her guards left Carina in Toren's care to secure Shadow. They weren't gentle, to Toren's satisfaction.

"The flash drive," Carina cried. "It's in his pocket!"

Shadow was briskly frisked, and one of the guards stepped back with the drive held up in his hand as the dog-shifter regained consciousness sluggishly.

"Well, that's a relief," Fask said, coming down the steps with Rian. They were both in human form. "Carina?"

"I'm okay," Carina said, drawing in a shaky breath. She clung to Toren. "I'm okay. He just got a lucky swipe in. Better me than one of you," she repeated.

Toren stripped off his shirt to wad into a makeshift bandage; Carina hissed as he applied it to her cut.

Drayger followed them and knelt beside the black dagger. He whistled, but didn't offer to pick it up. "Pretty risky having one of those around," he said.

"It was in our *vault*," Fask said crossly.

Arriving on the scene, Captain Luke stalked forward, secured the knife, and took the data drive from the guard who had retrieved it.

"Well, you aren't the only one who wants that drive," Rian said, holding out a hand to take it from the captain. "I was coming down to the vault to find you with the good news."

"I could use some good news," Fask said dryly.

"Amco Bank was already under investigation," Rian said. "I was contacted by a team from America's FBI. They've already got a warrant for the decryption software, so they'll be able to read the data and prove that it had been locked by their proprietary software. They hope to get the top executives not only on the money laundering charges, but also murder. You'd be cleared, Carina."

Carina closed her eyes and held tighter to Toren as Rian went on.

"Apparently, they already found proof that a whole lot of suspicious accounts had been deleted before they could get the key information about who had created them and who accessed them. That itself violated several policies, and would have gotten them a lot of stiff penalties and an official investigation. Carina's data is the smoking gun. It has proof of who was involved, and all the numbers they've otherwise wiped from all of their records. They're going to want this guy, too, I bet. I wonder if his fingerprints will turn anything interesting up. Like maybe something related to that murder you were accused of?"

Carina started to struggle in Toren's arms, and he quickly realized that she was trying to stand. He rose to his feet, lifting her gently with him, then let her go. She closed the distance to Shadow and everyone automatically stood at attention except him.

Shadow glared at her, hatred and frustration in his eyes and she stared him down ferociously, one hand holding the bloody shirt to her cut shoulder.

"I trusted you," she said firmly. "I gave you a home. I gave you my last hot dogs. And you *betrayed* me. I want you to contact your employers. And I want you to tell them that the queen of Alaska doesn't negotiate with criminals, and doesn't get scared, and doesn't give up! Tell them that I am coming for them, and that I will see *all of you* brought to justice. You are a *bad dog*, and if you ever set foot in this country again, you will be put *down*."

Toren could not help grinning and he caught even the iron-faced guards doing the same. Fask looked a little non-plussed and Rian's smile was admiring. Drayger made no attempt to hide his glee, whooping with laughter.

Shadow's face grew darker and darker as he looked around at their mirth. Then he smiled himself, a humorless, teeth-baring smile. "At least I got to piss on your grandfather's statue," he snarled, and Toren gestured with his hand for the guards to take him away.

"I'll go make some phone calls," Rian said, shaking his head.

"I'll take the drive," Fask offered.

"No need," Rian said. "I'm going to transfer the data to a secure server right now."

Fask looked like he might argue, then nodded. "I'll be happy to see the end of this," he said tightly.

Carina stepped back into Toren's arms and let herself sag into his embrace. "We should get you cleaned up," he said. "You might need stitches."

Carina moved the shirt, inspecting the cut. "I doubt it," she said. "It's almost stopped bleeding."

She eyed Drayger. "I was really hoping you'd recognize him," Carina said. "And I was really, really hoping that you were looking out the window."

"It's a helluva view," Drayger said offhandedly. "And that red hair is hard to miss. You've also got excellent lungs. But I wasn't able to do much at the end."

"You distracted him," Carina pointed out. "And...it means something that you tried."

"You might have saved her," Toren said grudgingly. "Thank you."

"All my guards are gone," Drayger pointed out. Only Captain Luke remained, and she looked furious. "Shouldn't you be calling for some more to drag me back to my rooms?"

"I can drag you myself," she snarled.

Everyone looked up at the shattered window three stories above. "Mrs. James is going to have words about that," Toren observed.

"She's going to have more words about what you did to her entrance hall floor," Rian said dryly.

"We'll put you in the north-facing rooms until we can get the window replaced," Fask said thoughtfully to Drayger.

"With guards?" Drayger teased. It was clear that none of them, except possibly Captain Luke, considered him a threat any longer. He winked at her. "Want to handcuff me?"

"There are still going to be guards," Fask muttered, and they all went inside, Captain Luke keeping a particularly watchful eye on the Majorcan dragon.

# CHAPTER 45

*T*oren took Carina to their rooms, and carefully took off her blouse, crusty with blood. It seemed like a lot of blood, for a mere human.

She felt so fragile, as he undressed her, peeling the layers of soaked fabric from her pale skin.

The cut was only barely bleeding now, the faintest stubborn ooze when he gently sponged the dried blood from her skin.

He couldn't resist kissing Carina as he worked, light kisses on her neck, at the corner of her eye.

He dried her bravely with one of Mrs. James precious white towels, and it came away clean. He daubed on antibiotic cream that he found in a cabinet, hardly daring to spread it.

Then he sat with his bride-to-be on the wide bed as she craned her head to try to see the raw gash.

"It might scar," he said, hopelessly. He had no idea how humans usually healed. "We should go to a doctor."

"I don't need a doctor," Carina scoffed. "And I don't mind a scar. It'll prove that I'm not to be messed with."

"You *aren't* to be messed with," Toren said with a crooked smile.

"I always knew that. From the moment you threatened me with your camp chair."

She pulled her bra strap back up over her shoulder and would have stood to find a clean shirt, but Toren drew her back. "There's something I've been meaning to do. Something I should have done a long time ago."

"We've done *that* a bunch," Carina teased, tipping her face up for a willing kiss.

"Not that," Toren said, and Carina stilled at his seriousness.

He took a deep breath, then slipped off the bed and knelt at her feet, bowing his head and taking her hands in his own. "Carina, you've changed my whole life, in every way for the better, even when I thought it couldn't. You are my fresh air and my open sky, you are…" he should have come up with a few more descriptions before he started, Toren realized. "…wonderful," he ended lamely. "I can't imagine living without you at my side. Carina…Carina, will you marry me?"

She was quiet for a moment, then said lightly, "Isn't it a little late to ask, after the big engagement party?"

Toren looked up and thought the smile dancing on her mouth looked tentative.

"I should have asked before," he said. "Every day I should ask you."

There were tears welling in her hazel eyes, threatening to spill over, and to Toren's horror, they didn't look like the joyous tears he had been prepared for. "What is it? What's wrong?"

One of the tears escaped down her cheek. "It's…it's…just…"

*Make this right,* his dragon begged.

Toren clung to her hands, desperate to fix whatever was causing her pain. "Tell me!"

"None of this is real," Carina whispered.

Toren blinked at her.

"This is just a fantasy," she said achingly. "It's just a magical compulsion, a thing you're forced to feel, because Alaska needed a queen, and your precious Compact thought I was the best choice, somehow."

"Well, you are the best choice," Toren said slowly. "But that's not how the spell works."

She slipped one of her hands away from him and dashed another stray tear from her cheek, wincing as the fresh cut flexed at her motion. "You said...it was a magical spell, a fate you couldn't escape."

Toren recaptured her hand, finally understanding. "The Compact doesn't *force* me to feel anything," he said. "I wasn't coerced into loving you, I was only allowed to see that I *could*, and oh, Carina, I did. You are so beautiful and so strong, and so smart, and so good, and Carina, I love you."

He squeezed her hand and shook his head. "I thought Raval had explained. It was a spell that made me *recognize* you, but it's gone now. No spells last, remember? Everything I feel now, everything you feel, that's *us*. That's *real*. I love you with my whole heart, not just my body, not just my dragon, not just a window to what might be, but now, entirely, with everything that I am, and that is not something that magic can even *do*."

There was hope behind the tears, hot and helpless as her eyes overflowed and Toren rose to catch her up into his arms and hold her close while she cried in relief into his arms. "Have you been feeling this *long*?" he begged. "The spell let me feel your emotions for a while, so that I would know you, and I've had to guess lately...I know you've had so much happening...we should have talked about it sooner..."

"I'm so stupid," Carina laughed and sobbed. "I couldn't feel what you were feeling anymore, either, but it never occurred to me that it was because the spell had *faded*. The *attraction* never diminished."

"Well," Toren teased, kissing her head, "I'm really hot. Everyone on my fan page says so. So of course you're going to keep wanting me. Who knows why I'm still attracted to *you*. One of life's mysteries, clearly." His playful leer belied his words.

Carina tickled him roughly, and kissed him, and they wrestled and laughed until they were wrapped up together and lying sideways across the bed.

"I have a theory," Toren said cautiously as he caught his breath. "I'm not a caster like Raval, and I don't understand the Compact like Rian, but when I looked at you, it was like I saw what could be, what was possible, like a little glimpse of the future. *This* future. When I first saw you, I saw how I feel about you *now*. Magic gave us a little head start, but it couldn't make me feel this. I love you with all of *myself*. For all of *yourself*."

"Oh, Toren," she said into his shoulder. "I love you, and I will always love you, and yes, I will marry you even if it means I have to be a queen and wear a fifty pound crown and terrible shoes…"

Then he was kissing her and she couldn't say anything else until considerably later.

# EPILOGUE

*C*arina unclipped the travel buckle and started to push up the pop-up top, hissing as her shoulder reminded her that it hadn't been that long since she'd been held hostage and slashed with a magic dragon-killing dagger.

"Let me get that," Toren said, stepping in behind her to take the bar and push it in place as he stood.

It was nice, she decided, having someone to help with the camping setup and chores. More than that, it was nice having a companion, a partner. Since he was standing with his arms on either side of her anyway, it was completely natural to turn and let him kiss her.

It was *particularly* nice having someone that set her body on fire with just a glance, and Carina looked forward to showing him how the bench seat lay out into a full-sized bed.

"You want to go make the fire?" she teased him.

"That depends," Toren said archly. "Can I light it my way?"

"Can you keep the fire safely in the fire pit?" Carina asked. "Because I don't want any visits from a nosy park ranger, and it would look pretty bad for the next queen of Alaska to burn down a forest."

"I'll have you know that I have very excellent fire control," Toren said, trailing a finger down her unharmed collarbone and following it with a kiss.

"I brought marshmallows this time," Carina said with an involuntary hiss. "And the macaroni and cheese with the squeeze packet. Do you want canned ham in it or chicken?"

Toren kissed her, deeply, and while she was still trying to get her breath back, suggested, "What if you show me where the bed is in this thing, instead."

"Duty first," Carina said reluctantly. "We've got to turn on the propane for the fridge and heater and set up camp before it gets dark."

Toren groaned. "I thought we were running away from 'duty first,'" he said plaintively.

"Only for a little while," Carina comforted him. "Did you really tell them we were going to be honeymooning in Costa Rica?"

"I don't think they believed me," Toren said. "Rian saw us driving off with the van, and Fask also observed that it wasn't standard to have a honeymoon before a wedding."

"Well, we had an engagement party before the proposal, so that seems to be our general theme," Carina said as she adjusted the controls on the tiny fridge. "Besides, we're rapidly running out of days before winter, so it was now or never."

The trees outside of the van were completely bare now, and the frost was persistent in the shadows. Clouds along the horizon teased at the idea of snow.

The van was parked near the edge of a bluff, overlooking the majestic mountain range to the south, faded blue in the distance as the sky above lost its color and the horizon took on hues of pink and orange.

It threatened to be a bitterly cold night, but Carina knew she wouldn't be chilled next to Toren's heat under the quilts they'd stolen from Mrs. James' linen closets. She was wearing her new parka, and the mittens in her pockets warmed her hands whenever they grew cold.

Toren heaved a great sigh and went to dump logs haphazardly into the firepit and shift to light them on vigorous fire.

"One of these days, I'm going to show you how to make kindling and build an actual fire," Carina told him, placing the grate over some rocks and starting the water. "Come help me hang up a tarp."

Toren turned out to be as hopeless at tying knots as he was at non-magical fire management, but he was excellent at standing and holding the far corners of the tarp while Carina guyed out the ropes. "I'll teach you all these tricks," she teased him. "But you have to promise to teach me to skate and play hockey."

"I thought the Queen of Alaska didn't negotiate," Toren mocked her.

"I don't negotiate with *criminals*," Carina corrected. "Are you a criminal?"

Toren smiled foolishly at her. "I stole America's greatest treasure for myself," he said with a shrug.

While the water heated, they sat close together near the fire—in fancy new camp chairs—and watched the last of the sun's rays disappear below the horizon. The sky above darkened and began to sparkle with stars.

"I kind of miss Shadow," Toren said. "I mean, as a dog. Have you thought about getting one? A real dog, I mean?"

"I've been thinking about a *cat*," Carina confessed. "I knew a guy in Oregon who went camping with a cat, and I could be on board with that."

"The squirrels might object," Toren chuckled. "Phoebe should be having her litter soon, we can pretty much guarantee a puppy of hers isn't an evil shifter sent to murder you."

"Will Mrs. James let me have a puppy inside?" Carina asked, sorely tempted.

"I'll make her," Toren promised.

"Oh, look!" Carina said, pointing. "Northern lights! Is that one of your brothers spying on us?"

"Let them," Toren said carelessly. He had one of Carina's hands in his. "Have we had enough duty now?" he asked wistfully.

Carina nearly tipped over her camp chair climbing into his lap. "I think it's your royal duty to take me into that van and make sure that your queen doesn't get cold."

Toren stood easily with her in his arms, making her squeak in alarm. "That's my favorite duty," he said with a laugh.

And he performed it *perfectly*.

~

*J*f you don't want to miss book two of *Royal Dragons of Alaska*, sign up for my mailing list here and read on for more information about my other pen names and a sneak preview of The Dragon Prince's Librarian. And if you liked *The Dragon Prince of Alaska*, you'll love Shifting Sands Resort…

# A SNEAK PREVIEW OF THE DRAGON PRINCE'S LIBRARIAN

This was going to be the greatest 'I told you so' in history, Rian thought. He was sweating in the Florida humidity and reconsidering the uniform that had seemed so sensible in Alaska in October.

"She's not your mate," his twin brother Tray had insisted. "She's a *pen pal*. The Compact already tapped a new queen for Alaska. Why would there be more than one? So that Fask could be king, maybe. You? No."

But Rian knew before Tania opened the door to her apartment that he wasn't here by accident. He hadn't imagined that undeniable pull whenever he thought of her, and his dragon was steaming in his head, absolutely certain and utterly focused.

*This is where we need to be,* he told Rian firmly. *This is the time.*

And when he saw her at last, she was weirdly familiar and entirely new; Rian couldn't stop himself from staring. She looked like her surreptitious photographs, wavy dark hair with fading blonde highlights framing a round, tawny-skinned face. Brown eyes with layers of gold gazed back under bangs that were too long.

Did she feel the same recognition that he felt? She didn't look particularly welcoming, but it was hard to parse around the flood of emotions and feelings he was simmering in. His? His dragon's? *Hers?*

Even his body didn't feel like it was entirely his own, which wasn't entirely *pleasant.*

"What do you want?" she asked, and her voice sent shivers down his spine.

"I tried to call," he explained. "And before that, I emailed."

It had only been emails, at first, starting from one carefully worded query about Tania's thesis—a thesis that had been wiped by Small Kingdoms agents from her university's database almost a year before.

Her first reply, more than a month ago, had been understandably defensive.

The document she had been working from was a secret version of the international treaty called the Compact, and had never been intended for general consumption. The public version had been greatly sterilized, removing all mention of dragons, magic, mates, and casters.

She'd written most of a thesis on the document before Small Kingdoms agents got wind of it, and operatives had moved in decisively, deleting the thesis, her copies, the copies of the secret Compact at the library, and even her prospectus in the university database. Her advisor had been amply paid off to pursue a sudden change of profession.

Once Rian had assured her that she wasn't crazy, that he had *seen* the same Compact she remembered, they traded a flurry of emails on the topic...and later went completely off-topic as they connected through a long string of letters. Rian's life had narrowed to her correspondence; he had never guessed he would meet anyone with her clever turn of phrases who shared his interest in books. Every email was anticipated more eagerly than the last, every red flag on his phone was a reason to shirk his duties and disappear. He read them over and over, composing his replies with care.

And then they stopped coming.

"The library froze my email when I got fired," Tania said coldly. "And my phone is off." Then, suspiciously, "How did you get my number? How did you know where I lived?"

Rian flushed. "I hired an investigator." He swiftly put up his hands. "Not that I was stalking you, but your emails started bouncing, so I called the library, and they wouldn't give me any way to contact you. I was worried for you. I couldn't sleep. I needed to know that you were okay." He ran his fingers through his hair in nervous habit. "I'm not making myself sound any less like a stalker…"

"I'm fine," she said, and in a rush, Rian realized that he knew she was lying. She was barely holding on. She was afraid, and she was in pain. He could feel the ache in her hips and her shoulders, and the exhaustion she was fighting.

"You're not fine," he blurted.

He really did think she was going to shut the door on him then.

"No, I'm sorry," he said swiftly. "You're fine. I mean, and you're definitely *fine*. I just don't mean…" Why couldn't he be suave like Toren or Fask? he wondered desperately. She probably thought he was leering at her, because he couldn't stop staring at her in wonder.

Tania's scowl softened a little. "You're not what I expected from a prince," she said, confirming that she'd long since figured out exactly who he was. It probably hadn't taken her a private investigator.

"I'm not," Rian agreed. "I mean, I'm a prince, but I don't fit much of the prince...expectation. Sorry."

"The uniform helps," she said, with a tiny quirk of a smile. "When you said you wore a uniform as part of your day job, I assumed you were in security." Then she glanced out into the hallway behind him. "No escort? No honor guard? Trumpets with long flags off the bottom?"

"I flew alone," Rian explained. Which wasn't much of an explanation, since she didn't know he was a dragon shifter. Yet. "I mean...ah…can I come in?" He certainly wasn't going to reveal that information in the dark, muggy common hall of her apartment building.

She gave him a deeply considering look and finally stepped aside, a little hitch to her step that Rian *knew* caused her pain.

Her apartment was small, just what Rian could charitably call cozy, and untidy. It was also completely lined in books. There were bookshelves on every free wall, a short shelf behind the couch, high shelves above the cabinets in the kitchen stuffed with cookbooks, even a narrow shelf just two books wide next to the door. Further piles of books were scattered on the coffee and end tables. Above the table, the only clear wall was decorated in old photographs and certificates.

It smelled like old books and vanilla, which seemed absolutely perfect.

"What do you want?" Tania asked again.

Rian thought it sounded less chilly this time, and more weary. He resisted the urge, just barely, to fold her into his arms and promise that everything was going to be okay now.

"I needed to talk to you," he said seriously.

"About the Compact?" Tania asked. "There are other scholars. Scholars of the *real* version, not the fanciful version I might have imagined."

"You didn't imagine it."

She seemed taken aback by his firmness. Rather than clearing him a seat, she sank into the one empty chair like she didn't have anything left for courtesy. Maybe she didn't. Rian took a stack of books with library bands off of the other chair and moved it to the table.

*Tell her,* his dragon hissed at him. *Tell her everything.*

She waited for him to go on, and Rian took a moment to compose himself and stuff his over-eager dragon back into silence.

"I'm really sorry about your thesis," he started. "It's…kind of my fault that it got scrapped. I mean, not mine personally, but…there are two versions of the Compact. The one you saw…you weren't supposed to see. I mean, I think you *were* supposed to see it, because otherwise I'd never have met you, but it's not for…public consumption."

Tania stared at him in confusion. "How is it your fault that there are two versions? I thought it was just an…older version. Why would there be two current versions? Why are they so different?"

"There are two versions to protect me. To protect my family. To protect our secrets. That stuff you thought was metaphor, about dragons and magic...that's real. We just don't share that copy with other countries because people would look at us...well, yes, exactly like that."

She looked deeply dubious.

"It's literal," Rian explained. "In fact, it's pretty exactingly literal, because it's a really long and involved spell, and you have to be really specific with spells or they can take off in unexpected directions."

Tania laughed. "The royal families of the Small Kingdoms, they are all dragons. And the Compact is a *spell.*"

Rian suspected that she was reconsidering her decision to let him into her apartment. "Please, hear me out! Magic is real, there *are* dragons, and I'm not a stalker!"

"So you keep insisting," Tania said, and Rian couldn't help but grin at her, because it was exactly something she would have written in an email.

"Do you believe me?" he asked hopefully.

"I shouldn't," Tania said, frowning at him. "I shouldn't, there is no practical reason that I would, and I don't understand why I do."

Rian smiled. "You will," he said confidently. "You will, so you do."

Tania stared at him. "Supposing this *is* all true, why are you here? What does any of this have to do with me?"

Rian looked at her and chewed over his options. "Do you remember the part of the Compact that talks about mates?"

"'When the need is great and the ground is fertile.' Very poetic stuff." Her eyes narrowed in suspicion. "I presumed it was a way to make an arranged marriage sound more palatable."

"It's a little more than that," Rian said. "When a change of power is needed, the Compact's spell chooses a partner for the heir. It's...not a compulsion exactly, but it makes sure that they meet. And that they know each other when they do."

"Like your brother, Torenayram." Tania was nodding slowly. "I saw the tabloids. Whirlwind romance, love at first sight, all the usual trappings. Was she really a murderer? That seems like a pretty big oversight on the part of a magic piece of paper. Isn't a mate supposed to be a perfect queen?"

"She was framed," Rian said. "The charges were dropped. But yes, Carina is Toren's mate. I have no reason to doubt it." Quite the opposite; now that he was sitting opposite from his own mate, he knew exactly what Toren had gone through.

"I'm still not seeing the relevance to me," Tania said, with an adorable scrunch to her forehead. "Surely there are people with more familiarity with the Compact than me. Even the real version."

"You're *my* mate," Rian finally blurted, and joy rose up in his throat at being able to admit it out loud. *The greatest 'I told you so' in history,* his dragon reminded him smugly.

Continue the story in The Dragon Prince's Librarian!

# Wolf's Instinct

## A DAY CARE for Shifters

# ELVA BIRCH

# A DAY CARE FOR SHIFTERS

*A Day Care for Shifters* is a swoony, sweet-hot series of standalone novels (and interconnected shorts) set in the small town of Nickel City, where shifters are trying to stay secret…something infinitely complicated by young shifters just learning their magical skills, right along with walking and talking and stealing hearts! These are gentle romances full of humor and feeling, perfect ice-cream-straight-from-the-container escapes. They can be read in any order, but this is the order in which they occur:

**Wolf's Instinct:** Roderick's toddler daughter and busy plumbing business keep him too wrapped up for romance and while he trusts his wolf, the magic of instinct can be like playing hot-and-cold with a kid who's forgotten where they hid the prize. Addison comes to Nickel City to take a job at a very special day care and finds a family to belong to.

**First Comes Love** (a mini-series!): Navigating on-line dating is hard enough for a single mom and first shift baker, but Chloe has a whole new set of problems when her little boy suddenly changes into a pushy baby penguin and Clay, a polar bear shifter comes to her rescue. This mini-trilogy includes three short stories: First Shift, First Day, and First Date. You can get First Christmas for free on my webpage!

**Dragon's Instinct:** Ian had enough trouble trying to write for a living and keep up with his daughter, Lucy, even before she started shifting into a squirrel. Now that she's turning two and breathing fire? The twos just got a lot more terrible!

**Unicorn's Instinct:** Tara just wants her mommy to be happy... and a puppy. Vivian doesn't have the heart or time for romance, let alone a puppy, but everything changes when she meets the new pediatric doctor at her clinic and learns his heart-breaking secret.

**Gryphon's Instinct**: A single dad chasing two kids - only one of them can fly, but the other one thinks he can...

# CHAPTER 1

*Don't swear in front of the kids, don't swear in front of the kids, don't swear...* Roderick wrenched his shoulder nearly out of the socket trying to reach through the tiny hole under the sink to get to the fitting. Inside his head was a far less censored litany.

"Uck!"

Had he said it out loud after all?

"Uck! Uck!"

Roderick craned his head around and saw a little girl with a blond halo of fuzzy hair standing in the door. She looked about the age of his own daughter, Gabby, but was standing confidently on both feet, a spit-soggy stuffed animal in one hand.

A spry middle-aged woman with salt-and-pepper and electric-blue pigtails swooped in behind her and lifted the child out of the way of the spreading puddle of dirty water leaking from beneath the sink.

"How did you get past the table?" Cherry demanded cheerfully of the child. Her wild-colored hair was at odds with her conservative country plaid shirt and plain jeans. Her feet were in socks, and she was careful to stay clear of the mess.

"Uck!" the toddler replied merrily.

Roderick looked sheepishly at Cherry.

"Yuck," Cherry agreed. "Yuck is right!"

*Oh, yuck. Yuck* was okay, even if it wasn't at all what Roderick had been thinking.

"What's the news?" Cherry asked, lowering her voice.

"Not good," Roderick said, shaking his head. He'd finally gotten his fingers around the fitting and could unscrew it and draw it out of the tiny access panel in the wet wall. "Whoever plumbed this building ought to be..." he glanced at the little girl chortling in Cherry's arm. "Yuck," he said. "Let's just go with yuck."

He wriggled out from under the sink and inspected the fitting. "I really should take a look at the rest of them, too. If they put these everywhere, you could have a big problem on your hands."

Cherry peered at the fitting. "What's wrong with it?"

"Besides the fact that this is a totally inappropriate fitting for this spot, it's the wrong material. Not to code for potable water."

"Is it toxic?" Cherry asked in horror, exchanging a look with the child in her arms.

"Uck!" the little girl added, trying to squirm free and play in the water on the floor.

"It's relatively harmless," Roderick promised. "But it should all be replaced if this isn't the only one. This stuff tends to wear out faster, especially if it goes through a lot of temperature changes. It also looks like maybe the system was frozen with water in it." He pointed out a crack in the fitting. "There may be other cracks."

"The place was empty last winter," Cherry said, looking around in despair. "Maybe it wasn't winterized first?"

"I hope you're not having second thoughts about expanding your day care business," Roderick said.

"No," Cherry said firmly, and she gave him a genuine smile. "I'm excited about it. I just dread explaining to Veronica that she's going to have to spend money on the place."

"It's a great place," Roderick agreed.

Cherry's scowl spread effortlessly to an excited grin. "I love it already," she said frankly.

Cherry had been babysitting for Roderick and other shifters in

Nickel City for decades, and he'd watched the demand for her services outgrow her house and her ability to watch them all on her own. She'd decided to make the leap to opening a day care downtown and hire a helper or two.

Roderick had been the one to find the place, despite his reservations about the landlord, and was sorry that her opening day had been met with a bathroom flood; he wished that he had better news for her.

The girl in her arms fussed and then seamlessly shifted into a fuzzy little owl chick, beating downy wings in protest of her captivity as she wiggled from her clothes.

"Whoops," Cherry said, easily tossing her in place as she gathered up the clothing. "Clever little Amy, but you still can't play in this mess, even as an owl! I gotta go check on the other kids. My new hire should be here in just a few minutes."

Roderick was surprised by a jangle at the fringes of his wolf's senses. Why would his shifter instinct be excited by *that* news? Sometimes he felt like instinct was a game of hot-and-cold with a kid who had forgotten where they'd hid something, with no hint of logic or direction. He'd learned to treat it with a degree of reserve—since a simple *that way* could lead him right off the edge of a cliff—but never to ignore it.

"Who did you get?" he asked, grabbing the mop to clean up the mess.

"Wendy—you know Wendy from the DMV? Her cousin from Buffalo was looking for work. I haven't even met her yet," Cherry confessed, "but her resume was impressive. She has a certificate in early education, and she worked as a nanny for a shifter family who gave her a glowing recommendation. Wendy said she'd suit me and, well, it's not like I have a lot of choices."

Hiring reliable help for a day care was hard enough. Hiring help for a day care for shifters? That could get complicated. Not only did they have to be part of a secret community, but they still had to meet all the usual human-world qualifications and pass background checks. Maybe his instinct was just confirming that Cherry had picked a good candidate. After all, whoever she was, his daughter would be spending time in her care, so she definitely mattered to his little family of two.

"I'm going to get my ladder and check out the other fittings in the ceiling," Roderick told Cherry. "I'll let you know what I find."

Why would his instinct insist that he was about to find happiness?

# CHAPTER 2

The only thing "city" about Nickel City was its name, Addison decided.

Her first day in the little town, she drove to visit several of the historical locations featured in the glossy brochure that her cousin Wendy provided for her. There were some quaint mining displays and a few interpretive signs about the brief prospecting rush that had built the town when stainless steel drove up demand for the mineral nickel. An entire bustling museum was devoted to nickels, boasting the most comprehensive collection of three-cent and wooden nickels in the United States. It had one of those commemorative coin-squishing machines out front and several laughing boys were putting it through its paces.

Each of the numbered destinations was more crowded than she expected them to be, with people who were obviously tourists snapping photos on their phones and dragging bored children behind them. There was a slightly surly feeling to the locals serving them, and Addison was surprised and a little delighted to run across not just one but two other shifters in her little self-guided tour, each of them giving her a little tingle of awareness at the edges of her nerves when they were close by.

They each exchanged a little smile and nod of recognition, but nothing more.

Nickel City had a busy little downtown with familiar coffee shop chains and fast food, but the office buildings didn't top four stories at the most, and the only box store was ten miles out of town. The little town seemed to be more trees than buildings, and indeed, a sign in town proudly pronounced it a member of "Tree City, USA."

In fact, one of the town's claims to fame was a particularly spectacular larch on a private estate near Belle Lake with a plaque declaring the fragrant pine the third-largest tree in all of Montana. It was open to visitors on each second and fourth Thursday, and Addison was surprised to realize that her timing was that perfect.

She visited it to satisfy her inner lynx's characteristic feline curiosity and wasn't sure what to make of the shiver of recognition that ran through her at the sight of it. It wasn't threatening, and it wasn't welcoming, simply weirdly aware. She reached inward, asking a question wordlessly, and her lynx gave an unconcerned feline shrug. Maybe any tree that old was slightly magic and it wasn't instinct at all.

A little older woman with fluffy gray hair and a bright red shirt stood beside her in the crowd, giving Addison's senses a not-quite-shifter tickle. "It's something, isn't it?" the stranger said proudly.

They stood a little apart from the other tourists, who were trying to take photos and selfies, complaining that you couldn't really see the scope of the tree in their pictures.

"I've never seen anything like it," Addison admitted. She didn't even try to photograph it, knowing that no snapshot could capture the sheer size and power of the thing. There was no way to even see the top.

"It's one hundred and seventy feet tall," the woman told her. "And the crown is thirty-five feet in diameter. It's almost a thousand years old."

She didn't look like a tourist, Addison decided. She didn't have a backpack or camera or even a purse. She was wearing something like a vintage pin-up girl, straight out of a World War II photo shoot. Did trees have docents like museums did?

Some of the tourists were circling the tree to show that four of them together could barely reach around the broad trunk, their friend taking shots on her phone. One of them gave a cry of disgust. "There's sap on me! Oh, gross, it's sticky!"

"That's what she said!" one of his friends chortled.

Addison giggled and glanced at the woman beside her to see how she'd take the joke and found that she had vanished. She looked around curiously but didn't see the woman's distinctive red blouse anywhere in the thin crowds.

～

*T*he following day, Addison found her new place of employment.

*Potential* employment, she reminded herself, looking up at the false storefront with a smile of amusement and excitement.

A block off of the main street, this area had clearly been made to imitate a gold rush town, with a quaint fake second story all along the street. She doubted that it was actually a historic district, but suspected that it was something more recent, to capitalize on the town's mining history, even though its real resource had been nickel and not gold, and the big rush had been in the 1950s and 60s, not in the 1800s. It was a curious mix of rustic and modern, with rough wood siding and chrome fixtures side by side. Addison suspected it would give an actual historian apoplectic fits.

She knew she was at the right place; a large sign above the door declared "Saloon" in an old-fashioned font. The windows to either side were obscured with colorful tissue paper in a bright, bold geometric pattern, allowing sunlight in, but not prying eyes. Instinct was humming in her veins, promising...Addison wasn't sure what, but she had to squash the feeling that she was exactly when and where she was supposed to be. Whatever instinct was good for, it could swamp her ability to speak logically, and she was here for an interview and wanted all her wits sharp and her mind clear.

The door was locked and there was a doorbell with a speaker

and the gleam of a camera right next to it, with a cheerful note that said, "Ring for Cherry!"

Addison drew in a breath and pressed the button briefly.

There was a static crackle of something that might have been Cherry's name, almost drowned by a child's shriek.

Addison depressed the intercom button again and said into the box, "This is Addison Carmichael," as clearly as she could.

The answer was completely garbled, but there was a little buzz and click at the door. Addison opened it cautiously and walked into an entryway fenced by walls that didn't quite reach the wood-paneled ceiling. She could hear laughter and children's voices beyond the divider, as well as the yelp of a puppy.

A poster of a bear wiggling weirdly human toes was the first thing that greeted Addison, with stencil letters that said: "'BEAR' FEET PLEASE. SHOES OFF." Beneath that was a handwritten note that said, "Please put socks in shoes if you are not going to wear them so they don't get lost."

There were two tiny, unmatched socks pinned up next to it.

Under the windows on each side of the door ran two low, unpadded benches, and facing each of them was a row of hooks. Half a dozen of them had bags and jackets hanging at them, and there were several pairs of shoes tucked under the bench.

Addison sat down at the bench and took off her tennis shoes, tucking them underneath neatly and pairing up the chaos of toddler shoes she found there out of general habit.

At the end of the hooks to the left was a doorway arch through the partial wall, blocked by a baby gate.

Standing guard at the gate was a toddler, a little older than a year, clinging to the molded plastic for balance as she bounced happily in place. Black curly hair covered her head, and she wore a green romper covered in frogs. She had clearly just discovered that she had knees and was testing them exuberantly.

"Gaba!" she announced when Addison approached and peered cautiously past her. "Gaba!"

There was a room divider, so that she had to step carefully over the gate and the toddler and take several steps before she could see into the room itself.

Inside was delightful pandemonium.

A big-pawed, mixed-breed puppy was tussling with a growling bear cub and a tiny, curled-up armadillo rocked under their feet, barely escaping from being trampled in the play. A gawky baby owl, not fledged yet, was bouncing in place, beating its fluffy wings in a percussion of joy. Tiny, downy feathers were floating in the air. Several older kids were in human form playing some arcane mixture of store, school, and doctor.

The spacious room itself was a charming mix of bold preschool decoration and the original saloon decor. The bar itself had been replaced with a row of low kitchen playware, but the original shelves remained behind it, crowded with stuffed animals and toys. Lit mirrors with arched tops above the shelves made the room look brighter and bigger than it was. There was a row of cages and cubbies backing the entryway wall, housing an array of classroom pets and a selection of birds who were chirping cheerfully into the chaos. A comparatively quiet nursery corner had several cribs surrounded by low walls and baby gates to keep disruptive older kids out. Heavy curtains could be drawn around the corner and there were rolled sleeping mats stuck in a wide bucket.

A reading corner by the nursery had shelves with board books along the bottom and paper books up higher. Big, fuzzy bean bags looked like inviting places to sit and cuddle with babies from the nursery or to read with older kids. There was one padded rocking chair as well. On the other side of the room were short tables and stacks of kid-sized chairs, plus a few highchairs. Locked storage cabinets were labeled with "Art supplies," "Glue and Paint," "Cleaning supplies," "Paper," and "Monsters! Stay out!"

A narrow hallway in the back led past two closed doors and opened out onto a high-fenced yard that let hints of sunlight and green-scented breeze spill in. One of the tables had been pulled and tipped over sideways to block the way to the hallway, and there was a stepladder filling the space. Addison had a glimpse of a very fine-looking ass in jeans that looked entirely too tight for carpentry. He was wearing only socks, out of respect to the no-shoes rules.

If Addison's instinct had been humming before, it was an electric sizzle now, and she wrestled her lynx's desire to caper without reason.

The rest of the man was up through the drop ceiling of the more modern rear of the building, cursing creatively. "Son of a monkey, I want to know what the guy who built this place was smoking."

"Son of a monkey!" one of the older children parroted. "Son of a monkey!"

"Smunky! Smunky!" a younger one echoed, and there was a chorus of nonsense from the school-grocery-hospital.

"Gaba!" the bobbing toddler at the door proclaimed generally. "Gaba!"

"You must be Addison!"

The woman who appeared from a back room past the ladder looked like a breath of fresh air in a checkered plaid shirt and a pair of age-softened jeans. Dark hair streaked with white and bright blue was pulled back in two ponytails that Addison's mother would have insisted were a sign that she was clinging too hard to youth.

Addison liked her at once.

"Yes, I'm here for the interview." She thrust a hand out and the woman, who could only be Cherry Aimes, shook it with a firm, kind handshake.

She didn't set off a shifter tingle of recognition, to Addison's surprise. Her cousin, a long-time resident of Nickel City, had told her about this job and recommended her for the position. Addison had assumed that someone running a day care specifically for shifters would be a shifter herself, but she didn't have that edge-of-the-senses prickle that all shifters shared.

Cherry looked at her hard and Addison felt like she was being evaluated in whole and hoped that she measured up. Her lynx was singing that this was where she belonged, this was the path to her happiness, that everything was right and true and *now*. It would be a shame if she blew that by falling on her face now.

"Would you mind skipping the interview and jumping right in with both feet?" Cherry asked plaintively. "My part-time help couldn't make it today, and we've had a plumbing emergency, and I got more kids today than I was expecting for our very first official day."

"N-not at all," Addison said. "Let's get started!" She was almost dizzy from the intensity of her instinct and the presence of so many young shifters.

Cherry gave her a slow, pleased grin, then called generally to the room, "Fingers and feet, everyone! Fingers and feet! I want you all to meet someone!" There was a big rectangular carpet in the middle marked on the edges with numbers and letters. "Everybody pick a letter!"

The bear cub turned into a boy of about four in coveralls and the dog he'd been wrestling was suddenly a slightly older girl wearing a sparkling skirt over a pair of jeans. The armadillo was abruptly a boy close to their age, stark naked. The owl flutter-skipped over to Cherry's feet and unfolded into a chubby toddler, reaching for her knees. The other children quickly gathered and claimed their letters, with a very brief struggle for the coveted "C," which had a picture of cherries.

The toddler guarding the gate seemed to realize that exciting things were happening without her and she gave a cry of protest, then let go of the gate to sink down to hands and knees and crawl to the colorful carpet, where one of the older children herded her to a letter and gave her a stuffed animal that temporarily mesmerized her.

"Thank you, everyone," Cherry said warmly. "Gil, what did you forget?"

Gil, the naked armadillo boy, looked down at himself in surprise. "CLOTHES!" he exclaimed. "I forgot my CLOTHES!"

"Please go find them," Cherry suggested. "We'll all wait, but I'm very excited to introduce you to our new teacher!"

Gil scampered into a corner where his forgotten clothing had clearly been accidentally shifted out of, while all the other children's attention settled on Addison, whose heart raced. They were a combination of curious and cautious. The owl-shifting toddler shuffled herself to the far side of Cherry, staring at Addison with round, golden-brown eyes.

Addison wiggled her fingers at the toddler, who giggled and hid her face against Cherry's leg.

Gil returned to the rug, awkwardly hopping on one leg as he tried to get his pants on the other leg. He took the letter "L."

"This is Teacher Addison," Cherry introduced. "I'd like you all to say hello."

It wasn't a terribly coherent hello chorus. Addison took mental note of which ones seemed exuberant and which acted shy. "You can call me Teacher Addy."

"I can add!" one of the boys volunteered enthusiastically. "Essept sevens."

"Sevens are very hard," Addison told him sympathetically. "I can help you remember them."

She was keenly aware of the scrutiny she was under, not only from the children, but from Cherry herself. She had gotten the interview easily, but she knew that it wasn't because of her qualifications; finding a shifter caretaker in a world where shifters were secret was tricky business. She might have been the only choice that Cherry had, and this was definitely a trial by fire. She was determined to prove that she was a good choice, not just a desperate one.

"I'd like you to teach her the rules, boys and girls," Cherry directed. "Some of you know them already. Tara, can you tell her the first rule of our school?"

Tara was one of the oldest girls at about five, with wavy brown hair and Asian features. She frowned self-consciously at the attention.

Before she could speak, Gil interrupted, "Fingers and FEET in FRONT OF PEOPLE!"

"I was going to say it," Tara protested, clearly hurt.

Gil didn't look particularly contrite.

"Let's go around and tell Teacher Addy your names," Cherry suggested. "Tara, would you like to start?"

Tara murmured her name at the floor in front of her.

"I'm GIL," the armadillo shifter shouted.

The boy next to him was Robert, and the dog shifter was Laura. Cherry introduced the owl-shifting toddler as Amy and Addison got a shy wave.

"That's Gabby," Cherry pointed.

The little girl who had greeted Addy when she arrived heard her name and abandoned the stuffy she had been examining to crawl in Addison's direction.

Addison sat down and Gabby went willingly into her lap, tugging experimentally at Addison's hair before snuggling happily into her arms. She wasn't a shifter, though she was close to the age that the transition usually happened.

"We've got two babies in the nursery right now," Cherry said, glancing towards the corner with the cribs. "Daria and Shane."

"Shane is my baby brother," Tara volunteered.

"Do you like being a big sister?" Addison asked her. "I was always the little sister."

Tara rewarded her with a slow smile.

In the hallway behind them, there was a sudden crash in the ceiling and swearing that had not been censored for children, followed by a swift, "Sorry, Cherry!"

"Let's go read a book!" Cherry suggested merrily. "How about a loud book?"

"TRAINS!" Gil hollered gamely.

Addison, still holding Gabby, helped corral the children over into the little library and sat to listen to a book with lots of audience participation and clapping. Gabby didn't pay a lot of attention to it, but she did like Addison's clapping and she joined in enthusiastically.

The little girl got restless during the next book, whining and straining in Addison's arms. Addison let her go, but Gabby immediately started to crawl for a gap by the table blocking the hallway towards the ladder. Addison laughed and chased her, swooping her up and making her chortle and shriek happily as the contractor started down the ladder, muttering and shaking his head.

Then he turned and looked at her, and Addison felt her giggles die at her lips.

It wasn't just he was genuinely breathtaking, with his warm, sepia skin and his jaw like a sculptor's dream. It wasn't even that he was a muscular specimen of male that transcended *guy* straight for *god*. It was that her instinct was humming in happiness and certainty, like she'd never felt it before.

# CHAPTER 3

*R*oderick knew he was staring, but it was impossible not to. Cherry's new hire was standing just across the table from him, holding his daughter in her strong arms and it was the most beautiful thing he'd ever seen. She had reddish-blonde hair in a sensible shoulder-length cut, pale, freckled skin, and a dimple in the middle of her chin. Her smile was crooked and eager, and she was wearing a blue skirt that looked green in the golden light from the back yard, over wild-patterned leggings.

She made his skin tingle, as every shifter did, but there was something more to his uncanny sudden awareness of her.

*What is this…?* He dived inward, calling for his inner wolf, as he folded the stepladder and moved aside the table.

*Here, now, this,* came the wolf's unhelpful answer. Roderick felt like his ears were pricked forward, his tail in a slow, eager wag, and he had to double-check to make sure his human body wasn't doing something ridiculous.

Every shifter had a sense of instinct. Just as certain birds knew when and how to migrate, and fish and turtles could find their way back to their birthplace, shifters had a subtle reaction to danger, a preternatural reflex that told them when something was wrong...and when something was right.

And oh, was this so *right.*

Some shifters—Roderick's mother included—believed in soul-mates, in the possibility of finding that one true love, and recognizing them when they met.

"That doesn't mean there aren't other ways to find love," his mother had been swift to add, "or that you couldn't screw it up irredeemably with someone who might have been your perfect partner. It's just a little extra jumpstart to romance that comes along with being a shifter. You ever feel that instinct, you listen to it good, because magic whispers, it doesn't shout."

It was certainly whispering now, more loudly than he'd ever heard it, urging him to take a chance, to risk everything.

But he'd screwed up trying to follow his instinct before, and it was hard to think straight because she was so pretty and his senses were all jangling.

It wasn't just attraction, though certainly she was all that he'd ever fantasized, with curves everywhere they ought to be. But beyond lust, there was such a feeling of comfort, of coming home. She was safety and shelter and...

"Gaba!"

Gabby had grown impatient of them drinking each other in and was straining against the woman's grasp. "Abababa!"

"I think someone needs a new diaper," the woman said practically, a mixture of shyness and smiling that made Roderick's heart flip-flop.

So much for romance.

"I can do that," he offered, holding out his arms. Gabby stretched towards him, leaning without fear. "I haven't technically checked her in yet, so it's still on me."

"You don't have to do that," she protested, shifting her grip on Gabby expertly so that she didn't fall. "It's my job...or at least, I hope it will be!"

"It's your first day," Roderick pointed out. "Cherry would never forgive me if I scared you away so soon."

"I *am* made of tougher stuff than that," she said, and her voice was made of laughter, but she offered him Gabby anyway.

She was, Roderick's instinct assured him. She was a coil of steel in silk, or a spicy candy, deceptively sweet and completely capable at the same time. He took Gabby, who babbled happily at the exchange. "Gababa babby."

"I'm Roderick," he said, tucking Gabby into one elbow and extending his other hand.

"Addison." She took his hand in a long, slow handshake that made his soul sing, and they smiled at each other foolishly. "The kids call me Teacher Addy."

"Addy," Gabby said firmly.

Roderick gave her a skeptical look. Gabby had been babbling for several months now, but it was hard to pick firm words out of the nonsense. Probably these were just random syllables, like adda *probably* wasn't dada, yet.

Addison laughed again, softly, and shook her head as she took her hand back self-consciously. "It's most likely..."

"...Just random babble," Roderick finished for her. "She's not really doing words or names yet, even though she has a lot to say. She's a gabby Gabby."

Now who was babbling?

Gabby was getting impatient and uncomfortable. "Ababa dabby!"

"Duty calls," Roderick said, only hearing how it sounded after it was out of his mouth.

"Duty does," Addison giggled, with a long ooo on the u.

*Diaper jokes,* Roderick thought. He'd just met the woman who completed him, and he was grinning with her over *diaper jokes.*

"Gababa," Gabby complained.

He forced himself not to look back over his shoulder to see if Addison was watching him as he carried Gabby to the little bathroom in the back of the day care. It wasn't the worst diaper she'd ever supplied for him, and he cleaned her up efficiently.

"Well, Gabby," he said as he wiped her down. "What do you make of this new development in our lives?"

Now that he wasn't directly facing Addison, doubts were crowding back as instinct ebbed in intensity. He'd been led down the wrong path before.

"Adaba bah," Gabby said conversationally.

"It does kind of complicate things," Roderick pointed out. "I mean, I hadn't really thought about dating again. Do you like her? Because it looks like you might see a lot more of her than I am." Was he actually jealous of a fourteen-month-old?

"Tuh-tuh," Gabby said, pointing at a turtle on the wall above the changing table. "Moo."

"Instinct isn't always *right,*" he told her, snapping the legs of her romper closed again. "Or at least, I haven't always been right about it. But I've got such a *good* feeling about this." A good feeling didn't tell him *how* to go about things; he knew it was possible to drive her away as easily as it was to win her heart. Instinct couldn't make up for sheer stupidity. Dana was proof of that.

Roderick wondered what Addison would make of him talking to Gabby like she was a grown-up, holding her own end of the conversation. All the baby books said it was good for their language skills and he didn't like to leave the television on, so he'd cultivated the habit when she was an infant, but he yearned for the day that she responded with more than strung-together syllables.

"Ababa boo," Gabby said reassuringly, and she gurgled happily as Roderick swung her up into her arms again.

"Let's go see Teacher Addy," Roderick said, wondering if she would echo the name again.

"Gabba," Gabby agreed. "Tuh-tuh."

Roderick's instinct suddenly gave a twang of unexpected warning and he rushed from the bathroom to find Addison at the front of the day care by the room divider, saying in alarm, "You can't come back here! No shoes are allowed back here, please! Let me get Cherry for you!" There was a note of panic and desperation to her voice, as well as understandable uncertainty.

A familiar voice said shrilly, "I don't know who you are, but I have every right to come in, and my boots won't hurt anything, don't be so *fussy.* Oh, just move!"

Veronica Chase, with her too-tight jeans and too-styled hair, looked appallingly overdone next to Addison's playful, easy beauty. She was stepping over the baby gate with her gold-etched cowboy boots, all but pushing Addison out of the way and Roderick glanced over the playroom to see in alarm that several of the children were in animal form. Cherry was busy in the nursery with a wailing baby.

In an instant, he was striding to intercept the woman at the gate, crowding up close as if he had no concept of personal space. He didn't mind being that close to Addison, but Veronica's proximity made his skin prickle in completely different ways. This woman was trouble, from her salon-styled bob to her ridiculous boots.

He didn't need instinct to tell him that, though. "Oh, Veronica," he said with a growl. "I had a chance to look at that leak. Let's have a word about the work that will need to be done. Out *here.*"

# CHAPTER 4

*I*t wasn't that Addison needed or wanted a big, strong, handsome guy to come to rescue her, but she had to admit that it kind of took her breath away when Gabby's gorgeous dad came and growled down the woman trying to push her way in. He *literally* growled at her, and Addison took entirely too much pleasure from the woman's look of affront.

Gabby made raspberries at her that were probably completely coincidental and growled in imitation. She seemed considerably happier now, and Addison found it hard to blame her. She'd be pretty happy in Roderick's arms, too.

She jerked her thoughts back to the confrontation in front of her.

"I found the problem, Veronica," Roderick was saying as he stepped in front of Addison. He put a weird emphasis on the name, and it was the second time he'd said it. "You've got a whole section of plumbing that isn't up to code, and there are probably more leaks just waiting to happen. What you really want to do is get in there and replace all the fittings, before you have an even bigger problem." He was angling the woman away, and Addison caught the barest edge of a shoulder shrug to her.

She understood his hint at once. Veronica wasn't a shifter, and her instinct to keep her out had been solid. She slid away, letting Roderick keep their unwelcome visitor at the room divider, and went back into the nursery to warn Cherry.

"There's a woman named Veronica who is trying to come back," she said, glancing around. "She had a key, I didn't buzz her in!"

Cherry grimaced. "Veronica Chase," she said with a sigh. "She owns all the buildings on this block and the main street one block over. She thinks that means free rein in any of them, at any time."

"Does she know...?"

Cherry shook her head and they quickly took stock of the children. Most of them were playing in human form, but Amy was hopping around as an owl and Gil was naked again.

Without consulting, they divided the tasks. "Fingers and feet, kids!" Cherry called cheerfully, as if it was nothing more than a nursery rhyme. "Fingers and feet!" She knelt to coax Amy back into human form as Addison went to find where Gil had shed his clothing and get him dressed again.

She left him tugging his shirt on to hurry back with Amy's clothing and found that it was too late.

Amy was still an owl, and Veronica Chase was coming into the room, with Roderick at her heels looking like a thundercloud. Addison noticed that she was still wearing her boots.

Cherry looked up and waved. "We're having a zoo day!" she called cheerfully. Unable to persuade Amy to shift, she had opened the cage doors for some of the real animals and gathered them on the carpet with the toddler shifter. A rabbit and a guinea pig were sniffing around, while Tara squealed and tried to pet them, and a large, slow lizard was testing the air with its tongue.

Veronica's gaze swept right over Amy without even noticing her. "You realize that you'll lose your deposit if I have to replace the flooring," she said with distaste.

"Of course," Cherry agreed mildly. "This is one of those protective waterproof carpets; the floor underneath should be fine, even if there's an accident."

The lizard started to creep slowly for the perimeter, and Veronica backed up with a hiss of disgust.

"The **REAL ANIMALS!**" Gil shouted, pushing around Addison to plop down in the middle of the carpet and try to pet the guinea pig. At least he was wearing his clothing again.

"I'm petting that one," Tara protested.

Robert, drawn from the library by Gil's loud pronouncement, came yelling into the circle as Addison tried to calm him. "We have to be gentle, Robert!" she reminded him. "Don't frighten the animals!" *Or Amy,* she added in her mind. The last thing they wanted was for the little girl to shift into human form right in front of Veronica.

"Did you need something?" Cherry asked Veronica pointedly. "We're in the middle of zoo day."

"Someone's liable to be bit," Veronica sniffed.

Personally, Addison hoped it was her.

"My contractor tells me that you need some plumbing fixes made," the odious woman went on. "But he says they are optional, and if I pay him to do them, I'll have to increase your rent."

Roderick sputtered. "That's not what I said."

"Optional," Veronica repeated. Then her voice sweetened. "But if it doesn't cost too much, of course, I wouldn't have to do that. I could take a small loss this month if I had to."

Addison was appalled. Even she could see that Veronica was playing them against each other, forcing Roderick to a lower price or Cherry to higher rent. Everyone knew it and could do nothing about it.

Gabby spotted Amy at that moment. "Abababababa!" she said, stretching her arms for the tiny owl chick.

Amy hopped up and down in recognition and Roderick, assessing the situation, swiftly said, "Let's talk about the invoice out here, Veronica."

Veronica, sensing a win, turned away just as Amy shifted into a naked toddler, lost her balance, fell over backward, and burst out crying in surprise.

Addison dashed in, swept Amy into her arms, and got a shirt

over her head in one swift motion as Veronica glanced back with a look of annoyance.

Veronica looked a little puzzled, but when her gaze swept down over the animals, she noticed that the lizard had advanced further on her and she gave a dramatic shudder and retreated out into the entry, muttering about chickens. Cherry took Gabby from Roderick and he followed her out.

Gabby, abandoned by her father, gave a wail of outrage, and Cherry and Addison breathed a sigh of relief.

"What a landlord," Addison said in an undertone, as she got a diaper on Amy and finished dressing her.

"She's a real piece of work," Cherry agreed. "But it was hard to find a place with a truly private back yard like this place has, that was central to where parents were working. Veronica owns a lot of property in town, and this was the only place I could afford." She smiled. "Besides, look at this great place."

Addison smiled up at the rough-cut ceilings, thick wood beams full of character, and the old bar features. "It's really perfect," she agreed. It had the kind of wear and weather that wouldn't bother children, and it was just the right size and configuration.

Roderick came back and Addison felt like he had brought sunshine back with him. He took Gabby easily from Cherry and tossed her a few inches in the air to turn her tears to squeals of joy.

"You shouldn't charge that woman less because of me," Cherry protested.

Roderick scowled. "That woman shouldn't pass that kind of cost on to you in the first place," he said. "It *should* have been done right to begin with." His face softened. "I'm still getting paid enough," he promised. "Not every job has to be at union rates."

Amy squirmed in Addison's arms and she put the toddler back on the floor so she could stagger to the bunny and sink down in a squat beside her to pat her ears with exaggerated gentleness.

Cherry rounded up the lizard and the guinea pig and put them back into their cages. The kids were reluctant to say goodbye to the rabbit. Cherry appeased them by letting them push lettuce in through the bars for her to eat.

Addison barely noticed, absolutely entranced by Roderick with Gabby in his arms. Like a sleepwalker, she closed the distance between them. She said quietly, "Thank you for the distraction. That was a close thing, with Amy."

"You acted quickly," he said, admiringly. "And Veronica can be a lot to handle."

"Instinct told me she was trouble the moment I saw her," Addison confessed, wondering if she put too much emphasis on the first word. "But I doubted it. I mean, I don't know anyone here and she had a *key*. Maybe she was someone Cherry knew..."

"Instinct was right in this case."

The air between them seemed to charge. Addison's skin was humming now, too strong to ignore, and she knew she was gazing at him besottedly.

They might have had that conversation then, the *you-and-me?* talk, the acknowledgment that they both felt something amazing, because it was really hard to deny that they were both feeling something amazing...but there was a sudden commotion in the school behind her, and the phone in Roderick's pocket gave a demanding buzz.

"I should get back to work," she said regretfully.

"I have another job I need to get to," he said, sounding every drop as regretful.

He started to leave, then turned back as he realized he was still holding Gabby. "You have to stay here, sweetie."

The hand-off was complicated by the fact that Gabby realized she was going to be left behind again and took double handfuls of everything she could reach. Roderick had to pry her off and transfer her, wailing and sobbing, to Addison, who had to take her without succumbing to her own desire to climb into Roderick's arms.

"I feel your pain," she murmured to Gabby, who wanted no part of her and actively tried to push off with all of her considerable strength.

Roderick stepped over the gate and stuffed his feet into his boots as Addison turned away, neither of them wishing to draw out their goodbye and prolong Gabby's misery.

Gabby settled almost as soon as he was out of sight, but fussed when Addison offered to put her down on the floor, so Addison carried her around with her for most of the morning.

# CHAPTER 5

For Roderick, walking away and leaving Gabby with someone else was always like being stretched on a medieval torture device.

Walking away and leaving Gabby with someone else when she was upset and crying piteously for him was like being doused in hot sauce after he'd been flayed. Even knowing that her protests rarely lasted long after he was out of sight was small comfort for the distress he was causing her.

Leaving her with Addison felt complicated because he didn't want to leave either of them, but he also knew, completely, that Gabby would be safe with her, safer than anywhere else in the whole world that wasn't his own arms.

Instinct could find him his soulmate, his mother had said. She hated the term mate and thought it made it sound like it was all about sex. "It's not about sex," she'd said frankly. Then, to his mortification, she had laughed. "Well, it's not all about the sex. It's about compatibility."

Addison...it was like she was a fit to all the puzzle pieces in his life. She could be the companion his life lacked, the breath of fresh air his stale existence desperately needed. She could be the mother that Gabby didn't have.

Roderick got into his pickup and paused without turning it on, still hearing the echo of Gabby's cries echoing in his ears.

Hadn't instinct told him that Dana was right, too? He'd thought that she was his one forever, and had trusted that they could get past their differences, if they both worked at it, and that they would make a life together. But the life that Dana had wanted wasn't what he had envisioned, and she didn't think there was a place for him, let alone for a child, which was something that Roderick didn't think he could ever forgive her for. Instinct had gone cold, like he'd been wrong about it all along.

So what if he was wrong about this, too? The sense was never obvious. It was a quiet whisper, a promise...but promises could be broken and Roderick didn't necessarily trust himself after the disaster of his last relationship. He'd never been sure if the magic had been flawed, if he'd misinterpreted it, or if he'd done something wrong. If he'd fought harder to stay together, if he'd been more accommodating...

The phone beside him rang, jolting him from his spiral of introspection and doubt.

"Douglass Plumbing," he answered.

It was an unfamiliar number and an unfamiliar voice, but a very familiar request.

"I've got a quick install job to do in that neighborhood," Roderick said, consulting his schedule. He liked an old-fashioned written calendar, and had a black-covered day planner that he laughingly called his little black book; plumbing jobs were as close to a relationship as he'd gotten to romance since Dana left. "I can be there about three o'clock."

He penciled them in and hung up, then finally started the pickup and pulled out into the quiet street.

"Hot Rod!" he was greeted at the door of his first job. "How's it hanging?"

Roderick had heard all the 'rod' jokes, but Ian Gadsby never tired of them. "I'm here to tighten your drains," he said mockingly, and they exchanged a rough, friendly hug before Ian stepped aside to let him in.

"Just be careful not to flush Lucy down the toilet, or let her climb into your toolbox. I spent two hours yesterday trying to find her while she was sleeping on top of the fridge."

"She's shifting now?"

"Yup. A squirrel like her mother was and as fast as a streak. I thought it got challenging when she learned how to walk, but let me tell you, this wall-climbing thing is giving me white hairs. How's Gabby?"

"Still only two legs," Roderick said with relief. "How's the writing going?"

Ian grimaced. "Not well. Lucy isn't napping so much now and I feel like I'm chasing her every moment I'm awake."

"Have you thought about putting her in day care? Cherry's got her business license and her shifter-watching is all official and above-board now. Well, the shifters part is hush-hush, of course, but the business is legal."

"It's tempting," Ian said wistfully. "I don't know if I'd be able to afford it, did I tell you that my landlord is planning to sell the house? Apparently, Veronica Chase is buying up a bunch of property in the area and made him a deal he can't refuse."

Roderick frowned, remembering Veronica's smug expression when she talked him into taking less for the repair job than he knew he should charge.

Ian shook his head. "Besides, I feel like since I work from home, I ought to be able to keep her here with me. Even if it's really hard getting anything done with interruptions every ten minutes to pull her off the top of the bookshelf or pry her out of the box she's gotten stuck in. And I worry, man, she can get into anything if I look away for a minute. Or out of anything." He gazed around the room. "Lucy!" he called, looking around at the tops of bookcases. "Honey? Remember Mr. Roderick?"

With just a squeak of warning, there was suddenly a tiny furry body launching itself at Roderick and he dropped his toolbox to catch a toddler, a little older than Gabby, as she shifted from a little reddish squirrel to a girl...right on his shoulder.

"Hot Rod!" she said in excitement, wrapping her arms around his head. "Gabby's daddy! Play with Gabby!"

"You forgot your clothes, Lucy," Ian said, mortified. "Let's go put them on again."

"You know, they teach clothing shifting at Cherry's," Roderick said, laughing as he handed off the little girl and picked up his toolbox again. "I can find the bathroom while you do that."

Clogged toilets were the least glamorous part of his work and honestly the most reliable pay because kids would put anything they could fit down them...and plenty that didn't. Roderick gave it a test flush, watching its slow progress, listening to the drain in the sink for clues to the location of the clog, and went to his truck to get the snake.

It was a simple job, and the clog pushed through without trouble. Roderick didn't even have to open up a pipe cleanout to get it cleared and he was done in a matter of minutes. "No charge," he said, shaking his head when Ian reached for his wallet. Lucy was dressed in a purple dress covered in little rainbow-maned unicorns and was sitting deceptively quietly on the couch, her bare toes wiggling as she flipped through a picture book. "Just keep me in mind when you have a real problem that I can charge you the moon for."

"I wouldn't take my business anywhere else," Ian promised, keeping his gaze knowingly on Lucy as they moved towards the door. When they were out of easy earshot, he asked, "So, is it still just Cherry with her daycare? I mean, I feel like I ought to be able to manage writing with just one small kid around, but maybe it would be nice if Lucy had more playtime. I do have a deadline coming up."

"She's got Shea Ando part time, and...it looks like she just hired someone new full time," Roderick said. Remembering how Addison had looked holding Gabby made him smile foolishly.

He hesitated, then asked, "Do you believe in...soulmates?"

"Like that mate nonsense that shifter girls sigh over?" Ian mocked. "True love and destiny," he said in a falsetto.

Roderick wasn't sure exactly what his face did then, but Ian didn't miss it. He sobered quickly. "The new hire at Cherry's day care? You think she's the one?"

"I guess there's no way to be sure," Roderick said sheepishly. It was sort of ridiculous to feel this crazy for someone he'd just met. Was it really a whisper of magic, or just a pretty face at a vulnerable moment? He felt full of bubbles, half-drunk with anticipation, and his wolf was wagging his tail in glee.

"So, tell me about her!" Roderick had all of Ian's attention now. "A shifter, I'm guessing?"

"Yes, but I don't know what. We've barely had a chance to talk. It was like recognizing another shifter, you know, but dialed up to eleven. I looked at her and...had feelings. I don't even know."

"She's hot?"

Roderick bristled. "That's not what this was. It was...more like hearing a song on the radio that you've been trying to remember for a year, or suddenly getting a joke."

"So, not hot?"

Roderick realized that Ian was teasing him, grinning knowingly. "She's hot," he said, shaking his head. "Kind of like a sexy Miss Frizzle mixed with Mary Poppins. Definitely a spoonful of sugar."

"Is it sadder that I know those references, or that they appeal to me?"

Roderick chuckled. "Nah, it's a single dad thing."

But he didn't want to be a single dad, Roderick realized rather suddenly. He wanted to go home to someone. And he wanted Gabby to have more than just him to look up to. Could he trust that Addison was that person? Was instinct enough for something *that* important? It hadn't been able to steer him right with Dana, after all.

"Lucy? Lucy?" Ian suddenly swiveled and looked back at the couch...where Lucy's book had been set aside and her unicorn dress lay empty. "Son of a..."

"Monkey," Roderick provided. "Son of a monkey."

"I gotta go find my monkey," Ian said. "Before she gets into the cleaning supplies or eats the taxes or something. Thanks for the plunge."

"Any time."

When Roderick shut the door behind him, he heard Ian calling, "Lucy? Who's the best squirrel? Who gets nuts for dinner if she comes out right *now?*"

# CHAPTER 6

*A*ddison spent the lunch period ripping the tops off yogurt tubes and opening lids. The range of dexterity was challenging, from kids who could manage their entire meal without assistance to toddlers in high chairs who were still exploring textures and smashing berries on their trays. As the older kids finished, Cherry had them clean their placemats, put away their lunch bags, and wash their hands.

"Who's ready to practice shifting?" she asked enthusiastically.

"I AM!" Gil called from his cubby, standing on tip-toe to shove his bag into the space above his coat hook with no care for the art papers that were already there.

"What are you going to remember this time?" Cherry teased him.

"My CLOTHES!" Gil laughed.

"Will you be alright here with these guys?" Cherry asked Addison, who was trying to convince one of the littlest children that berries were not better served on the floor. "I know I'm asking a lot for what was supposed to be a casual interview. This was not the day I had planned."

Addison wanted badly to impress Cherry, but she paused to

evaluate before she agreed too eagerly. The two babies were sleeping soundly, absolutely oblivious to the surrounding chaos, and there were only two toddlers remaining: Gabby and the shy owl shifter. One older girl, Tara, was dawdling over her food.

"No problem," Addison said confidently.

Cherry traipsed outside with the rest of the children and the comparative quiet in their wake was remarkable, even though their shouts and laughter could still be heard down the back hallway. Addison got several more mouthfuls of berries into actual mouths and chased them with cubes of cheese that were met with disdain until she pretended to eat them herself.

"So delicious," she said, closing her eyes and rubbing her stomach. The word delicious on her tongue made her think about the contractor, Roderick. What would he be doing now? When would they next have a chance to talk? "I love cheese so much! I'm going to steal it all!"

This had the toddlers hurrying to clear their trays, giggling and grabbing at their food with clumsy fingers as they stuffed it in their mouths.

Addison took the top level of their trays and brought warm, damp washcloths that were as much for amusement as they were for cleaning, swiping at faces and fingers in laughing games of peekaboo.

She finally released them from their high chairs and let them continue their chaos with the soft blocks while she washed the trays with half an eye back on their play.

Tara was still lingering over her lunch, eating one careful raisin at a time from the little cardboard box.

"Don't you want to go outside and shift with the other kids?" Addison asked as she wiped the table around her lunch mat.

Tara seemed to hunch up a little smaller, looking miserable in the way that kids that age couldn't hide. "I'm still eating," she protested.

"You could save the rest for your afternoon snack," Addison suggested. "You don't want to miss all the fun."

She remembered the shifter games she'd played as a child,

games designed to practice speed shifting, and the ability to do it in motion. There were tag games—shift-is-safe—and variations of Simon Says. Some of them were fast and dizzy, did Tara like quieter games? Maybe Tara wasn't very good at shifting yet, too slow for games, or frequently forgetting her clothing.

Was she being bullied by the other children? She doubted that Cherry would allow that to happen in her care.

"We could practice shifting in here, if you wanted," Addison offered warmly, sitting in the uncomfortably small chair across from her. "Gabby, please don't touch Amy if she doesn't like it!"

Tara only ate slower, and after a moment, sullenly shook her head, whispering something that Addison couldn't hear over the sudden cries of the toddlers. She stood up to moderate their argument over a coveted toy, and when she returned, Tara was still picking at her food.

She sat beside Tara this time. "What's up, buttercup? Do you like to shift?"

Tara's expressive face brightened at the cute name but fell again at once. "I'm ugly," she said despondently.

Addison felt her heart twinge in sympathy.

"Oh, honey—" she started.

Then Gil came running in, stark naked, shouting, "I have to use the POTTY!"

Addison swiftly stood to close the door to the little bathroom behind him and while she was doing that, Tara packed up her lunch and the rest of the class came streaming in, laughing and full of energy. One of the boys was carrying Gil's forgotten clothes.

Just then, a baby woke, squalling in dismay. Addison went to scoop her up and check her diaper as Cherry began the herculean task of getting a half-dozen wound-up children to calm down for story time. Tara sat quietly with the others, waiting for the book to begin.

# CHAPTER 7

*C*herry took her aside early that afternoon when the children were down for their quiet time. "You've been great, can you stay the rest of the day and then we can talk about the paperwork and pay and hours and all that? I'm happy to include today in your pay for this period, of course."

Addy felt a thrill of triumph, followed by a moment of uncertainty. She already loved Cherry's day care and every one of the kids, from precocious Amy to the very loud Gil who couldn't remember his clothes. She liked Cherry's policies, and the way she handled the children; she knew this would be a good place to work, a place where she could make a difference in people's lives, where she could teach and nurture. And most of all, she liked Cherry herself, with her unflappable humor and easy smile.

But Addison didn't have a place to live yet and agreeing to this job meant *committing.* This wasn't an under-the-table barista job that she could pick up and leave without notice. That was something she'd had to do before, but she didn't want to do that to Cherry.

The job also meant staying in Nickel City, and seeing Gabby's gorgeous dad again nearly every single day.

She realized that she hadn't answered Cherry yet, conflicted and swimming in feelings, with instinct like the hum of distracting electric lights confusing matters even further. Instinct didn't understand things like W2s or bills or stalker ex-boyfriends who hired private investigators. "I'll stay the day," she said cautiously. She wasn't promising anything long-term, not yet. She could spend the rest of the afternoon deciding for sure.

The children, however, had other plans for her, and instead of carefully pondering her options, Addy spent the remainder of the day running from diaper emergency to squalling baby, feeding, cleaning, and playing endless games of make-believe mixed up with math and letters and logic.

Once almost all the kids had been picked up, there was a lull in the activity and Addy immediately started searching real estate listings on her phone.

Nickel City had a fair amount of sprawling suburbs full of trees, it seemed, but there weren't a lot of apartments. Addy looked at some of the ads for cute little places with fenced yards and wondered what it would be like to have a place like that. She could even get a pet! She had always wanted a dog.

Then she looked at the prices of the rentals and regretfully browsed away. The apartment options were small and disappointingly overpriced. Addy had done a little research months ago, before coming all this way from New York state, but she must have misremembered the prices; it seemed like they were noticeably higher than she recalled.

"How was your first day?" Cherry asked from the doorway, one eye over her shoulder for trouble; the remaining children seemed to be playing peacefully. "You didn't run away screaming."

"Well, no one had to go to the hospital, except for the pretend one, so it wasn't too bad," Addy said, putting her phone politely away. "I don't suppose you know anyone looking to let a room? Wendy is going to want me off her couch soon. I thought it would be a lot cheaper to rent in a small town than it was in the city, but I'm finding that's not really the case." She wanted the job and the excuse to stay in Nickel City and see Roderick again, but it wouldn't really cover the cost of a place unless she could find a roommate or two. Maybe she could pick up some part-time work in the evenings?

Cherry glowered fiercely. "A lot of people I know have mentioned that their landlords have been raising the rent lately. I guess they've been getting sweet offers to sell."

"That Veronica woman who was here earlier?"

"She's the worst," Cherry confirmed. "She's setting up a bunch of short-term rentals that are crowding neighbors out of their communities to make a tidy profit. Nickel City got a little press a year or so ago when it won some kind of prettiest town in Montana nonsense, and it made some big lists for places to go antiquing. The extra tourism has been nice for the economy, but it's not so great for keeping secrets, and it has other downsides, apparently. Grace, at the Mine Hotel, actually says that she's doing worse business than ever, because everyone is renting full houses for not that much more than she charges for a room, and they don't have to meet the same kind of hospitality restrictions she does."

"Aren't there regulations that prohibit short-term rentals in neighborhoods?"

"Nickel City has never needed them before now," Cherry said, shaking her head. "We were off the radar of everything until we were suddenly in the running for town popularity contests or whatever. Oh, whoops, hang on." She went to untangle Gabby from the cord of the play telephone she was trying to use upside-down; it was too short to choke her, but she was getting frustrated trying to work the device. Tara was playing quietly with a doctor's kit and a stuffed animal and the remaining baby was wiggling on blankets and reaching for enrichment toys inside the safe-for-babies play area.

"Let me show you the shutdown routine and explain how the door lock works. You'll need to download an app to your phone in order to check the camera! And then I've got paperwork for you sign and we can talk about the work hours!"

Cherry walked Addison through sterilizing the toys and bathroom, vacuuming, and showed her the check-in system, each parent and authorized guardian carefully noted by each child. There were only nine on the roster so far. Roderick Douglass was the name by

Gabby's. No one else. Addison didn't think that he would have looked at her quite like that if he was *married*, but it had occurred to her more than once throughout the day that it was possible Gabby's mother was still in the picture somehow and she could not help but wonder how she would fit into that puzzle.

Cherry gave her the paperwork in her little private office and left her alone in the room while she watched the rest of the kids.

Addison read through the contract, which laid out the hours (plenty!) and benefits (nothing fancy) and the pay (a fair wage) and paused to listen for clues from her instinct.

And then she smiled, because she didn't need instinct to tell her that this was where she wanted to be. "Keep your secrets," she told her lynx, and she signed the papers with an extra flourish and went out to help pack up the next child who was going home.

Every time that the door chime rang, Addison's heart started pounding, and she eagerly looked, hoping to see Gabby's handsome hunk of a dad again. She signed out the other children, memorizing faces and names so that she could safely hand them over or buzz them in without checking with Cherry or seeing their ID in the future, and gave out warm hugs to the kids as they left. They seem to have gleefully accepted her as Teacher Addy and she was excited by the prospect of working here indefinitely...as long as she could afford it. As long as *Cherry* could afford it, with only nine kids enrolled, especially since the schedule indicated that not all of them were full-time.

"Here's a question for you," Cherry said, coming out of the bathroom to stash the cleaning supplies in a locked cabinet out of reach. There was a bottle of very diluted bleach left in reach of the older kids for wiping down placemats and art tables, but everything else was secured.

Addison tickled the baby with a gentle, socked toe. "Sure."

"Do you like A Flower Garden Day Care, or Little Haven for the name of the business?"

"I thought it was just going to be called Cherry's," Addison said in surprise. "That's what everyone has called it."

"I worry that it sounds like a strip club," Cherry said frankly. "And we're already set up in a saloon!"

Addison could not help laughing. The baby at her feet looked up in surprise and broke into a big toothless grin, then farted loudly.

Cherry and Addison both chuckled at that. "Well, I know his opinion," Cherry quipped.

Addison didn't hear the door chime over their laughter, but her lynx suddenly sat up within her and began to purr. She checked the phone app with her heart in her throat, and nearly fell down on top of the baby when her whole world seemed to tilt at the sight of Gabby's dad at the door, straightening his collar like he was arriving for a date.

She tried to stuff her giddiness down. "Gabby, your daddy's here!"

Addison herded Gabby towards the entranceway, walking her with each of her hands in her own.

He was waiting in the doorway to the lobby, obviously not wanting to take off the heavy boots that were forbidden in the back area and he crouched to meet her. "Hey, pup!"

Gabby had no shame in her delight at the sight of him and she screamed in joy and excitement, pulling her hands free of Addison's to sway in place and then throw herself down to crawl to him. He pulled her up over the gate into his embrace effortlessly.

Addison was busy trying not to scream in delight and crawl to him herself, then remembered that she had an excuse to talk to him. Cherry handed her the checkout clipboard with a tolerant, knowing smile. Cherry might not be a shifter, but Addison was sure that her flushed face and stupid smile were obvious clues for humans, too.

"I'll need you to sign her out," she stammered when she had closed the distance to the gate.

And Roderick looked up from Gabby and *smiled* at her.

Not just a smile, but a whole face glow like she'd just said something clever, which she clearly had not. He was as ridiculously handsome as he'd been that morning, and Addison thought that her knees felt as weak as Gabby's.

"Do you need to see ID?" he asked, in that gruff, teasing voice.

"No! No, I saw you this morning, I mean, and Cherry okayed you, and Gabby obviously...ah..." Was coherency too much to ask of herself? Addison wondered.

Gabby was laughing and babbling. She looked at Addison and said, "Gabba abby ADDY!" as she pulled on Roderick's collar. It was probably still just nonsense, not actually her name.

"Uh, her diaper bag is hanging there," Addison pointed out. "And let me just see if there were any notes..." If anything came up during the day—how long they napped, if a kid didn't like their lunch, or if something got damaged, or if there were any concerns at all—Cherry's form had a place to write a quick note to pass on to the approved grown-up.

"'Ask for his number,'" Addison read before she bothered to make sense of Cherry's swiftly written words. "Oh."

She looked up in mortification to find that Roderick's smile had split into a broad grin.

"I mean, I uh, have it here for your emergency contact," Addison floundered. "But that's obviously not, I mean, for personal use." She was such an idiot.

Gabby had enjoyed her fill of hugs and she struggled for freedom, arching herself backward and pushing away. "Abba gabba babba OOOOO!" Roderick tickled her to giggles and flipped her upside down to turn them into shrieks of delight.

"I'd like it if you did," Roderick said to Addison.

"Did what?" What was *he* thinking about? She knew what she was thinking about, and it made her entire body flush.

"Use my number for personal use."

"You want me to call you?"

"Or I could call you," Roderick suggested. "But I don't have your number."

"I could give it to you," Addison said swiftly.

"I'd like it if you did," Roderick said a second time, and they both laughed.

The most remarkable part of the whole ridiculous conversation was that he looked every bit as pole-axed as Addy felt, sort of stunned and gorgeous all at once, with a big wide smile like he'd just been given the best present in the world.

Addison had once been at a shifter friend's home in northern Wisconsin during a big snowstorm, and she'd stolen a chance to shift into lynx form and dive out into a yard full of deep, fluffy snow. It was better than swimming, rolling around in her cat form, leaping and batting at clumps of snow. She felt like that now, fun and free and entirely new. The play had all been...*instinctive.*

Her shifter instinct told her to trust, to make this leap. Roderick would catch her, just like he caught Gabby, and they could have the whole world.

# CHAPTER 8

*J*f it weren't for Gabby, squirming and laughing in his arms, Roderick might have kissed Addison right then and there, just on the strength of her gaze. She was looking up at him, with those sparkling eyes, like she was standing on a cliff of anticipation, poised to jump.

What was her shift form? he wondered, but it was considered impolite to ask among shifters.

Unfortunately, he needed at least one free hand to put her number in his phone, and when he reached for it, Gabby gave a herculean surge in her effort to escape. It took both limbs and tucking her backward under his elbow, tickling her to distract her, before he could extract his phone from a pocket.

He unlocked it and tossed it to Addison, who caught it in surprise. Did she think he was a complete knucklehead because he was having difficulties holding onto a twenty-pound squirming child? Gabby seemed to be doing her best to embarrass him, struggling mightily.

He righted Gabby and got her bag, bouncing her in his arms. "We're going to go home and have blueberries," he promised, which made her eyes get big. She smiled and was more cooperative after that, making the sign for *more.*

Addison had tapped her number into his contacts, and she shyly handed the phone back. "I didn't realize that she knew signs," she said, and she put her hand to the side of her head and then waved with it before giving a thumbs up with her free hand and pointing to Gabby. *Hello, how are you?*

"A little," Roderick said. "I learned some from YouTube. I heard that kids could get frustrated with speech before they were really verbal, and it seemed useful to know a few things. We use *more* a lot, *milk, yes, no*...lots of *nos.*"

"A lot of early educators use it now," Addison said approvingly, and Roderick felt like he'd been patted on the head. His wolf's tail felt like a metronome in his head.

Gabby looked back and forth between them, her brow furrowed. "Gababa," she interjected in protest. She wanted her promised blueberries.

Roderick slipped the phone back into his pocket and wished he had something half as intelligent to say to Addison. "So, I'll call you," he said, sounding like a complete dork.

"I'd like it if you did," Addison said with a giggle, and even though it was clearly the dumbest joke in the world at this point, Roderick gave a laugh that was too loud in the quiet entry and embarrassed himself.

"So," he said awkwardly, "Yeah, I guess I'll talk to you later."

She waved with her fingers, clutching the clipboard at her chest, with a big smile and bright eyes. Roderick forced himself to turn away and go.

Gabby wanted nothing to do with the car seat, struggling and whining as he buckled her into it. He distracted her with one of the many toys strewn across the bench seat. He'd bought a crew cab years ago thinking it might be useful for a plumbing crew. He just hadn't expected the crew to turn out to be one opinionated little girl who ruled with a drooly fist and could be football-carried under one arm.

"Let's go home and get you some blueberries," he said, once he had triumphed over her capture in the hated harness.

"Abbabbagab," she said in frustration, and she threw the stuffed turtle, then screamed because she couldn't reach it.

Roderick reached down, picked the turtle off the seat, and returned it to her. "I can't do that while I'm driving," he reminded her. He piled the rest of her toys in with her, even knowing that it wouldn't matter if she had a dozen other toys if she lost the one she wanted.

She was asleep almost before he had pulled away from the front of Cherry's still-unnamed day care.

Gabby slept the entire drive and stirred only minimally when Roderick unbuckled her and lifted her out of the car seat. She was starting to get big for the back-facing seat, but he had read that they were safer until they were two.

She woke up clingy and wanted to snuggle with Roderick, so he kept her in one arm while he puttered around the kitchen, heating the oven for his dinner and setting her food out on her highchair tray. It was slower working one-handed than putting her down, but he knew from experience that she would cry if he did that, and a later dinner seemed like a smaller price to pay.

"Is crabby Gabby ready for some blueberries?" he wanted to know, putting his phone on the counter longingly. Addison's number was in there, and he was dying to call her and hear her laugh again.

Gabby fussed a little when he clipped her into the highchair but was quickly distracted by the blueberries. She agreed to eat some of the cold elbow noodles he scooped out of the container in the fridge and chased a few garbanzo beans around without interest.

A week ago, she'd wanted nothing but garbanzo beans. Roderick had two cases of them now and feared they'd never get through them. When he pulled his own dinner out of the oven, she signed *mine* and reached for it.

"Oh, now we're *grabby* Gabby," Roderick laughed at her, but he cut off a corner of his calzone and put it aside to cool. "Not yet," he said. "Hot, hot, hot!" He signed it with his free hand and Gabby imitated him, spitting blueberry as she blew into her clawed hand.

"Ha! Ha! Ha!" she mimicked, then she cackled and squashed a garbanzo bean on her tray.

By the end of their meal, Gabby looked like a slayer of Smurfs and there was a radius of purple-blue-stained chickpea rejects on the floor around her chair. The corner of the calzone that she had been greedy for was met with disdain and Roderick had ended up eating it after all, stained violet from Gabby's fingers.

He left the high chair tray in the sink, slipped his phone back into his pocket, and carried Gabby straight to the bathroom for a bath. Once he had put her down in the tub with her favorite toys and a few inches of warm water, carefully checked for temperature on the inside of his elbow, he settled back on his heels and watched her. She was strong enough to sit up reliably in the tub now and loved the splashing. They played peekaboo until she got bored with him and scooted to entertain herself with the floating toys.

Roderick found himself fingering the phone in his pocket. Addison. She wasn't just pretty but smoking hot. He wanted to call her so badly, just to hear her voice again. Surely, it wouldn't hurt to see how she'd put herself into his contacts.

He sat on the toilet, keeping Gabby firmly in his sights, and unlocked the phone. Addison Carmichael, she'd put in, and then in the notes: (Teacher Addy).

And there was her number.

Roderick looked at it hungrily, and Gabby chose that moment to yell in triumph or frustration (it was hard to tell which) and bring a plastic shark down into the water hard enough to splash outside of the tub towards him. He jerked the phone to the side to save it from the water and put it on the counter as he rose to his feet. "Hey sweetie, let's not do that to your poor shark. Let's get the rest of your blueberries off and call it a night, okay?"

Gabby protested her extraction from the tub with a heart-broken wail, until he had her standing on her feet and wrapped in a towel and was playing peekaboo with her around the terrycloth.

Then, from the counter came a tiny voice. "Hello? Roderick? Are you there?"

He had accidentally dialed Addison.

# CHAPTER 9

*I*t wasn't that Addison was right next to her phone waiting for Roderick to call like a teenage girl with a crush, not really.

She just happened to be gazing wistfully at the lock screen when he called, that was all. Like she'd been gazing at it every five minutes since she arrived home at her cousin's crowded little house.

"Hello?" she said at once.

Distantly, a voice said, "—poor shark! Let's (something) blueberries (something) call it a night."

Then there was splashing and a shrieking protest that Addy knew entirely too well, which swiftly gave way to giggles and the sound of a peekaboo game. "Who's a wet little girl?" Roderick asked. "Who's going to be dry?"

Addison felt like an eavesdropper, realizing at once that Roderick must have accidentally dialed her number. She was overhearing an adorable moment between father and daughter, and it would be creepy for her to continue in silence.

"Hello?" she said cautiously. "Roderick? Are you there?"

"Shi—shoot!" came Roderick's far-off voice, then the sound of a phone fumbling. Then he was at the other end of the line in earnest, his voice sounding so close and warm that it sent shivers down Addison's spine. "I didn't mean to call you! I mean, not yet. I was going to call after I got Gabby down, I must've dialed when I fumbled the phone. I'm so sorry. Oh my God, I'm a dolt."

"It's okay," Addison was quick to reply sincerely. "That sounded like quite a struggle."

"There was a shark involved," Roderick said, sounding further away again. "Don't eat the towel, Gabby. It's not tasty."

"Ababa ababa!" Gabby replied. "Yuck! Yuck!"

"Yuck!" Roderick agreed, absolutely melting Addison. "Are you ready for a bedtime story? Who wants a book? Who wants a hungry, hungry caterpillar?"

Gabby's response was confused; Addison guessed that she knew it was a trap to get her into bed and she giggled.

"I could call you back," Roderick offered, his voice all hers again, but Addison thought he sounded reluctant.

"But then I wouldn't get to hear The Very Hungry Caterpillar," Addison protested.

It was ridiculous to think that she could hear him smile.

He put her on speakerphone and Gabby must have leaned very close because her voice was very loud as she said solemnly, "Gabby addy!"

Just nonsense noises, Addison reminded herself, but she couldn't quite keep the warm feeling of inclusion from spreading across her chest.

Getting Gabby into a clean diaper and dressed for bed sounded like another battle for the history books. Roderick gave it a sports play-by-play for Addison's amusement. "There's a leg in the romper! Score one for the dad! Whoops, there goes an arm! Score for the baby! No, no wiggling away! The penalty is tickling!"

At the final snap of the romper, he must have lifted her into the air, because Gabby gave a squeal of delight. There was a weird moment and a creak of a chair, then Gabby's breath sounded very near the phone as Roderick began to read.

Addison was in Wendy's over-crowded sewing room, lying back on the inflatable mattress, half under a table, surrounded by storage boxes. Some of them were her cousin's and some of them were her own. She closed her eyes and imagined Roderick with Gabby in the crook of his arm. His big, well-muscled arm, covered in soft brown skin. His long, clever fingers, turning the pages of the book. His beautiful mouth, his white teeth.

Was he *trying* to make The Very Hungry Caterpillar sound sexy? Addison had not guessed it was possible, but the low, easy tone of his voice reading, "On Saturday, he ate through one piece of chocolate cake, one ice-cream cone, one pickle..." set her blood on fire.

She wanted to be that ice-cream cone.

This wasn't *instinct*, she chided herself. This was just general desperation faced with the most gorgeous guy she'd ever met. Didn't she know better by now than to let herself get swept up in intense feelings?

Her lynx had other ideas, convinced beyond everything logical that this was the compass direction of their ultimate happiness.

"Are you sleepy?" Roderick asked.

"No," Addison said before she realized he was speaking to Gabby. She flushed, glad Roderick couldn't see her cheeks color.

Gabby made a grumpy sound that Addison recognized as fighting sleep. "Buh! Buh!"

"You want another book?" Roderick offered.

"Buh," Gabby insisted.

"Good Night, Good Night Construction Site?" The book must have been in reach because Roderick began reading it at once.

Gabby was snoring lightly by the end of that book. "Hang on," Roderick whispered, and there was the clink of the phone onto a table, the creak of the chair, and the rustle of blankets.

Gabby woke up as he lay her down and cried disconsolately as the phone was suddenly muffled in a hand and a door clicked behind him.

The toddler sobbed for just a moment, then went quiet. "That's always the worst," Roderick confessed quietly into the phone. He must have taken it off speakerphone because it sounded like he was right next to her.

"You're an amazing dad," Addison said softly in return. Questions crowded into her mind. Who was Gabby's mother? Was she still in their life? Would Addison ever be a part of that life?

They were silent a long moment, then both said, "So..." at the same time.

"Tell me about you," Roderick said first. "Where are you from? How did you come to Nickel City?"

Initially, Addison felt awkward talking about herself, but before she knew it, she was telling him about growing up in Kansas, moving to Buffalo in New York—she skipped the time in California—taking a job as a nanny, getting her degree in early education. "I didn't want to stay in the city," she said. "As soon as the kids aged out of me, I got my education certificate and started looking around for somewhere to live that wasn't so crowded, a place I could shift, maybe."

"What are—no, I'm sorry, it's rude."

"I'm a lynx," Addison offered shyly. "Canadian lynx. I wanted someplace quiet, someplace that got snow once in a while. A couple of months ago, my cousin, Wendy, told me about her friend who was looking to open a shifters-only day care and it sounded perfect."

"Wendy who runs the DMV?" Roderick guessed.

"That's the one," Addison said with a wince. Wendy could come on strong; did she have a good reputation in town, or had she made enemies here?

"Gabby likes her," Roderick said as if that was clearly good enough for him. "Are you guys close?"

"We were both kids in Kansas together," Addison explained. "She used to drag me into all kinds of trouble. But I hadn't seen her in years before I moved out here to work for Cherry."

"Are you planning to stay with her long?"

Addison chewed on her lip. "No, her house is really small, so I'm looking for a place. You don't happen to know anyone looking for a roommate, do you? I was looking at local rentals, but they're sky high. I didn't expect New York prices here."

"I have a spare room," Roderick said unexpectedly, and they were both silent for a moment.

Addison made herself chuckle when he did, but it was more from horror than humor.

She had made the mistake of moving right in with her last boyfriend, Owen. It had been convenient, at first, there was no reason for her to have her own place when Owen had the extra space and needed her, at least emotionally. He had a car and a credit card, too, and discouraged her from getting either. She never had any utilities in her own name, no credit, and it had trapped her in what had become a loveless power trip of a relationship for entirely too long.

Addison had to close her eyes and sort out what she was feeling; it was hard to feel her instinct through the guilt and anger she still carried, just as it had been hard to feel it over her sympathy and attraction for Owen.

She had craved love so badly that pity and chemistry overwhelmed the little tickle of her lynx's intuition. She wanted to believe that she was smarter now, that her instinct was stronger and her common sense more honed, but was that really true? How much of this dizzy certainty was just her loneliness and longing for family, her physical response to an inviting smile and a handsome face? Not to mention that amazing physique.

Instinct wasn't warning her now, it was a warm flush of encouragement, but she'd already spent years of her life recovering from her own impulsive actions.

"That wouldn't really be..." Addy said, just as Roderick said, "That's probably not a good idea."

"I appreciate the offer," Addison added shyly. "It's just..."

"...A little fast," Roderick agreed swiftly.

The whole thing felt absurdly fast, even though they hadn't even kissed. Every time she talked to him, every glimpse of him, every overheard moment with Gabby, Addison could feel herself falling harder.

But she barely knew the guy. She didn't know what music he liked, or what books, beyond The Very Hungry Caterpillar.

She had gotten burned moving way too fast with Owen.

Instinct told her this was different, but...instinct wasn't enough.

# CHAPTER 10

*R*oderick had never been big on phones. They were useful for work, and it was nice being able to snap a quick photo of Gabby, but the idea of conversing with someone for fun was completely alien. Calls were completed as quickly as possible.

Until Addison.

He sat down on the couch with the phone against his ear and eagerly listened for every word and telltale intake of breath.

Endorphins, he decided. There was a logical explanation for why talking to her felt so rewarding, and it didn't have anything to do with *instinct*, only brain chemicals. He'd been alone so long that the idea of romance was just kicking lots of hormones and neuro-transmitters loose or something.

His wolf had very different ideas, absolutely sure that Addison was simply equivalent to happiness. Explaining how chemistry and biology worked to his wolf had always been challenging. To his canine companion, everything was something to fight, to flee, or to claim, and why didn't matter.

"I think it's your turn," Addison said, once they had laughingly acknowledged that moving in together was simply absurd. It took

Roderick a moment to set aside the gorgeous fantasy of having her at his side every night, getting Gabby down together, retiring to...

"My...uh...turn?"

"I told you about growing up in Kansas. Where did you grow up?"

Roderick told her about the little town in the south where he'd lived until he was ten, his parent's divorce, moving to Nickel City with his mother, and her subsequent death a few years before Gabby's birth. "She would have liked you," he told Addy.

*Who* ***wouldn't*** *like her?* his wolf wanted to know. Roderick was beginning to think that his wolf liked Addison better than he liked Roderick.

*Obviously,* his wolf teased.

*Thanks,* Roderick replied.

"I'm sorry you lost her," Addison said sympathetically. "My dad died when I was in school, so I know how hard it is."

They talked about weathering grief and their coping methods. "I got mad at first," Roderick confessed. "Because it wasn't fair, you know. I made terrible decisions." He was shocked by how easy it was to say so out loud. Was it because of the facelessness of the phone, that it was less painful to confess things? Or was it because every sense in his body told him that Addison was *safe,* the way no one had ever been *safe* before?

"I got myself an awful boyfriend," Addison sympathized. "I quit school for an unhealthy relationship with a guy who didn't let me control my own money or drive a car."

Roderick tried to squelch his rage. "Who is he? Can I pound him for you?"

Addison laughed softly. "Owen is long gone. I had to dodge a private investigator and move across the country to get work under the table, but I was lucky enough to get out of it with a great job as a nanny and I never looked back. I haven't heard from him in years now."

Roderick hoped he never met this Owen character, because he wasn't sure he'd be able to restrain himself in the face of someone who had treated Addison so poorly.

They talked for a little while about college—Roderick had gotten a degree in art at the community college before taking an apprenticeship with the plumbing union.

"You're an artist?" Addison said in awe. "You'll have to show me some of your work!"

Roderick thought ruefully of his college assignments and the sketchbooks he hadn't picked up in months. "I don't have much. I loved the *idea* of doing art much more than I actually loved doing the art."

Addison commiserated. "I thought I might be a writer, for a while. I only got about four chapters in before I realized exactly how hard it was. My story went completely off the rails and I hated all my characters."

"Sounds like a best seller to me," Roderick teased.

It was easy to talk with her, picturing her expressions, remembering her shy, wiggly fingered wave when he picked Gabby up. He felt like he was sloshing with emotion, like his heart was full of anticipation and longing.

And then Addison reluctantly asked the question they had both clearly been dreading, "Who was Gabby's mom?"

To Roderick's surprise, it wasn't hard to explain. "Dana is an ad executive, and Nickel City was just a quick stop-over for her, a job on the way to the top. We...had a whirlwind romance and weren't careful. A big opportunity for her came up just as we found out about Gabby. Dana made it clear that her job was more important than a baby and wanted to give her up. I couldn't do that. So I chose Gabby, and she chose her career. It was...pretty much an amicable split, and I think we both feel like we got the better end of the deal. She got her freedom, I got a drooly little tyrant that I adore." He didn't mention instinct.

Addison was quiet for a moment and Roderick had a split-second fear that he'd said too much, been too raw. They really were moving too fast, and he'd just over-shared in a big way.

"Gabby's a lucky girl," Addison said warmly. "Are you...worried that Dana would ever come back for her?"

"I think that Dana was more worried that I'd come after her for child support or try to dump Gabby on her. She had a lawyer draw up papers and I have full custody, free and clear. Well, not free. My lord, diapers are expensive, and I nearly had a heart attack looking at the prices for college."

At the other end of the line there was a distant knock and the muffled cadence of a voice.

"I'm good, thanks," Addison called, away from the receiver. "I'm on the phone!"

The far-off voice sounded apologetic and Addison was back, "Sorry. Wendy was just offering a nightcap."

There was a moment of quiet on the line and Roderick wished he could see her face and try to read the emotions there.

Her voice was quiet. "So, do you think this is...? Do you feel...?"

"...Instinct?" Roderick guessed when she trailed off.

Her exhale was faint through the phone. "*Instinct.* Is this just...? I mean I like you, and I think that we could have something, but...?"

"My mother had lots of opinions about instinct and mates," Roderick said carefully. "And I've always believed that the magic of being a shifter gives me certain advantages."

"You don't think that the whole idea of mates is absurd?"

"I used to..." Roderick told her, and the air between them was so charged that he imagined he could feel her breath when she exhaled on the phone. He desperately wished that she was there, on the couch with him. But he also knew that it would be impossible to *resist* her if she was.

"What do we do from here?" Addison asked hesitantly.

"I've got that spare bedroom..." Roderick offered teasingly, then quickly added, "I'm kidding, I'm only kidding. That would be insane."

She laughed weakly. "Right, let's just move in together the day after we meet. That's sensible."

"My dear deceased mother would rise from the grave and beat some better sense into me," Roderick chuckled. "But I would like to take you out some time, and just...see where this goes. Can I take you out to lunch? Tomorrow?"

Addison paused. "Cherry mentioned that she had someone else part time who would be coming in tom—"

Roderick listened intently for several heartbeats before he realized that his phone had gone dead.

# CHAPTER 11

*A*ddison groaned and fell back on her mattress when the phone disconnected. She guessed his phone had run out of charge; they'd talked for more than an hour, and her own phone was protesting with a red battery warning.

Roderick.

He was gorgeous and funny and she was already head-over-heels for him. She hadn't been this nervous and excited about a guy since...well, since Owen.

Was this the same thing? A silly crush on someone she barely knew, willing to move way too fast because of intense feelings?

Just look where that had gotten her before.

But this time, her lynx was purring in her chest, happy and satisfied, sure of their fate. Addison had been willing to overlook her lynx's reservations before; their roles were almost reversed now. She was determined not to get swept up in anything too fast again.

It was just that when they spoke, when she saw him, everything seemed simple and safe.

Addison held her phone up above her and stared at the list of recent calls, then went in and added Roderick's name to her contacts. She considered giving him a special ringtone, then decided that was entirely too much.

She rolled to her feet and wandered out to find Wendy standing tip-toe on a step stool, pulling a box from the top of a cabinet.

Wendy loved projects. Sewing, knitting, crocheting, making dolls, sculpting...her entire house was filled with haphazardly labeled boxes full of supplies. "Oh, there you are!" she said cheerfully when Addison came into the kitchen. "I was beginning to wonder if you'd just gone to bed."

"No, I was talking on the phone." To *Roderick*. It was like having Pop Rocks in her chest, every time she thought of him.

"Did you find a place to rent?" Wendy asked, skipping down the stool with her arms loaded. "I mean, not that I'm trying to kick you out that soon. You're welcome to stay as long as you want."

Roderick had a spare room, Addison thought, and every time she remembered, her heart did a curious little flip, because she loved the idea of moving in with him, even as she cautioned herself that she'd never be able to resist him at that proximity and they were already moving at crazy speeds.

"No," she said reluctantly. "I'm looking, but most of the places around here are way, way out of my price range."

"I got an offer for my house in the mail today!" Wendy said. "'We're buying property in your neighborhood! Contact us for an offer well above appraisal!'" She plopped the box down on the table and opened the lid to riffle through what looked like leather scraps.

"Well, that doesn't sound shady at all," Addison scoffed.

"I didn't realize I'd be encouraging you to move here in the middle of a housing bubble," Wendy said apologetically as she found the exact scrap she'd been searching for and held it up triumphantly.

"Oh, don't worry about it," Addison assured her. "I already love it here. I can probably find some way to weather it until the bubble bursts. Some way that isn't hopelessly underfoot. There are some apartments in the warehouse district I could probably afford..."

"I am not letting you move to The Tails," Wendy was quick to interrupt. She scrambled back up the step stool with the box.

"The Tails?"

"It's a play on the nickel in Nickel City, heads or tails," Wendy explained as she wedged the box back into the space it had miraculously come out of. "The Tails are full of crime and poverty. Bad side of the tracks, if you will."

"I didn't realize Nickel City had anything like that," Addison said. "It looks so pretty and idyllic. There are so many trees."

"It's a nice place," Wendy agreed. "It feels good when you come here, but even really pretty apples might have a few bruises."

Addison's phone gave a buzz then, and she had a thrill of anticipation as she saw a text from Roderick on the screen and turned away to read it.

*Sorry battery went dead. Would lunch tomorrow work?*

Addison tapped in a reply. *I hope so. I'll confirm with Cherry in the morning.* Then she spent entirely too much time staring at the screen hoping for a reply.

"Who was that?" Wendy asked slyly as she turned back. "You're blushing."

*Great!* came the answer on her phone.

She didn't need to respond, Addison told herself, so she refrained from answering in a string of hearts or something else she would regret later. "Just a...guy. The dad of one of the kids at the day care."

"Ooooooo," Wendy said knowingly. "Is it *instinct?*"

Wendy wasn't a shifter, but she'd grown up with them, and she'd always given Addison a pale imitation of shifter recognition, a little warning tingle like a child who might start shifting soon...but she'd never actually manifested an animal counterpart.

Addison tried to brush it off. "I don't know," she lied as her lynx protested. "Probably it's nothing. He's just...asked me to lunch tomorrow."

"An hour on the phone the night you meet and a lunch date in the middle of your second day of work. Probably it's nothing," Wendy mocked her. "Addy has a ma-ate! Addy has a ma-ate!"

It was just the sort of ribbing that she would have done when they were kids together and Addison, still blushing, laughed and snapped towards her with a dishtowel.

"We're taking it slow," Addison insisted. "There's no reason to rush." She thought about Roderick's spare room rather wistfully.

"Well, good luck on your date," Wendy said kindly.

"Thanks," Addison said sheepishly. "It's just lunch…"

Wendy made a noise of disbelief. "Go on believing that, then." She bent to whatever she was in the middle of crafting on her kitchen table—it involved a hot glue gun, string, and feathers, as well as the leather scrap she'd found. She whispered, "Addy has a ma-ate, Addy has ma-ate."

Addy brushed her teeth, balancing her bathroom kit carefully on the ledge of the sink, and went back to her mattress in the sewing room. She changed into pajamas and cuddled down under one of Wendy's quilts.

She lay awake replaying The Very Hungry Caterpillar in her mind and was desperately hungry for all sorts of things that weren't food at all.

# CHAPTER 12

*a*ddison was every bit as adorable as Roderick remembered and he stood, craning to look over the gate at her for a long moment before she glanced around and saw them.

"Good morning, Gabby!" she greeted him cheerfully.

Gabby recognized at that moment that she was going to be left behind and buried her face in Roderick's collarbone with a cry of alarm.

"Oh, no!" Addison said lightly as she came to the gate. "Am I the big bad wolf this morning?"

Gabby peeked back at her, trying to decide if she was a threat.

"Grrr," Addison teased, and she made finger claws.

Gabby giggled, but she didn't offer to ease her death-grip on Roderick's shirt.

"Oh, shoes," Roderick remembered. "Not that she's walking on them yet."

"She's pretty close, though," Addison observed. "She's pulling up and she'll walk a little holding my hands."

Gabby was uncooperative about letting him remove her tennis shoes, but he managed to get them off of her feet and replace them with the elastic leather slippers that keep her socks on her feet for most of the day.

There were four unmatched socks pinned to the board that morning. Roderick was pretty sure at least one of them was Gabby's but would have been hard-pressed to pick out which one. Most mornings, he figured he was lucky to get two socks on her at all and he was glad to get her home with all her fingers and toes.

"I'm not sure if I'm actually looking forward to her walking or not," Roderick confessed. "It's going to take chasing her to a whole new level of difficulty."

Addison laughed and nodded. "Believe me, I know!"

There was a shy moment and Roderick finally dredged up the courage to ask, "About lunch…?"

"I can join you if you don't mind a late lunch," Addison said, just as bashfully. "The kids have a quiet time right after lunch and Shea will be here. I've got an hour break scheduled."

"That sounds perfect," Roderick said genuinely.

"Cherry promised it would be no trouble. And she got me to fill out a W2, so I think we're serious about this job now!"

Relief flooded Roderick. Addison was *staying.* She was staying in Nickel City and he wouldn't lose her any time soon. He hadn't even realized that he was worried about it until he wasn't.

"Great!" he said enthusiastically. "Great!" He was like a puppy, he thought, all but drooling on her feet.

"Ready to play some games, Gabby?" Addison asked.

Gabby looked between the two of them and her face crumpled.

"I'll be back before you know it," Roderick promised her.

Their handoff meant that they brushed arms, and it was every-thing that Roderick could do not to kiss her when their faces were unexpectedly close.

Gabby cried in earnest as he left, and Roderick could hear Addison saying soothingly, "It's okay, I know, I know," as she bounced the toddler in her arms. "It's so hard being little."

He drove a little way out of town for his next job, taking a winding way along through quiet neighborhoods. There were a lot of pending sales on houses, and he saw no less than three rental cars in front of places with cute names above their doors.

He only realized about halfway to his destination that he'd been unconsciously looking for houses for rent.

It was ridiculous and out of bounds to be looking for a place for a woman he'd just met to live, he scolded himself.

His wolf was just confused about why Addison wouldn't immediately come live with them, where she belonged.

# CHAPTER 13

*A*ddison blushed when Cherry caught her checking her phone for new texts for the fifth time and reminded herself firmly that it was only her second day of work and she ought to be more focused.

She put her phone up out of reach in the teacher's office so she wouldn't be tempted to keep checking it, then sat with the kids to help the youngest with the craft they were making that day, involving paper plates and dry noodles.

Tara helped her keep the littlest ones from trying to eat their supplies and gave Addison shy, hopeful smiles when Addison praised her.

Gabby spit out her noodle. "Yuck! Yuck!"

Each of the kids who was shifting had a sticker by their name at the cubbies that showed their animal. It was an easy way to share the information in a way that was non-incriminating if there were human visitors. While grown-ups might not volunteer what kind of shifter they were to each other, it was important to know what the kids were capable of, and what to look for if one went missing!

Addison wasn't sure where Cherry had found an armadillo

sticker, but most surprising was the sticker next to Tara's cubby—a delicate white unicorn.

She spent the morning focussing on that puzzle rather than thinking about Roderick or wrestling her doubts. "Why does Tara think her shift form is ugly?" she asked Cherry quietly when there was a brief gap in games, diapers, books, and keeping Amy from hitting other kids exuberantly with trains. They were sitting together on one of the benches letting the kids doctor them, which at this moment involved a great deal of consultation on the far side of the rabbit cage.

Cherry seemed surprised and frowned thoughtfully. "She does? She's a new enrollment, and I thought she just needed some extra time to get comfortable. They are new, and I think her mother is having a hard time. Did Tara say that to you? That she was *ugly?*"

Addison might have been pleased with Tara's trust, but she was more concerned with Tara's self-image. "Is she really a unicorn?" Addison knew that there were rare mythical shifters, but she'd never met one. "Have you ever seen her shift?"

"That's what her mother said," Cherry said. "But I've never actually seen her change. I just assumed that she wasn't sure we were safe yet, kids that age have heard lots of warnings not to shift in front of strangers and Tara is a cautious girl. Thank you for mentioning it, I'll talk to her." Then she regarded Addison more carefully. "Or you can. She seems to trust you. Can you get her to show you her form? Maybe there's something we can help with."

Addison slowly smiled back. "I'd be glad to try."

Then Cherry laughed in unexpected relief. "I'm so happy to have you here, Addison. I really am glad that Wendy suggested you, and I hope you'll stick around Nickel City." She slung an arm around Addison and gave her shoulders a warm squeeze. "My instinct tells me you're a keeper."

Addison gave her a sideways look of surprise. "Do you have instinct?" she asked in astonishment.

"Maybe not your shifter sparkly magic instinct," Cherry scoffed. "But I can get a good read of a person by how they act around children, and how kids react in return. Call it common sense or just experience, but I know a good person when I meet one, and you're the right stuff. I'm happy to have you on board and I know you'll fit in here in Nickel City."

Addison felt a wave of gratitude and pleasure wash over her and realized that she'd been desperately hoping for the praise but not expecting it. "Thank you," she said shyly. "I already love it here."

Then someone at the far side of the rabbit cage gave a cry of outrage and what had been a good-natured discussion turned into Gil shedding his clothing to turn into an armadillo as two of the older kids started shoving each other.

"No, thank you!" Cherry said firmly as she sprang to her feet and went to intercept them. "No thank you for touches that your friend doesn't want!"

She deftly got them all untangled and into line to wash their hands for lunch, which was like trying to thread a frayed shoelace into a hole that was too small on the best of days.

Addison watched the clock through lunch with the same eagerness she had been watching her phone for texts, counting down the minutes to lunch, and then naptime, and her *date*.

But lunch went swiftly sideways.

Gil unscrewed his water bottle to peer inside of it for no good reason and Robert knocked it over trying to fence with his cheese stick. As Addison grabbed paper towels to soak up the water, Amy swept her entire lunch off of her tray and cackled in triumph. Gabby less successfully tried to do the same, managing only to smear her food all over her sleeves.

Gil was shouting, Robert was protesting his innocence, Amy had realized that none of her food was in reach anymore and was crying, Gabby was just making noise to play along, and Tara was trying to sink into her chair...when one of the babies woke up and began to wail.

Addison tried to calm the boys and glanced at the clock in consternation as Cherry went to check on the baby. Roderick would be there any moment and she couldn't possibly leave with the day care in chaos like this.

"It's just water, Gil," she said, as soothingly as she could. "We'll refill your bottle just as soon as we clean this up! Robert, can you help your friend?"

"Gil wasn't supposed to open his bottle!" Robert said defensively. "It's not my fault!" He was gathering his lunch back out of the way of the spreading puddle.

"No one is saying it's your fault, Robert," Addison said, forcing herself to be patient. "I'd just like you to help clean it up. There are paper towels on the counter. Just a few at a time—!" She knew that the boys had a habit of grabbing off as many as they could, using dozens of squares for small jobs.

Amy was screeching at the top of her lungs now and Gabby clearly thought it was a competition. The second baby woke with a whimper and broke into a squall of consternation.

The front door of the day care gave a chime of warning and Addison scrambled for her phone to check the camera before one of the kids could shift out of sheer emotional reaction.

"That's Shea," Cherry called from the nursery area. "What excellent timing!"

Addison felt a curious calm settle over her at the sight of the woman who came in. She was a short, middle-aged Japanese woman with slate gray hair in a shoulder-length cut, and her eyes crinkled in amusement when she looked up at Addison.

Addison's anxiousness eased. Everyone in the room seemed to take a breath at the same moment and, although Amy resumed crying, it was with a fraction of her previous zest.

"I'm Addison," she said. She almost yawned, she felt so relaxed.

"Shea!" They shook hands and Addison smiled at her bemusedly.

The effect seemed to ease when Shea floated back into the nursery area and scooped up the second baby, who was only panting now and settled immediately upon being picked up.

Robert had indeed wadded up half the roll of paper towels to clean up the water, but Addison found that she didn't feel the slightest bit cross about it. She only laughed and helped everyone pick up their lunch bags as they finished and got up to wipe their mats down. Amy was re-stocked with cheese cubes and crackers and Gabby licked her squashed blueberries from her arms.

Then Addison's lynx gave a little shiver of happy anticipation and she heard the buzz of the front door.

# CHAPTER 14

*R*oderick would have jumped the gate to meet Addison if getting his boots off wasn't such a pain in the butt. They were solid work boots, with laces, so he stuck to the parent side of the gate out of respect for Cherry's no-shoes rule. He noticed on his way in that there were now six socks pinned to the "'BEAR' FEET" sign. Only two of them matched.

Addison appeared at the gate and stepped nimbly over, then seemed to hesitate.

She was smiling, but shy, and Roderick knew that he must look foolish, grinning like a loon right back at her.

"Hi," she said, coming to stand right in front of him. "My shoes are behind you."

"Oops!" Roderick chuckled and moved aside so that she could sit and pull a pair of practical tennis shoes out from underneath the bench.

He was still wearing his plain work clothes, and she was dressed in clothing appropriate to a day care; they had both considered this an informal lunch and Roderick was glad to find that their expectations had aligned.

When she had finished tying her shoes, Addison bounced to her feet. "Do you have a place in mind for lunch?"

"Do you mind walking a block?" Roderick asked. "I thought I'd take you to Heads Up Cafe. It's a little bakery that does great lunches. We should be there just after the main lunch rush and there are places to sit on the porch."

"I'd like that," Addison said, and they stood for a moment, smiling at each other. Roderick finally opened the door for her and wondered if it would be too forward to take her hand. He decided it would, and they spent a little awkward time figuring out how far apart to walk, how fast to stride, and how much to glance at each other as they went.

"Nickel City is so pretty," Addison said, as they had to walk closer together around a tree that dominated the sidewalk. "I know that Montana was supposed to be beautiful, but the photos don't even do it justice. All the mountains and forests, it's like being in a postcard."

"Have you been up to the overlook of Belle Lake?" Roderick asked, trying to decide if he should give her more space now that they were past the tree. He didn't really want to.

Addison shook her head. "No, I went to see the famous big tree out that way, but I didn't make it to either the shore of the lake or the overlook."

"It's worth a trip," Roderick assured her. "Sunset is pretty amazing there." He didn't add that it was a popular make-out spot among young locals, or fill her in on the other uncommon features of the forest; some things weren't topics for first not-dates like this, especially in public.

Heads Up Cafe was busier than he'd hoped, but they chatted as they stood in line, picking up where they'd left off from their phone call with the same easy friendliness that left him warm to his toes. They talked about Nickel City, and how it stacked up to Buffalo, Gabby and her love of blueberries, favorite foods, and how tastes changed.

"I used to hate olives," Addison said, "but I can't get enough of them now. I love a pizza covered with nothing but olives and cheese."

"I used to go by the name Rod," Roderick said with a grimace. "I thought it was clever."

"It's a bold nickname," Addison agreed, blushing and laughing.

"I decided it would interfere with my business aspirations. Who's going to take their plumber seriously with a name like Rod?"

Addison giggled. "I don't know, maybe it's got some truth in advertising, depending on the tools you use."

Roderick wasn't sure how she could look so innocent and still sound so dirty.

"I fear that I've doomed my daughter to the same kind of shame," he confessed. "But Gabriella seemed like too much of a mouthful for a baby, so it just sort of evolved to Gabby."

"It's a beautiful name! You'll have to hold it in reserve," Addison advised. "Full names for when she's in big trouble."

They got to the counter and there was only the briefest moment of hesitation before Addison placed her order and paid, not offering to split a ticket with Roderick. He ordered a club sandwich, and they took their table number and threaded their way through the people who were waiting for their takeout.

There was a couple just leaving a prime table on the porch and Roderick stepped in and claimed it while Addison got napkins and water glasses. He made sure that she got the seat with a view of the mountains.

They skirted the topic of politics carefully enough to establish that they had the same basic leanings and lingered over more fun topics, like favorite Beatles, and worst fashion mistakes from high school (sagging pants for him, ripped up jeans with lots of safety pins for her).

"Not again," Addison vowed.

"We'll never speak of it," Roderick promised.

Just as Roderick was starting to be convinced that their sandwich order had been forgotten or accidentally taken by a careless tourist, a harried waitress brought their plates and dropped them on the table in front of them.

"Thank you!" Addison said sincerely. "Oh, Rod, you weren't kidding. This looks amazing!"

Roderick groaned. "I'm going to regret telling you that name, aren't I."

Her eyes were crinkled with amusement and she must have read on his face that he wasn't really bothered. "I promise to use it only for powers of good."

Everything about her was good, Roderick thought, biting into his giant sandwich ravenously. He would have guessed she worked with children even if he hadn't met her at the day care; she had a quiet, relentlessly cheerful manner that suited handling pets and kids.

They talked more as they ate, about heavier subjects like loss and regret. Roderick coaxed a little more of the story of her last boyfriend from her, a tale that made him clench a fist in his lap because that Owen character had clearly preyed on her naivety and youth.

"You know the type," Addison said, deliberately off-handed. "Or, maybe you don't. The kind that seems just fine at first, just a little...needy. Flattering courtship with fancy dinners that he never let you pay for. And then it's been six months and you realize that he's gaslighted you away from having any friends that aren't his and emotionally manipulated you into not having any life or means of your own. I didn't have a car or credit or contacts or financial stability to be on my own..."

"I'd still deck him for you," Roderick offered.

"It's been years since I heard from him." Addison's look was complicated: thoughtful and grateful and a little afraid.

Understandably so.

Instinct was whispering again, warning him. If he pushed too hard, asked too much too quickly, she would run. Underneath that sunny smile and cheerful resilience, she'd been hurt. She'd given her trust too soon before, and Roderick didn't want to give her any reason to doubt his sincerity. He could be patient; his wolf suggested that it would be worth a slow courtship to win this woman.

"I have a date on Friday," he said, as off-handedly as he could manage.

Addison froze and Roderick could see her turning over that information, trying to decide what he meant by it.

"You'd be welcome to join us," Roderick added quickly, fearing the joke was too weak. "Gabby's not the jealous type."

Addison's face split into a laughing smile. "Are you asking me on a date?"

"Does it count as a date at a restaurant where you can color your own menu, with a fourteen-month-old chaperone?" Roderick asked.

"I don't know," Addison said, pretending to think about it. "Does this count as a date?"

Did it? Separate tickets, a simple sandwich? "Do I get a kiss at the end?" As soon as he said the words, Roderick wondered if it was exactly what he'd just warned himself not to do.

Addison gazed at him, her lips just slightly parted, like she was ready to say something but wasn't sure what.

"No pressure," he said quickly. "They are *your* lips."

The lips in question curved up at the corners. "Indeed," she said demurely. "And these lips need to get back to Cherry's by two-thirty."

They hastily bussed their dishes, and Roderick was glad that they fell right back into a comfortable conversation that carried them all the way back to the day care. There were seven socks on the "'BEAR' FEET" sign now.

Addison sat down to take off her tennis shoes and Roderick tried not to tower over her. "I had a really nice time," he said gruffly. "Thank you for joining me."

She smiled up at him like sunshine. "I had a great time," she agreed. "And I'd love to go out to dinner with you and your four-teen-month-old chaperone on Friday."

Roderick's heart leaped in his chest. "I'll pick you up at six?"

Addison cocked her head. "Why don't I meet you there," she counter-proposed.

Roderick extended his hand, and she shook it with a surprisingly strong grip. "Sounds great," he said sincerely.

Then there was the sound of something falling in the playroom behind him and there was the wail of an outraged child that might have been his own.

"I'm back to work!" Addison said, springing to her stocking feet. "Thank you!"

# CHAPTER 15

*N*ickel City felt like nowhere else that Addison had ever been, and she was pretty sure that it wasn't just that it felt like she'd come here to meet her soulmate. The air seemed to reach further down into her lungs. Her lynx was stronger here, her senses sharper. She had a brief chance to shift and play with the kids in the backyard of the day care that Cherry still hadn't settled on a name for and even shifting felt easier; she hardly had to think about it to flow into her lynx form.

Everything felt alive, full of magic and energy.

She'd never seen so many shifters in one place before, either. She ran into them unexpectedly—shopping in grocery stores, behind the counter of the bakery, jogging through the forest park in the middle of town—instead of just at the day care where she might expect them. It was no wonder they needed an actual establishment for shifter child care here.

There were plenty of humans in the little town as well, of course. But where she might sense another shifter once or twice a week in the bustling city of Buffalo, here, she ran into them half a dozen times in just her first few days.

They always gave each other friendly nods of recognition, a

grin, and a little tip up of the chin in greeting, and Addison felt like she belonged, like she'd come home, and her instinct said *here. Now.*

The surrounding humans weren't completely oblivious to the silent camaraderie, Addison thought, and she sometimes caught one of them giving a suspicious look after an unspoken greeting. She wondered if it didn't look a little cliquish, and she was more surreptitious in her acknowledgments after that.

Everything about Nickel City would be perfect if it weren't for the fact that she was living in Wendy's sewing room.

It wasn't that Wendy was a bad housemate—she didn't have unreasonable expectations on Addison's time or eat her food in the refrigerator. But it wasn't a lot of house to share, and Addison was very aware that it wasn't her space.

"Do you want me to bring back a sandwich?" Addison offered from the bathroom. She was attempting to tame her curly hair with a broad curling iron, an act severely hampered by the fact that there was no free surface in the bathroom to put the hot device down on. She had to fuss with each lock of hair one at a time, without a free hand to brush it loose. It was a laborious process, and Addison was not at all sure it was worth the time she was spending on it.

"No, you don't have to do that!" Wendy called from the living room. She was making...something...on a mannequin in front of the television. It seemed to involve a lot of sheer draped cloth and a whole lot of pins, but Addison wasn't ready to guess what it might be. "You're going on a *date!*"

"It's not really a date!" Addison protested. "I don't think you can call it a date when you're going with a fourteen-month-old and her dad. It's just a...dinner. At a family restaurant." With *Roderick.* "I really don't mind bringing you home a sandwich!"

She snatched the iron away from the ear she'd gotten it too close to and swore as Wendy said something. "Sorry, I didn't hear that?"

"I said this needs embroidered ribbon! I think I have some in your room."

But it wasn't Addison's room. It was the sewing room, and she was living out of a few suitcases. Her car was still full of all her moving boxes except the one she'd unpacked to find her curling iron. Did she have to have so much hair? Her arms were not used to this much primping, and muscles that she didn't usually use were starting to burn from holding them up so long.

"Go on in," Addison said. Wendy was very respectful of what space she had. She curled the last of her hair, liking the soft waves around her face and knowing that they were going to be gone as soon as she jostled her head. "Do you have any hair spray?" It was always a tossup between hair that went limp and frizzy immediately and having crunchy hair that didn't move in a breeze. Tonight, she was up for the crunch. She had even put on makeup.

"It's in with the art supplies!" Wendy called from the sewing room. "The box marked graphite!"

"Art supplies?"

"I use it as a drawing fixative!"

Of course she did.

Addison unplugged the curling iron and, when she could find no place to put it to cool, walked around with it in one hand to find the box labeled graphite and wrestle the hair spray out of it until Wendy came out and realized what she was trying to do. "Oh here, Addy, let me get that for you. This can cool on the kitchen counter. Don't you look gorgeous! Not a date, huh?"

Addison walked very carefully back to the bathroom, hoping to keep her hard-won curls from going limp too fast. She grinned at Wendy. "Not a *real* date."

"Well, you're going to wow him like it *was* a real date," Wendy said approvingly. "Is that what you're wearing?"

Addison had showered when she finished at the day care and changed into clean jeans and a t-shirt that said 'Donut Worry, Be Happy.'

"What's wrong with this?" Was the bakery name too terrible a pun?

"It's got no cleavage!"

"I'm going out to dinner with a toddler!" Addison protested. "I don't need *cleavage!*"

"The toddler will probably appreciate the cleavage as much as

Roderick does," Wendy scoffed. "They still think those things are made of milk. Hold on, I've got a shirt that you will *rock.*"

Addison knew better than to argue with Wendy, even if she could have made the point that Gabby must have been bottle fed, and she very, very carefully took the t-shirt off without disturbing her curls too completely. The shirt she got in return buttoned up the front, which at least didn't risk her coif.

"I think this is too *much* cleavage," she said, examining her reflection. "Shouldn't there be another button here?"

Wendy grinned. "Doesn't have one, sorry," she trilled. "Oh, look at the time, you'll be late if you take the time to change again!"

Addison looked at the clock in chagrin. Doing her hair had taken a good deal longer than she had hoped it would and she didn't want to keep Roderick waiting. She felt like she was buzzing with anticipation. It didn't matter that it wasn't a real date, or that Gabby would be in tow.

She ducked into her room to grab a sweater that she could wear if she got self-conscious, and her purse. "I'll be back before ten, for sure," she told Wendy.

"I'm not setting a curfew," Wendy said with a shrug. "I won't worry unless you don't check in with me before tomorrow. Say lunch?"

"I'm not staying over!" Addison protested over her shoulder as she left.

"But you could!" Wendy sang after her.

# CHAPTER 16

*R*oderick had always considered himself a punctual man. It was important to be where he said he'd be when he said it. It was part of how his little plumbing business had done so well; he was a contractor everyone could trust to run on time.

That was before Gabby.

It was uncanny how she seemed to know exactly when it would be most inconvenient to blow out a diaper, or knock something over that needed cleaned up right away, or pitch the kind of fit that required a lengthy calm-down period.

It was the first of these that made him late to the restaurant; a diaper so brutal it required a half-body sponge bath, to Gabby's giggling delight. "Yuck!" she said as she was being wiped down. "Yuck!"

"Well, I certainly hope that's out of your system," he told her, folding the tabs of the clean diaper around her with an extra tickle. He texted Addison to let her know they were running late.

*No worries,* she replied with a smiley face.

She was waiting at a booth with a high chair already waiting. Gabby took one look at the tantalizing silverware and the various condiments on the table and apparently realized that the high chair would keep her from all of them. Getting her into it was like trying to stuff a cat into a carrier before a trip to the vet, all impossible bendiness and outstretched limbs, complete with yowling.

It took distracting her with a stuffy to get her strapped in at last and she banged on her tray in protest until a waitress in a cowgirl dress brought a few pages to color and a box with four cheap crayons.

Then, at last, Roderick could slip into the booth across from Addison and drink her in. "You look amazing."

Addison's hand fluttered towards the expanse of bosom that her frilly blue blouse was exposing as if it embarrassed her and turned pink. Her hair was different, the curls looser around her face, and Roderick thought that she might be wearing makeup.

He'd felt that dressing up too much was probably inappropriate, but he'd worn a nicer-than-usual collared shirt and a bolo tie, and her appreciative look made it worth the effort.

"Sorry I'm late," he added.

"Oh, it's fine," Addison promised. "No worries. I know how it is, trying to get out of the house with little ones."

"You said you were a nanny," Roderick remembered. "How old were your kids?"

"Eighteen months and five, when I started, so only a little older than Gabby. I was with the family until they were both in school, almost five years. It's crazy how fast they grow." Addison talked about them for a while, and Roderick tried not to stare down her shirt. He forgot that they were there for dinner until the waitress came to take their order and he realized that he hadn't even looked at the menu yet.

Addison ordered a barbecue chicken wrap and a soda and Roderick hastily picked one of their country burgers, following suit with a soft drink rather than a beer, and got an order of chicken fingers for Gabby. "Rare!" he added, handing back the menus. "The burger, not the chicken fingers."

"No one wants rare chicken fingers," Addison giggled.

"Seasoned with salmonella!" Roderick joked weakly.

The waitress pretended they were funny to earn her tip and splashed water into their glasses. Gabby threw one of the crayons after her and Roderick went to pick it up. "We're not doing that right now, sweetie. Do you want to color?"

She wasn't quite to the point of scribbling with crayons, something that the developmental sites that Roderick followed assured him was just fine, like her stubborn refusal to walk. But she liked to pick them up in her fingers and crumple the coloring pages.

Most of the conversation centered around Gabby because Roderick's life did, but they talked a little about his business and Addison told him about her early care classes. "They don't want klutzes handling actual babies, of course, and one of our teachers decided that eggs weren't really challenging enough, so she sent us home with those personal-sized watermelons. Except that the watermelon she gave one of my classmates got eaten by her roommate, and when she came back to class, she was wearing a baby carrier with this behemoth thirty-pound watermelon. And she was cool as a cucumber, talking about growth spurts and weight milestones, even though it was totally obvious that it wasn't the same watermelon at all."

Roderick gave an embarrassing guffaw of laughter and asked, "Did she pass?"

"Flying colors," Addison promised. "I got docked points because one of the scarves I used got wet and it turned out the dye wasn't colorfast, so my precious watermelon-child had all these purple blotches on it."

"That seems unfair," Roderick protested.

"Well, I learned not to use hand-dyed things on kids. Haven't dyed a single one of them since then!"

They talked as easily in person as they had on the phone, laughing about the same things, including Gabby effortlessly in their banter. She added her own strong opinions, and when Roderick gave her a sippy cup of water, waved it around like a drunk with a tankard.

The meal was decidedly mediocre, but Roderick enjoyed it more than any meal he'd ever eaten, watching Addison's animated face as they chatted, Gabby beside him devouring chicken tenders like a small velociraptor.

"Dessert?" the bored waitress finally wanted to know.

"I couldn't," Addison groaned. "I am stuffed."

Roderick shook his head.

Gabby had slowed down and was playing with the last of her chicken. Her eyes were starting to glaze, and her fingers were getting clumsy. Clumsier.

On cue, she raised a fist and rubbed her eyes. "Oh, there it is," Addison said knowingly.

"The sleepy rub," Roderick agreed. "Think she'll stay awake all the way home?"

"I would not gamble a thin dime against it."

They got the bill, and there was a moment where they both reached for it and their hands brushed. Her touch was electric, and it was one of those slow-motion moments in a movie with swelling music.

"My treat," Roderick said firmly, not moving his hand.

"I'll get it next time," Addison conceded, and she took her hand back shyly.

Roderick belatedly remembered that her terrible previous boyfriend had always insisted on paying, as a method of control. "I'll let you," he promised.

"Ababa," Gabby said tiredly.

Roderick left cash, with a generous tip because of the mess Gabby made, and gathered up all of her things.

"That's a bold diaper bag," Addison said approvingly when he slung the fuzzy cookie monster over his shoulder.

"Never underestimate the power of a fuzzy blue monster to act as a necessary distraction when you're trying to get kicking legs in pants," Roderick said, unbuckling Gabby. "It's worked well for me."

They walked together to the door, Gabby in Roderick's arms, and he was keenly aware of how he and Addison were looking at each other and glancing away just as quickly, both of them smiling.

Addison walked with him to his truck and he strapped Gabby in. She was barely awake enough to protest, and she made some muddy signs with her hands that might have been more or berries or gorilla.

"I hope she doesn't take a power nap on the way home and then wake up prepared to keep you up all night," Addison said wryly. "Good night, Gabby."

Gabby's head was already lolling.

Roderick shut the door on her as quietly as he could. "She's usually a good sleeper," he said, "whether she's napped or not."

It had gotten dark while they were in the restaurant, only a hint of color left in the sky, and the street lights were on. Across the lot, a group of rowdy teenagers was gathered around a car shouting good-natured insults at each other.

"I had a good time," Addison said, wrapping her sweater around herself against the evening chill.

"Even with a fourteen-month-old chaperone?" Roderick teased.

"Especially with a fourteen-month-old chaperone," Addison giggled.

*Now, now, now,* instinct whispered at him.

Or least, he *thought* it was instinct. It was hard to separate wanting her from wanting to be with her, from his bone-deep certainty that they could be happy together, from his wolf panting in joy because everything was simply right in the world at this very moment.

She was gazing up at him, her lips just slightly parted, her whole posture invitation and excitement. He could kiss her now, he could wrap her up in his arms and taste her at last.

"Addison..." he started, because even instinct wasn't consent.

"Yes!" she said. Then, abashed, "I mean, yes?"

They met halfway between, the barest brush of lips to lips at first, then her soft arms were up around his neck and he was trying not to crush her against him and failing more than succeeding. "Addison..." he murmured, or tried to, but there was no space for words between them.

They didn't stop kissing until the teenagers across the lot started clapping and whistling, then hastily backed apart. Addison gave an embarrassed curtsy in their direction and Roderick tipped what would have been an invisible hat as they hooted their approval.

"Another time, another place?" Addison suggested quietly.

Every time, every place, Roderick thought longingly. But he could be patient. He was more sure now than ever that Addison was meant to be with him, and he could wait for forever.

# CHAPTER 17

*A*ddison reluctantly took her leave of Roderick, waving in chagrin to their audience, and skipped light-footedly back to her car full of moving boxes.

Of all the things she had expected to find in Nickel City, she had never seen Roderick coming.

She turned around and waved back at him when she got to her car, then slid into the driver seat and tipped her head forward to lean on the steering wheel.

She had always longed for...something of her own. A house. A family. Maybe a kid or two. She was terribly fond of all of her charges, but she always knew that they weren't wholly hers. And with Owen, she hadn't even felt like her own *self.*

Now, it felt like she had a chance. A chance at someone who looked at her like Roderick looked at her. A chance to be Gabby's real mother. A chance to be kissed like Roderick kissed her.

Her skin tingled with longing and excitement.

Instinct? Magic? A *mate?*

It was like she was in a fairy tale.

After a moment, she reminded herself that the teenagers were probably still watching her and Roderick had long since driven away to put Gabby to bed. She pulled out of the lot and drove back to Wendy's tiny house.

"How'd the shirt work out?" Wendy wanted to know. The mannequin in the living room had been abandoned and Wendy was knitting something in front of a sitcom. "Twelve, thirteen, hang on, I dropped a stitch, crap, here you are, fourteen, fifteen, sixteen, purl. I should know better than to try to do this and watch *Letterkenny* at the same time." She put the knitting aside and made room on the couch for Addison, tossing aside an afghan, her yarn bag, and two of the ugliest throw pillows Addison had ever seen. "I need all the dirt," she commanded. "Did you kiss him?"

Addison flopped onto the couch. "The shirt worked *great,*" she said honestly.

"I bet he couldn't keep his eyes off you for a second," Wendy said with great satisfaction. "How was the chaperone?"

"A good conversation piece," Addison giggled.

"And the kiss?" Wendy demanded.

The *kiss.*

Addison had certainly never been kissed like that before and she felt like her face would split from smiling. Her lips felt *used.*

Wendy made a noise like a steam kettle ready to boil. "Tell me about the kiss!"

"He has great lips," Addison decided she could safely say. Great lips, and a great mouth, and a great tongue, and a great, hard body that she could have pressed herself against all day.

"Great lips," Wendy said in disbelief. "That's what you put in a Yelp review. Did you get to second base?"

"You don't get to bases on a guy," Addison protested. "Man nipple just isn't the same."

"Fine," Wendy scoffed. "Then, did you let *him* get to second base?"

Addison shook her head a little regretfully, remembering how his hands had felt at her waist, not wanting them to move from there, ever, and at the same time desperate for him to touch more.

"Did you get a second date at least?" Wendy asked, exasperated.

"C'mon, Addison, I have no life and I have to live vicariously through you. Throw me a bone!"

"This *was* our second date," Addison pointed out. She used her opposite foot to pry each shoe off and tucked her stockinged feet up underneath her. "We had lunch two days ago."

"Good lord," Wendy said in frustration. "It's going to take you a month to get laid at this rate."

Addison hid her face in the ugliest of the throw pillows. "Wendy!"

"Just because I live like a nun, doesn't mean everyone needs to," Wendy pointed out. "Now, as much as I love having you here, we have got to get you your own place, with a much better bed, because that will probably help a lot. Air mattresses squeak."

Addison gave a groan. "Everything costs soooooo much," she complained. "I haven't saved anything yet for the deposits that they want, and I'm worried that if Veronica raises the rent on Cherry's place, I won't even have a *job.*" She looked at Wendy over the pillow. "I hate to impose. I really hoped I'd find a place in a week or two, but that's looking stunningly unlikely."

"Oh, yeah, about that!" Wendy bounced up and went to a pile of mail. "There's a municipality meeting in a few weeks. They're trying to pass some restrictions on the short-term rentals and put a freeze on rent hikes. Believe me, you are not the only one having this problem right now."

She handed Addison a flyer.

Addison took it and skimmed the information. "A town meeting? They still have those?"

"It's an assembly meeting with public testimony. You should give some."

"I've been here less than a week," Addison chuckled. "I have nowhere to live. I'm pretty sure I don't count as their voting public."

"Get your boyfriend to testify," Wendy suggested with an eyebrow waggle. "He lives here and probably wants to keep his neighborhoods for neighbors."

"Catchy slogan."

"Neighborhoods for neighbors? Oh, you should paint signs and have your day care kids march around downtown holding them. You can't lose!"

"I am not exploiting a bunch of children for cheap rent," Addison scoffed.

"Why don't you move in with Roderick?" Wendy said, laughing, but the joke fell short and Addison went cold.

She'd moved in with Owen for reasons of convenience, and just look how that had worked out. She wasn't going to make that same mistake again. Not based on something as uncertain and fickle as instinct.

Wendy wasn't oblivious to Addison's reaction. "Sorry, too soon?"

"Too soon is the story of my life," Addison said. "Last time—"

"Roderick isn't Owen," Wendy said unnecessarily.

"Not even close," Addison said with a little hitch to her breath. She didn't even need instinct to tell her that, though it was a humming undertone to her certainty. "It's just…"

"Once bitten, twice shy?" Wendy guessed, once Addison had trailed off.

"Once bitten, twice *smart,*" Addison corrected.

# CHAPTER 18

Roderick knew he was a lucky dad. He'd rubbed elbows with enough other parents to hear the horror stories about kids Gabby's age that refused to sleep. But most nights, Gabby went to bed with minimal fuss—a few moments of crying at most—and woke up full of bubbles and joy.

So he was surprised when Gabby woke him screaming at just past midnight, about a week after his first date with Addison.

Bleary-eyed, he staggered down the hall to her bedroom and opened the door. "What's wrong, sweetheart? What's the problem?"

Her diaper was dry and she refused food when he offered it. Picking her up didn't calm her, singing didn't work. He tried to settle her with a book, but she arched her back and fought him, kicking at the book and crying. He tried music, television, different food, changing her diaper even though it wasn't wet. "What do you need, Gabby? What's wrong?"

She signed for milk, then pushed it away, weeping in frustration, and by about three AM, Roderick was tempted to join her in pitching a fit. "I want to help you, baby girl, I want to help you, but I don't know what you want, darling girl."

At last Gabby seemed to run out of steam, and although she didn't seem interested in sleeping, she was content to sob against Roderick's shoulder while he paced the house.

"Poor baby," he told her, over and over again, and he tried to put her down in the crib twice before giving that up in the face of her distress.

Then he finally felt it, a little tickle in his tired head that made his wolf whine in understanding.

"Oh, honey, are you ready for this?" Roderick wasn't sure if what he felt was relief or fear. "Am I?"

Gabby was going to be a shifter.

Not today, probably, maybe not for days or even months, but she was starting the process. It was like teething, supposedly, but even worse, to hear Ian's stories. Gabby already had six teeth that had been days worth of agony apiece, but Roderick knew that it would feel like a walk in the park compared to what was coming next.

Would she be a wolf, like him? Or a domestic cat like his maternal grandmother? A throwback to something further back in his lines? Dana wasn't a shifter, and she had been gone, at least emotionally, before Roderick had a chance to talk about it. When it was clear that she wasn't going to be a part of Gabby's life, Roderick had seen no reason to bring up the topic with her. If she had shifter ancestors, he wasn't sure how to ask, and he didn't have a way to contact her now, anyway.

Gabby went limp on his shoulder, and he paced with her a little longer, not willing to risk disturbing her by putting her down. At least he had an answer now, that was some comfort.

When his shoulder was damp with her drool and she was snoring gently, he was finally able to lay her down in the crib and creep away.

~

The morning was exactly as awful as he guessed it would be, dry eyes opening to the shrill of his alarm.

The prospect of a date with Addison that evening was the only thing that made his breakfast bearable.

He sucked down coffee like a lifeline before daring to go in to wake Gabby, letting her sleep a little extra to make up for their fractured night.

She seemed no worse for their lack of sleep, though she was inclined to be fussy about food and was perhaps a touch more clingy than usual. Roderick was able to distract her without too much trouble and she sat quietly with a board book looking at her favorite pages while he texted Addison that they were going to be late, gathered up her diaper bag, checked his voicemail, and made a few calls to schedule repairs. He liked to have a free block in the morning for emergency calls that needed priority, and he smiled at the block on his calendar for the evening.

Addison.

Ian had agreed to take Gabby so that they could have an actual-factual, no-chaperone date. Roderick wished that he was facing the day with better sleep, but he was still filled with anticipation and excitement. Their single stolen kiss was like a promise, and he'd cleaned the house, just in case he brought her back here afterward.

"Ready to go, Gabby? Want to go see Cherry? And Addison?"

"Ababba addy," she replied, stretching her arms out to him. She probably wasn't saying Addy's name on purpose, Roderick told himself, but it still made his heart feel a size larger and he echoed his wolf's satisfaction as he scooped Gabby into his arms.

All the satisfaction vanished into shock and alarm when he came out of his house and found a woman waiting at his mailbox as if she was afraid to come to the door.

He recognized her from that distance, even though she was thinner than she'd been the last time he saw her, and her hair was shockingly short and in natural curls; she'd always worn it straightened, or tightly braided. Tamed, she liked to say.

There was something wilder about her now, and Roderick folded his arms around Gabby a little tighter and resisted his urge to swap sides with her to hold her a little further away.

She took one step towards him as he walked to his parked truck, then stopped and waited for him to close the distance.

"Dana," he said warily. "What are you doing here?"

He was desperately afraid that he already knew.

# CHAPTER 19

"Rough night," Roderick's text said. "We'll be late."

So Addison didn't worry at first when the morning went by without a sign of Gabby and Roderick. She texted him back a hasty thumbs up and chasing the kids kept her busy and distracted. When she did pause to think about them, it was with wistful longing for the evening ahead. A real date! At a restaurant without kids! And afterward...

Amy broke out in frustrated wails when the older kids refused to let her play with them, and turned into a sulky owl, screeching her displeasure. Addison scampered to distract her back to happy babbling and—most importantly—her human form.

She looked up when Tara appeared at her elbow, expecting her to want to play at some make-believe. But Tara didn't have a bandage to apply or a doll to talk to, she only gazed at Addison with her dark, solemn eyes and said, "I want to shift."

Addison gave a quick look around the room, doing a headcount of the kids. Cherry was setting up a craft and Shea was sitting with the babies. Addison stood up and Tara slipped her hand trustingly into hers.

Cherry looked up and met her gaze—she might not have shifter instinct, but she seemed to be almost supernaturally sensitive to everything that happened in her school. She nodded and called cheerfully to Amy, "Come help me count, Amy! One! Two! Three!"

Amy toddled eagerly to Cherry and Addison walked with Tara to the back door and out into the back yard. Addison sat on the grass near the middle of the lawn, letting Tara pick wherever made her comfortable to shift.

Tara didn't go for the corner of the yard that was in the bright sunlight, but for the shadow-dappled corner under one of the big, spreading maple trees and she stood still so long in human form that Addison thought she was going to change her mind.

Then she shivered in place and shifted, skillfully taking her clothing with her, and Addison finally understood.

Tara wasn't the pearl-white, golden-horned unicorn that her sticker showed, she was all mud-brown and covered in subtle rainbow-hued scales, with a fuzzy silvery-brown mane all around her neck like a lion. A short, furry crest traced her spine and ended in a tufted tail. She had small antlers on both sides of her narrow head, with one prong forward in a broad point.

Delicate cloven hooves lifted, one after another, and her big, deer-like ears flattened back against her head as it drooped sadly. Long whiskers around her muzzle floated in the air currents as if they were weightless. She looked a little like an Eastern dragon and a deer, mixed up with a Western unicorn.

"Oh, Tara," Addison said in wonder. "You aren't ugly at all." But she understood Tara's misplaced shame; she looked nothing like the books about unicorns on the day care library shelves, or the cartoons on the other children's' backpacks and t-shirts. "You *are* a unicorn, a Chinese unicorn. Do you know much about them?"

Tara's head cocked hopefully and shook a no, her undulous whiskers following her face.

"They're called *kirin,*" Addison explained. "To be honest, I don't know much about them, except that they are very rare and special. You are amazing, Tara. You have nothing to be embarrassed about. You don't have to show your friends if you don't want to, but I know that they would still like you."

Tara stepped cautiously closer and finally put her head in Addison's outstretched hand with a huff of breath. Then she shifted seamlessly into her human form and crawled into Addison's lap as a little girl.

Addison wrapped her arms around Tara, leaning over to comfort her and snuggle her in close. They sat quietly like that for some time, until the back door of the day care burst open and disgorged two boys, pelting out onto the lawn.

"We're going to play Simon-Says-Shift and I'm going to remember MY CLOTHES!" Gil announced.

Tara sat up and wiped a dirty hand across her face. Addison wasn't sure if she'd actually been crying, but there were no tears in her eyes now. She glanced once at Addison for support, then stood up and brushed off her heart-covered pants. "Can I play?" she asked shyly, and Gil and Robert didn't hesitate a moment to draw her to the starting line and start explaining the rules over each other.

Addison ducked her head into the classroom to see if there were any other children who wanted to play, and to exchange an enthusiastic thumbs up with Cherry.

None of the children reacted in the slightest when Tara shifted along with the rest of them. When she won the noisy game with a final fleet-footed dash to Addison on the finish line, Gil was inclined to pout, but Robert simply pointed out, "She shifts better than you do." None of them seemed even the slightest bit curious about what she was; she was still Tara, and she shifted better than the boys.

Addison gave her a sticker—a bear eating out of a pot of honey—and Tara proudly peeled off the backing and stuck it to her shirt.

Gil had to go back and collect his socks, though he had technically remembered the rest of his clothing, so he hadn't been disqualified from the game or sent back to the beginning.

Addison coordinated a handful of other games, cheerfully amending the rules when Amy came out to join them, toddling among them and shifting into her owl form to beat her downy wings at random points.

"It's book time!" Cherry called from the door. "Who wants to help me pick which book we read?"

"Firefighters to the Rescue!" Robert cried.

"Corduroy!" Tara shouted.

"Pigeon!" Gil shouted louder.

"Aaaaaah!" Amy added, falling over on her face when she tried to run too fast.

Addison helped her back up, picked up Gil's shoes again, and herded them all back inside, exchanging a grin with Cherry.

Three books later, after Addison and Shea had fed the babies and helped get everyone down for quiet time on their nap mats, she sat down in one of the undersized chairs at the far side of the room with a scrap of paper and a crayon and wrote down some ideas that occurred to her before she could forget them.

She was folding up the note to fit in her pocket when Cherry came to sit across the table from her.

"Did everything work out okay?" she asked quietly.

"It's all fine," Addison promised. "Tara is a kirin."

When Cherry looked at her blankly, she explained, "A Chinese unicorn. They look like a dragon and deer hybrid. Is there a library in town? I thought I might see if I could check out some books so she could see herself in print."

"Next block over, behind the bakery," Cherry said. "Her mother only ever said unicorn, and I never thought to ask! I had no idea!" She shook her head. "Here I was, showing her all the books with Western unicorns and pointing out Amy's shirt. Addison, I feel like a clod."

"You didn't know," Addison said kindly. "And I'm sure she'll face that a lot, I mean I didn't even realize they were *real.*"

"We can do better," Cherry said firmly, then louder, "Gil, we're pretending to be still like statues! Statues don't wiggle!"

There were some giggles from the nap mats. One of the babies in the nursery corner began to fuss and Addison got to her feet to go check on her. When she returned, Cherry asked, "What do you think of the name The Little Zoo for the day care?"

Addison considered, looking around at the cages of animals. "It would work," she said. "It does imply a certain amount of chaos."

"And maybe too much truth in advertising," Cherry chuckled. "I want to imply shifting, without coming right out and saying it. I'll keep thinking." She frowned briefly, looking for a moment very vulnerable and lost.

"Are you worried about Veronica raising the rent?" Addison guessed.

Cherry gave a bright smile that couldn't fool Addison. "We'll figure something out," she promised, but Addison could tell that behind her cheer she was quite concerned.

Addison glanced at the clock. Gabby and Roderick still hadn't shown up, and she wondered if she should be worried.

She shook her head firmly. All she knew about Roderick, she'd learned in a few not-really-dates and a couple of toddler hand-offs, plus the notes on his guardian-contact sheet and a handful of long, rambling telephone conversations and so many texts that she'd had to change her phone plan. It felt like she knew him, but what did she really know?

Maybe he tended to run late a lot. Maybe something had come up, and he didn't feel a need to send a second message. Lots of things might have happened.

Even if what they had *was* instinct, there was a limit to what they owed each other.

# CHAPTER 20

"*I* know what the papers say," Dana said defensively. "I know. I just...things came up, and I thought we could talk."

Roderick tried to resolve the woman before her with the whirlwind emotional upheaval that she had been in his heart before. The months before Gabby's birth had been a rollercoaster of simultaneously wanting to work out a relationship with Dana and being grateful that she wanted nothing to do with him long-term, trying to make sense of his instinct, or the sudden lack of direction from it. He had expected their next meeting to have the same kind of internal conflict and he was shocked that he didn't have any lingering feelings over the mother of his child.

When he looked at Dana, he measured her against Addison, a woman he'd only known a week, and didn't want her at all.

*Instinct knows,* his wolf said smugly.

"Why are you here?" he asked Dana. "Why *now?*" Gabby was starting to fuss, the tingly not-quite-shifter feel of her intensifying briefly. He bounced her gently, and she settled. It should take at least a few days before she was a true shifting risk, Roderick thought, but it would be just his kind of luck if she turned into a wolf cub *right now*. He was really hoping that she was going to give him a few weeks or months. Baby-proofing and wolf-proofing were similar, but not exactly the same, and he wasn't sure where house training fit with any of the rest of her milestones. The baby books were completely unhelpful on that topic.

"Can we go somewhere?" Dana asked plaintively. "Just to talk." She glanced back at the house but didn't suggest it.

"We're heading to the day care," Roderick said, not caring that he didn't sound particularly accommodating. "And I have jobs to get to."

"Later, then," Dana said quickly. "I can come back." But to Roderick's horror, there were tears welling up in her eyes.

Whatever ill will Roderick might hold crumbled in the face of her misery. "I already told the day care I was going to be late. Come on in and have a cup of coffee. Gabby needs a new diaper already, anyway."

Was he being a doormat? Gabby was staring at Dana with round stranger-eyes, doubtful and cautious. And why shouldn't she? Dana *was* a stranger to her. A stranger who just happened to be her mother.

He unlocked the house and stepped aside as she came in.

"It looks good," she said faintly, as he took Gabby back to her changing pad and efficiently took care of the gift she'd produced for him. "You look good."

Roderick gave her a suspicious, sideways look. Was she expecting to pick things up where they'd left off? Did she think that he'd spent the last year pining over her?

Her next words dispelled that worry. "I'm not here to get back together, or try to take Gabriella away from you."

"Then what do you want?" Roderick asked, not letting any warmth into his voice. He didn't particularly feel any warmth. He didn't bear this woman any ill will, but he didn't owe her anything, either, and her sudden return put worry in the pit of his stomach. Was she going to be trouble? Would she ruin what he was building with Addison? Even if he didn't think that Dana would deliberately try to sabotage Roderick's new relationship, having an ex around felt like a complication he didn't need or want.

They went into the kitchen and he turned on the coffee pot. He'd bought one of the coffee makers that used pods; he didn't like how much packaging he threw out, but he liked his second cup being as fresh as the first one. He put Gabby into her high chair and gave her a handful of crackers, then set a cup under the dispenser, waiting for the water to heat up.

"Boobuh!" Gabby said in disdain. She looked at her hands in frustration, put her fingers together, and twisted her wrists. It was as close as she had come to mastering the sign for blueberry.

Normally, he might insist that she at least try the food in front of her, but Roderick was desperate to forestall a fuss so that he could try to figure out exactly what was going on. He went to the fridge and got a few blueberries to put on her tray. She gave a cry of triumph and fell upon them. Roderick caught Dana staring.

"She's...so big," she said when she looked up and saw Roderick watching her. "I didn't expect... I don't know what I expected."

"I'm really hoping we can get to a point soon," Roderick said wryly. "Those aren't going to distract her for long, and I've got a job later this morning."

Dana licked her lips. "I can't have any more kids."

That certainly was a point.

It hit Roderick like a fist in the gut. First, he was sorry for Dana, for the terrible finality in her voice and the unexpected pain on her face. Fear followed on the tail of that sympathy. Did she want to stake some kind of claim on Gabby? Did she think that the two of them could pick up where they'd left off, like he hadn't moved on? Their time together had been fun, but they'd never had a relationship worth a name, and he couldn't imagine making a home with her. Should he ask *why* she couldn't have children? Wait for her to volunteer more information? His mind swirled with possible dangers in this minefield of a conversation.

"I'm sorry to hear that," he finally said, circling back to his first reaction. "Is there something I can do?"

To his horror, Dana began to cry. "I don't know," she sobbed. "I shouldn't have come. I can't take Gabby away, and I don't want to get back together, I don't think. I just...I had to come and see her. I wanted to know that I'd done one thing in my life right, to see her again, to know that she was...okay."

Roderick wanted to comfort her, but feared it would encourage something he didn't want to. *What do I do?* he asked his wolf, but his wolf had no advice. Where was instinct when he needed the damn thing?

He settled for making a cup of coffee while Dana found the paper towels hanging by the sink and loudly blew her nose.

When she had returned to her seat, the coffee finished brewing, and he put the cup in front of her. "There's sugar," he offered gruffly.

"No, thank you," she said quietly. She took a sip and cradled her fingers around the mug like she could use the heat to give her strength.

Gabby, having run out of blueberries, babbled into the silence commandingly. "Boobuh! Boobuh!" She smashed a berry-stained cracker.

"We're doing good," Roderick said. He brought the container of blueberries out of the fridge and tipped a generous helping out onto her tray.

Gabby stared at the bounty and then, almost grudgingly, offered him one. He took it. "Thanks, honey."

"Addy," she said in reply, then she was entertaining herself chasing the berries around her tray and putting them mostly in her mouth.

Roderick got his own cup of coffee and wondered if he'd regret the extra on top of a night that was low on sleep. He sat across from Dana, who was watching Gabby with a mixture of hunger and regret.

"Should we have a lawyer here?" he asked.

It must have come out more warningly than he intended.

Dana gave him a stricken look, then shook her head. "No. No, it's not like that. I'll go whenever you ask me to."

"You...don't want visitation rights or something?"

Dana wilted. "I don't know what I want. I thought I did, before. I was so sure. But this has...hit me a lot harder than I expected it to." She lifted her chin. "I've always been honest with you, Roderick. We didn't see eye to eye on a lot of things, but I never led you on, and I never lied. And I'm not lying about this. I honestly don't know what to do from here. My...my boyfriend left me when he found out, and it broke my heart. It scared me that...maybe I'd done that to you. I knew you'd take good care of Gabby, but I worried that I'd done you wrong and I don't like to leave debts."

Had she broken his heart? Roderick remembered how gutted he'd been, and how adrift those first few months had been...and how Gabby had been the glue that held him together. He looked at Dana, at the proud line of her neck and the set of her jaw. He'd felt betrayed, and he'd been angry at times, but he hadn't been broken, because he hadn't ever seen them with a future together...even when he'd desperately wanted one. Instinct had told him that they were meant to be together, then gone coldly, oddly silent when Dana chose a different path.

She'd tested his pride, but she hadn't touched his heart. Not the way Addison had in the short time they'd known each other.

Was it just instinct, the way he couldn't look at Addison without feeling like his feet were finally on the right path? He'd tried to force Dana to his vision of their destiny, and it had been the wrong future for both of them. Instinct was showed you a chance, his mother had told him.

Dana's face fell as she took his silence for rejection. "I'm sorry for everything that's happened, but I'm not sorry I came," she said quietly. "It looks like you've got everything under control and I'm really happy for both of you. It's enough to know that."

Roderick suspected that if he told Dana to go, she would go and that would be the end of it. He and Gabby would never see her again.

He looked at Gabby, who had dropped a blueberry in her lap but not noticed its escape and could not figure out why it was no longer in her hand.

And if Dana stayed, she would ask no more of them than he was absolutely willing to give.

His instinct, when he unfolded it from all the emotion swirling inside him, told him that she would do as she promised, whichever he chose. He was the one holding the cards.

"I'm not sorry you came, either," Roderick said gently. "And I can't be sorry for everything that happened, because if it hadn't, I wouldn't have Gabby." He wouldn't have been happy without Gabby, he realized, and instinct knew that.

Hearing her name, Gabby waved a fist. "Addy!" she said.

And without Gabby, he wouldn't have Addison, either.

"I've got a few things to catch you up on," he told Dana. "But first, let me introduce you to your daughter."

# CHAPTER 21

*A*ddison knew that something was wrong the moment Roderick walked into the day care.

No...not wrong. She tried to sort her instinct from her observations, and it did nothing but hum unhelpfully. There was something a little different about Roderick; his usual easy smile was missing. He looked distant and concerned.

"What's up?" she asked quietly, as she took Gabby over the gate so that Roderick wouldn't have to take off his boots.

"Addy!" Gabby sang. "Boobuh abada!"

Addison was grateful that Gabby had warmed up to her so quickly. Having her wail when Roderick left the first few days had been hard on everyone involved.

"Dana's in town. She came to see me."

It took Addison a moment to place the name. "Gabby's mom," she said, and it made a tangle of confusing feelings in her chest. Jealousy, worry, fear. She wanted to protect Roderick and fight for this new thing that they had, and she was terrified that maybe...she shouldn't. Roderick wasn't hers, not really. Maybe it would be better if he and Gabby's mother were together. Better for Gabby, better for Roderick.

Roderick frowned. "We're not getting back together," he said firmly. "You don't have to worry about that."

Addison wondered if she was that transparent. "Still," she offered gently, "this has to...complicate things."

Did they still have a date for that night? Was Dana here for long? Did she want to place some claim on Gabby? Questions that Addison didn't dare ask crowded into her brain.

What did this mean? Addison tried to focus on her shifter senses. She could feel that Roderick was tense, that Gabby was happy, that the other children were safe...but the magic gave her no clues, no draw towards the best thing to do. It also gave her no twang of warning, which she hoped was a good sign.

"I don't want it to," Roderick said, still frowning.

It took Addison a moment to backtrack through her thoughts and realized that *complication* was what he didn't want.

"You have to think about what's best for you," Addison said slowly. "And best for Gabby." Even if that wasn't *her*.

Roderick sucked in his breath and Addison thought that if the gate weren't between them, he might have reached for her. Cherry called a cheerful greeting from across the room just then and Gabby bounced in Addison's arms. She didn't seem at all bothered by the appearance of her mother and Addison envied her that innocence.

Then she abruptly recognized the nuances of what her instinct *was* telling her. "Gabby's...?"

"A shifter," Roderick finished. "Or will be, soon."

"You *have* had an exciting morning," Addison said sympathetically. Then, hesitantly, "Is...?" It would be nice if she could figure out how to finish her own questions.

"Dana's not a shifter," Roderick said, somehow knowing exactly what she was wondering. "We never got to the point where I told her about shifters, either."

Gabby was getting impatient and wanted down, so Addison set her down on her feet. Gabby held onto her knees for a few moments, looked like she was considering steps, then fell to all fours and crawled towards Cherry and the other kids.

"So *extra* complicated," Addison said, shaking her head. "With sprinkles of problematic." Did she even have the right to ask what he planned to do next? "Do you want to put off our date?"

When he didn't answer right away, Addison hastily added, "It's okay if you do. I totally understand. I know we aren't, we haven't, I mean...it's not like..."

She had unconsciously stepped back from the gate and Roderick looked like he wanted to step over it. "I'd still like to go out," he said. "This doesn't change anything between us."

Didn't it?

He'd said that he and Dana were never really a thing, but there had still been feelings—complicated feelings—and they'd had a *child* together. No one came through something like that without a little baggage.

Addison thought that he was sincere, that he still wanted her, the way that she still wanted him, but instinct didn't have a great sense of nuance, and she sometimes doubted that it understood mundane things like paying bills and car insurance...or negotiating custody. It had been a terrible conflict in her soul, not knowing *how* to leave Owen when she finally understood that every fiber of her being told her she ought to.

But Roderick wasn't Owen, she kept having to remind herself, and she wasn't the same naive girl that Owen had preyed upon.

"I'd still like to go out, too," Addison said, realizing that she had left him waiting long enough that he was shifting his weight from foot to foot nervously.

He looked relieved and Addison was surprised how much that soothed her own ruffled feelings. She flushed, suddenly remembering their passionate kiss. Would he have third-date expectations?

Did she want him to have them?

"I'll pick you up at six," Roderick offered. "I can show you the scenic route, point out a few of the Nickel City features."

Addison momentarily wanted to protest. Ever since Owen, she preferred to drive herself to dates, to always have an escape route, a way to get home on her own. But Roderick wasn't Owen, she remembered before she could answer. "That would be great." She trusted Roderick.

And despite the sudden return of his ex to add a whole new level of complexity to their budding relationship, Addison was definitely having third-date expectations of her own.

# CHAPTER 22

*G*abby was not nearly as excited about her playdate with Lucy as Lucy was, especially since she could clearly tell that Roderick was going to leave her alone there in an act of cruel abandonment. She cried piteously and pulled herself up on the couch.

"We'll be fine," Ian promised, already looking a little wild around the eyes. "Take your time. It's a weekend, so we can stay up late, or if it goes really well, just drop me a text, and we'll make her up a bed."

"Baby!" Lucy declared. "She can be baby!"

When Roderick fled, Lucy was trying to put Gabby in a crib for a doll and Ian was patiently explaining that she wouldn't fit and that Lucy had to play games they both liked.

"Good luck!" he called back to Ian.

"You, too!" he replied.

Feeling rather sorry for Ian, Roderick climbed back up into his truck and drove to Addison's cousin Wendy's house. It was a tiny house in a quiet neighborhood, the little yard cluttered with sculptures, gnomes, twirling pinwheels, and banners. There was some kind of knitted sweater around one of the trees in the front yard.

Addison must have been watching for him because Roderick had only just turned off the truck and opened the door when she came out of the house. Roderick had to pause before he stepped out because she looked like a vision.

She was wearing heels and a short dress that Roderick thought must be the little black dress that all women apparently wanted. It had a somewhat higher neckline than the blouse that had driven him so crazy on their last date, but it made up for it by caressing every curve and hugging every line of her beautiful body. She had done that thing with her hair again that made it soft, bouncy curls, and her lips were scarlet red.

Roderick remembered to get the rest of the way out of the truck and went around to meet her at the passenger door. He hesitated before he opened it, in order to drink her in. "You look...amazing," he said honestly.

She flushed but seemed to be looking at him with just as much admiration. "Thank you," she said shyly. "You, too."

Roderick had decided a casual suit wasn't inappropriate for the occasion, and he was glad of that, now, because she looked like she was ready to step into the pages of a magazine and he didn't want her to think he wasn't taking this every bit as seriously.

Because he was definitely taking this seriously.

This was the woman he had been working towards his entire life. Every decision had led to her, every choice, every whisper of his wolf that he'd listened to.

She smiled but squirmed under his regard and Roderick realized that he still hadn't opened the door for her. "Let me get that," he said quickly.

It was a tall truck, and Addison looked up at it in consternation. "Goodness, I hope I don't split my skirt getting up there. Why did I think heels were smart?"

Without thinking, Roderick said, "Here, I'll help you," and it was the perfect excuse to put his hands at her waist and lift her up into the truck.

She gave a squeak of delighted surprise and got her foot into the footwell and her hand on the grab handle. She smiled down at him. "That was fun," she giggled.

Fun didn't start to cover it; the feeling of her body in his hands was like delicious torture and Roderick didn't want to let go in the slightest.

He did anyway, waited for her to swing into her seat, and shut the door, glad that it latched on the first try so he didn't have to embarrass himself by having to slam it on her a second time.

"Where are you taking me?" Addison asked when he slid into the driver's seat. She was buckled in, with the straps making interesting accents to her skimpy dress.

"Larry's," Roderick said. "Best steaks in Montana, which is saying a lot, and they usually have a decent band if you want to do any dancing."

"Oh, gosh, I really *shouldn't* have worn the heels," Addison said, but she sounded delighted. "I haven't been out dancing since college."

Roderick drove her around the town the long way, pointing out some of the major sights. He took her to the overlook of Belle Lake and she hissed in her breath at the view. "I knew Montana was beautiful," she said in awe, "but this is...amazing."

The lake was a still mirror of mountains and forests, in more colors than mountains and forests ought to be. The sky above was just starting to fade from its mid-day blue, and a few picturesque clouds looked like a painter had carefully placed them in the sky. They watched it change hues until Roderick was afraid they'd lose their reservation.

Larry's was a better-looking establishment than the name implied, and they were met at the curb by a starch-suited man who valet-parked his truck without comment. The hostess checked their name in the log and led them to a private table by a water feature.

Addison held onto his arm as they walked and was lighter on her feet than her reservations about her heels implied she would be. "This is so nice," she said, as a waiter held her chair and spread a napkin in her lap.

Roderick took his own seat and napkin and gazed at her across the table as she ran her fingers over the fancy silverware and picked up her menu.

"Addison…"

She put down the menu and smiled at him.

He didn't want to ruin the moment, but, even more, he didn't want to leave stumbling blocks between them to catch them by surprise later, either. "About Dana…"

Her smile faltered but didn't completely fade. "You don't have to explain anything," she said. "I know that this must be a lot to work out."

Roderick took a breath and let it out carefully. "I don't want Dana back. I don't think I ever had Dana. I want you, Addison. I want us. Instinct tells me that you are for me in a way that I never imagined. You are my happiness, you are my destiny."

Her face went through a dozen different expressions, all of them fascinating to watch: astonishment, longing, wariness, confusion, desire…some that Roderick couldn't even identify.

"I feel that way, too," she said at last, so quietly that Roderick had to strain to hear her over the fountain. "But we don't have to rush right into it. Sort out what you have to do with Dana. I know you have to figure out what's best for Gabby first, and I'm…I'm not going to go anywhere while you do."

That tingling magic that was a little like recognizing another shifter was back, but like a whole swarm of bees in his chest, all of them together making a happy chorus of joy.

She was more than he deserved, so gorgeous and sensible and full of kindness.

"If roles were reversed, I am not sure I would be so reasonable," Roderick confessed. "I'd want to hit him in the mouth for hurting for you."

"I'd let you," Addison chuckled wryly. "But my ex was a controlling ass that I barely escaped from. From what you've said, Dana was just scared and confused and clearly didn't know what she was letting go of. It's her loss, frankly."

"I didn't really want to make our dinner about our exes," Roderick said sheepishly.

"Then let's not," Addison suggested, picking up her menu. "I'll remind you that this one is my treat."

Roderick had forgotten that promise. "I didn't mean to make you take the more expensive meal," he said with chagrin. "I wish I'd taken you somewhere...ah..."

"Cheaper?"

"Less extravagant," Roderick conceded. "I feel like I tricked you into something."

Addison smiled slowly then, and it was full of warmth. "I hope we'll have many chances in the future to make it even."

They talked about the menu choices, then, and ordered drinks, and didn't mention exes again that night.

# CHAPTER 23

*A*ddison's feet ached by the end of the night. Roderick persuaded her to dance for a few songs, but she thought that even just walking from the parking lot and back would have left her complaining about her shoes. They were terribly impractical and she could not wait to kick them off.

They talked over their meal, and while they were dancing, and it was just as easy in person as it had been with their very first phone call. Every story was new, every revelation was interesting. He liked very different music than she did, but they geeked out over the same television and movies. They compared reading habits and found that they had, perhaps not surprisingly, read a great number of the same baby books.

"Every one of my teachers hated the *What To Expect* books," Addison told him. "Genuine way to raise neurosis in any parent."

"They may as well have called them Fear-mongering for Fathers," Roderick agreed. "I own the one- and two-year-old books."

"Did you know they made a movie out of the first book?"

"How would you make a movie out of that book?"

"I never saw it, but I assume it was a horror movie," Addison said.

Roderick dropped his voice. "The call is coming from...the baby monitor!"

His phone gave a squawk then, and they both jumped a little and then giggled. It was a series of photographs from his babysitter: Gabby playing with a little girl several months older than she was. Gabby with food smeared across her face. Gabby with big eyes and a baby squirrel on her head.

They laughed until the waiter checked on them in concern.

"I've had so much fun," Addison told Roderick as she gathered up her purse and wondered if she would regret the second mojito she had ordered. Roderick had stopped at one beer, as the driver, but she had just enough to drink to feel slightly floaty. It was just too bad for her feet that it hadn't actually made her lighter.

She paid their bill, and they went outside to wait for the valet while the sky turned violet overhead. She shivered and Roderick wrapped his arms around her. He was so warm, so solid, so...he turned a little just as she recognized the specific pressure he was exerting against her accidentally and was suddenly, keenly aware of the tension between them.

She felt like her whole body was sizzling, and all she had to do was turn in his arms and he would take her, right there in the restaurant parking lot, they were both so on fire for each other. It was hard to say what was instinct, what was just attraction, and what was a warm friendship that was already blooming into trust. She'd come in his truck, to a place she didn't know, without a backup plan better than 'call Wendy.'

And it felt perfectly right.

The truck pulled up in front of them and the valet hurried around to open the door for her. Roderick lifted her up into the seat again, but let his hands linger just a moment. It was easy to lean over and he looked up at the right moment to catch her kiss.

His hand on her thigh tightened, but they kept the kiss light and teasing, a promise of more to come.

Roderick's phone gave an alarm then, and he glanced at it and then shared the photograph with her: Gabby asleep in a toddler bed with a squirrel in her arms like a stuffed animal.

"See you tomorrow morning," the text with it read. "I have plenty of blueberries for breakfast."

Addison licked her lips, wondering if the implication was what she thought it was.

Roderick's voice was low and full of gravel. "Would you like to come over?"

She should have him drop her back at Wendy's, Addison thought. That would be the sensible choice. The taking-it-slow choice. She surprised herself by saying, softly, "I'd like that."

Roderick's face lit up; he hadn't entirely been expecting her to say yes, and she decided that she quite liked that he wasn't making those third-date assumptions.

Their drive to his house was quieter than the trip to the restaurant, and more direct, going straight through town rather than around the hills surrounding it.

Addison wondered what he was thinking, watching his profile as he drove, occasionally catching his glances.

They were both thinking about sex, she knew. What would it be like? What would it *mean?*

Instinct felt like a neon arrow; it had never been so unmistakable.

Roderick's house was in a quiet neighborhood and it was considerably less...bachelor than Addison had envisioned that it would be. It was clearly Gabby-proof, with lower bookcase shelves full of board books and toys and higher shelves crowded with baby books next to thrillers and art references.

They were back to a place where they weren't quite sure what to do with each other, their longing warring with respect warring with their own respective histories. "I'd love to see some of your artwork," Addison remembered, eying the paintings on the walls. They were mostly landscapes; had he painted them?

Roderick got adorably flustered. "I've got some sketchbooks," he said hesitantly. "Would you like a drink?"

Addison's second mojito was almost worn off, but she declined.

She wanted whatever happened to happen with a clear head. "Is the artwork that bad?" she teased, instead, and she was glad when Roderick took it in the playful spirit it was intended.

"You'll have to be the judge of that," he laughed. He went into a back room and brought out a chunky sketchbook. They sat down at the couch, thighs just touching, and Addison made herself pay attention to the artwork, not just his sizzling presence beside her. They weren't rushing, she reminded herself. They had all night. They had their whole lives. It wasn't a race.

His art was an eclectic collection of subjects and themes, from comic book heroes and classical life drawings to animals and several pages of Gabby as a baby.

Addison exclaimed over them and turned every page in interest, feeling a little like she was getting to know Roderick with each picture as much as she had in each conversational exchange that they'd shared. Not all of them were successful, and many were barely more than gesture sketches, but all of them had appealing raw energy.

"Could you draw something for me?" it suddenly occurred to her to ask, looking at gesture sketch of a galloping horse.

Roderick looked wary. "What do you want me to draw?"

"Unicorns," Addison said.

Roderick blew out his breath in relief. "I could probably do that," he agreed.

"What did you think I was going to ask?" Addison had to ask, wild with curiosity.

He squirmed and Addison was reminded again of his proximity. "I thought you'd ask me to draw you," he said sheepishly.

Addison tried to decide how to take that and he saw her confusion and hastily added, "I'm absolutely terrible at making people look like they actually are. I'd give you uneven eyes or too big a nose or a crooked mouth and you wouldn't realize how beautiful I think you are."

"You think I'm beautiful?" Addison could not quite stop herself from asking.

Roderick almost crushed the sketchbook, gathering her into his arms at last, and Addison swiftly rescued it and reached blindly to put it on the coffee table as she tipped back and let him cover her mouth with his.

# CHAPTER 24

They made out on the couch for a ridiculously long time, until Roderick's mouth was burning and he knew that Addison's must be, too.

He kissed her and kissed her, letting his hands wander all the places he'd been gazing at all evening, the place where shoulder met neck, that place at her side just beyond her breast. Her breast itself, the glorious curve of it, the amazing cup of it in his hand, the way it met her body before her belly. Her thigh, firm and taut, and the way he could follow it to her ass when he pulled her skirt up.

Her hands were no less busy, her mouth no less demanding, and by the time that he had gotten up as high as her underwear—lacy, like she was hoping that he'd get there—and rub a thumb gently over her covered clit, she had gotten his shirt off and was kneading his shoulders like a cat.

"Bedroom?" he suggested.

"Bedroom," she agreed, and he was so happy with her answer that he couldn't let go of her for several moments, kissing her desperately.

He finally made himself roll off of her and draw her up by the hands, pausing as she kicked off her shoes with a hiss of pleasure, and then leading her back along the hallway towards the bedroom. He stopped to kiss her up against the wall several times.

"Rod," she said, sliding one hand over his cock, and he wasn't sure if it was meant to be a joke, but he didn't care, because she was caressing him through his pants and he could barely even think anymore.

*Bedroom,* he reminded himself and he caught her hands again so that he could pull her in, glad that he'd tidied up and made the bed, even though neither of them was exactly pausing to appreciate it.

He bent her back over the bed and her legs were up around him as he kissed her neck and tried to figure out how her black dress was attached.

"There's a zipper in the back," she murmured, and that was all the excuse he needed to flip her over.

His brain shorted out a little, her curvy ass pressing back against him as he held onto her hips and forced himself to puzzle out her clothing again. The zipper was tiny and delicate, and he slipped it down as slowly as he could manage, both because he didn't want to damage it and because he wanted to prolong the delicious exposure of her bare back, stroking it as he went.

She whimpered and ground against him. He had to groan and think fixedly about gross grease traps and clogged toilets a moment to calm himself down.

"Condom?" he finally remembered to ask. He'd stocked the bedside table hopefully.

"Implant," she assured him. "It's okay if you don't." Then she added, "But it's nice of you to ask…"

She rolled to face him and the dress fell away from her. Roderick had to unbutton his pants before he merely ripped them off and he wasn't later sure if she removed her undergarments, or if he managed to; he only knew that there was finally nothing between them, nothing but skin and his own hard cock.

They crawled up onto the bed together, kissing again, touching, making small noises of desperation and desire, and then he was in her and they were moving together.

Everything was pleasure and passion, instinct like the sugar sprinkle on a donut that was already decadent. This was where he belonged, buried inside of her, making her rise in ecstasy, her arms around him, her mouth hungry against his. This was where he belonged, making her his, giving her himself, drinking in the touch of her, the heat of her.

When he came, at last, he saw sunspots, and he cried out her name, and he knew that he'd come home.

$\sim$

*T*hey lay together breathlessly for a long time afterward, sweat cooling on their skin as they continued to caress and touch each other in happy exhaustion.

"You could stay," he said, and to his consternation, Addison went rigid in his arms. "Or I could drive you home," he offered swiftly. "I really don't mind."

She hesitated and then said tentatively, "I'd rather go."

He wanted to hold her forever and never let her out of his arms, but instinct gave a twang of warning. He couldn't force her to stay and he wouldn't want to. "It's no trouble," he said firmly, and he kissed her soundly on the neck. "Want a shower first?"

Addison giggled. "I can't decide which would be worse, going back to Wendy's freshly showered, or smelling like this."

"I like how you smell," Roderick told her, and he turned his kisses into licks into nibbles until they were tickling and giggling and, inevitably, kissing again.

"I should shower," Addison agreed with a contented sigh.

He showed her the bathroom and the trick with the shower knob.

"Isn't a plumber supposed to have the latest in perfectly working faucets and fixtures?" Addison teased him.

"The cobbler's children are the last to have shoes," Roderick countered.

"Are you going to watch me do this?" Addison asked when he

settled on the closed toilet to gaze at her through the steam-frosted door.

"Do you mind?" Roderick asked.

She replied by wiping the steam off suggestively and soaping her breasts.

Roderick was tempted to sketch her. She was so perfectly female, so everything that set him on fire.

But sketching in steamy rooms was hard on paper, and he lacked confidence that he could capture with a pencil that exact way that her back met her ass, the way her arms flowed, the lines of her legs. He satisfied himself with trying to memorize her instead and met her at the door when the shower turned off with a fluffy towel to wrap her in.

He put a kiss on her head and traded places, gratified that she seemed as interested in watching him shower as he'd been in watching her.

"You could do bachelorette parties," she suggested when he emerged. She found him a towel, and they dried each other off with plenty of distraction.

"Addison," Roderick said after she'd gotten dressed and was looking for her shoes.

She looked up with a dreamy smile, holding up her last shoe. "Yes?"

He wanted to ask her to marry him on the spot but hauled himself back. They were taking it slow, not rushing. He shouldn't declare his love yet, and the idea surprised him, not because he thought that he shouldn't, but because he wanted to.

He loved this beautiful, big-hearted woman to the very bottom of his soul, and it wasn't just the aftermath of their toe-curling sex or the curious tingle of instinct making everything faintly magical.

He simply loved her, from her smile to her nurturing spirit, from her strawberry-blonde hair—it was back into its usual crinkly curls after the shower—to her clever fingertips. This was the woman that would complete his life in a way he'd never even known he needed.

"It can wait," he said. "Let's get you home before curfew."

He left her on Wendy's steps with a lingering kiss and returned to his house, weirdly and unsettlingly quiet with neither his daughter nor his mate.

*It isn't home without them,* his wolf agreed.

# CHAPTER 25

*A*ddison floated into Wendy's house, not even caring that her feet still hurt.

Who even *needed* feet, after Roderick had done *that* to her whole body?

"I guess I don't need to ask how your date went!" Wendy exclaimed, coming out of the kitchen. She was wearing plastic gloves that went up to her elbows and an oversized shirt that had once been white and was now stained in clashing colors.

Addison kicked off her shoes and flopped down on a clear square of the couch. "The steaks were very, very good."

"A date with good *meat* is always a good sign," Wendy said with a wink as she sat down on the footstool across from her. "Why are you home? I didn't expect to see you until morning."

"It was just our third date," Addison protested. She didn't try to deny that she'd enjoyed her *meat*; her hair was still damp. "We're not moving that fast." Were they? Staying a night seemed further, faster than just sex.

"He's not Owen," Wendy reminded her.

Addison felt a flutter in her chest that she recognized as the reservations she was still holding onto. "I know," she said gravely.

"Owen was an asshole," Wendy said frankly.

"He didn't seem like an asshole at first," Addison protested. "He was so nice! Everyone liked him! What if...?"

"Roderick is not Owen," Wendy said firmly. "What does your instinct tell you?"

"You can't understand instinct," Addison snapped. She felt bad at once. "I mean...I don't mean..."

Wendy's mouth went to a thin line. "I'm not a shifter, so I can't understand what it's like to be one," she agreed, her voice carefully neutral. "But I know people a little, and I know you're still hung up on the fact that Owen took you for a ride. He gaslighted you and preyed on your trusting nature and isolated you from your friends and tried to control you, and you got *out*. Don't you let him keep his claws in you after all this time."

Addison looked at her hands. "At least I didn't marry him," she agreed. "Or have kids."

"But are you going to let him keep you from *ever* marrying or having kids? It's been years."

Addison could feel the truth in Wendy's words, the pointed observation. "It's not like Roderick and I are anywhere *near* the point of talking about marriage or having kids," she said defensively. It scared her that she wanted to be. She wanted to settle down to a home of her own, a family. And she wanted that with Roderick and Gabby. Was that yearning confusing her instinct? How much could she trust magic anyway?

Then she remembered, "Gabby's mom is back in town."

Wendy looked thoughtful. "But you're the one who had a date tonight."

That probably meant something. Addison hugged a throw pillow to her chest. "It's late," she said. "I should turn in."

She brushed her teeth and stared at her reflection. She shouldn't have given Wendy a hard time about not being a shifter. It galled her that she was dependent on Wendy's hospitality, she realized. Since Owen, she'd hated having to rely on anyone. It gave them power over her.

But trusting people—the right people—wasn't losing power. She could trust Wendy. She could trust Roderick.

Could she trust instinct?

Wendy was painting the kitchen—squeezing paint directly onto her brushes—when Addison came out of the bathroom.

"You know, you're right," Addison told her.

"I'm always right," Wendy teased, no hint of anger or resentment in her voice. Wendy never held onto anything, and Addison envied her that carefree attitude. "What was I right about this time?"

"Roderick isn't Owen."

"Good thing," Wendy scoffed. "The world doesn't need more than one of those. I'm not sure it needed the one, either." She glanced sideways at Addison. "That jerk took you for a ride and then chased you half across the country and it's no wonder you're a little gun shy. No one is going to object if you want to take it slow, least of all Roderick."

"Thanks, Wendy," Addison said sincerely. "For everything."

"Hotel Wendy always has a room for her favorite cousin," Wendy said, putting an abstract scarlet sweep across her canvas. "You're a good roommate. You don't eat too much and you pay your share of groceries. No noisy parties. No pet giraffes."

Addison hugged her from behind, mindful of the wet paint on her brush and hands. "Good night."

"Sleep well," Wendy said cheerfully. "I imagine you've got a lot to dream about!"

Addison settled into her creaking air mattress and stared at the ceiling. Wendy had painted a mural there, a colorful space-scape with shooting stars. One of the nebulae looked a little like a bird on fire.

How much more comfortable would she have been staying the night with Roderick? Was she letting her past keep her from the future she wanted, that her lynx knew was right for her?

She shifted restlessly, listening to the distinct squeak of the air mattress, and after a while, she got up to find a notebook and start writing.

# CHAPTER 26

*R*oderick woke up early, to a silent house, and couldn't get back to sleep. He checked his texts. Nothing from Ian. Nothing from Addison. Should he call her? Text her an eggplant or whatever it was that people did these days?

He puttered around in the kitchen, repairing a cabinet door he'd meant to fix for weeks now, checking the expiration dates of the food in the pantry. The quiet made him antsy. Surely Gabriella was chewing on electrical cords or strangling herself with dish towels or ordering pet gorillas on Amazon with his phone, being quiet this long. It was so odd not having her there.

He found music files he hadn't listened to since she'd been born, favorite bands and songs that weren't exactly child-appropriate, and after only a few songs, turned them off and put on a Baby Bop playlist.

He finally decided it was late enough and texted Ian, "I can come to get her any time."

Then he texted Addison, "Thought I'd take Gabby to the Nickel City memorial park, want to join us?"

Addison must have been holding her phone and possibly she fumbled it because the tease of her three dots typing something was on the screen immediately and lasted for so long that Roderick ran out of breath holding it.

Ian answered first. "Feeding her pancakes now. She's eating the blueberries out of them. Ready to go when you are. No rush."

Roderick texted him a hasty thumbs up in reply because Addison answered then as well: "I'd love to! Say wen." A second text followed: "When!"

Roderick dredged his mind for a clever reply. "When!" seemed too flippant. And maybe it would look like he was trying to correct her typo when she already had? "Picnic lunch at noon?" he suggested. It was already mid-morning, which would give him time to fetch Gabby and pack a basket.

"Sure! See you at the swings!"

He did not actually have a basket, but an insulated membership warehouse bag would do, and it had room for a few extra diapers and wipes, plus some ice packs and cold drinks. He made sandwiches in every flavor he had ingredients for, tossed in some squeeze applesauce and milk in a covered sippy cup for Gabby. And blueberries, of course.

He completely forgot about Dana until he got her text alert. He slapped the sandwich he was working on together and dived for the phone, heart in his throat. At first, there was only disappointment that it wasn't from Addison.

"Would like to see you and Gabby again," Dana wrote, with a sideways smiley face.

Was he wrong about her intentions? It was so hard to tell through a text, and instinct was no help right now.

He'd been clear with her that he wasn't interested in getting together, though he hadn't been sure what to tell her about Addison beyond a super vague 'I'm seeing someone.' He certainly couldn't explain to her about instinct; she didn't even know about shifters.

After a moment, he decided not to answer Dana. Not right away. He wasn't at her beck and call. He put the sandwiches in baggies and tucked them into the chilled bag, then sighed and tapped out a reply. "Busy today." Too brief? He didn't want to be too encouraging, so he decided it was good enough and sent it.

"Ok," was her equally brief reply.

Women were minefields, he decided wryly, and somehow he'd gone from one in his life that he could football-carry to three of them, all of them with expectations he barely understood.

Ian looked like he had survived the babysitting and the night, but just barely. "They slept great until about five AM," he said wryly. "Then we had a disco party, a tea party, a couple of fights over toys, and a fashion show, I think. There was a nap at about nine, so you might be safe until after lunch."

"I owe you," Roderick said sincerely. "I mean, I *really* owe you."

Ian grinned. "*Really*, huh? Well, good for you. Is that Cherry's hire at the day care? Miss Frizzle Poppins?"

Roderick grinned and didn't bother answering.

As fussy as Gabby had been about being left with Lucy and Ian, now she didn't want to leave them. She and Lucy tried to hide behind the couch, their legs sticking out.

"That's okay," Roderick said loudly, going to the door. "I'll go on a picnic by myself with allll the blueberries."

"Gaba ababa eeee!" Gabby gave a squawk of protest and crawled out over Lucy, straight to Roderick to pull herself up on his legs and stretch her free arm up to him.

"I dread the day that blueberries lose their bargaining power," Roderick admitted to Ian as they chuckled, and he gathered up all of Gabby's things and swung her up into his arms.

"Want to go see Teacher Addy at the park?" he teased her.

"Abab," Gabby groused, clearly suspecting that she'd been had.

～

*A*ddison was waiting for them on a picnic bench by the baby swings. There was a whole section of the park set aside for younger kids, with fragrant bark under low seesaws and short slides. A train-shaped jungle gym pulled a few platforms with plastic zoo animals on springs that could be ridden.

"I brought lunch," Roderick said, hoisting the overfull bag. "I wasn't sure what you wanted, so I made peanut butter, tuna fish, and turkey with lettuce and tomato."

"You give me the hardest choices!" Addison laughed and when she tipped her face up, Roderick gladly kissed her.

"Oh, but wait," Roderick teased. "I also have plain *and* barbeque chips to choose between."

"The agony!" Addison lamented.

"Ababa," Gabby said firmly. She had her eyes fixed on the giraffe. "Ababa!"

"Would you like to lay out lunch while we say hello to the local wildlife?" Addison offered, opening her hands to Gabby.

Gabby's initial interest in the big square-spotted giraffe swiftly turned to terror when she realized how tall it was and Addison took her instead to the lion, which Gabby was willing to pat and babble to.

Roderick had unpacked the lunch by the time they came back.

"You weren't kidding about the sandwich choices," Addison said, sitting beside him with Gabby in her lap. "What should I have, Gabby?"

Gabby reached forward and helpfully handed her a sandwich, pausing to maul it only a little bit before Addison could pluck it away. "Tuna fish! Good choice!"

Roderick took the turkey sandwich and offered a piece to Gabby, who stuffed it in her mouth and then looked at him dubiously. She chewed for a few moments, then reached into her mouth and extracted a piece of lettuce, which she offered back to Roderick. He and Addison laughed, and the lettuce was dropped onto the park bench and fell down to the ground.

That caught the attention of a squirrel, who braved the far end of the picnic table and eyed them warily.

Gabby stretched her hands out and strained against Addison's arm. "Ababa gabby eeeee!"

The squirrel wisely fled.

"That's not Lucy, honey," Roderick told her. "That's just a squirrel."

The rest of the picnic was blissful; it was a sunny day, with just enough of a breeze to keep bugs down. It smelled like late summer grass and pine trees. From across the park, older kids were noisily playing on the taller equipment and a few teenagers were pushing each other on the merry-go-round.

Gabby was not terribly hungry. She grudgingly ate a few bites of each of their sandwiches, then they let her down to play in the bark chips and skootch around the picnic table holding onto the bench. She didn't offer to let go and walk free-standing.

"I shouldn't be concerned that she's not walking yet, should I?" Roderick couldn't help asking.

Addison smiled knowingly. "Not in the slightest. Kids get to these milestones when they're ready, and walking late doesn't seem to have even a tiny impact on how they do later in life. I'd guess she's close, just look at her thinking about it!"

Roderick said sheepishly, "I see Amy cruising around, and she's younger."

Addison nodded. "Amy's also shifting already, she's got precocious gross motor skills, but she doesn't make a lot of sounds yet, and she hasn't mastered the same fine motor skills that Gabby has. Have you ever seen a dog try to get a whole pile of tennis balls in their mouth at once?"

Roderick had to laugh at the mental image.

"Kids are like that," Addison explained. "They're trying to hold onto all those tennis balls of skills, and they'll eventually master them all, but if they try to do them all at *once*, they'll just end up chasing them all endlessly. Gabby's doing great. I'm not the slightest bit concerned. One of these days she's just going to take off. You'll forget you were ever worried and wonder why you wanted to hit this milestone in the first place."

Roderick bumped her shoulder with his, grateful. "See, you should be writing those parenting books. The slobbery dog with a mouthful of balls is an image that is always going to stick with me."

Addison shuddered dramatically. "My books couldn't be worse than some of what's out there," she agreed. "Speaking of books, though, I wanted to talk to you about that project I had in mind."

They spent several hours at the park, putting their heads

together over Addison's notes and playing with Gabby on the equipment. The toddler was full of mixed feelings about the swings, tolerated being held on the seesaw, and was completely unwilling to let go of Roderick to slide down the short slide, no matter how they tried to coax her.

Her eye-rubbing need for an afternoon nap finally broke up the party.

"She usually sleeps for about forty-five minutes in the afternoon," Roderick told her as they gathered everything up and convinced Gabby they weren't abandoning Lucy the squirrel in the park. "Care to come over…?"

"I promised Wendy I'd help her transplant some peonies later this afternoon," Addison said regretfully. "But maybe tomorrow?"

Roderick winced, remembering Dana again for the first time since he'd brushed her off.

Addison was watching his face as he strapped Gabby into the car seat, and Roderick wasn't sure if her instinct made her guess, "Dana?"

Roderick frowned. "I'd rather see you," he said firmly, shutting the door on Gabby's squirrel-centered protests.

"It's not one or the other," Addison said gently. "You've got business to discuss, it's much more important that you settle…whatever needs settling. Text me if you're free in the afternoon, but I'm not an obligation. I'm not going to be jealous."

"You could never be an obligation," Roderick said sincerely. "I'll text you."

The following day, however, followed another largely sleepless night, and an hour-long screaming fit that meant Roderick scrubbed plans with both Dana and Addison, being vague with the former and honest with the latter: *Have lost my mind and haven't slept. Daughter possessed by demons apparently. We're taking a quiet day.*

She texted back with a heart emoji that Roderick tried not to read too much into.

No one had said anything about love.

# CHAPTER 27

The front door chime buzzed and Addison deftly fished her phone from her pocket, baby Shane in one arm and a cat tantalizer in the other; she was playing with several of the shifter kids practicing catch and chase dexterity in their animal forms.

Roderick was at the door, distorted by the camera but absolutely unmistakable. Just as Addison's heart leaped in her chest and her fingers reached for the unlock button, a strange woman walked up to him on the sidewalk and began talking to him. Addison wasn't quite swift enough in recognizing the danger to stop her own finger, and the door buzzed open.

Addison's lungs froze at their body posture. Roderick went as tense as a stalking wolf and the woman looked strung as tightly as a bear trap. Her accidental buzz had not gone unnoticed. Even without sound on her phone, it was obvious that the woman was asking to go in, and pointing out that the door had been unlocked. Roderick shook his head and set himself firmly in her way.

Addison swiftly did a headcount of the kids, assessing the danger. Most of them were in human form, but Jennifer was napping as a puppy and Robert and Gil looked dangerously near having a fight; shifting accidentally was most likely to happen when emotions were running high. They couldn't risk having someone in who didn't know the shifter secret.

It must be Dana, she realized, and she caught herself glaring at the woman's handsome profile. Addison had told Roderick that she wasn't jealous, but she hadn't realized that Dana would be so pretty and fashionable. She looked like she'd just stepped out of a salon. Addison had already been spit up on twice that day and Tara had spent some time 'styling' her hair.

Adrenaline surged in her veins, but none of it was instinct, Addison realized. She was alarmed, and jealous, and worried that she'd screwed up by buzzing the door open with a stranger nearby, but instinct wasn't one of the many emotions surging through her. She didn't have a danger sense, even though the situation certainly warranted one.

*You could have warned me,* she snapped at her lynx.

Her lynx only gave her an impression of pointedly grooming.

Addison got Shane down in a crib and after talking with Roderick a little longer, Dana finally left. Addison breathed a sigh of relief and unlocked the door again. Only after she had buzzed it open did she realize that it would be obvious that she'd been watching.

She went to meet Roderick at the gate with Gabby walking in front of her holding onto her hands. She stopped a little ways away, to give Gabby a chance to take steps on her own if she wanted to— she knew how much Roderick would enjoy seeing the moment!— but Gabby stubbornly fell down on all fours and crawled the final distance, babbling happily.

Roderick gave her a big smile and swept her into his arms for a hug, then sobered, looking at Addison.

"I told her about you," he said.

What did he tell her? Addison was wild with curiosity. Did he make her out to be his girlfriend? *Was* she his girlfriend? They hadn't really talked about it.

But maybe they should.

"What, exactly, did you tell her?"

"I told her that I was seeing you, that I was seeing you *seriously.*

And that this wasn't how I wanted the two of you to meet. It was all I could think of to explain why she couldn't come in while I got Gabby."

*Seriously.*

The word made her heart sing.

Addison wasn't sure what her face showed, but it must have concerned Roderick.

"I've been wanting to talk to you about this," he said. "About us."

Gabby patted his cheek. "Gaba aba baba," she said firmly.

"About all of us," Roderick agreed. "Addison, I know we said we weren't going to rush…"

The door behind him buzzed. Addison swiftly checked her phone. "It's Amy's mom," she said apologetically. "Shea's coming tomorrow, why don't we have lunch, the four of us?"

"With *Dana?*"

"I can't exactly invite her in here," Addison said practically. "Your place won't feel like neutral ground, and Wendy's would be…oh gosh, just no. If we're all going to be a part of Gabby's life, I should meet her, we should talk about what that's going to look like. Right?"

Roderick looked at her like she'd just hung stars in the sky. "Right," he agreed, a slow smile blooming over his face. "I'll text her and arrange something."

The door buzzed again, as Amy's mom got impatient, and she heard Cherry call from the playroom, "I got it!" and the door unlocked.

Roderick gathered up Gabby's things, then paused at the door long enough that Addison wondered if she should hop over the gate and give him a parting kiss.

The moment passed before she could seize it and she went to get Amy ready to go.

# CHAPTER 28

"Well," Roderick said with forced humor as he sat down at the table with their order number on a stick. "Here are all the women in my life in one place."

He winced, wondering if he should have worded it differently, but Addison didn't look offended, and Dana only looked a little skeptical, like she wasn't sure if she should laugh.

Gabby pounded her sippy cup on the tray in approval. "Ababba bee!"

If anyone had told him two weeks ago that he would agree to have lunch out with his fourteen-month daughter, her estranged mother, and his new maybe-girlfriend, Roderick would have doubted their sanity.

It had been Addison's idea, and he reluctantly decided that it was sensible. If Dana was going to be any part of Gabby's life, she was going to have to accept Addison's role in it, even if Roderick and Addison were still figuring out exactly what that was themselves. Gabby wouldn't understand their conversation, but she was the perfect neutral companion: a distracting element who was perfectly happy to be the center of their attention.

The fast-food restaurant at the edge of town, Burger-Z, was safe neutral ground; Roderick hadn't wanted to taint his enjoyment of Heads Up Cafe in case this meeting went terribly, terribly sideways, and the fast food chain had booths that were deep and private.

But he needn't have worried. Both Addison and Dana were both clearly determined to make the best of the meeting; they shook hands and smiled at each other from the beginning. His wolf gave a snuffle of amusement at his concern, content that things were happening exactly as they should. His instinct gave him no warnings even though logic told him this could be a very fraught lunch.

"I understand you're new to Nickel City," Dana said across the table to Addison. It could have been a slight, reminding her how new her relationship with Roderick was, but to his relief, Addison didn't seem to take it that way.

"Yes, I just moved from Buffalo, New York."

Dana whistled. "That's quite a change."

"I was looking for a change," Addison agreed mildly. "I just didn't realize how much of a change it would be." She cast a quick glance his way and blushed a little. Roderick considered taking her hand but thought that it might look too pointed.

"You work at the new day care that Gabby goes to?" Dana continued easily.

"Yes. Before that, I was a private nanny for a couple in New York."

Was Addison trying to prove her qualifications for taking care of Gabby over Gabby's own mother? Roderick had not realized what a minefield common topics could be, and he wondered how to tell her that she didn't have to prove anything, not to him, and not to Dana.

No one asked if Dana was staying long and they skirted politely around the topic of Addison and Roderick's relationship. They talked at length about Gabby, her antics at day care, Roderick's tribulations as a single dad, and his plumbing work. "So I pulled a red glove out of this drainpipe, and that's a little unusual, but not all that unexpected. But two weeks later, a second red glove, clogging up the inlet to a septic tank across town. What are the chances? It's eerie, is what it is."

He wasn't sure when he actually took Addison's hand, or if she had taken his, but he had to let go of her when their order arrived.

That led the conversation casually to food and Gabby added her own bubbly opinions of the meal and the company.

The topic went back to employment, and to Dana's advertising work. "My most lucrative work is for toothpaste companies," she said with a laugh. "If you ever need free samples, hit me up. But I also do public relations for nonprofits and charities. I did some of the advertising for Nickel City's tourist board when I was...last here."

She didn't have to explain what had happened the last time she was here, and Addison swiftly gave a forced laugh and observed, "It certainly was effective advertising. It's hard to find parking in town, and I'm still trying to find a place to rent."

For a moment, Roderick feared that the lunch was going to turn hostile, but Dana seemed as invested in making sure that things went smoothly as Addison was. "I'm staying at the Gold Mine hotel and they've got a lot of vacant rooms, but I've noticed that there are a lot of tourists. I guess most people are renting houses? I talked with the hotel owner for a while this morning. Grace, I think. She's quite a character. Lots of strong opinions."

"There's an assembly meeting on that topic next week," Addison said, suddenly snapping her fingers. "Something about adding some restrictions for short-term rentals and applying a rent freeze. Wendy—that's my cousin, I'm staying with her until I can find a place—she gave me a flyer. I was going to ask you if you planned to go to it, Roderick."

Dana glanced between them curiously—had she thought that Addison was living with him?

"I'd like to go," Roderick said. "I got the flyer, too. But the meeting runs through Gabby's dinner and bath time and I'm sure it will be a long one. Residents are pretty riled up it, and I'd like to weigh in. They're taking written testimony, and I figured I'd send some, but I always wonder how seriously they take it. To be honest, I imagine it's going to be quite a show and I'm sorry to miss it."

"It sounds like a major Nickel City event," Addison agreed. "I'd love to go just to people-watch."

The downside to sitting next to Addison was that it put him across the booth from Dana, and Roderick was trying hard to balance not staring at her and not pointedly looking away from her. He'd rather be gazing at Addison. But in that case, he'd be seated next to Dana, and that didn't seem any more correct. And the only other choice was to put both of them sitting together across from him like he was in a bachelor game show.

So he was watching Dana's face when he mentioned wanting to attend the meeting, and he saw the thought occur to her as she spoke. "I could watch Gabby."

Roderick and Addison went quiet. Gabby tried to fill the silence with her babble, excitedly eating the chicken nuggets on her tray at the same time with very mixed results and a spray of breading.

Dana seemed to recognize that she was taking a risk with the offer, and she quickly added, "I don't mean to assume that you'd trust me. I know that's a lot to ask. I'm sure it's too soon."

Roderick still didn't speak, conferring with his wolf curiously. His instinct was quiet, suggesting that there was no major risk. Dana would care for her daughter, and he didn't have to worry that she would run off with her or try to stake some kind of claim on her.

Without thinking about how it might appear, he turned to look at Addison, wondering what her instinct would tell her.

She met his eyes thoughtfully and Roderick tried to read what was there. She didn't look particularly worried, just intrigued. She glanced at Gabby, who was already getting bored with eating chicken nuggets and was just playing with them making various noises that weren't quite syllables.

"Does she know a lot of words?" Dana asked quickly into the silence that was beginning to feel tense.

"She says a lot," Roderick said, "but I'm not sure how much of it counts as real words. She has some animal sounds that she makes."

"Addy!" Gabby said, but she didn't look at Addison when she said it, so it might have meant anything.

"She understands a lot more than she can say, and she'll burst into real words before you know it," Addison said knowingly. "And then sentences, and then you'll wonder if she will ever stop talking, ever once, for a moment."

"Abababa gabba."

Everyone laughed, but Roderick could feel the underlying tension at the table. Dana thought she'd overreached and Roderick wasn't sure how to assure her that she hadn't. Addison wasn't sure if she should offer opinions on the subject. No one was exactly sure where they fit. Except for Gabby, who knew she was the center of all the attention and loved it. He wasn't surprised when she started fussing. "I suspect that someone needs a new diaper. We'll be back."

Roderick was glad that Nickel City was progressive enough to have changing tables in men's rooms at restaurants; he could only imagine how challenging it would have been for a single dad when he was a kid. He gathered Gabby from the high chair and picked up her bag. She shrieked and, although it was a happy shriek, they were still the object of a fair amount of attention as he carried her away from Dana and Addison, not sure which of all of them he felt sorry for.

"Sorry that this is so complicated, kid," he told Gabby after he had swabbed the table down one-handed and laid her down onto it.

She was cooperative for the changing, cheerfully holding her clean diaper for him and gravely commenting on the decor of the bathroom. "Tuh-tuh!" she said, pointing at a car.

"I want you to have a chance to know your mom," Roderick told her seriously as he got the wet diaper wrapped up on itself and took the clean diaper from her to unfold.

"I think it's important that you know who she is, and it's not the right thing to do to cut her out of your life. I know that she thought she didn't want you, but I can't really blame her for being scared, or for realizing later that she was wrong about it. We've all made mistakes along the way."

"Ha ha!" Gabby agreed.

Roderick smiled down at her. "My future is with Addison, honey, instinct knows. I'm not going to lose her, and I'm not sure how to make her understand that I'm not picking Dana over her by letting Dana see you. And now I have to decide if I'm comfortable having her watch you all by herself. Instinct says you'll be fine, but she's never been around kids, will she know what to do? You can be a handful, sweetheart, and you're nearly ready for your next big milestone."

She tingled to his senses, but only faintly, and his instinct wasn't warning him to whisk her safely home. Wouldn't it? He wrapped the new diaper around her, snugging the tabs around her waist and checking around her legs for any folds or wrinkles.

She giggled and kicked playfully. "Let's get you dressed, squirt," Roderick told her, trying to tuck a leg back into the leg of her pants. "One thing you can count on," he continued warmly, "I will always be your dad, and having two moms around isn't the worst thing in the world."

Then, to his chagrin, there was the sound of a flushing toilet from the single stall that he hadn't thought to verify was empty.

The gray-haired man who came out as he was trying to get Gabby's second leg into her pants looked as embarrassed as he felt, and they exchanged a sheepish smile. He wasn't a shifter, or Roderick would have sensed him, and Roderick cast back over his one-sided conversation with Gabby, hoping he hadn't said anything too incriminating.

"Pretty deep thoughts for a men's room in Burger-Z," the man said with a chuckle. "But she's a good listener."

"Gabba babba," Gabby agreed.

"You follow that instinct, son," the man said, alarming Roderick. But he didn't seem to give the term any unnecessary weight. "And keep taking care of that precious little thing."

"She'll always be the first lady in my life," Roderick agreed.

*Follow that instinct, son.*

He was a human. It probably didn't mean anything.

# CHAPTER 29

*A*ddy eyed Dana over the table and caught Dana eying her back. They pretended neither of them noticed the awkwardness, and Addy tried to prod her instinct into revealing...anything.

There was no sense of warning from her shifter magic, but no encouragement, either, which meant all she had to go on were her general impressions of Dana. Between Roderick's story and this brief meeting, Dana seemed to be driven, self-sufficient, and capable, but she was also forthright, and she seemed shaken and subdued.

Addy knew herself: she was a sucker for a story of grief. Owen had a compelling story of loss, too, and her sympathy for him had overwhelmed the warnings of her instinct. Well, that and her attraction.

But she didn't feel like she and Roderick were being played by Dana.

"This must be kind of weird," she said sympathetically when Roderick had taken Gabby to the bathroom, drawing all the eyes in the restaurant with their loud and adorable progress.

Dana gave a little snort of laughter. "'Kind of' doesn't even cover it." She chased the last of her drink with her straw and then went on. "I honestly thought I knew what I was doing when I walked away. I felt like *I* was the martyr, giving up nearly a year of my life. And I...just had no idea."

Addy refrained from reaching across the table to her. "It would have been so big and scary," she said, only thinking after she said it that she sounded like she was talking to one of the kids at the day care. Would Dana think it was insulting? "I mean, a baby is a lot." She wasn't helping, she feared, and she wasn't good at grown-up talks, even if she could carry on very long and meaningful conversations about socks and cupcakes.

"Roderick's done really well at it." Addy could hear the hitch in Dana's low voice. "And I'm glad I got to meet you. Gabby is a lucky girl, and I'm...really happy that she'll have such a great family."

The idea tripped Addy up.

A family. *Her* family.

She had thought about Roderick in that way, of course she had, but she'd been so careful to keep it one slow step at a time that she forgot to look at the finish line.

A family. The two of them together with Gabby.

Instinct swelled in her like music. That was the direction of her happiness.

"You don't have to worry about me," Dana said, oblivious to Addy's realization. "I won't try to get the papers changed or anything. I'll leave. I just had to see her, I guess, to know for sure that she was okay and I hadn't ruined her life. I thought maybe I could make it up to her somehow, or rescue her, but it turns out that me leaving was the best thing I could have done for her after all."

"She's in good hands," Addison agreed. Then she worried that it had come out wrong. "I don't mean mine, I mean Roderick's. I... to be honest, you caught us at a really weird point. We haven't been dating long, and we're still figuring out how we work together."

"I didn't mean to complicate things," Dana said firmly.

"I think it's just generally complicated," Addison chuckled. "But we'll figure it all out, the best way for Gabby, and..." Would it be too ridiculous of her to hope they could be friends? Was it too trusting and naïve of her? Magic wasn't giving her any help, but it rarely did unless the case was extreme.

Roderick returned with Gabby then, and all of them apologetically realized that they had places to be. Roderick had a plumbing appointment and Dana was meeting a girlfriend for coffee.

"Gabby and I have a nap time to attend," Addison said cheerfully. She wondered if Dana didn't think she was utterly inane, then wondered why she cared.

She carried Gabby out to Roderick's car and buckled her in while he talked solemnly with Dana at her car. She wasn't trying to watch them, but she saw them shake hands as they parted. Would it have been a casual embrace if she hadn't been there? Or something more?

Instinct gave a curious little twinge that wasn't warning, almost as if it was laughing at her insecurity.

# CHAPTER 30

"*J*'ve never been to anything *like* this," Addison confessed to Roderick several nights later at the assembly meeting. "Does it happen a lot in Nickel City?"

"This is kind of a big deal," Roderick said. "Most meetings have a couple of outraged people and a few gossips with nothing better to do. This is quite a turnout. Maybe the webpage helped?"

Addison and Roderick had put together a simple webpage called "Neighborhoods for Neighbors" laying out the issue and then posted the link on local social media. Roderick had designed a few graphics for it and Wendy had shared it with an entire army of local artists who had taken it viral.

The courthouse/conference room/community center was crowded, with every seat taken and the aisles filled with standing people. Addison's senses tingled; a surprising number of the citizens who had shown up were magic of some kind, she could tell, and the room was roughly divided; the shifters clustered together to one side and the humans filling the rest of the room, with only a few exceptions.

She recognized some people, Roderick said hello to many more. They crowded together behind the last row of seats in the shifter corner. A few of them had signs that said, "Neighborhoods for Neighbors."

As the meeting was called to order and people began to step forward and offer testimony, it became clear that the divide in the room was more than just magical.

The human side was against the legislation, almost entirely. Business owners cited the upswing in tourist trade as an economic boom that benefited everyone, realtors complained that they would lose their pending sales, landlords made swift, sometimes sideways complaints about how much new legislation would complicate their business, and what a hardship it would be for them.

The shifter side couldn't lobby directly for keeping their privacy for protecting their secrets, but there were several heartfelt statements about how neighborhoods should remain neighborhoods, how they felt unsafe with strangers perpetually driving into their cul de sacs, and how the visitors sometimes had large, unregulated parties, which called out local sheriffs. One of the speakers brought up the topic of increased theft, as the short-term rentals became a target of petty criminals and put nearby houses at risk as well. There were many glares to the far side of the room as people spoke passionately about being evicted from their houses and unable to find affordable options within an easy commute of their work and schools while the landlords who had spoken earlier looked stony and unforgiving. A few looked guilty but stubborn.

The testimony went on for several hours with no break, and Addison felt sorry for the assembly members, who were mostly human with just two shifters among them. They were all yelled at by both parties and struggled to keep the statements short and focused on the topic. At one point, she thought that two older men were going to come to blows over a property dispute that had exactly nothing to do with short-term rentals or lease regulations.

Roderick took a turn at the little table facing the assemblymen.

"I'm not saying that people don't need to make a living," he said, with a polite nod in general at the human side. "But there are ways to do things that are good for us all long term, and there are ways that aren't. We all rise together, and if we're squeezing solid citizens out in favor of riding a popularity bubble, we'll all suffer together when it pops. I think that the rental restrictions are smart and I want to keep my neighbors."

He received a smattering of applause and a few derisive laughs.

The assembly got more proactive about cutting people off when they got to their time limit. Addison wondered if she imagined their willingness to cut off the people in favor of restrictions more than the landlords and realtors, and eventually, they declared the meeting finished and invited citizens to submit further testimony by mail or email.

"I don't think it went very well," Addison said in disappointment when they left the building at last.

"Veronica has many...well, I don't know if I can call them friends," Roderick said unhappily. "She has a lot of influence here, owns a lot of property. It wouldn't surprise me that she has an assemblyman or two in her pocket, too."

"Do you think the webpage got them worried?" Addison asked.

"They seemed pretty organized," Roderick said thoughtfully. "Maybe it scared them a little."

"Why are there so many of...us...here?" Addison asked as she walked with Roderick to his truck. It was nearly dark now, the sun casting just a smudge of light in the sky, and they had parked quite far from the city center due to tourist traffic that had mostly dispersed.

Roderick unlocked the truck and considered her thoughtfully. "You ever notice how there are lots of trees around here?"

It had become normal at some point, Addison realized. Most of the trees in her neighborhood in Buffalo had been in straight lines or carefully enclosed in iron grates to prevent vandalism.

Here, however, the trees were everywhere. Streets meandered in organic lines around stands of them, as if the town itself were the afterthought to the forest. There was no yard that didn't have several stately guardians.

"I figured that's just how Montana was," she admitted. "Trees and cowboys and state parks."

"This is a pretty special place," Roderick explained. "That

famous tree out by Belle Lake is a dryad, Isadora Larix, and this is her forest."

Addison stood with her jaw dropped, staring around at the trees.

It made a certain amount of sense. That tingling feeling of belonging that was like shifter recognition, but not. That alive sensation she'd gotten the moment she drove into town. She thought at first that it was just the difference between a city and a small town with room for yards and gardens, but she'd been to other places with plants that felt nothing like this. Later, she thought it was her shifter instinct, because Roderick was here and he was the key to so much possible happiness.

"What a wonderful thing," she said in awe. "Does everyone know?"

"Not a lot of people, no," Roderick said. "My mother was told by a friend of hers who says that all the Tree City USAs are run by dryads. It's why Arbor Day is such a big deal here."

Addison laughed in delight and clapped her hands. "Every time I think that Nickel City can't get better," she said happily. She sobered to remember that she might not be able to stay if Cherry couldn't afford both the rent and her salary. She had unconsciously hoped that this meeting would solve all of her problems and magically fix the housing market that felt like her last obstacle to complete happiness.

Roderick opened the passenger door for her, and Addison thought that he was going to lift her up into the truck, but he paused with his hands at her waist and bent to kiss her instead.

It was challenging, finding time to be together that coincided with Gabby's naps or bedtime, without inconveniencing Wendy, who slept lightly and had to be up early, so despite several attempts to repeat their third date, Addison had to be satisfied with lingering kisses.

She thought this would be another of those, until Roderick pointed out, "I told Dana the meeting might run really late. She's not expecting us back just yet."

"The assembly did a pretty good job of keeping it short, considering," Addison said breathlessly against his mouth.

"We could go somewhere…" Rod suggested.

"A hotel?" Addison asked, drawing back in surprise.

"I was thinking the Lake Belle overlook," he chuckled. "But I could be persuaded…"

"Your truck is roomy," Addison said quickly, her disappointment in the results of the meeting turning to anticipation. "And it's a lot less expensive and also we probably won't meet someone you have to pretend not to know."

She didn't have to ask twice. Roderick lifted her into the passenger seat and went swiftly to the driver's seat. He'd barely parked at the overlook before their seatbelts were off and they were reaching for each other.

The truck wasn't quite as spacious as Addison had hoped; the passenger seat didn't slide back all the way because of Gabby's car seat, and the toddler's things occupied most of the bench seat in back.

But the console between the two bucket seats flipped up to reveal a narrow center seat, and Addison didn't care that there was a teething ring underneath her when Roderick got his pants down and her skirt up and they were finally, desperately, moving together.

He held her close, filling her in a way that made her whole body respond with joy and eagerness. She felt wild and fierce, and when her pleasure seemed too keen to bear, he took her higher, to bliss and release.

Best of all, it didn't ebb away to shame or regret afterward, but to pleasant contentment, her instinct humming in delight.

# CHAPTER 31

*R*oderick had some reservations about the idea of going straight home to see the mother of his daughter after passionate (and slightly uncomfortable) truck sex with Addison, but there wasn't much of a way around that unless he stopped at Wendy's to shower...and that sounded more awkward yet.

Addison was running her fingers through her hair as they pulled up, and she checked her reflection in the sun visor mirror briefly, then exchanged a rueful smile with Roderick. "I probably shouldn't care," she said.

"How about my hair?" Roderick asked teasingly. "Did I muss it?"

"Let me check," Addison said gravely and finger-combed his curls vigorously until Roderick was sure they were all standing straight out in a short afro. "That's better," she said breezily.

He kissed her and they laughed and Roderick felt utterly and completely content. This was how it ought to be, his mate at his side, coming home to Gabby after advocating for their neighbors...even if it had been futile. Of course, it wasn't Addison's home officially, yet, but after Dana left, he planned to ask her to stay the night.

Not for sex necessarily—though he wasn't averse to another round—but he wanted to hold her, sleep beside her, wake up with her easily in his arms, cook her breakfast. Maybe Gabby would sleep in a bit and he could kiss Addy awake and learn more about all her most delicious noises.

They walked to the door hand-in-hand and Roderick put the key into the door. "How do you think Dana did?" he asked before he turned it. "Is Gabby asleep?"

"Dana's capable," Addison said with conviction. "But she also had no idea what she was getting into. I'd give her even odds."

Roderick turned the key. "I told her not to worry if she couldn't get Gabby down, we weren't going to be that late."

But it turned out that they were entirely too late.

Dana was standing in the middle of the living room, her hair wild, her clothing disheveled. There was a look of absolute panic and despair on her face...and she was holding onto a tiny, wriggling wolf pup with gigantic paws who was trying to lick everything in reach.

"I'm sorry!" she wept. "I don't know what happened! She was growling and snapping and then...just...I didn't know what happened!"

"Oh, Gabby!" Roderick exclaimed.

Gabby's head swiveled as she recognized Roderick's voice and she gave a yelp and began to struggle in earnest.

"It's okay, you can let her down," Roderick said.

Bemusedly, Dana obeyed.

Gabby capered directly to Roderick and he bent and scooped her up into his arms, where she changed, giggling, back into human-Gabby, stark naked. "Ababa gabba! Tuh-tuh, aba addy!"

"She is *never* going to learn to walk now," he despaired. "Not when she can run everywhere on four legs."

Addison laughed warmly. "Don't worry," she said, leaning in to kiss Gabby on one of her fat cheeks. "All the shifter children I have raised have learned to walk with two legs, right on schedule, regardless of when they walked with four."

Dana was staring at them with wide eyes and something occurred to Roderick.

He glanced at Addison. "My instinct..."

"Mine didn't warn me, either," Addison observed. "I guess because it's not a problem?"

"Did you know she'd do that?" Dana said in outrage.

"Not tonight," Roderick said quickly. "I wouldn't have left her with you if I'd known. I knew she would soon, but I honestly thought I'd have longer." He'd trusted that he would have warning if Gabby was going to shift.

"Are you...can *you?*"

Some things were just easiest to show. Roderick knelt to put Gabby down on the floor and then flowed down on four paws as a big gray wolf next to her. Gabby grabbed onto the ruff at his neck as her legs swayed and threatened to betray her, then she was a puppy again, romping at his feet. Dana backed into the couch and sat down on the arm of it, staring.

Gabby growled and pounced at his paws, falling over onto her side and rolling back up. Her little whip-tail wagged furiously and she gnawed at his leg.

"You're...a werewolf?"

"Shifters," Addison corrected as Roderick crouched down to lick Gabby and nudge her with his nose, rolling her onto her side when she got rough. "We prefer to call ourselves shifters."

That earned her all of Dana's attention. "Then, you're a...shifter, too?"

Addison nodded serenely. "I'm a lynx, not a wolf. I could show you?"

Dana licked her lips and nodded warily.

Addison put her purse down beside the door and in one smooth move was a lynx. She sat down primly, in every way trying not to look threatening. Roderick sat down as well, his tail wagging. He'd never seen her as a lynx before, and she was simply gorgeous. He wanted to draw her, to capture that soft, plush coat and the big, tufted ears with a pencil. Her yellow-green eyes gazed back fondly.

Gabby, realizing that Roderick was ignoring her now, went to try to play with Addison instead. Addison stepped on her with one of her giant, soft paws and licked her soundly until she turned into a little girl again, squealing in equal parts delight and outrage. Addison shifted, as well, and gathered Gabby into her arms as she stood up.

"Addy!" Gabby said happily. Roderick was beginning to suspect that the sound really did mean Addison and wondered if he should be jealous that she had said it before dada.

Dana slid off the arm of the couch to collapse bonelessly onto the seat cushion next to it. "Well, that's certainly something," she said in wonder.

"Honestly, I didn't mean to spring it on you like this," Roderick said, shifting back into human form and standing. "I knew I'd have to tell you eventually if you were serious about being a part of Gabby's life, but I would have given you a little time first, built up to it."

Gabby reached for him, leaning away from Addison, and he walked over to gather her back into his arms, tossing her a little first. She cuddled happily against him, and he exchanged a knowing look with Addison when she started to rub her eyes and lean her head against him in a clear sign that she was winding down and running out of energy. Early shifts took a lot of steam.

"It's been a big day, little girl," he told her. "Your first shift."

"I'm sorry you missed it," Dana said. "I assume it's a milestone like walking or talking."

"One that they don't mention in most baby books," Addison added with a chuckle.

"No, I don't imagine you could," Dana agreed. She looked a little less stunned now, and she laughed and shook her head.

"Do you want me to put Gabby down?" Addison offered.

Gabby clutched harder at Roderick. "No," he said, "I'll do it."

He walked down the hallway and heard a low hum of conversation rise up behind him when he shut Gabby's bedroom door. He put her in a new diaper and a sleeper, snapping her in and then lifting her back into his arms. He held her like that for a long, peaceful moment, limp and trusting against him as she gradually fell asleep.

Filled to his ears with emotion and gratitude and love, he lay her gently down in the crib. She barely stirred, and he tucked her blanket gently around her and kissed her forehead.

She tugged at his senses.

His little girl was a shifter now, and as much as this complicated his life going forward, Roderick was glad for her and felt like he was made of contentment.

# CHAPTER 32

*I*t should have been awkward, being left alone with Dana in Roderick's wake. Addison expected to feel uncomfortable. Threatened, even. Roderick had made a baby with this woman, and Addison herself was still in weird not-committed limbo with him. But instinct told Addison plainly that Dana was no threat. The secret of shifting was safe with her, and she had no designs on Roderick or Gabby.

"Do you want a drink?" Addison offered. "I'm sure Roderick's got something around here."

They ransacked the kitchen and found a liquor cabinet above the fridge, with a bottle of wine and a half-full decanter of fancy-looking single malt whiskey.

"Both," Dana agreed and found glasses in another cabinet.

There was a dining room that looked like it had survived a toddler invasion, and they cleared off half of the table and sat down across from each other.

"So," Addison said, pouring glasses of wine and splashing whiskey unmeasured into the bottom of tumblers.

"So," Dana agreed. "Shifters."

"Shifters," Addison said. She took a sip of the whiskey and shivered and gasped.

Dana downed hers without so much as a wince and Addison gamely gulped the rest of hers down. It burned like fire and she resisted the desire to cough until her eyes watered. "It was probably kind of a shock," she wheezed, clearing her throat. She was such a dork.

"Are there...a lot of you?" Dana wanted to know. "Shifters, I mean?"

Addison still couldn't breathe. "Not many," she choked. "Most of them can drink better than I can."

Dana laughed at that, and Addison gradually got her lungs back under control. When she could smile and talk again, she answered all of Dana's questions.

"It's not werewolf-y like phase of the moon or silver or garlic— no, that's vampires, sorry. We just have an animal companion that we can change shapes with."

"Just one shape, then? Do you want some wine?"

"Yes, please. I should be able to drink that like a civilized person. We each only have one shape. It's genetic, with shifting forms passed from parents to children like hair or eye color. You'll get throwbacks sometimes, a wolf showing up in a line of deer shifters randomly, or an otter in a family of badgers. It usually traces back to that one grandmother no one talks about."

Dana nodded as if that made perfect sense and poured them glasses of wine. "And do you have super strength?" she wanted to know.

"We tend to be a little stronger," Addison explained, taking her glass and sipping it without embarrassing herself again. "But not superhero level feats or anything, just like some people are taller or shorter than others. My senses are a little keener as a human than my cousin's are, but not as good as they are when I'm actually a lynx. Most of my muscles are from slinging children, not from being a shifter."

"That day care Gabby goes to, where you work...it's for shifters, isn't it? That's why Roderick didn't want me coming in."

"You can understand why we have to keep it a secret. And it's especially hard with children who don't know better."

"Are there a lot of day cares for shifters?" Dana asked.

Addison shook her head. "No, not many. Usually, someone has to stay home with shifter children during that age, or a relative watches a few extra kids. I was a nanny for a shifter family. By Kindergarten or first grade, they know how to shift their clothing with them and understand how important it is to keep it all a secret, and babies don't usually shift until they are a year or two old. But I've never seen as many shifters in one town as I've seen here, and there's enough of a market for a full day care. I hope."

Dana nodded thoughtfully. "That makes sense."

They sipped wine in silence for a short time, and Dana finally said, "You said something when you came in tonight, about how your instinct didn't warn you."

Addison considered. "Instinct is hard to explain. I mean, lots of people—humans—have instincts about sketchy people or bad choices. But shifters have that on a different level, warning us of danger, or when to take a chance..." Addison looked up and realized that Roderick was standing in the doorway to the dining room. "Or pointing out a perfect opportunity."

Dana turned and looked at him thoughtfully. "And when we met...?" She looked at her whisky like she regretted saying anything and blamed it.

Roderick took the seat at the end of the table and reached forward to pour himself a shot.

"Instinct isn't an instruction manual or a blinking neon light. I wanted to believe that everything was straightforward like that, and it never is. But I know you were a part of my ultimate happiness because the magic knew that I wouldn't be complete without Gabby. I wanted to believe that meant we should be together, and I ignored it telling me we shouldn't." He downed the shot and looked at Addison. "And it knows that I wouldn't be complete without Addison."

Addison flushed but didn't try to deny a word of it. It was a constant hum now, familiar and comfortable. She was safe, perfectly where she ought to be. "Instinct knows," she agreed.

"Oh, get a room," Dana said, pretending to gag. Everyone laughed, as she meant them to, but Addison thought there was wistfulness behind her teasing.

They talked late into the night, about shifters, Gabby, the importance of secrecy, and how they would proceed.

"Don't change the papers," Dana said. "I'm already half-crazy for that girl, but she is indisputably yours and I don't want this to turn into a grab for power. You keep custody. You know best how to deal with her, by far. I'll be happy with whatever time you want to share. I don't even know what I'm doing with my life right now. I couldn't be in charge of someone else's."

"She should know you, too," Roderick agreed. At some point during the conversation, they had moved to the living room, and Addison was curled comfortably at his side with her feet tucked up on the couch while Dana sat across from them in an old recliner. "We can make that work if you're going to stay around."

"I think I might," Dana said, as if it surprised her, too. "There's something about this little town that I like. Maybe it's an instinct."

They lapsed into companionable quiet until Dana glanced at her phone. "Oh, gosh, it's really late. I should go." She slipped her shoes back on. "I'm okay to drive home now. Thanks for everything."

Everyone stood, and Addison evaluated her own state. She was tired, but the effects of the whiskey and the smoother glass of wine were long gone. She could drive back to Wendy's, too. She caught Roderick watching her out of the corner of his eye as Dana briskly gathered up her jacket and purse.

They walked her to the door and Addison impulsively gave Dana a swift hug, surprising all of them. Dana was stiff, but Addison thought she looked grateful when she stepped back.

She hung back as Roderick closed the door behind Dana, and the house had one of those moments where everything was weirdly quiet, no fridge running, no heater rattling, a small-town-at-midnight kind of silence outside where a dog barking somewhere blocks away was very loud.

Should she ask to stay? She knew she was still carrying baggage from her past, but if Roderick could be big enough to be friendly with the woman who had abandoned him with their child, couldn't she be big enough to remember that Roderick was not Owen?

Because he was certainly not Owen. He had never done a single thing that made her doubt herself or feel unsafe. He had never played her against anyone else or left her swimming in uncertainty. Her instinct was always in alignment with being with him.

She could gather up her purse and go back to Wendy's prying questions and knowing looks, and he would never question her decision or make her second-guess herself or manipulate her into staying.

Or she could trust him, and trust her instinct, and open her heart to the kind of happiness she had never imagined was possible.

"Do you mind if I stay?" she asked, and Roderick's smile was all the answer she needed.

"I wasn't sure if I should ask," he said, drawing her close. "But I was really hoping."

It was very late, and they had already fed their hunger, somewhat uncomfortably, in the truck, but it was still completely natural to tip her face up and slip her arms around him to kiss him passionately.

If they were going to get undressed for bed, they might as well do it slowly, lingering over one another with plenty of appreciation.

And if they were going to do that, they certainly didn't need to *stop* there. He was hard, and she was wet, and it was a very long time before any actual sleep occurred.

# CHAPTER 33

*R*oderick woke up feeling like all the pieces of his life had fallen perfectly into place.

Gabriella was making sleepy might-be-waking-up noises over the baby monitor. Addison was peaceful in his arms, all of her curves in all the right places against him. Everything was right in the world and exactly where it ought to be.

Then he remembered the disappointing assembly meeting and frowned, wondering if there was something else he could do to help his neighbors. And...maybe there *was*.

Gabby gave a cry of protest as sleep escaped her at last and Addison stirred and woke. "Oh, good morning," she said, as Roderick sat up. She rolled onto her back and smiled up at him. "I think your little tyrant wants blueberries."

Roderick wanted to insist that Gabby was *their* tyrant, not just his, but he feared that it would be too much to put on Addison at once. He felt like getting her to sleep over was enough of a triumph; he could make himself be patient for whatever else she was willing to commit to.

"What the tyrant wants, the tyrant gets," he said with exaggerated resignation. He kissed her and might have done much more, but Gabby turned her waking complaint into a true five-alarm wail.

"Duty calls," he said, crawling out of bed.

"Duty does," Addison agreed, drawing out the word like she had when they met.

There was a text from Veronica with an imperious request for his service at one of her rentals. Roderick had no problem letting her know that he had other plans. *Sorry. Taking Addison and Gabby to Belle Lake,* he replied. He didn't mind reminding her of her place in his priorities.

"I have an idea," he told Addison over breakfast. Gabby drank her milk and tried to spill it on her tray, banging her sippy cup upside down.

"But is it a *good* idea?" Addison wanted to know.

"I don't know," Roderick admitted. "But I think it's worth a try."

"Well, now I'm dying to know what it is." Addison's eyes always crinkled up when she was joking, and Roderick thought he'd never tire of watching it happen.

"It's about the assembly," he said.

As he'd feared, Addison's face fell as she remembered the disappointing meeting. "It's stupid that I care so much," she said wryly. "I mean I've been here a few weeks. It's just such a nice place and I'm worried that Cherry won't be able to stay in business if Veronica hikes her rent again. I want the day care to succeed. I want this to be a safe town."

"We still have an ace up our sleeve," he said, hoping to bring back the easy joy.

"What's that?" Addison asked plaintively.

"Isadora Larix."

~

*I*t was not a second or fourth Thursday, so there was a gate across the private access road that led to Isadora's prize-winning tree. But the gate itself was just a yellow truss on a hinge; there was no lock or cable on it.

"Are you sure this is okay?" Addison asked when Roderick climbed back into the truck after opening the gate.

"I guess we'll find out," Roderick said cheerfully. "My mother always said that you'd never get your heart's desire without actually pursuing it. Instinct only gets you so far without hard work and risk."

"I don't know much about dryads," Addison said, as they drove back to the parking area.

It was a good hike from the truck to the tree, and Roderick wondered if he should have brought Gabby's stroller or a baby carrier. She was starting to be an armful.

"It looks different without a bunch of tourists around it," Addison said.

The whole forest seemed to be sort of coiled in anticipation.

"Isadora?" Roderick called, feeling rather foolish. "Isadora Larix?"

Only the wind answered, and the branches of the monstrous tree rustled.

Gabby got bored in his arms and kicked her legs in frustration. "Abab bee addy."

"Maybe it wasn't such a *good* idea," Roderick conceded.

But as they turned to leave, they found that someone had come out of the forest—or simply appeared—behind them. Addison gave a squeak of surprise and squeezed Roderick's arm.

She was a white-haired woman with a worn, bark-brown face, wearing a simple Native dress of deerskin. Her feet were bare.

"You called?"

"I saw you!" Addison said in astonishment. "When I came to see the tree on my first day here. You were...dressed differently."

Isadora—it had to be her!—sniffed. "I was here for hundreds of years before settlers. I am not constrained to a limited window of human fashion."

"Of course not," Addison said swiftly. "I didn't intend offense."

"None was taken," Isadora said magnanimously. "But I'm sure you didn't call me to discuss clothing trends."

Addison smiled shyly. "I'd honestly love to some time, but no, that's not why we are here." She looked at Roderick.

Isadora smiled back and turned her gaze to Roderick as well. "Alright, then? What do you want?"

Roderick cleared his throat and bounced Gabby in his arms to calm her down. "I don't know how much local politicking you follow, but you may understand that your forest has been a refuge for many of...our kind."

"Shifters, mythics," Isadora said knowingly. "Yes, like is attracted to like."

"Well, progress has been coming to Nickel City recently, and there are conflicts between keeping our town safe and the people who want to develop it. There is...a bill before the local legislation that would give us some protection."

"You want me to interfere in mortal business for these petty little *property* disputes?" Isadora asked, arching one white eyebrow at him skeptically.

"More people and more development mean more incentive to cut down more forest," Roderick pointed out. "A less wild housing market would mean less."

Isadora's lips went tight. "Hm…"

"Ababa," Gabby said, stretching her arms for Isadora.

"A child," Isadora said fondly. "How quaint! And a shifter, too!" She reached for Gabby. "Young things are so odd."

Roderick's arms tightened reflexively, but a careful assessment of his instinct suggested that there was no danger and he let Isadora pluck the child effortlessly into the air and hold her at arm's length.

"Gaba moo eee!" Gabby told her, giggling.

Addison chuckled.

"She makes as much sense as most of you do," Isadora said, returning Gabby after a curious inspection from the distance of her arms.

Then, without any explanation or courtesies, she vanished as suddenly as she had appeared.

"Oooo?" Gabby said, looking around like a dog after an imaginary ball had been thrown.

"Did we get an answer?" Addison asked plaintively after a few moments of silence.

"Not really," Roderick said. "Which probably is our answer."

"It was worth a try," Addison said comfortingly, as she put her arm around his waist. "And it was a beautiful day to come out here."

They walked back to the truck through the forest, hand-in-hand.

"We don't have to go straight back, do we?" Addison asked wistfully. "There's nobody here…"

For a moment, Roderick's mind went very different places, and he wondered what Addison planned to do with Gabby while they—

"Oh, you mean we could shift and run around a little?"

Addison smiled like the sun. "When was the last time you had a chance to run around as a wolf in the wilderness?"

*Too long*, his wolf complained.

Addison stepped back from him and was rather suddenly capering around as a fluffy-furred lynx.

Gabby shrieked in delight, and Roderick only had to tell her once, "Want to be a wolf?"

He had to help extract her from her romper and diaper, because she didn't yet know to think them into her form with her, and a puppy was not nearly the same shape as a toddler. He got her down on the ground, folded her clothing, and left it on the seat of the truck, then he was bounding after his mate and his daughter on four legs.

# CHAPTER 34

*A*ddison didn't want to think about the fact that they'd lost their last hope for getting the legislation passed that would save neighborhoods for neighbors and, more selfishly, keep Cherry in business so that Addison could keep her job. It wasn't just that she loved the job, and the life she could see unfolding before her. She loved the day care, and the town, and Cherry herself. The future felt murky now; even her instinct felt muted.

It was a pretty day, and she concentrated on how lovely it was, and what fun she could have right now, ignoring all of her misgivings and disappointment.

Gabby was delighted to roll on the forest floor and dig with her giant puppy paws and scamper and growl and chase sticks and tails. For a long while, they all romped, a wolf, a lynx, and a puppy. Gabby got clumsier, after a while, and Addison caught her by the ruff and carried her to a patch of sunlight by the parking lot, curling up around her and licking her as the puppy growled playfully and protested.

Roderick looked like he'd just gotten started and he gave a sigh, his tail drooping. He turned back into a man and stooped to scratch Gabby's chin.

Addison jerked her own chin in the direction of the forest suggestively, putting one paw protectively over Gabby. *Go run,* she thought at him, purring, wondering if she would have to shift to convey the suggestion. Gabby was comfortably sprawled between her paws now, panting happily.

"You think I should go running?" Roderick asked hopefully.

Addison nodded.

Roderick looked conflicted, then grinned broadly. "Twist my arm," he said joyfully, and then he was bounding away as his long-legged wolf.

Gabby whined and tried to follow, but Addison groomed her firmly and she quickly settled.

Gabby didn't seem interested in sleeping, but she was happy enough to be wrapped in Addison's purring warmth, and she snuggled contentedly.

Addison's keen lynx ears heard the car as far away as the highway, and she expected it to turn away at the gate until she remembered that Roderick had left it open. Still, there was a big sign that said the tree with its plaque was only open on the second and fourth Thursdays, surely they wouldn't come all the way in?

It continued to approach and Addison grew worried. She couldn't just stay here like this, waiting for a stranger to spot a lynx with a wolf puppy. She shifted, gathering Gabby into her arms. "Sweetie, I'm going to need you to be a little girl again. Fingers and feet, like we do at Cherry's, okay? Fingers and feet!"

Gabby had absolutely no interest in being a girl again.

She chewed on the collar of Addison's shirt and wagged her little tail, squirming with renewed energy.

Any moment, a stranger was going to catch them. Could she pass Gabby off as a domestic puppy? Would she decide to shift at exactly the wrong time? The truck was locked, and the keys were probably safe in Roderick's shifted pocket, so even if she were a little girl, it would be weird that she was a naked little girl.

Then the car turned into the little lot, and Addison realized in horror and hot terror that it wasn't a stranger at all.

She stared at the familiar car as it pulled into the space at the end, opposite from the truck, and she immediately recognized the figure that got out of it.

"Owen."

He hadn't changed a bit. He was still tall and handsome and strode confidently across the lot to her. He didn't interest her the way that he had when they first met—how could he after Roderick? And even though Addison realized, as the shock of seeing him passed, that she wasn't scared of him the way she'd been when she finally left him, she didn't need instinct to warn her of the danger.

"Veronica said you might be here," he said chidingly.

"How do you know Veronica?" Addison asked in astonishment. "And how would she know where I was?"

"I know all the important people, darling," Owen said dismissively. "Apparently her *plumber* knew where you'd be."

Owen said plumber like it was some kind of insult, but Addison could only think that she'd take Roderick the plumber any day over Owen the jerk.

"Addison, honey, what were you thinking?"

"I was thinking I'd be glad not to see you again," Addison said. She was dismayed to find that her voice trembled, and she held Gabby closer to her. "How did you find me?"

"You did a good job staying under the radar," Owen said, his voice that same kind of reasonable snake oil as ever. "But I had a buddy keep an eye out on your social security number, and it looks like you recently got official employment."

It had been perfectly reasonable to give Owen all of her personal information. His reasons had all been completely legitimate, and Addison had ignored the twinge of instinct that suggested she shouldn't. Her job as a nanny had been under the table, so she wouldn't have shown up on his radar until she started working for Cherry. It was the first time that Addison had felt any regret for her new job.

"What do you want?" Addison asked. She did better at keeping her voice moderated that time.

"It's not about what I want," Owen said kindly, "it's about what you want, honey. You know I'll give you anything you need. You can leave this hick town and come back where you belong."

He always thought he knew better than she did about what she needed, and now it was painfully obvious how wrong he was. For a moment, Addison was more outraged by the "hick town" statement than the implication that she needed Owen.

Gabby was squirming for freedom. She wanted to run around again, and Addison worried that she'd struggle herself into human form. She'd never told Owen about being a shifter, not sure how at first, and later grateful for that reluctance to protect her secret. She bounced Gabby. "You're a puppy, you're a puppy," she murmured.

"Cute mutt," Owen said. "Is it house trained? I could let you have a pet if you needed something to nurture."

Addison actually laughed. She couldn't imagine a pet living with Owen. Dirty paw prints? Dog fur? Slobbery kisses? Owen was the exact opposite of that. And she was done with Owen "letting" her do anything.

"I'm not going back with you, Owen," she said firmly. "I'm not interested in you anymore. You were a jerk and I don't need you."

"There's no reason to exaggerate things," Owen said, in his terrible, suave voice. "I was so generous with you, so understanding. I gave you everything you ever needed."

He was standing uncomfortably close and Addison didn't want to give him the satisfaction of stepping back to get more space between them. "You were a jerk," she repeated firmly. "Get out of my space and get out of my life."

He knew how much his proximity was distressing her, the bastard, and he was enjoying it. "Nice doggy," he said, reaching towards her just to make her flinch back.

Gabby was tired of being held, and she could probably feel all the tension and nervousness in Addison. She took Owen's approach exactly as he'd intended it, and with all the self-control of a frustrated toddler, she surged toward his hand and bit down.

Owen screamed and leaped back, shaking his hand and swearing. Addison wished that she'd thought to bite him first and didn't scold Gabby, hoping fiercely that she'd stay a puppy, just a little bit longer.

Owen had never been violent with her. He'd never needed to, knowing exactly how to undermine her self-esteem and make her question her resolve.

So Addison was caught by surprise when he bent and picked up a thick fallen branch, advancing on her with fury in his eyes.

In her arms, Gabby barked and tried to speak. Addison took a step back in dismay, certain that the little girl was going to try to shift and that Owen might try to hurt her anyway. She had to protect Gabby—and Gabby's secret—at any cost.

# CHAPTER 35

*R*oderick thought at first that his anxiousness was from leaving Gabby behind. He always had mixed feelings about letting her out of his sight. But he trusted Addison with his heart and his life, he reminded himself, firmly ignoring the tiny flush of unease.

He just needed to run, to feel the forest floor under his paws and shake loose from his human form for a short time, so he forced himself away from where Addison was distracting Gabby.

And it felt good, letting his wolf stretch, letting his senses expand out ahead of him. He could smell the summer heat in the underbrush. It was cool, beneath the trees, and the soil had a distinct acrid smell to it that felt like home. He didn't follow a trail, just hurtled through the forest, leaping fallen trees and gorges with no particular destination.

When he slowed, near the ridge, all of his reservations came crowding back and he stopped, nose in the air, to listen.

This wasn't merely the nervousness of being away from his child, there was an undercurrent of instinct, strong and true, warning him with increasing volume of danger, risk, threat, MENACE.

Roderick turned back the way he'd come, running twice as fast, faster than a wolf was meant to go, until his lungs were straining, his muscles burning, and his paws aching.

*Danger, danger, danger...*

It drew him along like an arrow, back on a straighter path than he'd come, until he was bursting out of the thin underbrush like a mad creature, straight to where Addison, in her human form, was trying to shield Gabby, growling and yipping in her wolf form, from a man who had picked up a fallen branch and was advancing on them.

The stranger clearly reconsidered his attack at the approach of a snarling adult wolf but didn't drop his club or step back.

"I always knew you had secrets," he spat at Addison. "You fooled everyone else with your sweet, innocent, too-good-to-be-true facade, but I know what a dirty, trashy hussy you were."

"I wasn't the one doing the lying and manipulating, Owen," Addison said, and her own voice was a low growl.

*Owen.*

Roderick's impulse to punch Addison's ex had been replaced with a barely restrained desire to tear his throat out.

But Addison, even with her arms full of squirming Gabby, lifted her chin and advanced on him. "I don't need you, I don't want you, and you have no power over me anymore. You are a sad, worthless excuse for a man who didn't have any self-value unless he could dominate someone. I'm not sorry I escaped you, and I hope that I never see you again. You are delusional and weak. I deserved better."

With every word, Owen flinched, his fist around the branch going tense and white. Roderick kept his eyes on his throat, watching for any hint that he was going to attack, prepared to get there first. He was growling and panting...and Gabby suddenly realized he was there and gave a yip of excitement.

Several things happened at once: Owen lifted his limb, Addison turned, protecting Gabby in her arms and shielding her with her body, as the toddler shifted back to her human form, and Roderick charged forward.

Owen staggered back as Roderick leaped at him, snapping strong jaws with sharp teeth around his branch and ripping it from him by force. Owen fell back with a cry of horror and dismay, and Roderick dropped the stick as he straddled him and growled down into the man's stricken face.

Behind him, human Gabby was wailing in distress. Owen looked confused and terrified. Roderick glared down into his face, then deliberately stepped back, giving him space to get up and run.

Owen didn't need a second invitation, scrambling backwards on his hands until he could get up and stagger away, nearly falling before he got to his car. Roderick paced him, snapping his teeth in warning every time he slowed, until the car door slammed with Owen behind the wheel.

Roderick thought for a moment that Owen would try to run him down, and he waited on legs like coiled springs to dodge out of the way, but Owen chose the sensible path and peeled out from the parking lot rather than staying to prolong the conflict.

Once the sound of the car had died away down the access road, Roderick eased back into human form and turned to find Addison standing with a fussy, naked Gabby in her arms.

"I don't think he saw her," she said, her voice shaking like it hadn't once through the entire confrontation.

Roderick gathered them both into his arms, grateful for that at least, and felt relief surge through him on the heels of the instinct that had driven him back.

If Addison wept while he was holding her tight, she had controlled it by the time he was willing to let her go.

"How did he find you?" Roderick wanted to know.

"Apparently, he knows *Veronica*," Addison said.

That was certainly an unsavory connection to imagine.

"Abba aga gaba wheeee..." Gabby complained.

"We should get Gabby into some clothes," Addison said sensibly. "It's too chilly to be naked, and there are mosquitoes."

Roderick took his daughter and tossed her a few inches in the air to make her shriek in joy. "I bet *that guy* needs a new diaper, too," he said with satisfaction.

Addison laughed so hard that she had to hold on to him.

# CHAPTER 36

Tara's mother usually picked her up at exactly the time she said she would, dressed in her nurse's scrubs. She generally resisted efforts to draw her into conversation, though she was always kind and never impatient with Tara or her baby brother Shane.

Addison wasn't going to be brushed off this time, however, and she met Vivian Yang at the gate with something other than her baby.

Vivian looked at the little pile of paper that Addison handed her cautiously, as if she was expecting eviction papers or some kind of summons. "What's this?"

"I wrote this for Tara," Addison said, bursting with excitement and anticipation. "But I wanted you to see it first."

It was all she could do not to squirm as Vivian flipped through every page, reading each one carefully. Her expression was cool and Addison tried not to assume the worst. "Gabby's father, Roderick Douglass, did the artwork for it. He's a plumber, you wouldn't guess he was so good at art, too. He's got a lot of talent, I think. Of course, I'm a little biased."

Babbling, Addison recognized. She was definitely babbling. But

Vivian was paging through so agonizingly slowly and Addison was suddenly worried that she had overstepped, or misunderstood, or done something terrible. Should she have done more research? Maybe she had gotten something wrong. Vivian's hands turning the pages were starting to tremble.

To Addison's horror, she started to crumple the page, then lifted her gaze and Addison could see that tears were tracking down her face.

"I'm sorry!" Addison said in dismay. "I didn't mean to—"

"You made this for Tara?" Vivian's voice was full of grief.

"I haven't shown it to her yet," Addison said swiftly. "If you don't like it—"

Vivian gave a sob. "It is beautiful. It is a gift. I have never seen— I have never been—This is—Oh! I have gotten it wet and wrinkled! I am so sorry!" She tried to flatten the pages, still weeping.

"It's just a copy!" Addison was quick to tell her, not sure how to feel yet. "A few of the pages aren't finished yet. Roderick planned to add color to all of them."

"Mama?"

It usually didn't take the kids long to figure out when someone arrived at the day care, and Tara was standing with Gil, who was pulling his shirt on over his head and somehow had gotten both arms in one sleeve. Amy was toddling their direction and Gabby was crawling after, determined not to be left behind.

"Mama, what's wrong?" Tara's thin voice was worried. "Are you sad?"

Vivian cried harder, but she was quick to say, "No, honey, I'm happy, I'm so happy." She stepped over the gate, knelt down, and drew Tara into an embrace with her free arm. "Teacher Addy just showed me something that she made for you, and I'm so happy!"

Vivian showed her the first pages and Tara looked up at Addison in astonishment. "This looks like...me," she said shyly.

Addison could only nod, or she was going to cry as hard as Tara's mother.

"Will you read it to me?" Tara begged.

"'Cara was a unicorn,'" Vivian read, her voice wavering. "'But she wasn't like the other unicorns who lived in Heart's Hollow. Cara was a kirin—'" she had to stop and pull Tara close, burying her face in her hair.

"It's called *The Kirin who Could*," Addison said when it looked like Vivian wouldn't be able to continue. "It's all about what a kirin can't do, and about what she *can* do. I don't know if I got it all right. I wanted it to be a surprise, and I didn't know any unicorns to ask. I can fix anything that's wrong, of course, and we'll print you a fresh copy. Just let me know if you want anything changed. I also wasn't sure if it was too close to Tara's name, I can use something else."

"It looks like me," Tara repeated, and she was crying like her mother was, though she looked like she wasn't sure entirely why.

Amy and Gabby had reached them by now, and Amy was so distressed by the tears that she fell over and turned into an owl, peeping and hopping out of her diaper. Not to be left out, Gabby turned into a puppy and squirmed from her clothing to try to play with Amy.

The front door buzzed onto that chaos and Addison swiftly let Roderick in after checking the camera.

Vivian climbed back over the gate with the papers in her hands and fell weeping into his arms, then seemed to collect herself. "Thank you so much, Mr. Douglass. I can't say how much this means—It's so—I can't—!"

Rod, looking a mixture of alarmed and sympathetic, patted her kindly on the back. "Of course, Mrs. Yang. Of course. It was all Addison's idea."

Then Vivian was back to embrace Addison, and Addison really did cry in earnest at that and Tara began to bawl and Gil tried to stand on his head to cheer her up, shouting, "Look at me! LOOK at ME!"

"What on earth is going on?" Cherry demanded, coming from the back room with Shane, who was cooing happily in her arms. "Gil, is that your inside voice?"

Gil fell over, turned into an armadillo, and just as suddenly shifted back and shouted, "I REMEMBERED MY CLOTHES!" in what was very definitely not an inside voice.

Vivian proudly and tearfully showed Cherry the book and Tara crowded in to point out the pictures that looked like her while the other children ooh-ed and aww-ed.

Amy tried to eat the pages.

Everyone wiped their eyes and Vivian said thank you over and over while she gathered up Shane's diaper bag and Tara's backpack.

Addison felt about as tall as a tree and completely wrung out by the time they had gone. Roderick stood beside her and rubbed her back. "Was it everything you hoped it would be?" he asked.

"Even more," Addison said honestly. Her heart felt full.

"You've still got tears on your face," Roderick pointed out, and he used one callused thumb to wipe them away, then leaned down to kiss her cheek.

"Happy tears," Addison promised.

It occurred to her that Owen coming in on such an event would have made her feel stiff and uncomfortable. He would have disapproved of her tears and frowned at the noisy children.

She was getting tired of comparing Roderick to Owen at every turn. Roderick was a partner and his support was given without strings. Addison didn't even need instinct anymore to tell her that he was safe to love; he had proved it by respecting her at every step of the way.

She was quite sure that the doorbell did not ring, and that no one unlocked the door, but Isadora Larix was suddenly standing in the middle of the daycare, dressed this time in a fine wool suit dress straight out of the fifties, complete with a pillbox hat.

"How quaint," she said, looking around in interest. "The decor is not exactly historically accurate, is it?"

"The kids don't really care," Cherry pointed out. "Can I help you?"

If she was surprised that Isadora had abruptly materialized in the middle of her day care, she didn't say so, and Addison wondered if Cherry knew who—or what—the recluse was. None of the children seemed to find her sudden appearance unusual.

"You're Cherry Aimes?" Isadora stepped forward and offered her hand. She was wearing gloves that matched her suit.

"Ms. Larix," Cherry said politely, answering at least that question. They gravely shook hands.

"I was surprised to hear that there was a day care opening for shifters only," Isadora said without preamble. "I would like to enroll my daughter."

Roderick and Addison exchanged a look that suggested a daughter was news to him, too.

"I presume that she is not a shifter, but that she will have special needs that we can accommodate?" Cherry said without so much as a flutter of surprise, answering that question as well.

"Her range is not very far yet, but her sapling is still small enough to transport easily in a pot," Isadora said. "Otherwise, I imagine it will be the same consideration you would have for any young creature. Don't expose her to toxins or allow anyone to eat her."

Addison made an ungraceful snort trying to hold in her laughter.

She had composed her face, barely, by the time that Isadora glanced at her.

"Of course not," Addison agreed. "We discourage the children from eating each other."

"Very well," Isadora said. "Let us discuss payment."

"I have a fee schedule printed," Cherry said, starting to turn back to her office.

"I do not deal with mortal money," Isadora scoffed. "And I am doubtful that you would contract for sexual favors."

Addison's second attempt to hold in her laugh was even less successful than the first and Roderick made a choked noise at her side.

Cherry raised an eyebrow. "That is not a part of my usual business plan," she said very carefully.

"I came prepared to bargain," Isadora said, apparently not taking notice or care for their discomfort. "I understand that there is a resolution before the assembly that you have a particular interest in."

Everyone sobered.

"Yes," Cherry said slowly. "It would prevent rent increases above a certain rate. It...could mean the difference between continuing the day care and having to close it."

Isadora was nodding impatiently. "Yes, yes, and keep neighborhoods for neighbors. I researched the issue after these two brought it to my attention. I can ensure that it passes if you will allow my daughter to attend your school four days a week for a year. We can negotiate new terms at that time if I find it beneficial to her social development."

Everyone in the room was very quiet in astonishment, except the children, who were gleefully playing a game with the soft blocks that seemed to involve building walls around Amy, who hopped and squeaked in happy delight because everyone was paying attention to her. Gabby was dismantling the walls as fast as they could be erected and no one seemed to mind.

"How—" Roderick started to ask, then apparently he reconsidered.

Isadora answered anyway. "I have a certain amount of influence with the older citizens of Nickel City, including many who have contributed greatly to individuals with political aspirations. I haven't had a lot of interest in your petty mortal politics, but I do understand how they work after all this time. I can assure you that what I want, I *will* get. Do we have an agreement?"

Cherry looked stunned, and she hesitated. "No one will get hurt?"

Isadora looked affronted. "Of course not. Everyone will walk away convinced that they got exactly what they actually wanted."

Cherry nodded. "I think we have an agreement."

Isadora shook her hand decisively, then brushed at her skirt as if Cherry's hand had been dirty. "Very well. I shall bring my daughter on the first day of next week."

Then she vanished.

"Yes!" Addison pumped her fist in the air and danced around in a little circle.

Roderick felt like it was appropriate to kiss her soundly in celebration. "Veronica Chase is going to chew glass," he said, feeling smug.

"Why would she CHEW GLASS?" Gil wanted to know.

"It's an expression, honey," Cherry said soothingly. "I'm so impressed that you shifted with your clothes on earlier! Can you do it again for me?"

Gil promptly turned into an armadillo and rolled back into the fray with Amy and Gabby.

"Did you ever come up with a name for the day care?" Roderick asked.

"Shea suggested the Gingerbread House," Cherry laughed. "I was afraid that might sound like we ate children. Tater Tots was almost as bad."

"What about Tiny Paws?" Addison suggested.

A moment of silence met the idea. "I like it," Roderick said honestly.

"Yes," Cherry said, looking pleased. "It hints at shifters, without giving it away, and we can put paw prints all over the logo."

There was a buzz at the door, and Addison let Gil's father and Amy's mother in. "Please check for lost socks," she reminded them as they gathered up their things. There were ten small socks pinned to the board now.

Then the day care was quiet, only Gabby remaining. She seemed content to pile the blocks while Addison and Cherry did their rounds of the room, disinfecting and tidying. Roderick sat down with Gabby and helped her stack blocks until they were done.

He could not quite keep himself from watching Addison's happy caper around the room. Every so often, she would spin around, or impulsively hug a stuffed animal for no reason. She was so lithe and beautiful and lively, all of her emotions right there in her light step and beaming face. Seeing her so joyful did something inside of Roderick, made everything feel settled and perfect.

She finished the closing chores for the day care while Cherry retreated to do some bookkeeping and gathered up her own jacket and purse, meeting Roderick and Gabby at the door. Gabby was nodding off on his shoulder.

"Oh my gosh, I'm so relieved," Addison said as she pulled the door shut and locked it behind her. "Veronica won't be able to raise Cherry's rent unreasonably ever again, and I have some hope that I can keep my job. I wonder how many of those real estate deals are going to fall through now?"

Roderick thought about Ian and the sale of his rental. "I just hope that it isn't too late. Housing prices aren't going to drop immediately. It will take a little while for everything to stabilize back to something reasonable."

"I might have trouble finding a place to rent for months and months," Addison agreed. "Maybe even a year."

Roderick bit back his impulse to offer her his spare room again. He knew quite well why she was reluctant, why she wanted to maintain her independence, and he didn't want to push her too hard or question her autonomy. He respected her boundaries, even while he ached to always have her close.

So he was surprised when she very suddenly said, "Do you want to move in together?"

He'd been thinking about it so hard, reminding himself so firmly not to ask that he stared at her stupidly for several moments.

"We don't have to," Addison said swiftly when he didn't answer. "I just thought...it feels..."

"Instinct," Roderick said because it was humming like a motor between them now.

"It's the right thing, at the right time," Addison said quietly.

Everything seemed to click into place. "Addison Carmichael, will you marry me?"

For a moment he thought he'd gone too far, that instinct had pushed him too fast. He should have been satisfied with having her move in with him.

Then a smile bloomed across her expressive face and she beamed up at him in delight. "I will," she said softly. "I will!"

Roderick wasn't sure if he gathered her into his arms or if she stepped into them, but then they were embracing, Gabby wedged between them.

"I love you," he said to them generally.

The sleepy toddler reached out and patted Addison's cheek. "Addy," she said contentedly.

And everything in the world was right, with instinct singing in satisfaction.

# A SNEAK PREVIEW OF DRAGON'S INSTINCT

*Shots sizzled across the speeder's bow and Turnkey dove at the controls. "We've got a problem!" he hollered back to the engineer.*

*"You're telling me!" Tagrin shouted back. "We've got a coolant leak in the quarterdeck and a crack in the second hull! She's not going to hold together long enough to break atmo!"*

*"I know how to fix this!" Turnkey said—*

*J*an stopped typing, his fingers poised over the laptop.

He had no *idea* how to fix this.

It had taken him twenty minutes to re-read and remember where he was even going with his plot when he sat down to write and his brain felt shattered. He couldn't recall when he'd last gotten a full night's sleep or more than an hour of writing time in one sitting. Every time that he so much as started feeling like he was making progress on his book, his toddler daughter, Lucy, needed a snack, or a new diaper, or a hug, or a nap, or it was time for a meal or to do laundry or there was a toy that needed to be repaired.

Or, like now, there was suspicious silence, which was even worse.

Ian thought he'd have a little window of writing opportunity. Lucy had been happily playing with her food at the table, and as slow as she ate, Ian guessed he might be able to get a few hundred words written.

He didn't want to think about how a few hundred words at a time wasn't going to get him finished by the publisher's (third) deadline, or how many times he'd had to delete big chunks because he was incapable of holding the whole book in his head and his plot had gone straight off the tracks.

"Lu?"

Ian leaned back in his chair so that he could see into the kitchen.

Lucy's chair was empty, and her purple butterfly dress was hanging off the back of it. It hung neatly, as if she had taken it off before she shifted.

Ian swore under his breath and cheerfully called, "Lucy? Honey? Did you finish your food?" He should have kept her in a high chair a little longer, he thought woefully. But she was tall for her age and had convinced him that she was ready for a big girl chair. She was, but was he?

The sandwich that she'd been playing with had been disassembled and all the parts she liked had been eaten out. The halved cherry tomatoes were gone, of course, they never lasted long enough to be entertainment. Her sippy cup was on its side, a few drops of water on the table beneath it.

"Lucy, you know I don't want to play hide and seek right now. Lucy?"

Ian was equal parts annoyed and worried. There was so much trouble that a little girl could get into...and even more that a squirrel could. She'd been so safely occupied, and he'd barely looked away. He was the worst dad, he was a miserable failure, how hard could it be to juggle a stay-at-home career and one small child?

Pretty damned hard, it turned out. Ian scanned the top of the fridge and the cabinets in the kitchen; Lucy liked high places. But she wasn't in any of her usual spots, and Ian spread his search zone down the hall. "Lucy, please come out. Honey, are we playing a game? You know that Daddy needs to get his book finished, but if you want me to, I can read you one of *your* books. Lucy?"

The carpet gave a suspicious squelch, right in front of the bathroom and Ian flung the door open to find that there was water in a shallow pool all across the floor. "Argh!" He was wearing socks, and they were immediately soaked as he dashed across to the sink, where the tap was still running. There was a washcloth lying across the bottom of the bowl and when Ian pulled it out, the water in the bowl swiftly drained away. A few water-logged dolls sagged at the bottom.

"Lucy!!"

Ian made himself temper his voice. Lucy had probably realized that she'd done something wrong and was hiding as a squirrel in one of the million tiny places in this house where he'd never find her.

"Lucy, you aren't in trouble," he called as gently as he could. "I just need to know that you're okay!"

He pulled the towels down off the rack to start sopping up the puddle. He had a box fan somewhere, he'd better get it going in the hallway before they had a mold problem to add to the mix.

The phone rang while he was wringing out the towels for the second time. "Hang on," he said when the fan drowned out the caller.

"You sound like you're in an air tunnel," Wanda complained when he got the fan turned off. When Ian was feeling his most lonely and full of regret over their broken relationship, she usually managed to say just the right thing to remind him why they'd parted ways.

"Sorry," he said, knowing he didn't sound sorry. "What's up?"

"I wanted to talk about The Schedule."

She always said it like both words were capitalized.

The Schedule.

The Schedule was the calendar that dictated the days they had to see each other, the days that Lucy was hers or his. At first, Wanda had been adamant about getting every day allotted to her with their joint custody, and Ian had spent the days she was gone desperately missing his daughter. But Wanda got busier with work, her new boyfriend had kids, and Wanda had gradually adjusted The Schedule so that Ian had Lucy nearly all the time. He'd even thought about pressuring her for child support, but it had never felt like he was equal to the effort.

"After all," she'd said more than once. "You don't work, it's not an inconvenience to you."

Ian wasn't sure which part of her assumption he objected to most. That writing wasn't working? That raising a small child basically by himself wasn't a whole job all by itself? But like most battles with Wanda, it simply wasn't worth fighting anymore.

"What about it?" Ian sounded more surly than he meant. Was she going to want to talk to Lucy? Did he have to admit that he didn't know where she was and that she'd just flooded the bathroom?

Wanda sounded almost sweet. "I know I said I didn't want any of the holidays this year, but my parents invited us up to Helena for Labor Day. They'd like to see Lucy."

Ian remembered holidays with Wanda's folks. They were all squirrel shifters, and while he adored his daughter beyond reason, the ceaseless chattering and the way Wanda's family was always in constant motion always left him feeling like he'd been in a room full of mental vampires after only a few minutes. Having to stay with them had been a kind of fine-tuned torture.

Labor Day. "Let me check my calendar."

Ian didn't really have to look at it. Aside from the looming red BOOK DUE (really, this time!) entry on his calendar, it was just a trudging list of nothing. The closest he'd gotten to a social life lately was babysitting his friend Roderick's daughter Gabby, a little girl just younger than Lucy, while Roderick took his new girlfriend out on a date.

Sometimes, it seemed like everyone was moving on without him.

"That should work fine," Ian said.

"You're a peach," Wanda said sunnily. "I'll pick her up that Saturday morning and drop her off on Monday evening. Let me talk to Lucy."

*Dammit.*

"Hang on." He muted the phone, double-checking that he had,

and then hollered, "Lucy! Come talk to your mom! She's on the phone *right now!*"

A rustle at the baseboard gave him a few seconds of warning, and then Lucy shot out from behind the heater, her rusty red fur covered in dust.

She flowed up into a little girl, completely naked, and reached grabby hands for the phone.

"I'll hold it for you, honey," Ian said, thumbing the connection back on. He knew there were parents that would casually hand children Lucy's age a several hundred dollar phone—Wanda among them—but he didn't trust her attention span and he couldn't afford to replace it.

"Mummy! Bathroom's all wet!"

Ian couldn't hear Wanda's answer to that, and he oversaw half of a halting conversation before Lucy agreed, "Kisses!" and waved at the phone.

Ian checked to see that Wanda had hung up and put the phone back in his pocket. "You want to tell me about the bathroom?" he asked.

Lucy eyed her escape route back under the heater and Ian made a note to try to block it up with something. His entire house had become an obstacle course of trying to keep her out of small places and dangerous things. The cabinet locks were a constant frustration, as much for him as they were for her, and she could climb *anything*.

"You're not in trouble," Ian promised. "I just want to make sure it doesn't happen again, honey."

She wilted and mumbled something about dolls, carrots, and possibly a trombone.

"Just make sure you ask me before you play in the bathroom," Ian begged. "And turn off the water. We don't want to waste it!"

Lucy looked up at him hopefully, then said, "I'm hungry."

It was her get-out-jail-free card. Ian wasn't going to deny her *food*, no matter how recently she'd eaten, and he bent and scooped her up into his arms. "What did you forget, sweety?"

Lucy put two fingers in her mouth and said, "Clothes?" around them.

"Clothes," Ian agreed. "You're supposed to take your clothes with you when you shift."

Ian found himself at eye level with the business card magnet that Roderick had given him the week before as he opened the fridge. Cherry's new day care for shifter children, Tiny Paws, apparently taught kids to shift with their clothing.

A day care for shifter children.

Maybe he could talk Wanda into helping to pay for it. Maybe, if he could finish his damned book, he could pay for it himself. It would be good for Lucy to get more socialization. He couldn't just go set up playdates with the neighborhood kids when she was so good at shifting and so terrible about knowing when she was supposed to.

"Do you want a yogurt squeezie?" Ian offered. He knew she would.

When he put her down for a protesting nap, an hour later, he went back to his laptop. There were sticky squirrel footprints on the lid.

*I know how to fix this,* he thought hopefully.

He opened up his phone and punched in the number for Tiny Paws.

"Hi," he said when Cherry answered. "I was wondering if you had any openings…"

Continue the story in Dragon's Instinct!

# SLIPPERY WHEN WHAT?

# THE WORLD OF INSTINCT

A Day Care for Shifters takes place in a much larger world where shifters are secret and there are other bits of deeper magic like dragons and elementals and unicorns—I have several spin-offs of this series planned, and this short lesbian tale gives a glimpse of one of them!

This story takes place at a small, remote research camp in Alaska called Silver River, staffed by both regular humans and shifters trying to hide their special abilities...a task complicated by their isolation and close quarters.

THE WORLD OF INSTINCT

# CHAPTER 1

"*It's dead, Jim.*"

Felicity was sure that Star Trek references did not do anything to improve her reputation as an irredeemable geek, but Gina seemed more concerned about the broken ATV than she was about Felicity's social status anyway.

"Mostly dead? Or all dead? There's a big difference."

Was Gina making a *Princess Bride* joke? Felicity gave her a suspicious sideways look but got no clues from Gina's cool, perfectly made-up face. Gina, a botanist who was at least five years younger than Felicity, was very reserved and never joined in on campy movie nights, so it seemed unlikely. She was the kind of person who would only watch snooty documentaries and read serious literature with no sex scenes whatsoever. Personally, Felicity didn't really see the point of that kind of book.

Gina was not only really hot, but also a hard worker, and she never complained about the rustic conditions of the research camp, Silver River. It was still painfully clear that she was used to a considerably higher standard of living and she insisted on putting makeup on every morning, long after the other researchers had given up on all but the most basic hygiene. Felicity's beauty routine was running fingers through her short hair every morning and slathering on some deodorant. The camp had limited resources and showers were strictly rationed.

But even Silver River was going to seem like a luxury resort compared to a night out on the Alaskan tundra if their transportation was really dead.

They were fifty miles from the camp, which itself was a hundred miles from civilization, on windswept tundra dotted sporadically with stubby, stunted little spruce trees, clumps of alder bushes, and lichen-covered rocks. The mountains that should be towering around them in all directions were shrouded in threatening clouds. The only thing that counted as structure anywhere in sight was the science station they'd come to take readings from. It was a tower barely as tall as Felicity with a little solar panel at the top and an array of antennae and access panels, all of them tightly sealed against the inclement weather and possibility of curious bear molestation.

"Let's see if a chocolate-coated pill will revive the four-wheeler," Felicity said, testing her *Princess Bride* theory.

Was that a *smile* at the corner of Gina's lipsticked mouth?

Felicity pulled the seat up off the ATV so that she could get to the tool kit, and the cowling wasn't so rusted that she couldn't get it off, even if it took a little unladylike swearing.

Gina was a quiet and capable assistant as Felicity went through her minimal arsenal of repair tricks, even if the botanist did wipe her fingers off every time they got dirty. How could someone so fastidious like plants? Felicity's experience with gardening was that it was messy and unruly. At least Gina's nails were short and practical, and she knew the difference between a Phillips head and a flathead screwdriver.

"So, what made you come to Alaska?" Felicity asked, as she started poking around for loose wires or other obvious problems. "Promises of glory and fame?"

Gina was quiet so long that Felicity worried that she'd said something wrong.

"You don't have to say," Felicity assured her. "Lots of people come to Alaska to get away from their lives. They either turn tail and leave immediately or can never live anywhere else again."

"I just…had a feeling," Gina said evasively.

Felicity thought she could guess why Gina was embarrassed to admit she made a major life decision over something woo woo like a *feeling*. She was very analytical and careful with her research, scrupulously scientific, and Felicity wasn't sure she *had* feelings. She was the absolute embodiment of an ice queen, with perfect, straight black hair and lips like red fruit of temptation. Every attempt that Felicity made to get to know the woman behind her facade had ended with Gina looking at her with her big, startling green eyes and finding an excuse to leave—something challenging in a small camp of a few dozen people. She was as slippery as an oiled otter.

Gina also seemed to know exactly when she stopped being useful and left Felicity to her swearing and desperately amateur dismantling of the ATV to collect samples and take field notes while her devices still had a charge.

"I think it's the starter," Felicity finally decided, a few hours later when she had exhausted everything she could think to try and Gina had run out of samples to find. What they could see of the sun through the cloud cover was still high in the sky, but at this time of year, above the Arctic circle, the sun wouldn't set at all. Felicity's stomach was starting to growl, and her watch claimed it was nearly six. They should be arriving back at camp about now. "There's plenty of fuel and the lines look good. There's charge on the battery. It's just not turning over."

Gina glanced back at the way they'd come. "Do we have to *walk* back?" she asked in horror.

Felicity shook her head. "We're about fifty miles from the research camp," she said. "We'd be better off camping here and waiting for the helicopter."

"How long will *that* take?" Gina wanted to know. Her expression clearly said *I'm disgusted but don't want to lower myself to complain about things*. It was a common look for her.

Felicity checked her phone, even though she already knew that it wouldn't have any signal. "They were expecting us back for dinner, but they probably won't start looking for us until morning. Lots of field parties get delayed by weather or wild animals, and we've got enough supplies to last a few days in a pinch."

Gina's chin actually trembled and Felicity was quick to add, "They know right where we were going, though. It shouldn't take them long to find us once they get started. Jay can probably fix the four-wheeler and you can go back in the helicopter with him and Sigrid."

"You shouldn't have to drive it back alone," Gina said quietly.

Felicity glanced over, trying to decide what the tone of her voice really meant. Part of her fascination with the young woman was that she didn't fit in any of the boxes that Felicity expected her to. Gina was from Atlanta, with city-girl sensibilities, but she was stronger and quicker than her soft Southern voice and sweet, round face suggested. Felicity was often surprised by how much Gina carried at one time when they were unloading a supply flight.

Maybe she did a lot of yoga or pilates or whatever was vogue in civilized places.

"Anyway," Felicity said, trying very hard not to picture Gina in tight Spandex doing bendy things, "let's finish what's in the cooler for dinner and then set up a camp. We can save the MREs for breakfast."

They'd planned to be back at Silver River by dinner, so it was just the remnants of their lunch that they had left to split—half a sandwich, some vegetables, an apple, an orange, and a chocolate protein bar. Felicity poured the water in the cooler that had melted from the ice cubes into travel cups, knowing that their supply of fresh water might need to be stretched.

Gina all but held her nose, but drank the water and accepted half of everything left courteously. Felicity took the apple and Gina delicately peeled her orange while Felicity thought about how they were apples and oranges.

Felicity almost dropped her wet apple when Gina licked her juice-covered fingers, and reminded herself furiously that she should not be fantasizing about other things Gina might lick. "Oops," she said, catching the apple gracelessly.

Felicity put it back in the cooler, nervous that they might be hungry before their rescue, gathered up all their trash to seal away from attracting hungry animals, and stood to survey the landscape. A gentle, persistent wind was just strong enough to keep the mosquitos to a dull roar. The ground was flat here, rocky and patterned in lichen and little clumps of moss and grass.

None of it looked very comfortable or inviting, and it had rained recently enough that everything was faintly damp.

Gina opened the emergency duffel and looked through the contents skeptically. "I think there are some things missing. Is this *food*? There's not a tent."

"Sure there is," Felicity said, looking over her shoulder and pulling out a tiny stuff-sack. "It's not much, but it will be shelter for a night."

"There's a tent in there?" Gina said in astonishment. "Is it one of those magic expanding capsules? Just add water?"

On cue, the sky opened up and it began to pour.

# CHAPTER 2

*A*s the raindrops got faster and fatter, Gina yanked her raincoat hood up and helped Felicity stuff everything back into the duffel in a vain attempt to keep as much dry as possible. She was keenly aware of Felicity's proximity and the sheer limitless energy of her.

*This is your fault,* she told her inner fox as she grew more soaked by the moment. ***Your*** *instinct is what brought us here. Move to **Alaska**, join a research team, see the world, find true love.*

Her fox only cackled in pure mischief, not at all bothered by the downpour or the proximity of the woman she kept insisting was their destiny.

Gina still had doubts, even if her fox didn't. Alaska had been a culture shock to say the least, and Gina wasn't convinced that this was where she should be, even if Felicity had captured her heart from her first warm greeting and Vulcan salute. The camp residents had all been kind, but they were all so closely knit that Gina couldn't figure out where she fit, and her awful natural nervousness meant that she hadn't really made friends, even among the other shifters at the camp, no matter how desperately she wanted to belong.

It didn't help that she dissolved into embarrassment every time that someone had to explain something basic to her, like how the outhouse worked, and why it didn't get dark. Why was she so *awkward?* If this was where she belonged, why wouldn't instinct make her *smoother?*

Sometimes instinct was a flash of insight, an urge to look up at the right time, or a choice that was suddenly lightning clear. Sometimes it was a hesitation that wasn't her own saying *don't go there,* or *don't lend that guy any money.* And sometimes, like now, it was a sweet, unreasonable yearning, a promise that this one person could bring her more happiness than she'd ever imagined...if only she could bring herself to make that first leap of trust.

But Gina didn't know how to *do* that, and instinct didn't come with instructions.

The tent unfolded into something only marginally more tent-like than the hand-sized sack, and proved to be basically a flexible space blanket tube. "How is that going to work?" Gina asked, trying not to sound too panicked. Felicity looked like getting caught out in the wilderness with a scrap of aluminum foil for shelter was no big deal. Gina was sure they were going to starve to death, unless they froze to death first. And there were *bears* in the area.

"We need two things to tie out to," Felicity said, looking around. "About ten feet apart. Maybe twenty."

There were no two trees close enough together to support a tent, except the ones that were too close together to be useful.

"The science station?" Gina suggested. "We could put the ATV in neutral and push it close enough to tie out to?"

"I would accept certain death before I tie a tent to a seven hundred thousand dollar science station and have to face the wrath of Jay. We're worth a lot less than that equipment. But moving the ATV is a good idea."

They got the four-wheeler into neutral and shoved it by sheer will and ill-concealed shifter strength on Gina's part to a spot near one of the sturdiest looking little trees and turned sideways. "That ought to hold," Felicity said with satisfaction, and in a competent little flurry, she had a line tied out between the tree and the ATV, with the emergency tent strung up on an unfolded horizontal pole.

With careless disregard for conservation, she stripped a few branches from one of the stunted trees and tore up several lumps of mossy sod to cover the worst of the rocks beneath it.

Now, instead of a tube of tin foil, they had a limp tube of tin foil on a *string*, on top of a lumpy, wet bed of spruce branches and moss.

"What do we do now?" Gina asked helplessly, searching the bag for more parts. The brand of the tent was Don't Die in the Woods, and she thought it was a very morbid name indeed.

But that was apparently all of the tent that there was, and Felicity was tossing the duffel into it.

"Crawl in, princess! There's plenty of space!"

Whatever else there was, there was not plenty of space.

The bag claimed it was a two-person survival tent, but that was two *very* friendly people. Felicity had anchored the bottom corners of the tent with rocks so that it made a saggy tent-shaped triangle, the shiny surface facing in to presumably reflect heat back in, but it definitely wasn't a sit-up-play-card-games dry space.

Gina tried not to think about *horizontal* games as Felicity wriggled into the tent tunnel and adjusted the branches under the tent surface beneath her. There was a space blanket in the duffel that Felicity unfolded.

*I'm smaller,* her fox reminded her. *We could just shift.*

*We could not,* Gina insisted. Even as a fox, it would be a snug fit; she was a cross fox, which was larger than a red fox and silver-black in color.

"Don't worry about your boots!" Felicity said, squeezing over to one side and patting the space beside her. Neither end of the tent had a door, but it was long enough that they ought to be able to stay dry if they stuck to the center.

Instinct had been pushing Gina in Felicity's direction from the day she'd landed at Silver River, airsick and out of her depth. Even before that, the magical tingle of instinct had made her choose a remote Alaskan research camp instead of a nice cushy lab in a college town somewhere.

She wasn't sure what held her back the most: Felicity's absolutely ballsy independence, which made Gina doubt that there was room for romance in her life, or Gina's deeply seated belief that protecting the secret of shifters was an imperative and her unwillingness to be dishonest as a first step in any relationship. This made the idea of courtship feel impossible. And Felicity, despite her obvious preference for women, had never made so much as a pass at Gina.

Gina had tried, a few times, to make conversation, but every time, she was seized by indecision. Should she just blurt the truth out to Felicity? "Hi, I can change into a fox and I think you're really cute?" Dating in the tiny, rustic research camp was hard enough for straight girls who *weren't* shifters when there was little privacy and even less opportunity for romantic escape.

And maybe Gina wasn't Felicity's type. Gina was boring and uptight and anxious. Felicity was *fun.*

And now Gina was still standing outside of the tiny tent, getting wetter by the moment, trying to figure out what to do next. She probably looked like a dolt. "Shouldn't we...ah...make a fire?"

Felicity gave her a deeply skeptical look. "In this?"

The rain had slacked off from its initial fury, but it was still coming down steadily.

"I'm...really wet," Gina protested. Her cheeks heated at her unintentional double entendre.

"You're not getting any drier," Felicity pointed out. "I mean, if you want to stay out there in the weather, you've got a raincoat and probably won't die of hypothermia, but we're stuck here for the night. Might as well crawl in and dry out while we wait for the weather to let up."

Gina still hesitated. Instinct said *yes,* but she was starting to think that instinct was just her fox's sense of humor, leading them into non-stop trouble, just for the fun of it.

"Look, I'm not going to feel you up or anything," Felicity said frankly. "I may be the gayest thing since sandals with socks, but I can keep my hands to myself."

*What if I **want** you to feel me up?* Gina thought, but she couldn't bring herself to say it out loud. She shook off the worst of the rain and went to shimmy in next to Felicity.

# CHAPTER 3

he problem with her promise was that Felicity wasn't sure what to actually do with her hands once Gina was in the trumped up tarp tube that called itself a tent.

Getting both of them in the tight space together required a certain amount of bumping and *oops!* and *sorry, let me just…!* until Gina had wriggled her way in and was snugged in close by necessity.

The least invasive way to lie together was side by side on their backs, which was wretchedly uncomfortable even over the ground padding that Felicity had been able to cobble together.

They lay there a while, listening to the raindrops tapping a rhythm on the plastic surface of the survival tent. The ends of the tent didn't actually close, so there was a fine spray of rain over their feet and face when the wind was just wrong, but for the most part, they were dry and cozy.

"All the comforts of home," Felicity said, when the silence between them had gotten horrifically awkward.

"Except pillows," Gina pointed out. "And coffee makers."

"Oh!" Felicity reached down the tent and fished out the duffel bag with the rest of the emergency supplies. "*Voila*, a pillow!" She managed to elbow Gina as she got it positioned under their heads. "Sorry!"

It was a narrow pillow and they had to squeeze closer together than ever to share it. After a few attempts, they found that they could lie back-to-back, the space blanket stretched over both of them. Gina was warm against her back, and Felicity found that while her clothes were slowly starting to dry, other parts were wetter than ever.

She spoke desperately into the rain-pattered quiet, hoping to distract them both. "So, what's the best movie ever made, and why is it *The Princess Bride*?"

Gina giggled. "It's just sweet and silly. Have you read the book?"

Was she the kind of snob who felt like the film could never do a book justice? "I can't say I've had the pleasure," Felicity admitted.

"It's just as good," Gina said. "There's an entire Zoo of Death that they have to navigate to rescue Wesley in the book. And there's a hilarious bit imploring readers to write to the publisher for a copy of a deleted reunion scene. I like that it doesn't take itself too seriously."

Felicity's crush on Gina expanded exponentially, and they talked about other surprising media overlaps. Gina wasn't fond of *Doctor Who*, but she enjoyed *Star Trek* and loved *Galaxy Quest* unreasonably.

"I like fanservice and stories that break the fourth wall," she admitted. "It's hard to pull off convincingly, but when it works, it's so...*satisfying*, you know?"

Felicity was definitely thinking about how satisfying it would be to roll over and crush Gina in her arms.

Gina was so sexy and soft, and the natural curl of two bodies meant her butt was right up against Felicity's. She would fit just right against Felicity's belly and in her arms if they were spooning.

"I have a rock under my hip," Felicity said, after she had resisted the urge to move so long that her limbs were going numb.

"I have one under my shoulder," Gina said plaintively. "And under my knee. I am dying to roll over."

There was one of those fraught silences, where they both realized that rolling over would bring them face to face, and Felicity wasn't sure if she'd be able to resist kissing Gina. She'd promised to keep her hands to herself, but she hadn't said anything about her lips.

"You could, you know," Felicity finally said.

"Could *what?*" Gina squeaked.

Had their silence been *that* long? What was *Gina* thinking about? "Roll over if you need to. I'll stay here."

Gina hesitated a moment, then started the arduous process of carefully rotating in the confined space. There was another flurry of *oops, sorry, my bad* as they renegotiated the space blanket and the boughs beneath them and settled again, closer than ever.

Felicity wasn't at all cold anymore, at least, even if she felt far too keyed up to ever sleep.

To her surprise, she did sleep, and when she woke up, she found that they had renegotiated their arrangement unconsciously, and now she was wrapped around Gina, and Gina wasn't wearing her raincoat any longer...in fact, she had somehow found a damp fur coat, which is when Felicity came all the way awake and realized that she was curled up with a large, dark cross fox.

It had stopped raining at some point, and there was a glint of sunlight outside that said nothing at all about what time of day or night it was above the Arctic Circle. There were mosquitos buzzing nearby, and there was an irregular dripping sound that was probably water off of the emergency tent, which was sagging over them.

And Felicity had a fox in her arms, and it wasn't the same kind of fox she'd gone to sleep not-quite-cuddling.

She lay for a long time trying to make sense of the situation, waiting to wake up from some kind of delirium. Maybe she'd unknowingly gotten hypothermia after all, and this was all an illusion.

The fox stirred in her arms and stretched, then seemed to come completely awake and suddenly Gina was there again, trying to get away from her in a tent where there was absolutely no room.

"I'm sorry!" Gina cried, tangling in the space blanket and nearly pulling the tent down on both of them. "I'm so sorry! *Crap!*"

It was as close to swearing as Felicity had ever heard from her, and in one swift scramble, Gina slipped away and Felicity was alone trying to make sense of her *entire life.*

# CHAPTER 4

*G*ina stood trembling outside of the tent because there was *nowhere* to run.

A clever fox could have found a hole in the open tundra, and if she'd wanted to lie down in a puddle as a person, she could have found a place to hide, but there was no *escape* for her here, trapped in the wilderness with a woman she had a ridiculous crush on who was probably now questioning her own sanity.

She'd blown any attempt at a *measured* reveal about shifters, and she felt like fool for shifting in her sleep. She'd just been so... comfortable in Felicity's arms, with the vibrant woman snoring lightly in her ear. It didn't matter that there were still hard rocks beneath them, that the boughs had slipped so that one was poking her in the thigh, that it was daylight bright even though it must be nearly midnight, that the blanket and tent and raincoats rustled noisily at the slightest motion, or that her stomach was growling with hunger. It mattered that Felicity was warm and perfect around her, and Gina felt like she was exactly where she belonged. She must have shifted as she drifted off to sleep herself.

The emergency tent was rustling madly as Felicity struggled out of it, cursing and untangling herself from the plasticky fabric.

Gina was tempted to shift and flee randomly out onto the tundra.

*Stay*, her fox urged.

How could so much of her want to run away when so much of her wanted to stay?

Felicity looked much the same emerging from a night of roughing it in what barely qualified as shelter as she did every morning: vivacious and beautiful, with her short hair in a hazy brown halo around her head.

"At least it stopped raining," she said cheerfully, taking off her raincoat.

Gina looked up in confusion. The sky was lighter, and she couldn't figure out how much of that was clearing cloud cover and how much was that the sun was higher. It hadn't set all night.

Wasn't Felicity going mention the whole *woke up with a furry animal* thing?

Could they let the topic just slide away, like the rapidly evaporating rain?

She could ignore it just like Felicity was, or…

Instinct was like a leaning weight, not a neon sign or an imperative, just a magnetic pull. She had to decide what to do with it herself.

"I wanted to tell you, before," Gina blurted.

Felicity froze with one arm of her raincoat still on. "Tell me what, exactly? Because I mean, there's not a lot about this trip that has gone according to plan and I'm sort of wondering what's even real right now."

"I'm a fox shifter," Gina said softly. "I have a fox in my head who can change shapes with me, and I wanted to tell you because I…really like you but being a shifter is a pretty big part of me, and I didn't want to start anything with a bunch of secrets, but it's a secret I've always had to keep and I didn't know what to do."

Felicity just stared at her.

*Why wasn't the helicopter there yet?* Gina wondered in misery, though she still had no idea what time it was.

Felicity very slowly took the rest of her raincoat off and slung it up over the tree they'd tied off to. "So, that wasn't...just a dream."

Should Gina have pretended that it was? It was too late now.

Felicity's eyes narrowed. "Are there a lot of shifters?" she suddenly demanded. "Because this would explain a lot of crap at Silver River that I've thought was some kind of elaborate prank."

Now that she was being honest, Gina couldn't seem to stop. "Yes. Shifters recognize each other, it's part of what we call instinct, and there are several at the research camp."

"Who—" Felicity stopped herself. "No, I don't want to know. It will be more fun to figure it out myself, and it's clearly a taboo subject. Look at you squirm! It's adorable! But this definitely makes a lot of things make sense now and oh my God, I am going to make the most of this." She rubbed her hands together in dramatic anticipation.

"You don't seem...as surprised as I thought you'd be," Gina said, wringing her own hands.

"I always thought you were a fox," Felicity said merrily, with a sly sideways look. "I just didn't think it was literal." Then she sobered. "When you said you *liked* me..."

If Gina hadn't been watching Felicity so closely, she might not have noticed the flash of uncertainty and longing that crossed the older woman's face. For one brief moment, she looked vulnerable and unsure, just like Gina felt.

Realizing that maybe Felicity wasn't impervious from doubt gave Gina the courage to admit. "Yeah, I like you. Like, *like* you." But she had no idea what to do after having said the word *like* entirely too many times in a row.

Fortunately, Felicity did, and she closed the distance between them in two long strides and put her hands on either side of Gina's face so that she could kiss her passionately.

*Told you so*, her fox said gleefully, and Gina didn't even care, because she could put her arms around Felicity and kiss her back just as deeply, touching and caressing everything she could through Felicity's flannel.

Finally Felicity pulled back. "Do you hear something?"

The pounding of her own heart? The laughter of her fox? No, there…it was the distant *thump thump thump* of a helicopter, and Gina felt a moment of frustration and annoyance. Could Jay and Sigrid not have waited one more hour? She *still* wasn't sure what time it was.

"It will take them a little while to get here," Felicity said, squinting at the horizon. The clouds had lifted enough to show the regal mountains, and sound carried a long way; the helicopter was just a dot in the distance. Rain was steaming away in the rays of sunlight breaking through the clouds in misty, magical streaks across the grand landscape.

"We should break down our tent," Gina suggested with a sigh. What had seemed ridiculously inadequate and flimsy seemed like a haven of safety now.

"Or we could *use* the tent," Felicity suggested with a grin.

"It's *wet*," Gina said, knowing that she was playing straight into her reputation of being fastidious and uptight.

"So am *I*," Felicity said frankly. "I'm willing to risk some mosquito bites if you are…"

Then she was kissing Gina again, and Gina was willing to risk much more than mosquito bites. She was willing to risk *belonging*.

SUDDENLY SHIFTERS

# Something in the WATER

## ELVA BIRCH

# SUDDENLY SHIFTERS

Anders Canyon is an unassuming little town where big things are afoot! This series includes completely self-standing novellas and shorts, each a quick, fun read with a full emotional arc and a satisfying conclusion. All of them weave together into a compelling mystery, and you'll see familiar characters in every book.

Each tale has a romantic core, a diverse cast, and unexpected twists. They aren't all straight, but they are all straight-up fun, every story a perfect bite-size adventure full of laughs and heart.

Many of the stories overlap on the timeline and although they can be read in any order, this is the order they may be most enjoyable:

Something in the Water
Throw Me a Bone
Abruptly a Bear
Hare Today
Suddenly Squirrel

Forthcoming: Wolf Without Warning!

# CHAPTER 1

*J*ulia stomped on the brakes at the last moment, knuckles white on the steering wheel, as her heart tried to leap out of her chest. For a moment, everything was bright and sharp and Julia had to remind herself to breathe.

Her car was safely at rest again; she hadn't been going that fast. The rain had already died to a minor drizzle, and the wet driveway sluggishly reflected her headlights and the yellowish lights above the doors of the duplex. In that pool of light there was a dog, still standing there, staring at her in stupid, frozen fear. It was some kind of black and white, wolfish-looking husky, with upright ears and bright eyes over a narrow white muzzle. Four long legs were splayed out in a posture of sheer shock.

"Damn," Julia said, as her pulse returned to normal and she reassured herself that she hadn't actually hit it. She rolled down the window. "Get out of the way, mutt!"

It looked down at its feet like it had forgotten that it had them and gave a yelp of what Julia could only identify as surprise. It ran for her neighbor's stoop, seemed to hesitate at the closed door, and then dashed around the house into their backyard, tail tucked between its legs. After a moment, she heard the distinctive sound of a door opening and slamming shut behind the duplex that she shared with her neighbor.

Julia gingerly took her foot off the brake and pulled her car up the drive. She put it in park, turned it off, and sat for a long moment, her hands trembling with adrenaline. She turned the car briefly back on to roll up the window.

"Dumb dog," she said, gathering her purse. "The homeowners association is going to have kittens if the neighbor got a dog and is letting it run wild."

She tripped over some sodden clothing that was lying on the driveway, frowning down at it. Was it some kind of prank? Was someone out streaking in the rain? She kicked it out of the way and pulled out her house keys.

There was already a notice taped to her front door, and it looked like there was one on the neighbor's, too. The soccer moms and nosy old biddies of the homeowners association hated their duplex and their fence and the fact that they had mismatched cars and took every opportunity to complain about any tiny violation.

But this wasn't one of their saccharine handwritten notes with hearts on the i's, it was an urgent-looking note with a government seal.

Julia skimmed it in dismay. Thallium? There was *thallium* in the groundwater? Julia had written a research paper on water contaminates and their treatments for an upper level class in medical school, but her focus had been on common bacterial pollutants, not heavy metals. The alert was a dense, official-looking notice, and there was a dire warning across the top not to drink tap water from any wells in the area.

Anders Canyon was a fairly old community and some of the suburbs, including this aging duplex, still clung to well water, though most of the town had gone to centralized water from the treatment plant. Julia drank most of her water at work, which was hooked up to the city system, and she kept a gallon of distilled water in her fridge because the well water tasted so terrible.

She glanced over at her neighbor's door.

The guy next door was already quiet, his lights out. Julia didn't know much about him; he kept to himself and never got misdelivered mail, so Julia hadn't snooped out his name yet.

She kept meaning to introduce herself, because he was pretty cute and had a great laugh, but their hours were completely incompatible. She came home after he'd gone to bed and tried to tip-toe without making too much noise; their walls were stupidly thin, and the only wall her entertainment center fit on was the one they shared. He'd never actually complained, but Julia had heard him stomping around one night after trying to watch a movie, and it was impossible to miss him getting up at the crack of dawn every morning, even though he wasn't particularly noisy about it.

He was even nice enough to mow the backyard that they shared, pushing the mower around and whistling cheerfully while Julia put a pillow over her head and cursed people who got up before noon in a general sense.

Julia had considered taking over a plate of cookies or a casserole as a thank you for the mowing, but there was a rush at the clinic the week he moved in, and by the time she could catch her breath, it had been months since he moved in and it felt like it would just be weird to introduce herself. She was also not a very adept cook, and she wasn't sure if appearing to poison him would be the best way to try to make friends.

Julia sighed as she went inside, flipping the light switch on with her elbow. She put her purse down and kicked her shoes off at last. She should have stopped for takeout. Calling for delivery would take too long, and everything in the fridge looked like too much work. A sniff suggested that the milk was still good, so Julia poured herself a bowl of cereal and went to eat in front of an entirely-too-quiet sitcom with the subtitles on. She could hear the new dog next door; its nails clacked loudly on the floor and every so often it would whine.

The sitcom humor didn't translate well to captions and Julia turned it off as soon as her cereal was down to the last unappetizing soggy wheatballs.

She saw the groundwater notice on the table next to her purse and frowned at the kitchen sink, then went to the bookshelf in the living room. Her organic chemistry textbook was unhelpful, so she booted up her laptop and did an Internet search for thallium.

Thallium was used as rat poison, a fatal heavy metal that could be leached into local water from ore-processing plants. Anders Canyon didn't have one of those, but it did have a mysterious government facility up in the mountains that had been shut down a few years ago. Julia refreshed herself on the symptoms of thallium poisoning. Hair loss, vomiting, diarrhea...they weren't things she'd seen in the clinic that day, at least, or any time recently. Mostly they'd had a few cases of the flu, a kid with a rash, and a few minor injuries. And Mrs. Harrison the hypochondriac, of course, who kept self-diagnosing on the Internet and demanding that Julia test her for obscure diseases that she didn't have.

The government warning didn't have anything helpful regarding the actual contamination levels or how long it had been around, but if it was severe enough to let people know, it was probably above the recommended concentrations. The terrible taste of the groundwater probably kept most people from drinking it, but kids in the neighborhood drank out of hoses in the backyards all the time. Julia had to expect to see symptoms showing up and she wanted to be ready with answers for their parents about long-time effects and treatments.

There wasn't anything about it in the local news yet, but Julia was sure it wouldn't be long; there were already alarmed posts in local community social media groups from other people who'd gotten the slips. She followed rabbit-hole links around the web for about an hour and ordered an online personal water test for thallium so she could get her own numbers. Then she somehow ended up reading smutty fanfiction of a popular television show where everyone mysteriously worked in a coffee shop, and finally felt tired enough to go to sleep, creeping into bed like a thief in her own house.

# CHAPTER 2

*F*rancis got to the back door of the duplex and skidded to a four-legged stop, heart hammering in his chest.

Now what?

He tried to figure out how to open the door as a dog—as a dog! He was a dog!—and as quickly as he tried to picture reaching a hand for the handle, he was a human again. A very naked human, and it was raining. He yanked the door open much harder than he meant to and slammed it behind him again.

Then, still completely naked and soaking wet, he sat down on the floor and tried to make sense of everything.

Monday, he'd been sure that the biggest news of his week was going to be his latest book release, which had unexpectedly hit a bestseller list. What could possibly top that thrill? He hadn't been able to tell anyone about it, which was a minor let-down, but he'd watched his stats obsessively and cracked open a lonely bottle of wine.

Then he'd randomly developed a weird itchiness, eaten an entire ham that was supposed to last through the weekend, and slept for a full day.

That, in itself, was pretty odd.

Francis tried to calm his breathing and think logically through the following events.

Still tired and groggy, he'd gone outside to grab the mail. It was raining, but he didn't bother putting on a coat for the short trip. He hadn't gotten more than a few steps outside before he'd stumbled. The disorientation was intense, and he'd felt trapped in his clothing, struggling and hearing seams rip as he fought free.

While he was standing there, slowly realizing that he was on four legs and had a tail hanging off his ass, he'd almost gotten hit by his hot next-door neighbor. And now he was here, with what was left of his clothing still lying out in the driveway.

Francis chuckled weakly. That was not at all one of the scenarios that he'd imagined for meeting Julia. He knew her name because he'd gotten her mail once, but he'd lost his nerve to knock on her door and give it back, and settled for slipping it into her box, instead.

He'd lived in the duplex for almost three months and he still hadn't worked out how to meet her without looking like a crazed stalker. All of his carefully practiced conversations died on his mouth when he saw her coming home in the evening, so he usually pretended to have gone to bed too early and hated himself for being a coward.

It was easier to think about Julia than it was to face the fact that he'd just turned into a dog and back.

None of this made any sense at all.

Then he pulled his arm away and stared at it.

He'd never been particularly fit. He hated exercise for the sake of exercise, and his writing career was—if satisfying—quite sedentary. He tended to the skinny end of the spectrum and had abandoned his aspirations of strength with his dreams of superpowers and becoming an astronaut.

So it was quite a shock to see an arm with definition. And not just minor definition; Francis made a muscle and gaped at the shape it made. He looked down to see that his whole body had transformed. He'd gone from scrawny to the tawdry descriptions in a trashy romance novel, six-pack and all.

He scrambled up to his feet. The only mirror he had was in the bathroom, the one above the sink that he used for shaving, and it didn't do much to show his body. His face was pretty much unchanged, though there was actual muscle in the neck, and what he could see of his shoulders was frankly impressive.

After a few contortions, trying to figure out how to see the most of his new physique, Francis laughed at his reflection.

He was a werewolf!

Well, were-dog. He'd gotten enough of a glimpse of his canine self to know think that he looked much more mutt than regal wolf.

Was it a phase of the moon thing? It was too cloudy to see it, but Francis thought that the full moon had been a week or so ago. Before he got dressed, he wondered if he could do it again.

He stretched out his arms. "Transform!" he said.

"By the power of canine!" he tried.

"Woof!"

He stared at his very human hands and nothing happened.

But he was still naked, still wet from the rain, and still weirdly buff. He'd *been* a dog, he was sure. He remembered what it was like to feel pavement under the pads of his feet, and how the rain hadn't bothered him, buffered by a coat of fur.

A sudden wave of dizziness made him fall forward and run headlong into the cabinet under the sink. His dog body was longer than he'd expected, and what felt like taking a small step propelled him further than he expected. His tail complicated matters, too, banging against everything as he rotated in the small bathroom and tried to escape the confined space. It smelled *overwhelmingly* of deodorant and aftershave and toilet cleaner.

He found himself staring at a doorknob again, and as soon as he thought about reaching for it with a human hand, he was.

He tried changing shape again in the bedroom, where there was more room, and this time he felt that it went much more smoothly. He just had to remember some sensation of the form he wanted to switch to—the strong smells or the feeling of four feet, or the way it felt to stand up and brush his hands off—and he could shift between them almost effortlessly.

Maneuvering as a dog was a lot less effortless. He had expected four feet to be easier than it was, more stable and quicker, but it was a lot of feet to keep track of, and he face-planted more than once and knocked his phone onto the floor with his tail no less than three times as he navigated his house.

He finally got dressed, in human form, and sat down at his laptop.

Supposing this was real, and something that actually happened to other people, not just a complete fluke of nature, where would he go to find more information?

He turned off the Internet blocker and gazed at the field in the search engine. How exactly do you research "I'm suddenly able to turn into an animal?"

Well, it wasn't all that much weirder than some of his keyword searches.

# CHAPTER 3

The next morning, Julia found a new notification taped to her door, a duplicate of the first. If they knocked, she had slept through it. She glanced at the neighbor's front door. A second notice was taped over the old one.

As late as she was for work, Julia hesitated. She couldn't just let him keep drinking the water in oblivion.

Julia knocked quietly the first time, but when there was no answer, she leaned into it, pounding as hard as she could. Looking around, she saw dog paw prints in the soft earth by the sidewalk where the grass was thin.

Still no answer.

Maybe the homeowners association would have his phone number. She started to turn away, and the door jerked open.

"Yeah?"

Julia had to stare for a moment. He wasn't wearing a shirt, which wasn't too unusual for him; he'd mowed the back yard shirtless a few times.

She was pretty sure he hadn't looked like this, though, with broad, muscular shoulders and strong arms...and a six-pack that drew her eyes down towards his jeans. He'd been cute, but if he hadn't had the same crooked grin and adorably tousled hair that he'd had before, Julia would have thought she was talking to a different person.

"Wa-wa-water!" she managed intelligently. She swallowed and told herself not to think about nipples. Not hers, and definitely not his. "I wasn't sure if you'd seen the notice on the door. There's something in the water. Thallium. It's a heavy metal. Poisonous. We're not supposed to drink it."

"Thallium?"

"The water," she said stupidly. "Don't drink the water."

He was staring at her, kind of the way that she was staring at him, and it was a moment before she could swallow. "There was a notice," she tried to explain. "There *is* a notice. On your door."

She was noticing. She was noticing the way his muscles bunched up under his skin with every little movement, and the way he was shifting on his feet sort of uncomfortably, probably because she was still gawking at him. "Anyway," she squeaked, dragging her eyes away, "I just wanted to make sure you saw it. And maybe you shouldn't let your dog drink it, either. They're giving away jugs of water at city hall."

"I don't have a...oh, right, my dog." Color flushed his skin. "We'll stick to bottled water," he agreed. "Thanks for letting me know," he added.

Julia blushed. "It seemed...uh...neighborly." She remembered. "And on that subject, thanks for mowing the lawn."

"You're welcome."

They stood there for a long, weird moment.

"So, I'm going to work," Julia said, finally backing away. "I work at the clinic. We're open late. Because people work, you know." Then she turned and fled, feeling like a complete idiot.

She berated herself all the way to the clinic, nearly running a red light because she was picturing her neighbor—whose name she still didn't know!—in all his shirtless glory.

# CHAPTER 4

*F*rancis spent the morning turning back and forth between man and dog until he had a good handle on how to do it reliably. He wasn't immediately good at dog things; the tail in particular took some getting used to. He impatiently waited for Julia to go to work so that he could try running around in their backyard without an audience.

When she rang the doorbell, he'd already gotten undressed in anticipation of her departure and he had just enough self-possession to put on pants.

She was just as gorgeous in person as he had imagined from the tantalizing glimpses he'd gotten of her, all curves and confidence. Her eyes were brown and her hair was dark blonde in a sensible bouncy bob.

And she stared at him like she'd never seen a guy without his shirt before.

Francis would have felt pretty good about himself if he could have managed some decent dialogue to go with his new abs, but apparently whatever magical spell or alien ray had transformed his body and given him shapeshifting abilities had not made him any better at talking to women.

He spent the brief conversation trying to figure out whether or not he was imagining that she looked interested, and how to actually ask her out without being creepy.

She finally backed away because he was gazing as dumbly at her beauty as he'd stared at her headlights the night before. "So, I'm going to work. I work at the clinic. We're open late. Because people work, you know."

Francis waved lamely and when he closed the door, he leaned his forehead against it and banged it there a few times. He hoped he hadn't said anything too dumb because he honestly remembered nothing of their actual conversation. Oh, she had warned him about the water, and he'd stumbled over her assumption that he had a dog.

He opened the door—she was long gone—and peeled the well water warnings off of his door, frowning at them thoughtfully.

Was it coincidence that he had these crazy new abilities at the same time that something like this was happening? Francis wasn't big on coincidence. Coincidence was lazy plotting.

The notice wasn't terribly helpful, and the symptoms it specifically mentioned didn't match his whatsoever, but Francis wasn't willing to say they weren't related. He hadn't turned up anything terribly enlightening in his searching the night before; a lot of terrible werewolf fanfiction, and a lot of active furry forums full of hopefuls, but nothing that matched his own transformation in any way.

Maybe it was something local, though, something literally in the water? Wasn't this exactly the kind of warning he'd put out if he wanted people to stop consuming the groundwater if it had some other kind of effect on people? Something like giving them the ability to shift forms?

Then it occurred to him that *Julia* might be going through the same thing he was.

It was a comforting thought, and a little thrilling.

But how did you open up a conversation like that? "Hello, good day, I am newly able to turn into a dog and was just wondering if you were also." Or perhaps, "Great weather we're having. Feeling a bit like changing into an animal these days?" It was the worst come-on that Francis had ever heard, even in his own head.

He sighed and slipped off his pants. He'd been dying to see if rolling on the lawn felt as good as it looked when he caught dogs doing it.

# CHAPTER 5

*J*ulia saw four people during that afternoon who complained about feeling itchy and tired and abnormally hungry but didn't exhibit any symptoms that might match thallium poisoning. No fever or rashes, and their vitals were otherwise perfectly fine. She authorized a few labs to check for abnormalities. Anna, the nurse, started calling it the itchy-munchies by the fourth patient.

Mrs. Harrison's latest self-diagnosis was a brain tumor. Julia patiently explained that her headache was much more likely to be dehydration and wrote her a prescription for Motrin.

Between patients, Julia investigated thallium further, and fantasized helplessly about her hot neighbor's bare chest. Oddly, her order for the thallium water test came back into her inbox; the company was unexpectedly out of stock. She'd have to try a different company when she had time, later.

"We've got another possible itchy-munchy case!" Anna announced unexpectedly.

"Nipples!" Julia yelped in surprise as her vision of the hot neighbor's sculpted pecs dissolved into paperwork.

"Sorry, what?" Anna looked understandably confused.

"Nothing!" Julia said quickly. "Never mind!" She had no reason to be thinking about her unexpectedly gorgeous no-name duplex-mate. "Who is it?"

"One of the Hanson kids, the oldest one, I think." James Hanson was one of the most eligible single dads in town, with two kids in middle school. He owned the local hardware store and spent most of his days battling off single (and sometimes not-so-single) women who thought he must be lonely after the tragic death of his wife.

Stepping into the examination room, Julia found herself critically thinking that he wasn't half as good-looking as her neighbor. She wrenched her thoughts back to the business at hand.

"I haven't seen you in a while," she said directly to the son, Andrew, after flipping through his file. "Staying healthy? Eating well? Any problems?"

Andrew, predictably for the age, rolled his eyes. "I'm *fine*," he sighed.

"You ate half a roast during the middle of the night and I couldn't wake you up this morning," his frazzled-looking father protested. "That's not fine!"

Julia ignored him, continuing to talk to Andrew. "Feeling itchy?"

He shrugged, but after a moment, he reached up to scratch the back of his neck. "A little, I guess."

Julia turned her attention to James. "Are you folks on city water?"

James slowly shook his head. "We've got a well."

"Did you get the notice about the contaminated water?"

"I saw it in the newspaper this morning," James said in concern. "You think this is related? Does he have heavy metal poisoning? We drink bottled water, the local stuff just tastes bad."

"It's gross," Andrew agreed.

Julia frowned. The symptoms didn't match in the slightest. But a sudden outbreak? At the exact same time? "It doesn't seem likely, but I think we should run some labs in case it is."

Andrew looked at her with owl eyes. "Radioactive heavy metals? Am I going to get superpowers?" He looked like a combination of trying to look cool and unaffected, and genuinely excited by the idea.

"That seems even more unlikely," Julia chuckled. "I'll set you up with the lab, we'll need urine and blood samples. Stay away from drinking the tap water, and let me know immediately if you notice your hair falling out, or if you have any vomiting, diarrhea, or weakness." She winked at him. "Or superpowers."

"You've got a visitor," Anna told her, when she came to get the next chart.

Julia told her hopeful libido that it wasn't going to be her neighbor. And if it was, he would probably be wearing a shirt.

To her surprise, it wasn't a patient at all.

The two people waiting in her tiny office looked suspiciously casual. The enormous man looked like he was trying very hard not to accidentally break anything in the room, his hands carefully clasped behind him. A woman who would have seemed tiny even if she hadn't been contrasted with him was sitting in the only chair across from Julia's desk, her short hair pulled back in plain silver barrettes. They were both dressed in civilian clothing that was just a little too pressed.

Military, Julia guessed at once. They were very fit.

The woman jumped to her feet and offered a hand to shake.

"I'm Lena, this is Torque. We're with the EPA," she said, just a little too cheerfully.

The aptly-named Torque offered his own hand without comment and then ominously closed the door behind them.

"You've seen the news?" Lena asked leadingly. "About the thallium contamination, I mean?"

"No," Julia admitted, sitting at her desk. "But I got a notice on my front door."

Lena nodded, her short hair bobbing at her exuberance as she sat back down in the chair. "Naturally, we're very concerned about the findings, and we'll be coordinating cleanup operations. We wanted to make sure that you hadn't had any patients coming in with anything concerning."

Julia felt the hairs on the back of her neck rise and she resisted the temptation to scratch it. "No vomiting or diarrhea today, or anything else particularly worrisome in the past week," she said, as neutrally as she could manage.

"We'd be interested in other unusual symptoms," Lena said. She didn't quite bat her eyelashes at Julia, but it was close.

"I'll keep my eyes open," Julia promised. "I thought I'd order up some doses of Prussian blue just in case. That's the standard treatment for exposure."

Lena smiled at her as if Julia was a dog that had demonstrated good training. "I'll have some stock sent over first thing in the morning," she promised. "We've got a very *large* settlement to distribute for this project and a lot of interest in seeing that no one suffers unduly." She slipped a business card across the cluttered desk. "Please give us a call if you see anything that's not normal! However minor or unusual you think it might be!"

Lena must have seen Julia's hesitation and she was quick to add, "Naturally, we have all the authority we need to request medical records and we'll go through all the proper channels. You don't need to be concerned about privacy or authorization."

Proper channels were not at all what Julia was worried about, but she smiled and hoped that her nod was convincing. "Yes, of course! I'll give you a ring if anything out of the ordinary comes in."

Lena seemed satisfied, and she stood and shook Julia's hand again. "I look forward to hearing from you," she sparkled.

Torque also shook her hand. "A pleasure," he grumbled.

Then they were gone, and Julia breathed a sigh of relief. She was pretty sure that the EPA didn't go around cleaning up toxic spills *personally*. They were in the business of issuing fines and filling papers. And if they were going to get involved, they'd bring lawyers, not muscle like Torque. Something was definitely up.

A conspiracy, she thought. It must be. But the pieces didn't fit together yet. Why would you lie about something like a heavy metal contamination? That was the kind of thing most people tried to cover up. So there must be something even worse that they were attempting to hide. What was worse than poisoning the wells? And if they weren't with the EPA, who *were* they with?

She absently scratched the back of her neck and closed her eyes in pleasure at the sensation. The tingly nervous feeling had turned into a full-blown itchiness and Julia felt a little like she wanted to rub off her own skin.

Her fingers froze as she recognized the symptom, and she immediately self-evaluated.

No fever, no shakes, heart rate was fine. She wasn't nauseous...but she was ravenous. True, it wasn't all that unusual to be hungry at this time of the day. She just...itched.

It could be coincidence, but Julia wasn't convinced that it was. There was already entirely too much coincidence for comfort. She pondered getting a blood sample to send to the lab, but if Lena and Torque were already sniffing around here, would they be able to get information on the labs she requested, too? She'd have to get it done quietly.

After staring for a little while at the business card, she called to order takeout, to be delivered just after she arrived at home, and fell into all the final paperwork of the day.

# CHAPTER 6

*F*rancis was writing when the doorbell rang, and he scowled at the screen and typed even more furiously for several moments because he knew that if he didn't get the words down the way they were falling into place, he'd lose them forever.

The doorbell rang again, and he growled and closed the laptop in defeat. He shoved the chair back, forgetting about his new strength, and nearly smashed it into the bookcase behind him before stalking downstairs.

"What?" he demanded, opening the door.

A car was pulling out of the driveway, which made Francis realize that Julia's car was parked next door. There was an amazing smell wafting up from a heap of takeout bags at his feet. It looked like enough food to feed a small army, and there was a credit card receipt stapled to one of the bags. Julia's name was on it, and it looked like the driver had gone ahead and given himself a middle-of-the-road tip.

Francis closed his eyes, astonished to realize that he could pick out individual scents from the fragrant bags. Peanut oil, chicken, pork, garlic, onion, even the cabbage in the egg rolls. Could he smell rice? He frowned down, opening his eyes again. It was a rather impressive amount of food, and he remembered the crazy hunger that had him eating the cold ham in his fridge down to the bone.

Was Julia going through a weird transition, like he was? Was she going to end up a were-dog like him?

Francis felt an odd mixture of delight and anxiousness. Maybe she'd appreciate talking to someone who'd been through the same things. Maybe he could coach her through the most peculiar parts. Maybe she'd look at him again the way she had that afternoon, like she was seeing him for the first time...and liked what she saw. He'd gotten so used to being a dog that he fully expected to feel his tail wagging behind him.

And he had the perfect excuse, he realized, looking down at the bags. He just had to bring her the food she'd ordered.

His resolve stuttered.

What if he was wrong? How crazy would she think he was, if he started talking about shifting into a dog and suddenly having keen new senses, if she hadn't experienced any of it? He'd look like a complete madman. The nutty guy next door. She might pepper spray him.

He reined in his flailing imagination. He'd start safely: just bring her the food she had ordered and see where it went from there.

And if the conversation just happened to get around to shapechanging, well, that was a bridge he would cross when he got there.

# CHAPTER 7

*J*ulia was so busy reminding herself not to scratch at her skin on her drive home that she almost didn't notice the large, dark shape in one of the yards as she drove past. She didn't think to come to a stop for several moments, and when she did, looking back in astonishment, the thing had vanished. Surely there wasn't a bear in the middle of Anders Canyon, just sitting on someone's front lawn. She took her foot off the brake slowly and finished her drive.

She didn't remember her unexpectedly hot neighbor again until she had arrived home, and by then, she was too hungry and itchy to do more than glance wistfully at his closed door. She glanced at her phone; she probably had enough time to take a quick shower before the food got there, if she hurried. As she was stepping into the shower, it occurred to her to take her temperature (normal), and jot her list of symptoms down on a sticky note with the date and time. She stuck it to the fridge.

She was dressed again, in flannel pants and an oversized tee, when she heard the knock on the door. Her stomach was growling demandingly and she ran down the stairs two at a time. The shower had not done much to ease the increasingly annoying itchiness.

"Yes!" Julia exclaimed, flinging open the door.

It wasn't the delivery driver.

It was her coveted food, but it was her neighbor holding the bags. He was, unfortunately, wearing a shirt again.

"They delivered your food to my door," he said apologetically.

Julia was busy remembering what he looked like without a shirt. "Oh, um. Sorry. I. Thanks?" She was briefly embarrassed that she had ordered as much as she had.

Then he smiled, and Julia experienced a whole new kind of hunger. "They just left it on my doorstep, the credit card receipt had your name on it."

"You know my name?" At the moment, Julia wasn't sure she knew her own name.

"Julia."

That was it.

"You want to join me?" Julia blurted impulsively. She regretted the offer at once, keenly aware of her less-than-sexy attire.

But to her surprise, he accepted. "That's...neighborly of you," he said. "I'm Francis."

"Like the pope?"

He laughed at the weak joke, and Julia tried to figure out if she should try to take the bags of food from him and risk touching him. Her itch seemed to have changed to a different sensation entirely; she was tingling and it took all of her self-control not to stare at him. She stood aside and pointed him to the kitchen table.

"You got a lot of food," Francis said innocently, as he put the bags on the table.

Julia shot a glance at him, trying to figure out what the underlying note in his voice was. Was he trying to make a dig on her weight? Just making conversation?

"I was thinking about leftovers," she said. Really, everything on the Thai menu had just sounded amazing. "Let me get some plates."

"Spicy?" Francis said hopefully, taking out a clamshell marked with something indecipherable that might or might not have been in sloppy English. He inhaled deeply and Julia tried not to stare at the neck of his shirt.

"Medium," Julia said with a smile. "Sorry, I have weenie taste-buds. But there's sriracha in the fridge."

"You don't need to refrigerate it," Francis pointed out, going to get it. "Can I get you a drink?"

"Don't drink the tap water," Julia laughed weakly. She'd almost forgotten about the conspiracy. "I'll take an orange soda." That was safer than beer, she thought.

He brought one back for himself as well, and sat across from her at the table. "Thanks for dinner," he said, looking shy as he piled a perfectly modest portion from the open clamshells onto his plate. "You'll have to let me host next time."

"I look forward to it," Julia said ungracefully around a mouthful of food.

If she hadn't been so starved, she probably would have been too addled to eat; Francis was freaking gorgeous, and he ate like he was being photographed. Tidy forkful of food, dab the corner of his mouth artfully, and then, oh lord, he was licking his lips.

Julia, on the other hand, had to hold herself back from wolfing down the food in front of her and then eating her plate. She tried to take a normal-sized portion, but it just didn't look like enough, and it took all of her will not to simply shovel curry and pad thai directly into her mouth out of the carton.

"So," she said, swallowing and making herself say something rather than just make a complete fool out of herself. There was one thing she was dying to know: "What do you do for a living?" Under-wear model, she hoped.

Francis, to her astonishment, blushed like she'd just asked if he was a virgin.

"I'm a writer," he said, almost squirming in his chair.

Not a good one, Julia guessed, by his acute embarrassment. "That's awesome," she said encouragingly, not wanting him to be uncomfortable. "What do you write?"

She caught him with a mouthful of food and he sheepishly swal-lowed before admitting, "Science fiction."

Science fiction didn't warrant that kind of color in the cheeks, Julia thought suspiciously. "Would I recognize your name?" she asked, before she could stop herself.

"Ye—no," he said firmly. "It's kind of...I mean, the last book has sold maybe a hundred copies. Self-published."

Julia could tell that he was definitely failing to tell her everything. Secrets seemed to be the theme of her day. But she didn't get the same polished deception feeling that she'd gotten off of Lena and Torque, and she didn't care as much about his writing career as she did about the food in front of her.

She had to force herself to bite from the eggrolls rather than simply try swallowing them whole like a snake. Only Francis, sitting across the table from her looking sort of shy and awkward, kept her demonstrating any manners at all.

"So, you're a nurse?" he asked, when she failed at conversation.

"A doctor," Julia corrected, making herself pause between bites with effort.

"Sorry," Francis said swiftly. He blushed way too often for a guy that gorgeous. Julia thought she could spend a lot of time watching his skin turn color.

Thinking about his skin reminded her of his nipples again and Julia was pretty sure that she was blushing as hard as he was. Her own nipples were completely hard. "It's okay," she assured him.

Her plate was empty, and she was too self-conscious to take another helping as he more sedately polished off his serving.

"Thanks for the food," he said sincerely. "I've been hoping to meet you, but it seems like we have sort of incompatible hours."

"I hope I haven't been too noisy coming home," Julia said, abashed.

"Not at all," he said quickly. "You've been really courteous."

Julia didn't feel particularly courteous. She was divided between wanting to scarf down the rest of the takeout like a rabid raccoon at a trashcan buffet and wanting to crawl across the table and put herself in his lap.

"Well, you know, trying to be neighborly," she said lightly.

They smiled at each other, and Julia felt like Francis was trying to decide if he should say something, opening his mouth and then closing it. "Can I help you clean up?" he finally offered.

Julia guessed that wasn't what he had been thinking about saying.

She wasn't good at flirting because she rarely cared to, but Julia thought that maybe he was trying to hit on her. He had this devastating combination of friendly and shy, and Julia felt her ovaries clench every time that she caught him wrenching his gaze away.

They loaded the dishwasher talking casually about books. She admitted that she mostly read trashy historical romance, and they agreed that reading on a tablet might not have the same visceral pleasure of a paper book, but it helped to keep the collection under control.

Listening to him say the words *visceral pleasure* made Julia's knees feel weak.

Then they were out of inane conversation and the leftovers were all put away and they stood there in the kitchen together not quite staring at each other.

He wanted her, Julia thought. Maybe as much as she wanted him.

His hands flexed and balled into fists, and he looked everywhere but directly at her. He swallowed and licked his lips and Julia couldn't help but wonder what they'd taste like. Spicy?

She wished she were a different person. Someone who would take that moment and live it, not think too hard about how impractical it was to feel this hot for someone she'd just met.

"I should go," he said. His voice was low and sort of rumbly.

If Julia were someone else, she would have said, "Should you?" or "Don't go." Or possibly, "Take your clothes off!"

Instead, she walked him to the door, trying to keep just the right distance from him. His shirt didn't do that much to hide the fact that he was devastatingly built. How had she never noticed? It wasn't like they'd met, but she'd caught glimpses of him. Glimpses that hadn't done him justice. She desperately wanted to reach out and pet him. His hair was just long enough to thread fingers into, and she imagined she could feel the heat of him as she brushed past him to open the door.

It was late, and the rain had stopped. A car, unnaturally loud, drove quickly by, ignoring the "Children at Play" sign warning them to slow down.

"Thanks," they both said at once.

It was the moment Francis should leave, but he hesitated and Julia didn't shut the door. "If you...ah...need anything..." he said haltingly. "I mean, tomorrow. You'll...ah..."

Struck with sudden doubt, Julia wondered if she'd been reading his signals incorrectly. He looked more worried than flirtatious. "Is something wrong?" she asked.

Francis looked like he would burst with indecision. Was he conflicted over whether or not to kiss her? Julia wondered with sudden hope. It was kind of like a first date, her flannel pants notwithstanding. Should she try to kiss him?

Before she could screw up her courage, he shook his head firmly. "No. Nothing. Thanks for the food. I'll...see you. Call me!"

Then he was striding away, just next door, and Julia was kicking herself for missing her chance to throw herself into his arms.

She closed the door and leaned against it, feeling dizzy. She should check her temperature again...and then she remembered that she'd left the sticky note with her list of symptoms on the fridge where Francis could easily have seen them. What would he make of that?

The itch had returned, and Julia spent a moment trying to decide between an ice water bath and going directly to the fridge to finish all the Thai food leftovers. A wave of exhaustion swamped both desires and it was everything she could do to stagger to her bed and pass out.

# CHAPTER 8

$\mathcal{I}$t wasn't until Francis got back into his own half of the duplex that he realized he'd told Julia to call him...and had not actually bothered to give her his phone number.

"I am such an idiot!" he said to no one. "Argh! What is wrong with me?"

How was it possible for him to write intelligent characters and be so completely dumb?

He found his phone and stared at it as if it would somehow send him back in time and let him fix the hash of that...could he even call it a date? It was a meal, and it had been an interesting conversation. They hadn't talked about anything particularly deep, but it was obvious that she had a quick mind, and she was even prettier when she laughed and smiled at him than she was scowling at her phone or hurrying to work. And he was almost sure that if he'd tried to kiss her when he left that she would have let him.

"A coward, too," he chided his blurry reflection in the shiny phone.

He didn't have many doubts left that she was heading down the same strange journey that he'd just been through. The notes she'd left on the fridge indicated she was just a day or two behind him, and the way that she ate her food like she thought he was going to take it away suggested that she would very shortly drop into the long, deep, cocoon-like sleep that had resulted in the Brave New Francis.

(Except, of course, that he clearly wasn't all that brave.)

Maybe when she woke up the next day, he could screw his courage back up and go over to talk to her about it.

He was still staring at his faded face in the phone screen when it rang, and he nearly dropped it in alarm.

"Hi there, is this Francis Albert?" The voice that greeted him was so cheerful that Francis immediately distrusted it.

"May I ask who's calling?" he asked formally.

"My name is Lena. I'm calling to follow up on the notifications we left at your residence." Bubbles. She sounded like she was made of sugar and bubbles. Totally harmless and not the slightest bit suspicious.

Francis was not fooled. "Okay," he said unhelpfully.

"We'll be in the neighborhood next week installing special filters at absolutely no charge to you. We wanted to make sure you had an alternate source of water until then, and also to check in and make sure you didn't have any puzzling symptoms. We have a team of specialists on hand, and we want to catch any problems as early as possible."

"Uh," Francis flailed. It seemed perfectly innocent. They were just following up on a possible contamination...they surely didn't mean 'do you turn into a dog' when they were asking about 'puzzling symptoms.' "I seem to be in fine health," he said vaguely. Better than fine, he thought, unable to resist flexing one of his arms. "I've got bottled water."

"Great!" Lena said effervescently. "When can we schedule you for the water filter? We'll need access to your house for a short time to get the installation done, so you'll need to be home from work at that time."

"I work at home," Francis said cautiously.

Lena suggested a date and time, Francis reluctantly agreed to it. Whether the thallium was related to his sudden new superpowers or not, it probably wasn't a great idea to have heavy metals in his water.

"Should I be worried?" he asked. "I won't drink it, but what about...I don't know, showering?"

Lena was quick to assure him that only ingestion was problematic.

"Thanks," Francis said.

"We'll take care of everything!" Lena sparkled at him. "Be sure to call if anything comes up!"

It was just a little too friendly and forward to be genuine, and Francis hung up and looked at the time. It was unusually quiet next door; Julia didn't have the TV or music on, and wasn't moving around at all.

Asleep? Francis figured it would be late the next afternoon before she woke up and hoped she wouldn't miss work for it. He wasn't naive enough to think that this thallium issue was unrelated to suddenly being a werewolf, but he couldn't figure out how they fit together.

His Internet leads were all dead ends, and after he tried to order a home thallium water test (they were oddly all out), Francis booted up his tablet and settled in for a different kind of research.

# CHAPTER 9

*J*ulia's first waking thought was regret.

She really should have tried kissing Francis when she had the chance. He was hot, nice, lived conveniently close by, didn't seem to mind that she'd been dressed for a slumber party and ate like a barely house-trained pig…

Her second thought was that she still itched, but it wasn't nearly as bad and she made a mental note to update her symptoms log.

Her eyelids were nearly gummed shut and it was an effort to finally open them, blinking in confusion.

Julia struggled with her comforter for a moment before she could twist out of it and stand up to go to the bathroom. She hadn't bothered getting undressed, and her t-shirt felt curiously wrong over her shoulders. She was trying in vain to straighten it when she passed her mirror, and she took two full steps before backing up in astonishment.

Her reflection stared back.

Her face didn't look much different, and her hair definitely looked well-slept in, but the reason that her t-shirt didn't feel right was that it was tight over her shoulders. She blinked, trying to decide how it could have shrunk overnight, then realized that the shape of her shoulders had changed. It wasn't just too much Thai food; she flexed her arm and gaped at the muscle that popped up.

Hesitantly, she lifted her shirt and stared at her tummy. It was, to her disappointment, no less padded than usual, but when she turned, there was definition in the muscles at her side that she'd never seen before.

She looked like a body-builder.

She poked herself in the stomach. Well, a slightly chunky body-builder. Sleeping in her bra had left marks in the soft flesh beneath her breasts.

Julia dived back towards her bed. She had weights that she almost never used under there somewhere and she was dying to know if she was actually stronger than she had been.

The next moment was a confusion of cloth and panic, and for a worried moment, Julia thought she was being kidnapped by an unknown assailant. She twisted and fought, and was somehow emerging from a tent of her own clothing to look...up at her bed.

She froze in alarm, suddenly in a giant's bedroom, and gradually became aware of a weight on her...tail?

She turned her head slowly, and found the back end of a cat with her t-shirt, now enormous, still draped over it. Her flannel pants lay in a heap beneath her. When she shimmied out of the shirt, a fluffy tail emerged, a fluffy tail that was *attached* to her.

The huge bed and bedroom and clothing slowly made sense.

She was a cat.

She rotated, trying to catch a glimpse of herself, and then scampered for the mirror.

It was too far up off the ground for her to see her whole self at once, but she found that she could balance carefully on her hind feet, with that crazy tail out behind her, and verify that indeed, she was a long-furred, tabby-striped feline.

She fell back onto all fours in utter astonishment and stared around.

Her vision was curious, sharp and discrete, like she was focusing a telescope with every glance, and her nose twitched at the assault of smells.

She was a *cat*.

Questions tumbled through her mind. Was this permanent? Was this related to the hunger and the itchiness? Was it magic? Science fiction? Was it all a dream?

It certainly didn't feel like a dream. She could feel the texture of the carpet under her paws, and the curious ruffle of her own fur. Her whiskers were an amazing, fascinating source of information; she could feel little variations in the airflow all around her. When she walked too close to the door frame, her face exploded into an overflow of sensation.

She was a cat!

The doorbell was a sudden assault on all her exquisite new senses, and Julia had just enough time to wonder how she could open a door when she was standing up as a human again. Her bare skin started to goosebump in the cool air almost at once. Was it the simple act of imagining herself as human that triggered the transformation?

She closed her eyes and thought about how it had felt to be warm and cozy in her own fur coat and was not as surprised as she thought she probably should be when she opened her eyes and found herself staring at the top of the short boots by her bedroom door.

The doorbell rang again, and she startled back into human form, only remembering to grab her clothing and yank it on at the last moment before she dashed down the stairs to answer the front door.

She was not surprised to find Francis there; somehow, he was the only thing that whole day that seemed to make any sense at all.

"You're your own dog!" she blurted, putting all the pieces together.

He looked painfully relieved. "Did it happen to you, too?"

It looked like it was late afternoon. "What time is it?" she asked. "How long did I sleep?" She realized that she was dressed in the same rumpled clothing that she'd been wearing the night before, and that she hadn't bothered with underwear in her rush for the door. Francis didn't seem to care, he was looking her over like he was trying not to. Did he notice her new physique? Could he miss it?

"I slept almost nineteen hours when it happened to me," Francis offered. He looked like she'd just confirmed his deepest fear that he wasn't entirely insane, which was a lot like how Julia felt. Also, she still kind of wanted to kiss him, and wasn't sure if that was adrenaline, sheer relief that she wasn't alone in this madness, or just the fact that he was really adorable.

"Come on in," Julia invited, and she let him close the door behind him. "Do you want a drink? It's late enough for a drink, isn't it? I must have slept all day."

"I would love a drink," Francis said. "Just, maybe not the—"

"—tap water!" Julia finished with him. "This can't be caused by a thallium contamination," she said skeptically, opening the fridge. "I mean, there's no way!"

She found two craft beers in the back from a multi-pack she'd bought a few weeks before and offered Francis his choice of them.

"Kind of funny that this all happened at the same time, though," he observed.

"Not funny, and not a coincidence," Julia said firmly. "I had five cases at the clinic with some of the same symptoms." She found a notebook in a drawer and flipped it to an empty page to start jotting down notes. "I think it's a cover-up. Tell me what you went through!"

Francis blinked at her authoritative tone, then slowly smiled. "You'll think it's weird."

"I'm a doctor," Julia told him. "I just turned into a cat. I think we're well past weird."

Francis pulled the bottle cap off with his hands—it wasn't a twist-off—and tossed it onto the table as he sat across from her. "It started a few days ago. I just felt...off. I was itchy, but there was no rash, really tired, and absolutely ravenous. Then I slept for most a day, went outside and kind of stepped out of my own skin. You almost hit me with your car, right after I tore off my clothes."

"Sorry," Julia said absently. She was writing down the details of Francis's transformation, and putting down all the vitals she remembered from her patients. She didn't write any names, suspiciously remembering Lena and Torque. She didn't put it past them to break into her house and snoop.

"Your turn," Francis prodded her.

Julia looked up, into his gorgeous brown eyes. Unlike last time, he didn't shy away from her gaze. Apparently, sharing secrets like this meant that they were past tiptoeing around each other. She realized that he'd been awkwardly trying to figure out if she was going through the same thing he was, the night before, without sounding crazy. She liked this more-confident him.

It made her want to kiss him even more.

"I, let's see." Now was not the time to fantasize about his lips, Julia reminded herself. "I noticed that I was itchy towards the end of my shift at the clinic yesterday evening, and yes, also very hungry. I didn't have a fever, vitals were fine. I ordered a lot of Thai food, which you were kind enough to bring over, and then I slept all day and when I woke up I got trapped in my own clothing and came out a cat." Julia looked away first, ostensibly to write down her own symptoms. She remembered all over again that she wasn't wearing underwear.

She flipped over another page. "Okay, so we've got thallium as a red herring, and the so-called EPA is sending muscle to shake out information about it."

"The EPA?"

"Probably not the EPA," Julia explained. "I got a visit in my office yesterday from two way-too-helpful government officials who wanted to know about *unusual symptoms.* They even wanted to provide us with antidote, for free, and no one does that. Well, no one except drug companies who think it will pay off."

"Oh, I got a phone call from a ridiculously chipper woman named Lena. Did you tell them anything?"

"I told them I'd report back if anything came up."

"Who do you think they were really with?"

Julia tapped her pen on the pad. "Some kind of secret government agency? I definitely got a black van and suddenly missing neighbors sort of vibe off of them. I wasn't going to throw a couple of high appetites and possible allergies at them." She found herself watching the newly defined muscles in the back of her forearm. "You know, they were both really fit. I thought they were probably military, but they could have both gone through...whatever this is. What do we know about people who turn into animals? I mean, anything?" She liked the idea that Lena and Torque were shapeshifters, looking for others of their kind to protect, but she didn't exactly trust that they were, and she didn't want to end up in a cage in a laboratory by trusting the wrong people.

"Fiction, or otherwise?" Francis wanted to know. "There's werewolf legends, of course, and, ah, a whole subgenre of shifter romances."

Julia watched his ears turn pink and knew there was something he wasn't telling her again. "Have you been bit lately?" she asked. "That's how werewolves usually happen, right? They get turned?"

Francis shook his head. "Nope," he said. "And most of the stuff I've...uh...been reading has shifting as a genetic quirk, passed on to children. As far as I know, my parents were perfectly normal pharmacists who never turned into anything more exciting than rabid sports fans during football season."

Julia had to laugh. "Yeah, my dad is way too fastidious to be a shapeshifter. Cat fur? Not in his house."

"Where did you grow up?" Francis wanted to know.

"Chicago suburbs," Julia told him. "A couple of blocks from the El. You?"

"The other side of Anders Canyon," he said with a shrug. "But I spent four years in California going to school."

They talked about their childhoods, briefly, trying to determine any shared exposure that might have explained their new circumstances. "I didn't witness any strange meteors or come wandering back from a cornfield with no memory," Julia quipped. "And that wouldn't explain why other people in Anders Canyon are suddenly turning up with these symptoms, all at the same time like this."

"I tried to search the Internet," Francis volunteered. "There are Reddit forums that would be all over something like this if it were happening everywhere, and there hasn't been a peep."

They opened a second round of beers, and then a third, while they put their heads together over Julia's notes, adding anything they could think of.

The more they worked, the more Julia liked Francis. He listened to her craziest hypothesis (experimental drugs leached into the groundwater from the closed military facility), countered them with an even crazier hypothesis (the beginnings of an alien invasion), and then logically hashed through all the facts with her.

It didn't seem like a possible contagion. Julia knew where her five patients lived, or at least the general area, and they didn't have much in common. "And I haven't actually been drinking the water," Julia said thoughtfully, "so it's unlikely to transmit that way."

She called Anna at home and asked a few questions about the patients that had come in the previous day. None of the labs were back yet; Anna was the one who received the text alerts and she hadn't gotten any. "Yeah, I know it's a day off, I just got curious," Julia explained. *Curiosity killed the cat,* she thought.

She asked a few leading questions about Anna's own health, but Anna seemed puzzled and distracted.

"There could be a lot more people affected than those who have come into the clinic," Julia said thoughtfully after she hung up. "I'm not sure the symptoms were severe enough that everyone who had them would bother visiting a doctor. A lot of Anders Canyon would just tough out a little itchiness. I'll call my patients on Monday during the day to follow up and see if any of them have weird lingering symptoms."

"Weird lingering symptoms like changing into a domesticated pet?" Francis said dryly.

"That's one for the medical journal," Julia laughed. "Oh, I thought I saw a bear on the way home last night. So maybe it's not just domestic pets." She was starting to feel the beers, a pleasant overlay of contentment. They finished off the rest of the Thai food. Her appetite wasn't even a fraction of what it had been the night before, but she had just slept through an entire day, so she was still hungry.

It was surprisingly comfortable to have Francis there. They

moved to the living room after eating and sprawled at opposite ends of the couch as they continued to chew on their mutual puzzle. She still wanted to watch his every movement, and was thrilled to sometimes catch his glance lingering over her hopelessly un-sexily-attired body, but she didn't feel as tightly wound as she had before.

It felt oddly *domestic*. It was nice to have someone around, and Julia had never realized how empty and lonely her half of the duplex felt, and how much she rattled around in it by herself. She'd considered getting a pet a few times, but it felt unkind to get a pet around her clinic hours.

She put her head down and giggled. Now she was her own pet, how about that?

"What are you thinking?" Francis wanted to know.

"I was just wishing that I'd have lost some of this weight in my magical transformation," she said lightly. "I mean, I'm clearly stronger and more fit and flexible, but I didn't end up all...ah..." She couldn't figure out a safe way to finish the sentence and gestured blushingly at Francis.

"Maybe you were already perfect," he said gravely.

Julia made the mistake of looking up at him in surprise and then couldn't take her gaze back as her breath stilled.

It was a charged moment, and he didn't look away either, even though he looked a little like he wanted to, shy and uncertain.

"You know those shifter fiction books usually have a fated mate in them," he said hesitantly. "A shifter knows their one true love when they meet."

"Do you think that happens?" She could barely speak above a whisper.

"Destiny seems complicated," Francis said slowly. "But maybe it's...possible."

The space between them on the couch seemed like an insurmountable distance. "It could just be a shift in hormones or body chemistry," she said. "I mean, we did just go through a pretty intense physical change. Probably, it's not something to build a fairy tale out of." She realized after she said it that she was going to kill any mood that was there by being boring and scientific, and when Francis stood up, her heart fell.

*Way to go, Julia,* she scolded herself, standing to probably see him to the door.

But he didn't move to leave, he came to stand before her. "I'm pretty sure that this doesn't have to do with turning into a dog," he said quietly. "I've had a crush on you since I first saw you."

"You...have?" Julia said stupidly.

"Can I kiss you?"

She misjudged the distance between them, or maybe he was moving in at the same time, and their lips crashed together with a kiss so desperate and hot that Julia couldn't have said how they got back to the couch.

He was everything under her fingers that she'd thought he'd be, all hard muscle and soft hair. His kiss was hungry and demanding. Almost as hungry and demanding as hers was; Julia was not sure she had ever been so completely turned on. The mass of his cock against her thigh confirmed that he was equally excited, even through their clothes.

The couch was unequal to their eager struggle, and Julia dragged her mouth away long enough to command, "Upstairs. Now!"

He came willingly, ripping his T-shirt off over his head before they made it to the bed. Her shirt followed, in a flurry of kisses and nibbles. Julia lay back, throwing her arms up, and let him kiss down between her breasts, cupping each one and worshipping the nipple before exploring further. His fingers were nimble and clever over her skin and when he reached the waistband of her pants she realized he was growling.

She was stronger than she knew; the headboard gave a warning creak under her hands as Francis slipped fingers down to slowly caress her clit. She let go in a panic, and then had nothing to hang on to. "Francis," she cried softly.

Then he was kissing her again, his body over her. A brief fight with his jeans resulted in the sound of ripping cloth. "Sorry!" she said, not certain if she'd been the cause of it. But literally ripping off clothing was certainly a very werewolf sort of thing for them to do, and she was laughing...and then they were both finally naked.

There was a pause, both of them drinking each other in, breathing hard. He was straddling her, propped up on both hands, staring down at her, and she realized that she could make out every line of his sweet body even though she'd never gotten her bedroom light turned on. She was keenly aware of his closeness, of every touch of his skin against her, like she was made of her sensitive cat whiskers.

"Julia..." he said, and she reached for him, giving his very impressive cock a stroke with her hand that made him jerk and groan helplessly.

She spread her legs, drawing him down onto her, guiding him into her wet, hungry entrance, whimpering in need.

He was achingly big, and it had been a very long time since Julia had been with anyone, but he slipped in with gentle persistence, finding a delicious, perfect rhythm, deeper with every stroke, harder and hotter until she was crying out without the slightest bit of shame.

As the tremors of her orgasm slowly ebbed away, she giggled. "Good thing the neighbor isn't home," she said, twining her arms around Francis's neck.

He laughed with her, still buried deep.

Impulsively, Julia twisted her leg around his and flipped him easily onto his back. She loved being stronger and faster than she had been, though she suspected that it would have been more chal-lenging if he had resisted.

Straddling him, her hands on his fascinating chest, she sank onto him.

He made a deep, guttural noise of pleasure and his hands clenched at her hips and abruptly let go with a frantic, "Sorry, sorry!"

"I'm not," Julia told him, and then she was riding him, harder and faster, crying out as another orgasm flooded through her. It almost felt like she could ride Francis' release to her own as he came, hot and frantic.

# CHAPTER 10

Since they were already naked, Francis didn't feel odd asking, "Can I see your cat?" Well, not completely odd.

"I don't have a—" Julia stopped herself. "Okay, my life has taken a weird turn."

"I'll show you mine..." Francis teased.

They fell out bed together and then regarded each other curiously from new heights. Francis had to resist the urge to lick the top of her furry head. He couldn't quite keep himself from lowering his nose and snuffling at her. She gave a little mew of protest, then rubbed the top of her head against his jaw, walking between his legs and letting her tail trail over his nose. She wound around one leg and returned to look up at him.

He didn't even try to keep from licking her that time and she shifted under his tongue to say, "Ew!" and then they were both human and he pulled her playfully back onto the bed with him, pretending to keep licking as she squirmed and squealed.

They snuggled for a while, and Francis marveled at the perfection of her curves in his arms.

"What do we do now?" Julia asked, tracing her finger along his chest contentedly.

"Right now, or in about thirty minutes?"

"I mean about this whole shifting thing," Julia said in exaspera-
tion. But she giggled, and didn't seem to mind the suggestion.

"Well, we're a cat and dog," Francis said archly. "We should
probably start fighting."

Julia pinched his closest nipple and they giggled and wrestled
together for a moment, ending in lingering kisses.

"Seriously, though," she said, when they had settled somehow
even more comfortably again together. "There's some kind
of...weird contamination or contagion that is causing *people* to turn
into *animals*. There are agents from a mysterious department that
isn't the EPA sniffing around. I'm pretty sure that one of our neighbors is a brown bear."

Francis wound locks of Julia's short hair onto his finger. He
couldn't get enough of touching her, marveling at all the amazing
parts of her. "I don't really mind it, do you?"

Julia snorted in helpless laughter. "No, I honestly do not mind
suddenly being twice as strong and flexible and able to see in the
dark and turn into a cat. It was the second-best thing that happened
to me this week."

"What was the best?" Francis wanted to know, hardly daring to
hope.

Julia hesitated, then admitted shyly, "You."

Francis propped himself up on one elbow and looked at her in a
mixture of fear and delight. He'd been afraid that it was nothing
more than great chemistry and hot sex, like she'd suggested. While
he didn't honestly object to any of that, he desperately wondered if
there was something more and wasn't sure how to ask.

"Me, too," he finally decided to say. "I mean, you were the best
thing that's happened to me. And it was a helluva week, I have to
confess. You beat out some really stiff competition."

"What else happened this week?" Julia wanted to know, as
curious as her cat counterpart.

Francis hesitated. If she knew...would it change how she looked
at him? Would he be a laughingstock? He drew a breath. He wanted

this to be more than just a casual hookup, and he wasn't going to keep secrets from her. "I made a bestseller list. Well, one of my books did."

Julia sat up in astonishment. "You told me your books sell like a hundred copies," she said, crinkling her eyebrows together. "I mean, it's great, congratulations! I think I have a bottle of wine in the cabinet. But you made it sound like you weren't doing all that well."

"My science fiction books don't sell well," Francis said. He could feel the heat in his face and ears. "But I have a pen name…"

Julia looked at him expectantly, raising her eyebrows.

"I write science fiction *romance*," Francis said reluctantly.

"Your books have romance?" Julia said, clearly not seeing the reason for his hesitation. "Like, sex scenes?"

He sighed and fell back into the pillows. "No. I write books about buff scaled alien men who kidnap helpless earth women for kinky sex experiments and learn how to love."

Julia gaped at him.

"Don't judge me," he begged, propping up on one arm again. "They sell really well. Hard sci-fi doesn't pay the bills unless you're Poul Anderson."

"I have three of them on my tablet," Julia confessed. "How could I possibly judge? What's your pen name?"

"F. M. Lovelace."

Julia shrieked almost as loud as she had before. "You wrote *His Human Captive Mate*! I own that book!"

Francis wondered if he'd made a terrible tactical error and broken Julia before he could even ask her to be his girlfriend.

"No wonder you were so amazing," Julia said, giggling hysterically. "That was one of the hottest books I've ever read."

It was a compliment, Francis decided. It was definitely a compliment, and when he reached to gather her back into his arms, her uncontrolled laughter faded to snuggly chuckles. He'd never held such a perfect armful, he thought, breathing in the scent of her hair.

"I suppose this doesn't quite answer the question," she said after a moment. "What do we do next?"

"We could contact our friendly EPA representatives," he suggested reluctantly.

They both shook their heads in unison.

"I don't trust them as far as I could throw them," Julia said. "Even if I could throw Lena pretty far now."

"And what do we do about all the people who might suddenly be shifters?" Francis asked. "Do we try to contact others?"

Julia rolled out of his arms and stared up at the ceiling. "I'm worried that Lena and Torque already know what's up. They said they had the proper authority to request medical files, who knows what other powers they have. I hate the idea of one of my patients ending up spending their life in a padded cage, if that's what they're planning!"

"Can you delete or alter their files?" Francis asked. "I ask as a fiction writer who doesn't know a thing about how the system actually works but uses it as a plot device all the time."

"I could," Julia said thoughtfully. "Anna would know, though."

"Would she...react poorly to the truth?"

"No," Julia said promptly. "Anna's solid."

Francis sat up lazily and ran fingers through his hair. "Maybe what we need is a secret society. We could pretend to be an AA group or something. We can coordinate our stories, cover for each other, have a secret handshake. With sword fighting! I've always wanted to be part of a swashbuckling secret society."

Julia smiled slowly up at him until Francis began to get nervous. "What?"

"Not just a secret society," she said slyly. "A book club! The Anders Canyon Book Club! You can be our first celebrity guest writer."

"Nonononononono," Francis protested. "I'm not good at that."

"All you have to do is sit there and look broody," Julia teased him. "Just like an alien lord!"

"I will never live this down," Francis moaned. Then a thought occurred to him. "You know, though, I have read a half a dozen shifter books in the last few days. I probably could write one. You know, one with the real details that other people this happens to could use to figure out what's going on. I could call it Real Shifters or something."

Julia laughed in delight and clapped her hands. "I never thought I'd be so happy that my boyfriend writes bodice rippers," she said.

Francis felt his heart lurch in his chest. *Boyfriend?*

"I'll talk to Anna," Julia continued, as she rolled away at last and started to pick through their clothing. "And I'll call my patients and get to work on making their records less obvious if the EPA comes snooping. Some of them have labs coming in tomorrow or the next day, I'll see if any of their levels are out of whack. You want a shower?"

Francis was still hung up on *boyfriend.* "Julia…"

"It wouldn't surprise me if hormones were high, given the physical changes. Maybe endorphins and catecholamines, too. I didn't specifically script a test for any of those. I should send in a sample of my own blood and see how it comes back. I've got a friend at the lab who would be able to do it quietly."

Just hormones? Francis was on a rollercoaster. "Julia?"

She held up his jeans. "We ripped them," she said sheepishly.

Francis stood up and took them from her. "I don't care," he said honestly. "Julia, I've always thought that destiny was lazy writing. It's something you only find in novels and movies."

Julia licked her lips and Francis had to reach out and brush his thumb over the place her tongue had been.

"I like you, Julia," he said. "I like you a lot. You're smart and funny and hot, and I think this could be something amazing. But I…is this just a moment to you, or is this something momentous?"

"Is that a line from one of your books?" Julia asked in a whisper. She was doing that adorable thing where she was trying not to gaze at him and failing.

"It will be now," Francis said. "It was pretty good, don't you think?"

She looked at him then, really looked at him, and burst out laughing as she reached to put her arms around him. "Oh, Francis," she confessed, "I'm half in love with you already!"

He bent to kiss her, deep and hard, and she kissed him back like she meant it.

Francis wasn't sure if they'd find others going through the same things they were, but he was really glad that they'd found each other.

"Look out Anders Canyon," he said. "You're getting a helluva book club."

# A SNEAK PREVIEW OF THROW ME A BONE...

*H*ally was ecstatic when Lucas rather suddenly started turning into a wolf.

It was, in her little part-Collie canine mind, the very best thing that could happen to her friend and feeder, and she could not understand why he wouldn't be overjoyed to finally be able to romp with her on four legs.

Lucas was far less happy about the transformation, at least at first. "I don't have time to be a werewolf," he protested, trying to scratch off his own skin. "This fucking sucks."

Fortunately, after a day of unbearable itching and ravenous hunger and an extra day of sleep, the phenomena seemed to have settled into a weird combination of new talents and physical enhancements. Lucas was deeply relieved that he didn't seem inclined to revert to a slavering, feral beast, largely because he was pretty sure that the homeowners association would complain. He'd already gotten notices about the length of the grass (one quarter inch too long) and the fact that his door jamb needed re-painted.

And as far as weird curses went, it wasn't that bad. The worst of it was no more terrible than a bad hangover. He only missed two nights of his job, bartending at the local bar, creatively named The Canyon Bar, and the poor lighting did an admirable job of hiding the fact that he was rather suddenly ripped. He'd been in decently good shape, but had gone from basically fit to brawny in the space of the last week.

"You can stop touching your biceps," Sheilah said, looking annoyed as she brought a tray of dirty dishes to the bar. "So you've been working out. Everyone is *really* impressed." Sarcasm was pretty much Sheilah's only brand of humor.

And okay, maybe the bad light *didn't* hide it very well.

"You trying to get the attention of your gorgeous neighbor?" Sheilah asked, putting the dishes by the sink, but not actually offering to wash them. "What's his name? Shaun?"

Lucas flushed, and was glad that the crappy lighting would at least cover for that. "He's probably straight," he said, trying to sound nonchalant. Hally, lying under the bar, thumped her tail in delight at the sound of her master's voice.

"Nah," Sheilah said. "No straight man has hair like that."

Privately, Lucas thought that Sheilah only suspected he was gay because she hadn't had any luck getting his number and she had a pretty tall estimation of her own wiles.

Shaun lived three houses down from him. Their street backed onto a green belt with a slough where Lucas could let Hally run, and he often walked along it after dark. If you could judge a guy by his yard, Shaun was uptight and totally unapproachable. Every blade of grass was exactly the same length, and the hedges were perfectly shaped; he'd probably never once gotten a nastygram from the homeowners association. The image was only enhanced by his nice clothes and perfect hair; Lucas suspected he was some kind of big shot at one of the technology firms in town.

Shaun came into the bar a couple of times a month for shows (Anders Canyon didn't have a lot going on), and he and Lucas ran into each other at the store once in a while, or saw each other down the street taking out the recycling at the same time, but Lucas had never dared to do more than nod in a friendly fashion and professionally take his drink orders.

Hally was rolling on her back, kicking her feet in the air, and Lucas bent to rub her exposed tummy. "Just a few more hours," he promised, and he went to wash the dishes that Sheilah was pretending didn't exist.

To win his mate,
he'll have to put
his foot down...

# The Flamingo's Fated Mate

## ELVA BIRCH

# LAWN ORNAMENT SHIFTERS

This is the book I wasn't writing. I made the cover as an April Fool's prank…but it swiftly became my most demanded title and after threatening for an entire year not to write it (and sharing bits of what I wasn't writing with my mailing list and Facebook group), I released it as a surprise for the following April Fool's! Then I had to write it a sequel…

Short, hilarious, and full of heart, fall in love with the quirky characters who run Wilson Kinetics, world famous artists and lawn ornament manufacturers. Shifters meet their fated mates in these clever, quick-paced stories of adventure and romance, set in a world with shifters, gnomes, and more! There isn't really an overall series arc to this one, but you'll see characters again, so it's best read in order:

The Flamingo's Fated Mate (book 1)
Gnome Sweet Gnome (book 2)
A Bear in a Birdbath (not that I'm writing it…)

# CHAPTER 1

*T*here were two thousand cupcakes in the back of Anita's van.

It was a lot of cupcakes.

Anita stared at the results of her labor over the last day and a long, sleepless night. There were boxes of cupcakes on every shelf and even in the aisle between them, each of them with tidy rows of lemon and mint, chocolate and cherry, vanilla and peach. Every cupcake was perfectly iced with an artistic swirl and topped with a tiny garnish and a little flag with her bakery logo.

It was six in the morning and just starting to snow. Anita's wrists ached and her back had a warning twinge that reminded her that she wasn't twenty anymore; bending over pastries with a piping bag was harder work than it looked.

It was hours and hours before the charity event started and there were no other vehicles at the back loading dock where Anita had been instructed to bring the cupcakes. She had a moment of worry that no one was going to be there yet to let her in, but she'd always rather be early than late, and this was her opportunity of a lifetime.

Today, two thousand of the city's biggest muckety-muck businesspeople were going to be eating *her* cupcakes, and staring at *her* branding, while they emptied their pockets for charity and rubbed elbows with the other elite and upper class at the Wild and Wet Charity Gala.

It was the kind of thing that could make or break a little bakery like hers, and she wasn't going to blow it by being late because the weather was bad.

And it was *dramatically* bad.

Anita frowned up into the snow and wondered if she should wait until she made contact with the event coordinator before she started actually carrying boxes in. The loading dock had a little overhang protecting it, but it was windy and she didn't want the boxes to get wet with snow.

She closed the van door and climbed up the ramp to the little man door next to the big rolling doors for unloading semis. Her first knock was timid, but she leaned into the next one. She wasn't going to get anywhere in life if she didn't take chances.

There was no answer, so Anita put her hand on the handle and pulled. Just as she decided it was locked, it sprang open with a clang and she went staggering back.

The janitor on the other side of the door looked as surprised as she was, but as soon as Anita caught her balance, she was quick to say, "Oh, thank goodness! Don't let the door close! I have two thousand cupcakes that need to go inside *right now*, and it's starting to snow!"

"C-cupcakes?" the man stuttered, staring at her. He was handsome enough, but seemed a little slow.

"Cupcakes," Anita repeated. "Tiny little cakes with frosting. Hold the door, please!"

She scampered back to her van and wrenched the back door open, pulling the first two half-sheet boxes carefully from the floor and bumping the door closed again with her hip. As fast as she could, she was back at the loading dock, carrying in the cupcakes. The man followed her bemusedly inside, and Anita looked around. There was a kitchen to the right and a long, dark hallway that must lead to the ballroom. No one else was there yet.

"Do you know where these should go?" she asked the janitor.

He gazed at her a moment and she repeated, "The cupcakes. Where should I put the cupcakes?"

"The kitchen?" the janitor guessed.

"The kitchen," Anita said kindly. "Good idea." The kitchen was enormous, probably three times the size of her entire bakery, and shiny with chrome. The janitor turned the lights on and Anita put her bakery boxes on the nearest counter. "I've got to get the rest of them in here before the snow gets any worse!"

She left him struggling with a doorstop for the outer door and got a second armload, passing him as she came back up the ramp. Together, they unloaded box after box, hurrying as the snow came down thicker and thicker. The janitor found a wheeled cart, and they stacked it as high as they dared and pushed it together up the ramp through the gathering slushy snow.

By the time they brought in the last boxes, the snow was ankle-deep and her van looked like it had been covered in a fluffy blanket.

"That's it, then," Anita said with relief, as they stacked the final cupcakes. "We made it, all eighty-four boxes. Thank you so much for your help." She cheerfully offered the janitor her hand to shake, and he did, holding onto it considerably longer than she expected him to, as shy as he'd been.

"I'm Anita," she said with a grin. "I own Donut Worry, Be Happy." She laughed at herself, feeling punchy and exhausted. "I say *own*, but really, I'm the whole thing. Just me."

"I'm Frank," the man said, smiling slowly. "That's a lot of cupcakes. You made them all yourself?"

"It was a lot of work," Anita admitted, finally taking her hand back and realizing that she had dyed her fingertips with pink food coloring. "I haven't slept."

"I'm really sorry," Frank said.

Anita rubbed her throbbing wrist. "It was worth it," she said with satisfaction. "This is my big chance. The kind of thing that could launch my bakery to greatness, you know? It was crazy of me even to apply. I thought for sure that Harriet Slade at Patty Cakes would get it, but I had to try, anyway. You've got one life to live, my mother always said. And now, not only can I pay the rent, but Frank

Wilson the gazillionaire and all these really important people are going to eat *my* cupcakes and see *my* dorky name. It's probably the most exciting thing that has ever happened to me!"

Frank was still sort of staring at her like he couldn't quite help himself, but Anita wasn't sure if that could be blamed on his mental state. She was kind of babbling, and she could come across a little strong even when she had gotten a good night's sleep.

He winced. "No, I'm *really* sorry," he explained. "The charity event was canceled."

It was Anita's turn to stare. "Canceled?" she squeaked. "It was *canceled?*"

"There's a giant snowstorm blowing in. We're supposed to get three feet by the afternoon and they're already warning that the power might go out when the wind hits. Didn't you get the cancellation notice?"

Anita felt a wave of despair. "How was it sent? I've been kind of busy making two thousand cupcakes, and I haven't had a chance to check my email. I forgot my phone at home."

"Didn't you hear the news? There's a travel advisory on every channel!"

"Two *thousand* cupcakes!" Anita protested.

"I am *so sorry,*" Frank said, and he seemed to be taking it really personally for a janitor.

"I'm sure it's not your fault," Anita said unhappily. "It was just...my big *chance.* And what am I going to do with two thousand cupcakes?"

"I'll still pay you for them," Frank said firmly.

Anita, who had been looking at the food coloring stains on her fingers, looked up at him in alarm as the details finally snapped into place in her tired mind. Frank the janitor. Like Frank Wilson. "You're—"

"Frank Wilson, the gazillionaire," he said sheepishly.

And all the lights in the building went out.

# CHAPTER 2

*I*t actually took Frank a moment to realize that the power in the building had gone out. His flamingo was certain that the light in the world had simply gone away because they had caused their mate such bitter disappointment.

His flamingo had woken him frantically and driven him into the quickest clothing to hand—the jeans and stained shirt he wore to work on machinery. *Flock! Flock!* his flamingo kept shrieking, and that had made it very hard to think indeed when he met the adorable, plucky little baker who put him to work carrying cupcakes under the assumption that he was some kind of janitor.

She was his mate, he realized. His one true love. He'd always doubted the concept, figuring it was a comfortable fiction for people unwilling to put work into a relationship. But one look at her sparkling brown eyes, and he and his flamingo were both lost.

And then he'd offered her money, like that would solve everything.

*Fix it fix it fix it,* his flamingo was insisting now.

Anita squeaked in the darkness and Frank reached forward for her automatically and caught her arms reaching out for him. Her touch was like an electric shock as they grasped each other by the forearms and held on, waiting for the lights to come back.

*Snuggle,* his flamingo suggested, but Frank knew that would be too forward of him.

*Snuggle!* his flamingo repeated.

"Don't you have a generator or something?" Anita asked when it became apparent that the lights weren't going to come right back on.

"I have no idea," Frank said. "I just rented this place."

"Well, do you have a flashlight?" she asked practically. "The last thing I want to do is run into a pile of cupcake boxes."

Frank wracked his brain. Probably this wasn't the kind of kitchen to have a junk drawer full of useful things like that. "My phone!" he exclaimed. He had to let go of one of her arms in order to reach into his pocket and was gratified that her other hand seemed to hold on to him harder. Was she afraid of the dark?

He found his phone and fumbled to turn it on one-handed and find the control for the flashlight. It wasn't much, in the big, dark kitchen, and jagged shadows fled before the beam. Anita stepped closer to him with a hiss of alarm. "Oh," she breathed. "It's actually scarier this way. I feel like I'm in a horror movie. Do you hear a bloody hook on the back door?" She laughed weakly. "Sorry, I talk too much and have too active an imagination."

*Snuggle!* Frank's flamingo was all but stomping his feet.

Frank wasn't actually averse to the idea of snuggling. He was, in fact, quite enamored of the idea. Anita was curvy and looked like she'd be a delight to hold in his arms.

"I can't believe the power is out!" she said, stepping tantalizingly close as he swung the beam of the flashlight around in the weirdly reflective kitchen. "I mean, bad enough that the event was canceled, and I'm probably stuck here all day because I'm not sure my van would make it through the snow, but now there's no power! And with you! Of all people! Oh no, I mean, not like that, I'm sure you're fine, and you're certainly *fine,* it's just…"

She put her hand over her face and Frank realized he'd just watched someone actually, physically, facepalm.

"I'm sorry, everyone is always telling me I have no editor, and it's apparently even worse when I haven't slept. I should always stop one sentence earlier."

"I rented the penthouse upstairs," Frank said.

"I am *not* that kind of girl," Anita said tartly, snatching her hand off of him. "You bought cupcakes, mister gazillionaire, not me."

It was Frank's turn to be flustered. "No, of course not. I didn't mean, no, never, definitely not."

"Well, you don't have to be *that* sure," she muttered, just as Frank realized he'd said it much more firmly than courtesy dictated.

It was hard to think around Frank's flamingo, who was still stuck on the snuggle idea, and besides that, was pretty sure that the way to her heart was through dancing. If there was one thing Frank knew, it was that he was completely making a hash of this introduction and that bobbing his head and flapping his elbows was very unlikely to improve matters.

"Look, this has all gone terribly sideways," he said honestly. "Can I just start over?"

Anita looked at him suspiciously. "Like, we've just met, and you weren't pretending to be the janitor?"

"I never pre—yes, let's do that. Let's say that I was never a janitor and you've just arrived. 'Hello, Miss…?'"

Anita giggled cautiously. "Townsend," she supplied.

"'Hello, Miss Townsend, welcome to the Wild and Wet Charity Gala, which, while we're pretending, hasn't been canceled. I'm Frank Wilson, the gazillionaire, and I've hired you only for your cupcakes.'"

*Snuggle,* his flamingo muttered.

# CHAPTER 3

*a*nita was surprised by how strong and confident Frank's second handshake was, given that he sometimes looked like he was having an argument with someone in his head...and was losing. She was really glad for the touch, though, because the dark kitchen and the weirdly quiet building were making anxiety and terror swell in her, undoubtedly exacerbated by being sleep-deprived and half-starved.

She held onto his hand longer than she meant to and then let go rather sharply and felt adrift in the darkness. "It's really spooky," she blurted. Remembering their charade, she quickly added, "'I mean, I am so pleased to be here, Mr. Wilson. What a delightful party you throw! Such excellent taste in cupcakes!'"

"It's probably lighter in the ballroom," Frank suggested in his real voice. "All those big windows will let in any daylight that there is." He cleared his throat. "'Would you like to accompany me to the party in a very non-penthouse sort of way, Miss Townsend?'"

Anita took the janitor-celebrity's offered arm and strolled with him down the hallway towards a room that opened up only slightly less black and more gray. It was dark outside for the hour, and blowing snow obscured the view of the river. "'It's a lovely day for a charity ball, I believe,'" she said in a terrible British accent. "'Not snowing at all!'"

"'I ordered the very best weather with my gazillion dollars,'" Frank said seriously. "'May I offer you refreshment?'" They stopped at a folding table clad only in a white tablecloth and he poured her a drink in an imaginary glass from an imaginary bottle.

"'I'm charmed!'" Anita declared, accepting it. They toasted each other and pretended to drink. "'I understand you have purchased only the most delectable foods and beverages. Such a swanky event. What a crowd! Look at all these famous people!'"

"'I hear the host is something else though,'" Frank said, straight-faced and snotty-voiced. "'He pretended to be a janitor, can you imagine?'"

"'Shocking!'" Anita giggled. "'Shall we mingle?'"

Frank offered his elbow again and Anita thought it wasn't too forward to snuggle rather close to him. It was, after all, a little chilly in the drafty room.

"'Oh, there's the mayor,'" he said, suddenly steering Anita in another direction. "'He's campaigning again and wants me to endorse him. Let's go hide behind these people or he'll talk your ear off. That's the chief of police, but that's definitely *not* his wife.'"

Anita played along. "'I see Victoria Hennings, the TV anchor. She didn't let me park in her spot once. I had to carry seventeen cakes almost a block. Let's snub her.'"

"'I hate her forever,'" Frank promised. "'I'll never watch her morning show again.'"

"'Oh no,'" Anita cried, clutching his arm. "'That's Harriet Slade. Hide me!'"

Frank was happy to let her duck to his far side and press up against him as they walked.

"Who is Harriet Slade?" he asked, forgetting his voice. "I mean, 'Who on earth is Harriet Slade?'"

"'Harriet Slade is my arch-nemesis, of course.'"

It was hard to believe that someone as adorable and cheerful as

Anita had an arch-nemesis. "'Has she threatened your family honor?'" Frank asked, miming a sword at his waist.

"'Nothing so common,'" Anita said with impressive snootiness. "'We are *cupcake* rivals.'"

Frank let his imaginary sword go. "'I did not realize that baking was so competitive,'" he confessed.

"'She owns the Patty Cakes chain of bakeries downtown and my store is quite new and apparently rather threatening.'" Anita raised her chin and tipped her head like they were passing another couple. "'The cupcake business is quite cutthroat!'"

"'Shall I have security throw her out?'" Frank offered in a whisper.

Anita giggled. "'I don't suppose that will be necessary,'" she said. "'But perhaps you could have her car towed? She has a very fancy car.'"

They had circled the room and were at a low stage that had a weird collection of shapes draped in cloth. In the muted light from the window, they looked like cheap Halloween ghosts.

"Would you like to see the latest of my sculptures?" Frank had dropped his fancy voice and actually sounded shy.

Anita knew that Frank Wilson's fame and fortune had come, in a non-linear way, from lawn ornaments. His outdoor, articulated metal sculptures had been art collectors' items at first, selling for hundreds of thousands of dollars apiece at auction. He'd shot to greatness, quickly becoming a celebrity in exclusive art circles.

He had shocked the art world when he declared that he was going to start mass-producing the pieces and he bought up an abandoned car plant in the city and employed factory workers at union rates to make smaller, simpler versions from recycled parts and scraps.

Critics swore he would bankrupt himself and devalue his sculptures, but the market turned out to be surprisingly receptive and the Wilson Kinetic line of home decoration had skyrocketed him into riches and recognition. Every year since, he unveiled two versions of a new design—a large and complicated sculpture that he auctioned for a charity of his choice, and a smaller home version that would be generally affordable and available throughout garden shops across the country and in parts of Canada.

"'I'd be delighted to see it,'" Anita said in her best snooty voice. "'I'm considering purchasing it with my cupcake money.'"

"'I don't know, it might cost penthouse money,'" Frank said skeptically, with a sly, sideways look. "'The bidding can get very high…'"

Anita pretended to choke on her imaginary champagne and glared at him as long as she could keep from laughing—which wasn't very long.

"I'm glad you thought that was funny," he said, with his authentic voice full of relief.

"I'm pretty punch drunk," Anita admitted. "I was up all night making cupcakes, so everything is funny." Then she leaned close to confess in a whisper, "Okay, no, I'm this much of a dork all the time. I can't blame it all on the cupcakes."

Frank had really nice teeth, bright in the dim light, and a genuine smile. "I won't tell," he promised just as quietly, looking around like their pretend audience might overhear. "'Oh, it's time for the big reveal. It's my moment of fame!'"

Anita clapped loudly and turned to hush imaginary people. "'Quiet in the peanut gallery! The gazillionaire is going to uncover all the big metal stuff! Stuff it, Victoria Hennings!'" She turned back to Frank. "You're up, stud. Knock 'em dead."

Frank sprang to the stage, waving and blowing kisses to all the people that weren't actually there. He started to speak several times, play-acting that there was too much applause to continue. Anita clapped until her palms stung, whistling and hooting. It was absurd in the empty, echoing room, but then, everything about this day already was and it could only be about seven in the morning.

"'Without further ado, I give you this year's Wilson Kinetic Sculpture!'" Frank yanked the sheet aside and Anita froze in wonder.

She's seen photos of his work—who hadn't?—but there was nothing quite like seeing something like this in person. It was larger than she thought it would be, and much more intricate.

"It's supposed to be lit up," Frank said nervously, as Anita real-ized she'd stopped clapping. "It should have colored lights from there, and there, and there would be music, of course. Some kind of loud march. It would all be very impressive."

Anita clambered up onto the stage. "It's a flamingo!" she exclaimed in joy.

# CHAPTER 4

Frank had unveiled a lot of Wilson Kinetic Sculptures by now, but he had never been as invested in the audience as he was in this one. The critics he'd been desperate to impress, the investors he'd been frantic to woo...none of them mattered even a fraction as much as his mate. The delight in her glowing face was the reward he hadn't even known he was craving.

"I thought it was appropriate," he said shyly. "For a lot of reasons..."

"Well sure," Anita said eagerly. "You have a lawn ornament business. How could you not have a flamingo in the line? Will you...?" She flapped her hands eagerly.

Frank reached up and pulled on the crank, not taking his eye from Anita for even a moment. He watched her squeal in glee as the wings fluttered and the neck snaked down and back up gracefully. One leg extended and tucked back up. Lapping metal feathers shivered down the back. The clockwork was so smooth it barely made a sound, just a ticking rustle as the pieces whispered together. The mechanism took only the tiniest amount of pressure, all so perfectly balanced and counterweighted that it continued going for several minutes after he let go.

Rose quartz and pink topaz gemstones were set in several places, and even in the non-ideal lighting, it glimmered and flickered.

Anita crowded close, clinging happily to him as she watched its dance. "It's amazing!" she said, almost sounding choked. "I've never seen anything so wonderful in my life!" Then she looked up at him in awe, and Frank had never seen anything so wonderful in *his* life.

This was it.

His purpose, his entire happiness, was here in the arms of this amazing woman. He'd been one of his own sculptures, moving through the motions of life on a mechanical track, act and counter-act, waiting for some purpose to make him more than a machine.

And here she was, the vibrant, unstoppable woman who was his mate, with her forward, funny heart on her sleeve and her indomitable spirit obvious to anyone with eyes.

"'I bid one thousand dollars!'" she said loudly, raising her hand imperiously.

"Anita…"

"That's way, way too low, isn't it," she whispered back in her true voice. She was gazing at the flamingo sculpture again, still looking awed. "What should I start with? Like one hundred thousand? A million? I'm not letting Victoria Hennings outbid me."

"Anita, there's something I have to tell you…"

"It's for a good cause!" she protested. "I mean, I'll be in debt the rest of my life, but I'll have this gorgeous flamingo to make me happy, and it saves wildlife habitat, right?"

"Anita…" Frank could not help but chuckle.

"I suppose it comes with delivery for that price?" she asked anxiously. "I think it's too tall to fit inside my delivery van. Oh, maybe I can screw it onto the top like ice cream trucks have those giant cones! Oh, yes! It will be my new trademark look. People will buy my cupcakes just to get my van parked in front of their buildings for a little while. But what will that do to my car insur-ance? Do you think they'll hike up my premium because of the increased risk of theft? Of course, it will be hard to sneak that thing away. Oh no, what if it gets knocked off going under an overpass?"

"Anita!" Frank had to resist the urge to take her by the arms and kiss her to make her listen.

Anita put a hand over her face, giggling hysterically. "I'm sorry," she said sheepishly, peeking through her fingers. "Punch-drunk and hungry. Do you have, like, an energy bar or something? I think I'm going to crash really soon."

*Feed her!* Frank's flamingo insisted with a hiss.

"We have food!" Frank said instantly, for once in complete agreement with his inner animal. "In the kitchen. We've got all the hors d'oeuvres and two thousand cupcakes, and if we don't eat everything in the fridge it will go bad."

Anita snorted. "I know I'm a little fluffy, but I definitely cannot eat two thousand people's worth of hors d'oeuvres."

"I didn't mean that you'd have to eat it all!" Frank said, horrified that she'd think that was what he'd been trying to imply. "I just meant, don't feel bad for eating as much as you want."

It was dark down the back hallway to the kitchen, and Anita clung delightfully to his arm. Frank was distracted by how warm she was against his side, and how good she smelled, like sugar and lemons.

"Did you ever think about how hors d'oeuvres is spelled?" she chattered. "I mean it doesn't look a thing like it sounds. I must have been in college before I realized that it wasn't pronounced whores devours! I thought it was some kind of kinky French thing for an embarrassingly long time and never put it together with snack food for a party, which clearly should be spelled o-r-d-e-r-v-e-s. Do you know at one point I thought about a food truck that only served finger food? I'd call it Orderves spelled like it sounds and they'd be really super fancy and served on square plates with sauce drizzles but made out of, like hot dogs and Jell-O. Oh, it's dark in here."

The kitchen was all reflective angles and racing shadows in the light of Frank's phone.

"Let's pack a picnic lunch and go back to the ballroom," Frank suggested. It wasn't exactly light there, but it was better than this.

"You're full of brilliant ideas," Anita said. "Got a basket?"

They couldn't find a basket, and it was challenging but kind of fun ransacking the cabinets with Anita firmly attached to his side. They did find a serving tray, and a few bags of high-end croutons.

"As kitchens go, I'm kind of underwhelmed," Anita said. "I couldn't cook anything here! There are no spices, no flour, no sugar, no talking mice or singing crabs!"

"It's a rental," Frank said apologetically. "I guess you're supposed to bring your own talking mice and singing crabs."

"I'd kill for a bag of chips," Anita said with a sigh, peeking over Frank's shoulder into a cabinet. "But I guess croutons will do. What's in the fridge?"

This, at least, was a treasure trove, and they heaped the tray with artful swirls of cheese and cold cuts and tiny foods that Frank couldn't even identify.

"What's this one?" Anita asked, holding up semi-transparent globes on toothpicks with pink plastic flamingos on the end.

"They look kind of like pickled pearl onions?" Frank guessed.

There were skewers with fruit interspersed with white cheese, drizzled in some kind of dark sauce and sprinkled with something green.

"What's on this?" Anita asked raptly.

"I have no idea."

"How can you not know what you're serving at your own party?" Anita asked.

"I have people!" Frank protested. "They handle stuff!"

"I had no idea you could put so many *things* on toothpicks," Anita said as they loaded their serving tray with a few of everything that looked good. "Oh, that looks like it's wrapped in bacon, grab me three of those. And some of those tiny shrimp! We'll need something to drink!"

"Wine..." Frank started, and he finished in chorus with Anita, "Probably too penthouse," and they both burst out laughing. He found a few bottles of water.

"Glass bottled water," Anita said skeptically. "That *is* fancy. But I suppose it's better for the environment? I try to be mindful of that, but I have to admit I have one of those K-cup machines at home for coffee."

She took one of the boxes of cupcakes with them as they hurried back to the ballroom with Frank carrying their loaded tray. Anita glanced behind them frequently. "Did you hear something?" she asked. "I felt a cold draft."

Their own sounds were all that Frank could hear in the weirdly silent building. "Bloody hooks?" he asked, and while he loved that Anita squeaked and pressed even closer up against him, it nearly made him drop the heavy tray of food. "Whoops! It's probably just the building creaking as it gets cold."

"Are we going to freeze to death in here?" she wanted to know morbidly. Then she brightened. "Oh, but that will keep the food from going bad, at least!"

Frank wondered if suggesting that they could huddle together for warmth was going too far in a penthouse direction, and then they were stepping out into the relative brightness of the ballroom and he was looking for a table to put his tray down on.

Beside him, Anita gave a tiny shriek of fear and dropped her cupcake box.

# CHAPTER 5

*A*nita didn't want to be a complete scaredy-cat in front of the nice, rich man who was so tolerant about being mistaken for a janitor and then pretending that the event was still on, just to humor her. He put up with her cuddling up to him for comfort in the terrifying dark in far too familiar a manner, but didn't for a moment act like that meant he could take liberties. Anita wasn't sure if she'd really mind liberties from him, and even suspected a few times that he might want to take them, the way he smiled sideways at her.

She'd always thought that *dancing eyes* was some kind of outrageous flowery description, but Frank's golden-brown eyes really did look like he was poised on the brink of laughter, or breaking into a foxtrot.

She was letting herself think about those eyes, trying to remind herself that being trapped by a storm in a giant empty building with no power was not at all frightening and probably there was *not* a serial killer locked in here with them in the dark and ghosts weren't real and...

They stepped into the ballroom, which was at first a great relief because what light there was outside in the storm was filtering in through the tall windows, and then Anita's heart seemed to stop.

She wasn't aware that she'd screamed and dropped the cupcake box until it hit the floor, moments after Frank's heavily loaded tray crashed to the table where he'd poured her fanciful champagne.

"What is it?" he asked, snatching up one of the heavy bottles of water like a club and turning with impressive spryness.

And then he saw it, too.

When they'd left the ballroom, the great mechanical flamingo had come to a rest, and they had never gotten around to uncovering the smaller, commercial version.

Now both of them were uncovered, and both of them were moving as if they had each just been wound.

Frank looked around in alarm. "Hello?" he called into the shadows, brandishing his bottle. "Who's there?"

Only silence answered as they both held their breath and listened.

Even empty buildings usually had a background of sounds. Pipes creaking, fans whirring, distant HVAC systems, the hum of lights. Anita strained so hard to hear that she felt herself getting dizzy, and all she could make out was the constant batter of snow being blown against the windows, the creak of the slowing kinetic sculptures, and the pounding of her own heart. Her stomach added an embarrassing groan that was loud in the room.

"Sorry, that was me," she whispered.

Both of the flamingos ponderously came to a stop again, and no sound replaced their creaking.

"Did you rent a *haunted* event hall?" Anita hissed. "Or did you build a giant enchanted flamingo that can start itself?"

Frank chuckled dryly and put the bottle down. "I didn't think I'd done either of those things." He picked the bottle right back up, then marched across the room to the sculptures.

Anita had never seen anything so brave or stupid. She gave a squeak of dismay at being left behind and scrambled after him, nearly tripping over her abandoned cupcake box. Frank put a hand out to her, and she gratefully took it, twining her fingers easily into his as she caught up.

"Maybe Tobias attached some kind of mechanism to make the unveiling more dramatic," Frank hypothesized. He put the bottle down and got his phone in his other hand again, moving the light over the sculpture and frowning in concentration.

"How'd the other one get uncovered?" Anita wanted to know.

Frank shrugged. "Maybe the covering jiggled off when the mechanism was activated? I'm going to bill my heart attack to that jerk, if that's what happened. He could have warned me." He had opened up a panel in the flamingo's breast and was eyeing the gears and cables inside the cavity. Finally, he snapped it closed again. "Well, whatever it is, I don't think it will happen again. Let's have some food to settle our nerves."

Anita wondered if he was trying to distract her, and realized that he hadn't confirmed that there was some kind of *mechanism*, but she didn't have a more reasonable explanation for what had happened, and her stomach was starting to make a whole host of embarrassing noises in the quiet room. "Food sounds great," she agreed plaintively. "Let's make a fort and put our backs up against a wall."

Frank, to Anita's surprise, took her idea for a fort quite literally and tipped over a few of the tables to make a barricade around a blank spot of wall that faced the stage. Anita rescued the cupcakes and brought the tray into their cozy new corner as Frank ransacked a supply closet and found a whole armful of drapes and table cloths. "You look cold," he offered.

Anita wasn't sure if she was cold, if all of her nerves were shot, or if her blood sugar had just reached new record lows, but she was actually shaking. She wrapped a royal blue semi-velvet drape around her like an emperor's robe and padded a place for them to sit on the floor with the rest of Frank's cloth. They could just see the flamingos over the comforting protection of the table, and the eerie statues didn't move once while they fell upon the contents of the tray.

It was easy to be distracted. Not only was Anita starving, the food was absolutely amazing, and Frank himself was more and more interesting to watch as the hunger in her belly was slowly sated. She had never realized how sexy someone eating things off a stick could be.

"I would never in my life have paired some of these things," she said, teasing a ball of cheese from her skewer with her teeth. "Dates and bacon should never be served separately again. And I am glad we're eating here instead of in the kitchen, because I probably actually would try to eat two thousand people's worth of these hors d'oeuvres and you wouldn't be able to fit me back out the door when the snow finally stops and we can leave."

"There's the big sliding cargo door at the loading dock," Frank said, doing something with his tongue to get his food off his toothpick that made the breath catch in Anita's throat. "I'm going to need it to leave myself because I cannot stop eating the tiny food on twigs. Have you tried the pearl onions?" He held one out.

It was perfectly natural to lean forward and eat one off the toothpick that he offered. Anita didn't realize until her lips closed around it that a) this brought her incredibly close to him, b) she probably could have just taken the toothpick with her hand, and c) that he smelled *fantastic*.

He was watching her avidly, like he wanted to eat *her*.

Then he turned pink and looked abashed, realizing that he was staring.

Anita managed to stab herself in the mouth with the toothpick as she turned the moment into something completely graceless. "Ow," she said around her pearl onion once she was at a safe distance.

"I'm so sorry," Frank said, looking like a dog that had just been snacking from a plate of cookies.

Anita wasn't sure what he was apologizing for. She wasn't sure *he* was sure what he was apologizing for. She ought to say something, but she couldn't figure out what that was supposed to be until the moment had gotten weird and she decided to say nothing.

He opened one of the bottles of water for her, and Anita took a long, grateful swig.

This, unfortunately, illuminated a new problem that Anita was having.

"Are you okay?" Frank asked after a few moments while Anita cursed her tiny bladder and the cups of coffee she'd drunk to stay awake all night frosting cupcakes.

She gave a noisy sigh. "I have to pee," she said plaintively.

# CHAPTER 6

 rank made a sound that probably betrayed that he was trying to decide whether to cough politely or laugh and didn't quite manage either. It was very un-gazillionaire of him. "Let's go find the ladies' room," he offered gallantly. "I think it's on the second floor."

Anita unwrapped herself from the velveteen drape and stood up. "I'm really sorry," she said, looking embarrassed.

"Bodies," Frank said with a shrug. "They always want inconvenient things, like food and sleep." *And sex,* his flamingo added hopefully.

*That's not helping anything,* he replied with gritted teeth.

He offered her his hand to help her over the sideways table and was delighted when she accepted it. He was even more delighted when she left it there as he led her to the back of the event hall where the stairs went up to the second level.

"I think it's back this way," he said when they got to the top of the stairs, hand-in-hand.

It got darker as they went further down the hallway, and Anita drew closer and closer to him as they walked. He had to pull out his phone again to use the light and find the doors to the bathroom, two of them together with fancy silhouettes for his and hers.

They stopped before the ladies' room and Anita gave a little squeak as she seemed to realize that Frank wasn't going to go in with her. "You can take my phone." He held it out to her.

She reluctantly let go of his hand and took the phone. "Thanks," she said quietly.

"Are you reconsidering?"

"I am," she confessed, fidgeting in place. "My bladder is not."

She raised her chin in an impressive show of bravery and opened the door, letting the beam of light swing over the bank of sinks and stall doors. "Here I go," she said. "In by myself."

"There you go," Frank agreed.

"Really, I'm going in," Anita insisted without moving.

"I know you can," Frank encouraged.

"I am ridiculous," Anita said, and she finally marched in and let the door swing closed behind her.

Frank wondered at how bereft he felt when the door latched between them.

He'd known this woman a few scant hours and already, he could not imagine his life without her unquenchable sunshine.

It was also very quiet without her chatter, and Frank was aware of the vast emptiness of the building around them.

All the hair at the back of his neck suddenly rose. At first, Frank was confused by his warning instinct, thinking that it was just that his mate was out of his sight for the first time since they'd met and his flamingo was being protective. Then he realized that he was hearing footsteps.

Someone else *was* in here with them.

He didn't want to frighten the already high-strung Anita, so he hadn't admitted that he still didn't have any idea why the sculptures had been in motion when they returned to the ballroom. There didn't appear to be any sign of tampering and his off-the-cuff theory that there was some kind of last-minute automation had proved at a glance to be wrong.

But the conjecture had been comforting to Anita and Frank had decided that it was better to let her continue to believe it than squash it before he had a better idea of what had actually happened.

The footsteps seemed to be coming towards him from around a corner down the dark hallway and Frank reached for his phone, wondering if it was pointless to call the police in the middle of a snowstorm that had already taken out the power and probably closed every major road for miles. Then he remembered that Anita had his phone anyway, just as there was suddenly a shrill scream from the bathroom.

He slammed into the bathroom door before he remembered how door handles worked and it groaned at his impact, probably only frightening Anita further.

He fumbled for the latch and got it open, peering into the inky darkness of the bathroom. "Are you all right?" he called.

He had to blink for a moment to adjust his eyes and could finally pick out the silhouette of her head peeking from behind a stall door.

"Yes," she squeaked. "Your phone light turned off, and it scared me. That's all. Sorry."

Frank's whole body was sizzling with adrenaline, and he could not quite keep himself from stepping further into the bathroom and sweeping Anita into his arms. It only occurred to him after she was there that she had stepped to meet him, and he wasn't sure who was trembling more.

"I didn't mean to frighten you," she mumbled into his collarbone, along with other words that Frank only partly heard, something about *ladies' room* and *washing hands*.

She belonged in his arms like this; she fit him perfectly, all soft curves and perfect height. He could cradle every part of her, lean his jaw into her hair. Frank's tremor swiftly became less about fear and more about need. She was warm against him and yielding in all the right places.

If she tipped her head up to meet him, he'd be able to kiss her... but she didn't and after a few moments, she gave a shuddering sigh and stepped back instead.

Frank's flamingo gave a keen of regret, but Frank let her go.

He only realized that certain parts had grown unmistakably hard when there was space between them again, and he wondered in chagrin if she'd noticed.

# CHAPTER 7

*a*nita noticed Frank's hard-on.

It was hard *not* to notice.

Anita promptly rearranged the emphasis in her head.

It was *hard* not to notice.

And he felt even better all snuggled up in a comforting hug that he had when she was just casually clinging to him like a scared rabbit. He was so deliciously built, with seriously impressive muscles underneath his janitor-comfortable clothing. It was the strongest, sexiest hug that Anita had ever had.

Peeling herself out of that embrace took all of her crumbling self-control. "Sorry I scared you," she said sheepishly. "Your phone just ran out of juice and I guess I screamed. I mean, I seem to be screaming a lot. I didn't think of myself as a...uh...screamer, but here we are."

Now she'd said *scream* way too many times. She fished the dead phone out of her pocket and handed it to him, trying not to think too hard about how he might make her scream, or read too much into a kind hug that suggested he might actually be into her.

Because guys who were into her were always trouble.

It was fun and games when things were friendly and funny and flirty, and there was the brief thrill of feeling attractive instead of just goofy, but after that, it always got weird. *She* made it weird. And she didn't want it to be weird with Frank.

Besides the fact that he was really cute and fabulously rich, they were trapped together in a rapidly chilling event hall in the middle of the storm of a century, and there was nowhere to run if he turned out to be a serial killer.

And honestly, she really liked Frank and didn't want to ruin what she was actually starting to feel was a blooming friendship. He had a great sense of humor and he was sweet and willing to be silly with her. Anita felt comfortable and safe with him.

He was being really quiet now, so probably she'd already done the deed and gone from adorable and fun to be sequestered with to someone who screamed too much and had a bladder the size of a tomato. It was hard to make out his expression in the dark, spooky bathroom. It was hard to make out even the shape of him. There was a tiny frosted window up near the ceiling, but it let in almost no light.

"Sorry," she mumbled.

"For what?" he asked promptly.

"For screaming? For being terrified and terrible with people?" She probably should have kept the second thought to herself. Normal people kept those confessions on the inside.

"I'd have screamed too," Frank admitted. "All alone in a bathroom when the light went out."

Anita couldn't help but scoff, "You would not. You have probably never screamed in your life."

"I have," Frank insisted. "Like a *girl*." He swiftly added, "Not that there's anything wrong with girl screams."

He was so *nice*.

"I have to wash my hands," Anita said firmly. She fumbled her way to the sink and turned on a tap, rinsing her fingers longer than usual because she couldn't see if she'd gotten the bubbles off. It was ice cold and she splashed a little on her face, getting her shirt wet as she did. "I feel like an Antarctic explorer," she said. "In one of those research stations where they study penguins."

She couldn't remember where the towels were, so she dried her hands on her pants and turned back to the dark, looming form of Frank.

"Do you…like birds?" he asked unexpectedly.

Anita guessed it wasn't the oddest question he could have asked; she was the one who'd brought up penguins. "Sure," she said. "I mean, on a case-by-case basis. I have a neighbor with a parrot that bit me once when I was watching their house, but for the most part, yeah, I like birds."

"I have something I need to tell you," Frank said hesitantly.

*Here it comes.*

Anita felt her heart drop down into her toes. Was it going to be the familiar *I don't think of you that way* speech? The *I wouldn't mind doing it because we're trapped together and there's nobody better, but please don't assume it means anything* pitch? Frank seemed too kind to use the *I'm sorry for you so I'll sleep with you* line. And they'd already had the penthouse talk; only her cupcakes were for sale.

Also, she wasn't sure what any of that had to do with *birds.* Unless maybe he thought she didn't know about the birds and the bees?

*Snick, snick, snick.*

In the silence that stretched between them, the sound of footsteps in the hall was suddenly very loud, even though the person outside was clearly trying to sneak by. Anita knew from experience that sneaking in heels was very challenging.

*Snick…*

The sound stopped abruptly, right in front of the bathroom door, like they'd just realized that the conversation inside had quieted.

Anita stuffed her hand into her mouth to keep from screaming again. Frank took a swift step towards her and then turned so he could brandish his phone towards the door as he put an arm around her shoulders protectively.

They were definitely not alone in his haunted event hall.

Anita was shivering now, between the freezing water and her nerves. Why was someone here with them? Who was it? Her imagination, a runaway train at the best of times, was happy to supply the possibility of a serial killer, or an angry spirit, or a ferocious monster in high heels with a taste for baker's blood.

And nothing happened.

After a few moments, Frank left Anita's side and stalked bravely to the bathroom door, groped for the handle and flung it open… onto an empty hallway.

He peered out in each direction, and Anita crowded close behind him.

No one was there.

"I heard footsteps," she insisted. "I did."

"I did, too," Frank said. "And earlier, when you were in the bathroom alone."

Because *that* wasn't terrifying.

"The flamingo sculptures didn't start on their own, did they." Anita didn't say it like a question.

"I didn't want to frighten you," Frank said, with a grimace that she could see. It was brighter in the hall, and she could make out his features. It was always astonishing how handsome he was, even when he was looking sheepish.

Anita knew there were several ways that she could take that. He could be just a generally dishonest guy. He could be one of those guys who thought he knew what was best all the time and thought he was protecting her with omissions of fact.

"I really want to be honest with you," he said softly.

He might be the kind of guy who had trouble being honest when Anita was perfectly happy leaping to assumptions like 'you're a janitor,' and 'there's a logical reason for this really creepy thing.'

"It's usually the best policy," Anita said. She kept swiveling her head, looking to each end of the hallway suspiciously. It was eerily quiet again, not even the tiniest little *snick* of footsteps or any sounds other than their own conversation and breathing. She could barely even hear the storm anymore, this deep in the building.

When Frank slipped his hand into hers, it felt like the most natural thing in the world, and Anita let herself twine her fingers with his. It made sense to let her think there was a reason that the flamingos had been wound up. A reason that wasn't 'we're stuck in a building with a ghost or maybe a murderer.'

They headed back down the hallway towards the stairs that went down to the open ballroom below and Anita felt safer in the brighter and more familiar territory. Their table fort looked undisturbed from above, though they couldn't see the possibly haunted sculptures from here.

"What did you want to tell me?" she asked as they got to the top of the staircase. It was the kind of staircase that a princess might walk down to make a grand entrance. Anita was more focused on not tripping down it because she was wired to eleven and her exhaustion was rapidly catching up with her.

Frank stopped right at the top of the stairs, and then drew her back a short way. "I think I should show you." He said it shyly, like he was getting ready to demonstrate a magic trick that he wasn't really sure about.

He took his hand back, and while Anita was still feeling a little lost and uncertain without having it to cling to anymore, he suddenly sort of shivered in place and she was staring into the yellow eyes of a gigantic, prehistoric pink bird.

*I'm not going to scream, I'm not going to scream, I'm not going to scream.*

Anita was concentrating so hard on not screaming that she forgot they were standing at the top of the stairs and nearly fell down them taking a big step backward.

Frank transformed back to human and caught her by the waist before she could humiliate herself by toppling ungracefully down the steps, doing a super careful dance of *touching-but-not-bad-touching-saving-you-ack!*

"You're a shifter!" she exclaimed, taking both of his hands in hers. "You're a *flamingo!* That's why you asked about birds! Oh, you're a *shifter!*"

# CHAPTER 8

*F*rank wasn't absolutely sure that Anita would have fallen down the stairs if he hadn't caught her and pulled her back, but he *was* absolutely sure that if he'd let go of her, she would have fallen shortly after, she was capering so carelessly.

His flamingo was triumphant. *She's dancing for us! Our flock!! Our mate! We please her!*

Frank managed to guide her away from the most dangerous area, laughing helplessly as she clung to both of his hands and bounced like a sugar-high toddler.

"You're a shifter," she squealed in absolute glee. Frank was not sure he had ever witnessed such happiness. "I've never met a shifter before. I mean, I think one of my neighbors is one, because I never saw him at the same time as his cat, but nobody who was out about it, you know? Except on television, like that crazy bendy guy with the talk show. He's, what, a leopard? A flamingo is so much cooler!"

Shifters were not exactly secret anymore. They had been when Frank was a baby, but the shifter equality laws had been in effect by the time he was walking and shifting. Shifters didn't have to disclose themselves, and most of them chose to go quietly about their lives to avoid discrimination; there were still circles of people who thought that shifters were unnatural or demonic. For the most part, though, there were enough shifters, in all walks of life and privilege, that it was as generally accepted as being a characteristic rather than a quality.

Frank had only a very small circle of close friends and artists who knew that he was a flamingo, and they were all shifters themselves, some of them quieter about the knowledge than others. Tobias was trying to pressure him to go public with it, in order to improve the general impression of shifters using his prestige.

Anita sobered suddenly. "Could there be another shifter in here with us? Like...a mouse shifter or something?"

"It's possible," Frank agreed. That would explain how they'd stayed out of their way this long, but it didn't really do much to illuminate why there was someone here at all, or what they wanted.

"You don't have some kind of—" Anita flapped her hand. "Sonar? Telepathy?"

Frank shook his head. "Sorry to disappoint," he said.

"You do *not* disappoint," Anita said quickly. Frank thought she blushed then, but it was hard to make out in the gloomy light.

He was still holding her hands. Should he risk a kiss? She'd been so happy that he was a shifter, and not the tiniest bit disappointed he wasn't some kind of massive, manly shifter like a bear or an elephant or something. Was she blushing in invitation?

"Should we try to find them?" Anita proposed. To Frank's disappointment, she took her hands back at last and he missed his chance to draw her close and kiss her.

"Our only flashlight is dead," Frank pointed out. "I mean...we could?"

Anita looked nervously down the shadowed hall. "I think I'd rather go back to our fort," she confessed.

"You look cold," Frank agreed.

*Snuggle*, his flamingo suggested.

# CHAPTER 9

The flamingo sculptures were not moving when they cautiously descended to the ballroom, and Anita drew in a deep breath of relief. "I was half-afraid they would have come entirely to life this time," she confessed. "We'd come out to find that they were stalking around wrecking up the place."

She mimed a stiff-armed, stiff-legged robot and Frank did something more zombie or dinosaur than robot until they were both laughing so hard that the empty ballroom rang with it. If there was someone lurking around in the darkness, they had to know by now that they weren't alone and that Frank and Anita weren't scared of them.

Well, not very scared.

Okay, maybe Frank wasn't scared. Anita was still on full five-alarm alert. Plunging into the darkness alone in an unfamiliar bathroom was probably the most terrifying thing that had ever happened to her.

"Are you still hungry?" Frank asked when they had arrived back at their table fort.

Most of the *hors d'oeuvres* had been *hors devoured*, and Anita shook her head. She was full and, now that the jolt of adrenaline had eased, she really just wanted to sit down for a little while in the comfortable-looking pile of curtains and tablecloths.

Frank, true to his bird nature, vaulted into the fort and made her a proper nest, then extended a hand to help her scramble over.

She found the bottle of water and took a good swig as she settled down into the cozy little space and pulled a tablecloth around her. When Frank looked like he might hover uncomfortably or set up some kind of perimeter march, Anita patted the spot beside her. Finding out that he was a shifter had made her feel safer with him than ever. All her very favorite stories had featured shapeshifters, and although he'd been very alarming as a flamingo —nearly as tall as she was and with a beak like a battle axe—she felt like he'd do a very solid job protecting her in either form.

Even from murderous ghosts.

He settled gracefully at her side, not quite touching, and they both leaned back against the wall behind them.

The box of cupcakes had survived being dropped, suffering no more than a little frosting lost to the lid. Despite saying that she wasn't hungry, Anita opened it and took out one with pink frosting that matched her stained fingertips. She handed the box to Frank, who selected a blue one.

That prompted her to say, "Can I ask you something that might be a little personal?"

Frank shrugged as he peeled his cupcake wrapper off. "Anything." He took a bite then, and his look of rapture delighted Anita. "This is the best cupcake I've ever had," he said earnestly.

"You paid enough for it," Anita sniffed. "And I'm worth the cost." That seemed like a very penthouse thing to say. "I mean... ah...you've got one thousand and ninety-eight of them left, at least?"

Anita concentrated on eating her cupcake so she wouldn't watch Frank eat too avidly. He licked the blue frosting off his own fingers, and she remembered her question.

"So, I learned that flamingos get their pink coloring from a kind of algae that they—that *you* eat, and that in zoos if they don't get this—*you* don't get this—not that you'd be in a zoo—they go white.

*You* go white. Do you eat special algae diet to keep you so handsome and pink?"

His cheeks certainly didn't need a special algae diet. Even in the gray snowstorm light from the big ballroom windows, they were flamingo pink. "I take a supplement," he confessed quietly.

"You don't have to say it like that," Anita told him in an identical whisper. "I take melatonin and magnesium."

"It's kind of vain of me," Frank told her, laughing but maintaining their stage whisper. "It doesn't do a single thing but keep me pink, but it just…doesn't feel right to be white."

"I don't think it's any worse than dyeing your hair," Anita assured him. "It's totally fine. You're totally fine." She reminded herself to shut up a sentence earlier. "I mean, you're a fine flamingo."

Frank glanced shyly sideways at her. "Thanks," he said sincerely.

"What's it like being a gazillionaire?" Anita asked wistfully.

She didn't think that it might be a rude question until Frank didn't answer right away. "I'm sorry, that's probably—"

"Oh, you're fine," Frank hastened to assure her. "It's just that I'm kind of a new gazillionaire, and it's mostly on paper." He looked around surreptitiously and whispered to Anita, "I hope I'm doing it right."

Anita had to scoot closer and pat him on the arm. "I'm sure you're doing great," she said comfortingly. He had a really great arm, and she didn't really want to stop patting it. "Everyone says you're a really nice person. Very generous."

"They have to say that," Frank scoffed. "I'm a gazillionaire. Who's going to say bad things about someone who might impulsively buy them a swimming pool and an antique car?"

"Not me," Anita said. "You've been very kind. And I'm not just saying that because you might buy me a swimming pool or an antique car."

Frank was warm. They were kind of leaning into each other now, and Frank had an arm around her.

"Do you want a swimming pool or a car?" he asked, and Anita was alarmed to think he might be serious.

"No," she said. And in a feat of stunning self-control, she did not say what immediately popped into her mind, which was, *I only want you.*

It was a ridiculous thing to want this guy.

Well, no, it wasn't ridiculous to want *him*. He was good-looking and possibly the sweetest man that Anita had ever met, not the slightest bit stuck up, despite being impossibly rich and also a shifter. He was funny and smart and built like a cover model for a dirty book, on top of being a famous artist who donated most of his money to charity.

It was just ridiculous to think that she wanted him to want her.

Anita wasn't sure when she slipped from consciousness, thinking about how impossible everything about this whole day had been.

# CHAPTER 10

*I*t didn't take more than a few moments for Anita to fall asleep, and Frank almost stopped breathing because he didn't want to accidentally jostle her and wake her up. At first, she was just leaning heavily against him, then her head was lolling against his shoulder.

She wasn't exactly light, but Frank didn't mind holding her at all, propping her up with one arm and letting her head nestle against his collarbone. Would it be too forward to kiss the top of her head? She had the softest-looking hair, with tiny little dark brown curls escaping her French braid like a halo. Surely it wouldn't be too bad to tuck a few of those locks behind her perfect little ear, and if that meant brushing his fingers over her velvety freckled cheeks…

*Snuggle*, his flamingo said, in perfect contentment.

For a long while, Frank was happy just to sit and hold his mate. Then his brain returned to the puzzle of the person in the hall with them.

He and Anita had not been quiet at all. If someone had been trapped in the building with them, why wouldn't they join forces? Frank was happy to have Anita to himself, but it indicated a certain amount of *not supposed to be here* on the part of their mysterious companion that put Frank on edge.

It was someone who could vanish silently.

It was someone strong enough to wind the great flamingo sculpture, so not a child, even supposing a child had gotten in.

Frank thought best writing things out in notes and sketches. He patted his sweatshirt and found a pen and a Wilson Kinetic promo notebook in a deep pocket. Anita was occupying his right side, but he was fortunately left-handed and could balance the pad on his left knee and take some notes.

*Stealthy*, he wrote. *Shifter?*

Why would they wind the flamingos if they were trying to stay out of sight? Impulse? Curiosity? Maybe they just thought that Anita and Frank would be gone longer?

Was it someone he'd hired for the charity ball? A server who hadn't left in time and was embarrassed to admit it? Frank made more notes, with lots of question marks, then moved on to less plausible ideas, unwilling to eliminate any possibilities.

*Ghost?*

If it was, it wasn't obviously haunting them.

The wound-up flamingos were pretty alarming, but the interloper had clearly been trying to sneak past the bathroom, not terrify them further. Why would they tip-toe past at all when they could vanish so convincingly a moment later?

It was hard to concentrate on the puzzle, which seemed largely harmless now that there was no sign of their mysterious companion. The building was still and silent, except for the gray noise of the storm outside. The wind whistled and moaned and battered snow against the windows.

Anita was warm and solid against him, everything about her making Frank feel like everything in his life had just fallen beautifully into place.

*Flock*, his flamingo murmured.

She was everything he'd never known to miss. He thought his career had been fulfilling, that his success had been satisfying, but now that he'd met Anita, he understood what it meant to be complete.

He frowned, remembering her vehement penthouse protest. It was definitely still possible to scare her off.

*Flock*, his flamingo repeated.

He had to figure out how to properly court her. He had to convince her that she was his everything…and he had no idea how to do that.

He had never dated all that much, and he wasn't sure what it entailed. Dinner? Drinks? Dancing? If his phone still had power, he'd text Tobias to see if he had any advice. For a guy who was barely five foot four and sported a beard like a lap rug, he had no trouble finding female companionship. If anyone could give him direction, Tobias could.

*Dancing*, his flamingo was sure, but Frank was already having trouble wrestling back his bird's occasionally overwhelming instincts. Maybe he should write her poetry, or sing under her window.

Probably, he shouldn't try singing.

But he had pen and paper at hand and great incentive not to move while his mate napped at his shoulder.

Frank carefully turned the page and started writing.

> *My flamingo thinks you're swell*
> *To tell the truth, I do as well.*
>
> *You came into my life with snow*
> *You brought with you a happy glow.*
>
> *I know you are my destiny,*
> *Please say you will stay with me.*

Frank looked at the words he'd written and groaned quietly. Singing was looking better and better.

He flipped the page back and frowned at the notes he'd made for their unwelcome visitor.

Then he frowned at his flamingo sculpture. Although he sometimes had trouble remembering it, his work was worth fabulous amounts of money. Could someone be skulking around with plans to *heist* it?

Frank wrote down *thief*.

Then he shook his head. There was no way that anyone could get away with a three-hundred pound mechanical sculpture in the middle of a snowstorm. It was possible that they could pry out a few of the larger gemstones, but the real value of his pieces lay in the clockwork mechanism and the grandness of scale. There was also no resale value in huge, distinctive, one-of-a-kind statues. Theft didn't really make sense.

He crossed off *thief*.

Then he flipped back to the poem and crossed over it with two big strokes.

He wasn't going to try to be something he wasn't. He was just going to *tell* Anita that she was his everything and promise to love her forever.

*Flock*, his flamingo said happily.

# CHAPTER 11

$\mathcal{A}$nita woke up drooling on a billionaire's shoulder and chagrin jerked her up out of his arms so fast that she knocked his chin with the top of her head.

"Ow, sorry, ow," she said. "I'm graceless."

"Hi, Graceless," Frank said with a smile. "Nice to meet you. I'm Frank." He was so gorgeous, and his mouth was so genuine. "I'm a janitor here at the Wild and Wet Charity Gala and Sleepover."

Who *wouldn't* have been able to smile back at that? Anita wondered, putting a hand to her head sheepishly. "Oh," she said then, because it finally occurred to her that she could see Frank really well now, and that was because sunlight was streaming in through the big bay windows.

The storm had broken, and from their vantage in the table fort, Anita could look up into the sky where big, puffy clouds were breaking apart like giant golden cupcakes.

"It's gorgeous," she said, and that was even before they both scrambled to their feet and could look out over the river and the valley far below. The landscape was covered in deep, fluffy drifts of snow, all silver and tinted in pastel blues. It was a painting, or a childhood memory, a perfect moment frozen in time.

"I wish I was an artist," Anita said wistfully. "I wish I had any hope of capturing this view, this moment, this..." she ran out of words and flapped a hand uselessly.

"It's beautiful," Frank said, but when she glanced over at him, he wasn't looking outside at all, only gazing at her, like she was the painting.

The power was still off, and the wind had stopped, too, so it was eerily quiet.

"How long was I asleep?" Anita asked, touching her hair self-consciously. She'd braided it the night before, so it was probably doing that thing where she looked sort of fuzzy all over. Frank's hair looked perfect. Her fingers were still pink, she realized, and that reminded her that Frank was a flamingo. She just kept herself from squealing.

"A few hours, I think. My phone is dead and I don't have a watch." He was rotating his arm like it was still asleep, and it probably was if Anita had been leaning all of her weight on his shoulder for a few hours.

"I'm so sorry," she said. Then she remembered something else. "Is there any sign of our creepy creeper person?"

"Not a peep," Frank said. "The only sound I heard was wind, and you snoring."

"I didn't!" Anita was mortified. "Tell me I didn't!"

Frank held up his fingers, close together. "A little?"

Mortified but laughing, Anita stretched and yawned. Maybe they had imagined the footsteps. Maybe the flamingo sculpture had...been some kind of mechanical fluke? The hall certainly felt a lot less haunted with brilliant sunlight streaming in.

"My foot's asleep," she said, wiggling her toes and feeling the warning tingle that would come before the painful stage. "I bet the roads are all snowed in, too."

"It will be hours before they get the plows up here," Frank guessed. "Maybe not even until tomorrow. We're kind of off at the end of things here."

"Brrr," Anita said. "It's sunnier, but it's not a lot warmer." Frank had been more than just fun to cuddle up next to, he'd also been a great source of heat. Her foot was coming awake, and she stomped it to work the blood back into it.

Frank bounded back into their fort and found a tablecloth that he folded into a manageable cloak that he masterfully wrapped around her.

"I feel like an Irish princess," Anita said, swirling around in place. "'Come, Frank. Is the Wet and Wild Charity Gala still on or did I sleep through it?'"

"'Frank, the Irish janitor, at your service, m'lady,'" he said gallantly, with an utterly terrible Irish accent. "'You snored through the boring speeches and now the mingling is in full swing and I can hear the orchestra tuning up. Can I carry your train?'"

"'No, no,'" Anita insisted, gathering the dragging cloth and draping it over one arm. "'You are Frank the Janitor and you bow to no tablecloth and'…ow…my foot."

It was the sort of pain that made Anita giggle and gasp, not genuinely in agony, but so deeply uncomfortable that she couldn't ignore it and had to limp around with Frank hovering helplessly over her while she tried to force circulation back down to her toes.

"Okay, okay, it's better," she finally said, clutching at Frank's arm. "I'm such a dork. I bet real Irish princesses never let their feet go to sleep."

"I imagine that royalty has servants to follow them around and rub their extremities while they sleep," Frank said. He snapped his fingers. "I should have massaged your feet while you slept."

Anita figured he wasn't serious, but the idea of a guy like Frank rubbing her toes brought up a lot of those penthouse feelings that she'd been trying to ignore.

# CHAPTER 12

rank had loved having Anita snoring on his shoulder, even when half his body went numb from her weight and she drooled on him.

But he loved having her awake and so full of life that even a giant deserted ballroom didn't feel empty. She filled up the whole space with her energy and playfulness.

"We should do something," he proposed impulsively. "Play a game or something."

"Not a—"

"Not a penthouse game," Frank laughed. "Truth or Dare, or I Spy, or Simon Says."

"It's still kind of dark for I Spy," Anita observed. "And Truth or Dare seems risky with you. How do you play Simon Says with two people?"

"I, er, guess you just tell me what to do and I lose if you don't say Simon says and I do it?"

"Simon says stand on one leg, flamingo-man."

Frank obediently stood on one leg.

"Now put it down."

He caught himself just before doing it, and Anita gave him a golf clap.

"Simon says hop," she challenged.

Frank did, to his flamingo's delight. *We're dancing for her!*

*It's a game,* Frank tried to explain to the joyous bird. *We can only do what Simon says and we lose if we do what she says, but Simon doesn't.*

Frank's flamingo was not happy about the idea of losing.

"You're good at this," she said, after sending him through a series of increasingly complicated commands, failing to trick him into doing what Simon didn't say. She let him stop hopping, but she didn't say a word about putting his foot down.

Frank had to concentrate, still balanced on one leg while he patted his head and rubbed his stomach in a counter-clockwise direction. An idea suddenly occurred to him.

"Now change directions."

Frank might have failed the test on his own, but his flamingo was adamant. *She didn't say Simon says, we do **not** change directions.*

"We should make this interesting," Frank suggested, once he'd verified that his hand was not going to change directions without his conscious control.

"Strip Simon Says?" Anita asked innocently.

*She said strip!* his literal-minded flamingo shrieked. *Simon says!!*

It took every shred of Frank's concentration to continue rubbing his hand across his stomach and patting his head while still maintaining his balance on the one leg.

*That's not what she meant,* Frank said firmly. His flamingo pouted.

"I meant a bet," he said carefully. "If you can get me to do something Simon doesn't say, you can have the flamingo statue."

"The flamingo statue worth a gazillion dollars?" Anita blinked at him in astonishment.

"Sure. It would be yours." Forming words while making his hands do opposite things and standing on one foot was the absolute limit of Frank's attention span.

"What would I do with it?" Anita wanted to know.

"You wanted to put it on your van."

"Not seriously," she protested. "I couldn't afford the insurance.

Besides, it's supposed to be auctioned off for charity. I can't steal it from the orphans! Or the flamingos! Or the orphaned flamingos, or whatever!"

Frank's flamingo was a little miffed that she didn't want the giant statue of him.

"Fine," Frank compromised. "You can have one of the little yard-sized flamingos."

Anita considered. "Do I have to pay taxes on it?" she wanted to know. "I know that it can be complicated when you win sweepstakes."

"I'll have my accountant pay the taxes for you," Frank promised.

"What do you get if you win?" Anita said skeptically.

"A date," Frank said, squashing his flamingo's alternate ideas.

"A penthouse date?" Anita asked suspiciously.

"No, just a date," Frank said swiftly. "I'll take you out to a swanky restaurant, your choice, and we can go dancing if you want…"

He nearly lost the bet at that exact moment as his flamingo all but exploded into feathers of glee.

*Dancing!!*

# CHAPTER 13

*A*nita was impressed.

Frank would have been pretty awe-inspiring under most circumstances, but here he was, being funny and coming up with good ideas while she was making him stand on one foot doing crazy things with his arms. And he was playing for a date? That was pretty flattering.

The pile of fabric in their fort was looking pretty tempting, actually, and Anita had a hot moment wondering how far she could get Frank to go with Simon Says. Would he take off his sweatshirt and shirt so she could see if his chest was as gorgeous as she imagined it was? Would he kiss her if she told him to? Or lay her down and make sweet love to her?

It would probably be hard to do on one leg.

Frank was gorgeous—and a shifter!—and he was so nice that Anita wanted to trust him and let herself feel all those bedroom feelings.

But she didn't dare.

She was running out of things to challenge him with and it occurred to her that it was probably as bright in the building as it was going to get.

"Do you want to go exploring?" she asked, trying not to stare at Frank too obviously. "It's light right now. Maybe we should look for our ghost before it gets dark and raid the kitchen before everything goes bad."

"An excellent plan," Frank agreed cheerfully.

Anita half-expected him to stride out, forgetting about her stand on one leg command and she held her breath in anticipation.

But he was still patting his head and rubbing his stomach as he turned and hopped towards the back hallway.

"You can stop rubbing your stomach," Anita told him as she caught up with him, wondering how on earth he was managing to keep his limbs all synched up.

He gave her a cheeky smile and continued with his jerky hop-rub-pat.

"Simon says you can stop rubbing your stomach," Anita corrected.

He did, with a sigh of relief, and they continued on.

They made it out to the front entrance, and Anita gaped around. It was not well lit, but there were enough windows letting in light to see the marble floor and the fancy art. There were sculptures in alcoves all around the big lobby area, and everything was velvet and gold, like pictures she'd seen of old opera houses.

"If we're explorers, we should be thorough," Frank said, marching one-legged to the first door on the right. It was locked. "Probably a closet?" he guessed.

"You're the janitor," Anita pointed out. "You should know!"

The next door opened onto a coat check room, and there was one lone coat hanging there, a ticket on its sleeve suggesting someone had mistakenly left there it long ago. Frank offered it to Anita, but she demurred in favor of her Irish princess cloak. There was a broom in the corner, and Frank hefted it thoughtfully, then brought it with them.

If he'd been heroic with a bottle of water, that was nothing compared to Frank wielding a broom like a sword. On one leg.

The following door was a large storage room, and it was full of folding chairs and tables and spooky dark corners. Frank hopped bravely in, hollered, "Show yourself, ghost!" and then tripped over a low dolly he hadn't seen in the dark.

They left that room laughing and clinging to each other. Anita didn't penalize him for putting his leg down to save his balance.

# CHAPTER 14

*A*lthough it was brighter than it had been, not all the rooms had windows, and as they left the lobby and the ballroom behind, the halls got darker and Anita found herself closer and closer to Frank.

That wasn't such a bad thing. He leaned on her a little as he hopped along.

"It's often rented as a conference center," Frank explained. "These are all the meeting rooms back here, and they have walls between them that can pull back and forth for bigger and smaller classes. I've attended a few trade shows here. Truly yawn-worthy stuff, with panels like *Accounting tips for wholesale import of small titanium screws from Elbonia* and *Obscure regulations for selling depictions of fowl in the state of Kentucky.*"

They peered into a few of them, letting their eyes adjust to the darkness, but there were no sounds or signs of people, just echoing empty rooms with industrial carpet and low popcorn panel ceilings.

Frank gave his challenge to each empty space, brandishing his broom. "Show yourself, ghost!"

No one showed themselves. There were no sounds of footsteps that weren't theirs.

They wandered quickly to the end of that long hall and found that it stopped in a T-intersection. "That's the way to the kitchen and the back entrance of the ballroom," Frank said, and he turned the other way. There was a meeting room to their right, with a dozen doors along the hallway opening into it and all the interior wall panels folded away so that it was one giant space instead of half a dozen little ones.

To their left, as they walked, was a bank of windows. They were on the not-sunny side of the building, and deep drifts of snow obscured the window, but there was enough light that it was all just a little eerie, not truly frightening.

It helped to have Frank at her side, and sometimes, when he wasn't imitating a one-legged sand creature from Star Wars with his broom, they were holding hands.

Not romantically, Anita told herself. It was just…convenient. Friendly. It wasn't a *penthouse* thing. It was just that she was helping him balance, because she was really starting to wonder if he was going to stay on one leg forever if she didn't release him. Did he really want a date with her that badly?

"I wanted to ask you something!" Anita remembered, as they got to the end of that hall, which bent around to return to the lobby.

"Anything," Frank said promptly.

"This charity event was to preserve wetlands for wildlife," Anita said. "Are those…like wild family members? Do you have a flamingo wife and kids down in Florida or something?"

Frank burst out laughing even as Anita recognized how absurd the question was.

"No," he assured her. "As far as I know, the flamingos down there are only flamingos, not shifter flamingos. Tobias is the one who picked the charity, because I'd already done the sculpture, and he has a weird sense of humor."

"Tobias is your friend?" Anita said wistfully. She didn't have many friends left since she'd moved.

"My very best friend," Frank said without a moment of hesitation. "He runs Wilson Kinetic because I'm hopeless at it and he was the one who said it would work."

"Does he know what you are?"

"Yes," Frank said. "But I don't know what he is. He jokes that he's a gnome, but no one believes him."

"Like…a garden gnome?"

Frank shrugged. "So he says. And who am I to judge? I turn into a giant pink bird. I have to figure it's *gnome* big deal."

Anita felt her mouth quirk into a smile. "Gnome sweet gnome."

"There's no business like gnome business," Frank countered.

"I'll be gnome for Christmas!" Anita sang, badly.

Frank replied with, "Country road, take me gnome!"

They were back at the lobby now, having walked the full circle of the convention rooms loop.

Frank took her hand and drew to a stop in front of her, his face sobering.

"Anita, it's kind of on that topic. That is, I want to be perfectly frank with you…"

Frank's sudden seriousness made Anita nervous. "Are you being Frank? Cause Anita moment." She paused, not sure if the joke had rung true. "Get it? Anita? You're Frank and…I need a moment…"

He laughed more like a loon than a flamingo, a hooting, honking, helpless laugh that had tears rolling out of his eyes as he clutched her and shook with humor.

"It wasn't that funny," Anita said, giggling along anyway because maybe it was. It was nice having someone who *got* her stupid sense of humor. It was also kind of nice being held up close to him in the throes of his amusement, even with the broom against her back. He was really *well-built* for a gazillionaire.

"You really are perfect for me," Frank said, wiping at his eyes. His gaze gained intensity. "I cannot imagine anyone I could love more. You're my destiny."

"Woah, woah," Anita said, freezing in his arms. "I mean, this has been fun, and you're really cute for a janitor, but we had the penthouse talk, and oh—" She stared back at him. "That *mates* thing. It isn't just a crazy story?"

There were a lot of rumors about shifters, and Anita wasn't clear on what was real and what was sheer speculation. Some people insisted that they were mutants with superpowers, some that they were aliens from outer space, or their descendants. She'd seen claims that they all had X-ray vision and incredible strength, that they were all secretly cannibals, or farming people for food, or that they had mind-control powers, or that they were part of a conspiracy to take over the government. The talk show shifter had certainly had some freaky flexibility.

But one of the more pervasive and considerably less believable stories was that every shifter had a fated mate, one true love that they recognized on sight. It was a beautiful fairy tale, and in Anita's opinion, entirely too good to be true.

But Frank was nodding slowly, and his grin had taken on a dreamy, besotted cast. He looked like he wanted to kiss her, and as much as Anita wanted him to do that, the whole idea of it terrified her.

She'd already tried being someone's *destiny* and that had been just *awful.*

"Oh, no," Anita said, carefully pulling herself out of his grasp. "No, no, no, no."

"No?"

"It's a one-syllable word for not a chance, mister."

# CHAPTER 15

*F*rank had to stare. Even his flamingo, for once, was struck dumb. This wasn't how mates were supposed to work.

He was supposed to tell her that she was the one, perhaps in interpretive dance, and then...

*Snuggle?* his flamingo said hopefully.

Anita, however, was clearly not interested in snuggles and she stood apart from him with her arms crossed over her breasts. "Look, you seem really nice," she said, in that way that some people said babies were cute when they actually looked like squashed hams.

"But I don't believe in true love, and I'm not looking for a relationship, and I am especially not interested in being some kind of shifter trophy. I know you're a gazillionaire, and we're stuck together in the middle of a snowstorm, and that probably seems really romantic, but I'm not the kind of girl who swoons over a guy and please don't turn out to be some kind of creepy stalker who isn't going to be able to take no for an answer. Especially while we're trapped in your haunted event hall."

Frank was not going to be that kind of creepy stalker. That was the last thing he wanted to be. "I can take no for an answer," he said gruffly.

"You won't call and call and call and text me and then text my parents and lean on all my friends when I don't want to date you anymore and start hanging around my work and look for rentals in my apartment building and leave notes about how pretty I looked when I was jogging and stalking all my social media until I couldn't post anything publicly or get my mail without putting on a sweatshirt?"

Frank was outraged. "Wait, someone did that to you?"

Anita sat down on one of the tables by the front door and drew her legs up so she was cross-legged, everything about her posture looking uncomfortable. "Sort of. I mean, they said it was my fault because I was nice, because I wasn't good at saying no, and I'm better at that now, and the answer is no. That's why I'm not nice to people now, too."

"Who said that?" Frank wanted to know. "Who said it was *your* fault?" His flamingo honked in fury.

"My parents," Anita said mournfully. "My friends. The *police.*"

"They failed you," Frank snarled, and for a moment, Anita looked genuinely afraid. Frank had to remind himself that she was a young woman trapped alone in a powerless, possibly haunted building with a complete stranger. "And you seem really nice to me," he added more gently.

"It was a business thing," Anita protested. "I'm allowed to be nice for money. And I don't mean that in a penthouse way." She buried her face into her hands. "I'm so bad at people."

"You aren't bad at people," Frank countered. "People were bad at *you*. You should be able to be nice to people without turning them into crazy stalkers. I *want* you to be nice."

Anita peeked through her fingers. "Everyone says I'm too nice," she said. "I've got no sense of boundaries. Too forward, too much, I mean listen to how much I'm over-sharing right this very moment. I'm sort of proving the exact point here."

"Is that why you moved here from California?" Frank asked quietly.

Anita nodded. "I figured he wouldn't follow me across the country. I mean, I'm a catch, but not a *moving expenses* catch. And I could make new friends that weren't *his* friends. I hoped."

Frank wanted to tell her she was utterly irresistible and that he'd certainly follow her across the country in a red hot minute, but he realized it was in bad taste considering what she'd been through.

*Snuggle*, his flamingo said mournfully. *Flock.*

Frank didn't have the slightest doubt that Anita was meant for him. Whatever else his annoying flamingo was good for, he trusted the bird's instincts and could not disbelieve that she was absolutely the most perfect mate in the world.

He also knew that if he pushed her too far, he'd lose her forever, and the last thing he wanted to do was scare her or have her put him in the same box as her previous pushy would-be beau.

She had wilted and was as expressively morose as she'd been irrepressibly full of joy just moments before. She was a tempest in a teacup, Frank thought. So much heart and personality in such a perfect package. He was angry at the idea of someone frightening her and making her feel like she had to dampen even a tiny bit of her beautiful spirit.

Then he glanced behind her, to one of the little alcoves with a statue in it.

If the power had been on, it would have been the focus of a spotlight, but with the power off, it was dramatically shadowed, each of the pieces of art barely discernible. Most of them were stone figures, vaguely Grecian, and some had animals.

So Frank had to stare at this one for a moment to realize that what had caught his eye was the barest glint in the shadowed recess. The reflection of an eye.

While he watched it, ostensibly trying to look as if he was only gazing at Anita, the shape resolved into a pale bird, exactly the shade of the stone figure holding a vase that it was perched on top of. It was an owl and its shining eye was completely unblinking.

Frank gripped his broom tighter.

An owl could fly silently. It might have even passed over their heads in the hallway, causing a brief, icy draft. A shifter, undoubtedly, and one with some kind of ill intentions, or they wouldn't be skulking around this way pretending to be pseudo-Greek stone.

"Look, you don't have to feel sorry for me," Anita said, probably assuming the worst from Frank's sudden silence. "I'm a big girl with big girl pants on, and I don't mean that in a *fat* way even if I am. I've made a new life for myself and I got this great gig for a charity event that might have gotten me out of debt if I could use it to reach some big new clients, and even though it's canceled, maybe I'll still be able to make it because—"

Whatever she was going to say next was cut off with a scream because the owl that Frank was keeping tabs on had finally blinked and confirmed that it was alive.

He charged forward with his broom and a war cry.

# CHAPTER 16

*a*nita thought for one horrible moment that she'd completely misjudged Frank, the way she completely misjudged everyone, and she really had been trapped in an event hall with a serial killer—but it was *him*.

He came charging at her with a furious cry and Anita screamed, confirming that she was much more of a screamer than she'd ever guessed, and not in a good, sexy way.

She should never have been friendly with him, she thought, as Frank raised his broom. Or maybe she shouldn't have refused him. Maybe she should have just gone along with his crazy *mate* delusions until the power came back up and she could find a phone and call the police.

If the police even believed her.

As she winced and closed her eyes in anticipation of Frank's blow—morbidly wondering if it could hurt worse than her disappointment—he sprang to the top of the table she was sitting on and speared the sculpture behind her with his broom handle. Anita fell to the side in astonishment as a bird rose out of the alcove with a haunting hoot.

It was quickly out of Frank's range with the broom, circling the high ceiling around the chandelier, and Anita thought that would be the end of it.

She'd forgotten that Frank was a flamingo.

Or maybe she'd forgotten that flamingos could fly.

She definitely forgot to be afraid for herself as Frank launched himself into the air after the bird and spread giant pink wings.

The other bird was an owl, Anita realized, watching them circle each other, a white and black-barred snowy owl. It was far more maneuverable than Frank was, and a little smaller, but Frank was surprisingly agile for a waterbird, and he was holding his own whenever they met mid-air.

Honestly, as alarming and horrifying as it was to watch, Anita could not help but overlay the action with a comic musical soundtrack in her mind. The two of them smashed into the walls and lights, sending the chandelier into tinkling song, and they flapped their wings at each other and turned dizzying somersaults as they fought. Neither of them seemed invested in truly hurting each other, but Frank wanted to catch the owl and the owl didn't particularly seem to want that.

Frank honked, and the owl screeched until the lobby echoed with their cries and Anita had to stand up on the table and cheer him on, the tablecloth that had been wrapped around her slipping off as she jumped up. She grabbed it as it tried to slither away, just as the two fighting birds swooped alarmingly close. She flung the billowing cloth at them desperately, not entirely sure if she was trying to protect herself or insert herself into their battle.

It was a lucky shot, and the fabric swirled out over both of them as if she was some kind of graceful Amazon and not just a plump baker with dye-stained fingertips.

They fell together onto the floor in a tangle of tablecloth and squirming lumps of bird and wing. Anita wasn't sure which was which when it landed, so she simply flung herself over both of them with her arms spread, hoping to stop the fight and capture the owl.

"Ow, ow, ow!" It was a woman's voice, and a woman's form underneath her now, and Anita rolled to pin her down as Frank shifted and wrestled his way out from underneath the other side of the tablecloth.

"Mercy!" the woman cried. "Ow, your *elbows!*"

Anita immediately felt terrible, never mind that the owl shifter had been haunting the hall and scaring the bejeebus out of them and possibly plotting their grisly deaths. She rolled away just as Frank grabbed the broom and got to his feet. They flanked the draped woman and Anita reached forward to pull the tablecloth away, feeling like a frumpy Vanna White.

*The prize behind sheet number one is…*

"Harriet Slade?!"

Her arch-nemesis was dressed in a slinky silver dress and matching heels, and her bright red hair looked considerably worse for the wear.

She sat up slowly, eyeing the business end of Frank's broom warily and holding her shoulder.

"Hi, *Anita.*"

Anita felt like her head was doing a record screech sound. "Harriet Slade?" she said again, sitting back on her heels. "What are you doing here?"

"This is your cupcake rival?" Frank said in astonishment. He didn't offer to lower the broom. "What are you doing here?"

Harriet glared between them, then decided that Frank wasn't going to immediately hit her, slowly getting to her feet with her hands spread. Anita scrambled up with considerably less grace.

"Answer the question," Frank growled, taking one threatening step towards her. "Why are you here?"

Anita watched Harriet weigh her options, glancing up at the ceiling and rubbing her sore shoulder. Finally, she heaved a sigh and glared at Anita. "I was here to sabotage your cupcakes."

"My cupcakes? *Sabotage?*"

Frank let the tip of the broom droop. "Why would you do that? She was up all night making those cupcakes!"

Anita was warmed by his defense.

"Because cupcakes are a cutthroat business," Harriet protested. "Because she just waltzed into town and stole the event contract and half my sales and everyone…likes her cupcakes more." She had her arms wrapped around herself and looked for all the world like a kicked puppy.

Anita reminded herself not to feel sorry for her. *Sabotage!* Her *arch-nemesis!* "What were you going to do?"

Harriet reached into her cleavage and Frank immediately drew his broom up. "Careful," he warned.

"It's not like I have room for a gun in this dress," Harriet said, slowly drawing out a small plastic bag filled with sparkling powder. "And if I was going to kill you, I'd have done it earlier, while you were snuggling in your little fort."

Anita blushed at the idea of Harriet spying on them. It was lucky that she hadn't done anything more risqué than drooling on Frank in her sleep.

"Wait, you were going to drug my cupcakes?" Anita's imagination suggested that it was crack or cocaine or maybe some kind of mind control powder. "Is it poison?" Was arsenic white? She thought it was supposed to be odorless and colorless.

"No!" Harriet said in outrage. "It's vinegar powder. I was just going to ruin them."

Frank gave an angry growl and poked her in the shoulder with his broom. "How dare you?" he bristled. Anita wondered if he'd be so gallant for just anyone, or if it was because she was his mate. He seemed like a gallant kind of person, so probably she shouldn't take it as personally as she wanted to.

Harriet's look was flatly unimpressed, but she winced when he made contact. "Look, I had the best cupcake shops in the whole city until she showed up! I was going to lose my biggest clients! And anyway, that was before I heard the whole stupid sob story about how you had to move here because of a creepy stalker." She looked at Anita then, and her gaze was golden-brown and unblinking. "I'm sorry you had to go through that."

She held out the vinegar powder packet like a peace offering. After a moment, Anita put her hand out and accepted it.

Frank didn't seem as willing to forgive. "Why did you come when the event was canceled?" he asked suspiciously.

"I wasn't exactly on the guest list," Harriet sniffed. "So no one bothered to tell me that it was canceled. I strained my wing getting here just before the storm. My plan was to come early and hide until the party got started, then mingle with the guests."

"You wanted to watch them hate my cupcakes," Anita said, feeling a complicated amount of respect for Harriet.

"Yeah," Harriet said sheepishly. "I thought it would be hilarious. Sorry."

"It would have been hilarious," Anita agreed. "I can't say that I would have done the same thing, because I'm not a jerk, but I still bet it would have been amazing. All those celebrities spitting out their cupcakes into their napkins!"

"They'd probably dare each other to eat them," Harriet said enthusiastically. She lifted an imaginary cupcake to her mouth. "'I'm sure it isn't as bad as Victoria Henning's hair,'" she said in a perfectly snobby voice as she mimed taking a bite.

Frank looked between the two of them and finally let his broom rest on the floor again. "If you didn't want us to know you were here, why did you wind the flamingos?"

Harriet spread her hands as if it was perfectly obvious. "I didn't expect you to come back to the ballroom! There's a penthouse upstairs. I figured that you'd go straight up there after you hit the kitchen. Duh. And I'd never seen one of your fancy machines in motion and I didn't think I'd ever have the opportunity to again." She squinted at them. "Why *aren't* you up there?"

Frank was doing a bristly protective shuffle in place like he wanted to come and stand between them. "I don't want to make Anita do anything she doesn't want. I only bought her cupcakes."

"I wasn't asking you, you cotton candy goose," Harriet snarked.

Anita blinked. "Me? Well, you heard..."

Frank really did come and stand between them then. "She doesn't have to answer you."

"Don't get your feathers in a twist, hot legs," Harriet said. She craned her head to look around him at Anita. "I just want to point out that this guy is clearly not the jerk who chased you onto my turf. He's been a total gentleman with you. He's hot, you're into each other, what's the holdup? He even wrote you really awful poetry."

Frank gave a little jolt. "You saw that?"

"Owls have really good vision in dim light," Harriet said as if it was really obvious. That seemed to be her default tone.

"You wrote me poetry?" Anita said to Frank's back.

"It's kind of terrible," Frank said, turning to look down at her. "Sorry. I'd already decided not to inflict it on you."

"I kind of want you to inflict it on me," Anita confessed.

"Oh my god, you two are disgusting. Just *neck* already."

# CHAPTER 17

*F*rank was definitely happy to have an answer to the
riddle of the haunted event hall, and he loved the idea
that Harriet thought that he and Anita were 'into each other,' but he
wasn't all that pleased with the rival baker's constantly conde-
scending tone. His flamingo was outraged that she'd come here to
ruin their mate's culinary reputation, though he was a fan of the
necking idea.

"What are we going to do with you?" he asked generally.

"We could call the police," Anita suggested. "Except that your
phone is out of power."

Frank looked thoughtfully at Harriet, who gave a bark of
laughter and met his gaze with challenge. "I'm not going to give you
my phone so that you can call the cops on me. Besides, I haven't
actually done anything wrong. You're the one who assaulted *me* with
a broom."

"You're trespassing," Frank pointed out. "You didn't have an
invitation."

"Oh help, I got lost in the snowstorm of the century! I needed
shelter! All I tried to do was stay out of your way!" Harriet's innocent act wasn't terribly convincing. "Look, I didn't hurt anyone, and

I didn't take anything, and you've still got two thousand unmolested cupcakes, for all the good they'll do you. I didn't *have* to tell you what I was planning to do, that was a gesture of good faith. And I decided not to do it anyway."

"I don't want her to get in trouble," Anita said, because she had a heart seven times the size of the flamingo statue.

"I thought you said that cupcakes were a cutthroat business," Frank said, mystified.

"A whole lot of Westerns would have been much shorter movies if they'd just built a town big enough for the two of them," Anita laughed. She extended a hand to Harriet. "Look, I hope there are no hard feelings. I didn't mean to encroach on your territory. Maybe we can work out...like a customer custody schedule or something."

"I feel bad for planning to destroy your cupcakes and crush you like a bug," Harriet said just as frankly, taking Anita's hand and giving it a sharp shake. "I've been wanting to specialize in fancy wedding cake decorating more anyway. I'll send you my extra cupcake business." She made it sound like a careless concession.

"And I'll send you my extra wedding cakes," Anita said kindly.

"Just weddings?" Harriet asked shrewdly.

"I'm not going to give up the rest of the holiday cakes for a few measly cupcake orders," Anita protested.

Even as Frank admired Anita's keen business sense, Harriet burst out laughing. "You're alright, sugar queen."

"You're not half bad for a baker baron," Anita retorted.

"Maybe...we can be friends?"

Frank didn't trust Harriet for a hot moment, but Anita bounded forward and impulsively hugged her.

"Oh, sorry," she said, when Harriet patted her awkwardly and squirmed away.

"You weren't kidding about being bad with boundaries," Harriet said.

Frank rather liked that about Anita, and he thought that Harriet looked a little like she did, too, sort of embarrassed and delighted and disgusted all at once.

"It's been kind of a long, weird day," Anita said frankly. "And I'm a hugger."

Harriet met Frank's eyes over Anita's head. "Enjoy *that*, super pink."

Frank wasn't sure what to say to that. "Thanks? I will?"

"Well, this has been real," Harriet said, brushing off the skirt of her sparkly silver dress. "It looks like the storm has cleared up enough for me to get home, strained wing or not and as fun as this has all been, I am going to jet before I die of sugar poisoning."

Not really sure what else to do, Frank walked her to the front doors and courteously opened them for her. A great deal of snow had drifted up against them, and it took Frank his full weight on the door to get it open.

"Miss me!" Harriet called, shifting back into an owl and bypassing the hip-deep snowbank by lifting up into the air. She flew somewhat raggedly, but was gone by the time Frank had wrestled the door shut again.

Then he really was alone in the deserted event hall with only Anita.

All he had to do now was win Simon Says and get his date with her so that he could sweep her off her feet.

*Dancing!* his flamingo said hopefully.

# CHAPTER 18

"Well, that's the mystery solved," Anita said. "I feel like Scooby Doo. Velma of course. The short, nerdy one." She looked sideways at Frank. "You're Fred, of course, all handsome and rich."

"If it weren't for us meddling kids," Frank said knowingly. "I guess this means we're back to Simon Says." He made a show of stretching, like he was about to start a sprint. He arched his fingers together over his head and then lifted one leg after the other as he tilted his head to each side. "Whenever you're ready, Simon."

He picked up one leg and started patting his head. "I believe you had released me from the stomach rubbing," he said hopefully.

Anita smiled at him. "Simon said you could stop rubbing your stomach," she agreed. This would be a joke that they always had, she thought happily, before she could remind herself that Frank was a gazillionaire and she made cupcakes. If he won this game, as he seemed determined to do, he'd take her on a date, and...what then?

Was she really his mate? Was any of this real? If she Simon Said that he should take her over to their sideways table fortress and make love to her in a pile of curtains and tablecloths, would he do it?

What if this was just a silly diversion, like Simon Says itself, and she was just a ridiculous girl building it all up to too much in her own head?

Would there be anything left when the power came on and the roads were cleared and everyone went back to their own lives?

"Can I see the poem you wrote me?" she asked shyly.

Frank ducked his head. "I guess," he said sheepishly. "But I promise I'm no Wordsworth or Rumi."

"Interesting choice of poets," Anita said, glad that she'd at least heard of both of them.

He patted himself, nearly falling over on his one leg to twist for his back pocket. "I don't have it," he said in dismay. "It must have fallen out of my pocket. Maybe it's back at the fort."

He hopped on the one leg all the way back to the ballroom, still patting his head, and Anita took pity on him and squirreled in under his arm to help support him. It didn't feel weird to be up close with him, after their long adventure.

"It's a lot less scary in here now that we know what the ghost was," she said, as they came out of the shadowed hall to the ballroom. "Oh!"

If the view out the windows had been awe-inspiring earlier, it was enchanted now, with the sun starting to set. The clouds had gone from fluffy and slightly gold to rich smeared hues of orange and pink, the sky above fading to purple. The snow-filled valley reflected every color in a soft palette of the most magnificent painter ever.

They had both drawn to a stop, Frank leaning on her just a little. He was a big guy, but he didn't make her feel afraid for a second. He was just exactly as he was supposed to be, somehow.

"Oh, here it is," he said, and he somehow managed to crouch down on the one leg to pick up a tiny promotional notebook with his logo on the cover.

Anita had done enough yoga—it didn't take much!—to know that even for a shifter, his leg must be aching. She ought to take pity on him. She was being entirely too cruel. He'd done every weird thing she told him to without so much as a hesitation, and he hadn't done anything too forward or presumptive, even after he'd leveled that whole mate thing on her.

Especially after the whole mate thing.

She'd said her piece, and he'd taken it for absolute gospel.

And he wrote her poetry.

He'd also crossed it off, Anita discovered, when he reluctantly flipped it open and handed it over to her.

"I'm sorry it's so awful."

"It's not awful," Anita protested.

"You haven't read it yet," Frank pointed out.

> *My flamingo thinks you're swell*
> *To tell the truth, I do as well.*
>
> *You came into my life with snow*
> *You brought with you a happy glow.*
>
> *I know you are my destiny,*
> *Please say you will stay with me.*

Anita read it, making it sing-song in her head. It was silly and sappy and didn't scan perfectly.

"See?" Frank seemed to take her slowness in reading it as proof.

"It is sort of awful," Anita conceded. "But I love it anyway."

It was genuine, like Frank himself. It was straight from his big, beautiful heart.

Harriet, bless her competitive soul, was right about him. He *wasn't* Anita's past, and he *was* really hot, and they *were* totally into each other. She didn't want to waste a perfectly good opportunity, trapped in snowstorm without power, and regret it for the rest of her life.

"You should kiss me," Anita said boldly, and it was delicious to watch Frank's face light up.

She was confused that he didn't lean forward then and close the space between them. He had a really nice mouth and Anita was dying to know if it would feel like she imagined it would against hers.

"You didn't say Simon says," he reminded her.

"Simon says to kiss me," Anita said impatiently.

Frank, still on one leg, still patting his head, reached forward with his other arm and pulled her close. He lost his balance and nearly fell over, but Anita was sturdy and used to accidentally almost knocking people down, so she kept them upright until his mouth was brushing her lips and her whole world went away.

Anita hadn't kissed a lot of people, but she was pretty sure this was an amazing kiss by *any* criteria. He smelled so good and he felt so good, with one arm around her, and when his lips touched hers she felt like she'd been lit on fire.

Good fire, though. Fire blazing through her veins like special effects in a movie. It wasn't scary or overwhelming and she didn't once stop to think that she might be doing it wrong or worry that she would taste bad, she was so happy and excited and he was holding her so close.

Anita didn't realize that she was rubbing herself up against him until he groaned in her mouth and she realized exactly what it was that she was rubbing herself up against.

"I'm sorry," she said breathlessly, pulling back and trying to look anywhere else. Too much. Too forward. Too fast. That's what everyone said about her.

Frank let her go and nearly unbalanced. He was still on one leg and doing a terrible job of patting his own head. "Simon said," he gasped.

Did he only do it because she'd told him to? It was hard to think that he didn't want her the same way she wanted him because of the way he looked at her, and the way he talked about being her mate.

# CHAPTER 19

*A*nita tasted exactly like Frank had expected her to: like cupcakes.

*Algae and plankton and saltwater,* his flamingo sighed happily.

But it wasn't just the flavor of her, it was the heat of her mouth, and the eagerness of her tongue, and the way her whole body was along for the ride. She was so much person in such a perfect package, and she had a dozen expressions dancing across her sweet face now. How could a complete stranger be so familiar and so comfortable and still feel thrilling and new? He felt like he'd known her forever and just met her, all at once.

He wanted her like he'd never wanted anything else in the world, wanted to capture her in his hands and cage her in his heart forever.

But he knew that it wouldn't work if he trapped her. He had to tame her to his hand, not hide her behind bars.

She licked her lips and smoothed back the hair around her face. Her braid had gotten progressively more wild as the day advanced, and she had curls everywhere. "I'm sorry," she repeated.

"I don't want you to be sorry," Frank said. He wasn't even sure exactly what she was apologizing for, but he knew what he had to do at last.

"Anita," he said, hopping backwards a few feet.

He made sure that she was watching him and stopped patting his head.

Her eyes widened in horror. "I didn't say Simon says!" she warned him, as his foot lowered to the floor. "Oh no!"

Then she looked up at him. "You did that on purpose!" she exclaimed in surprise. Her face fell. "Oh. Oh, you didn't...want to win."

*Fix it fix it fix it!* Frank's flamingo shrieked.

"I didn't want to win," Frank agreed, stuffing his irritating bird back into his head. "I didn't want you to go out with me because you had to, or felt obligated, just because I am clearly the world's greatest Simon Says player. I want you to go out on a date with me because *you* want to. Not because you're my mate and I'm a billionaire, but because maybe we get along really well, and you want to see where we could go *together.*"

She was silent, which was so ridiculously un-Anita that Frank was a little frightened.

His flamingo hid his metaphorical head under a wing.

"You don't have to," he assured her. "This isn't a trap, and if you tell me you don't want to have anything to do with me, that's what will happen."

She was still quiet.

"I won't call or stalk you," he promised. "I'll never order cupcakes from you again, if that's what you want."

Why wouldn't she talk?? Was he doing this all wrong?

He cleared his throat and started again. "Anita, I want to be frank with you. If you *need a* moment..." He waited to see if she laughed at the joke again, then plowed further on when she didn't, "I'll give you all the moments you need. I'll be patient as it takes. You can have space and time. This is your choice to make."

*Could* she speak? She was still staring and every so often, she would blink, but her mouth didn't move.

Frank was out of things to say and flailed after what to do next.

*Dance?* his flamingo suggested hopefully.

Frank didn't have a better idea.

He cleared his throat and bowed to her. "'Miss Townsend,'" he said formally, "'seeing as the Wild and Wet Charity Gala wasn't actually canceled, would you like to dance with me to the music of the lovely orchestra I hired. It sounds like they are starting a waltz.'"

Her smile was so careful that Frank felt a little like he was watching it in slow motion.

"I'd like that," she whispered, and she put one hand into his.

Frank took her gently into his arms, not wanting to spook her.

As sure as his flamingo was of their dancing skills, Frank knew well that he was mediocre-at-best at socially acceptable forms of dancing. He could cut a rug at a wedding where flailing elbows and lots of hugging were expected, but he would never be the surprise winner of a ballroom dancing competition or the star of a reality show that involved footwork. He could do a foxtrot and lead a basic waltz, in a pinch, and he vaguely knew the hand motions to the Macarena.

But without music, completely distracted by the feeling of Anita, who was stiff in his embrace, he was worse than ever.

He tried humming, to give himself a sense of rhythm, and ended up stuck in a repeating refrain of "I'm a little teapot..." before he collided knees once too often with Anita and she offered, "Do you want me to lead? Or possibly, sing?"

If a flamingo could die of embarrassment, Frank's would have perished on the spot.

"I'm not usually *this* terrible," he said with chagrin.

"I did just make you hop around on one leg for like an hour," Anita pointed out as she drew him in a circle. "Duh duh duh duh duh. Duh duh. Duh duh. Duh duh duh duh duh. Duh duh. Duh duh..."

She led him off in circles that got increasingly wide as they sang the refrain to Blue Danube, over and over again until they were both laughing and dizzy and Frank's flamingo was yodeling happily in his head.

"I love you," he told her, when they had slowed to a more sedate pace. He didn't really mean to, but it just bubbled up out of him. She was close in his arms and they were swaying in place. She had to tip her head to look up at him, but she didn't draw away.

"I'm sorry," he said, seeing the conflicted emotion on her face. "I won't press."

"I...kind of do want you to press," she admitted. "I like you a lot, Frank, and I don't think I'm at code level love yet, but I could sure get there in a hurry. You're the nicest, cutest guy I've ever crushed on, and...you kiss really well."

"Could I kiss you again?" Frank asked.

"Simon says that would be acceptable," Anita said demurely, and her smile was slow enough that it was still in the act of curving up as Frank caught her mouth with his.

It was all a great deal simpler when he was kissing her, that was for sure.

She was fluid in his embrace, soft and strong and sweet, and she slipped her arms up around his neck like they belonged there.

If their first kiss was magic, this one was wild sorcery.

# CHAPTER 20

$\mathcal{A}$ nita had been trying really hard to be the kind of person who didn't rush into things, but everything about Frank made her want to tear off her own clothing and fling herself at him. She'd spent the entire day wrestling back her intensifying attraction, trying to dampen her own reckless impulses with common sense and life experience.

But the more she was *herself*, the more Frank seemed to like her. He liked all the weird, wild things she came up with, and he didn't seem to think she should always stop talking a sentence earlier. If his hard-on, apparent again, was any indication, he found her as hot as she found him.

And she wanted this guy, in all the dirty-sweet ways that she could imagine. He checked every single one of her boxes for animal desire. He had a body she wanted to climb and wrap her legs around, and he had a face she would have postered on her ceiling so she could go to sleep with him as the last thing she saw before dreaming. His smile was like a magazine cover, and his clever hands made her whimper.

But it was his laugh that made her weak. When he threw back

his head and chortled with her, Anita felt like she'd grown wings of her own and could fly.

His second kiss was even hotter than the first one and Anita let her hands wander up so she could feel the muscles in his back and grind herself against his leg and its friend.

His hands wandered, too, from chastely at her waist to take a handful of her ass, and she absolutely loved it, kissing him harder and clawing him accidentally.

"Anita," he said, drawing away for a tantalizing, terrible moment.

"Simon says take me to the penthouse," Anita said, before she could remember her resolve to take things slower and be less forward.

Frank drew away just far enough to shock her by sweeping her up entirely into his arms and marched with her down the back hallway toward the elevator.

They kissed passionately and made out against the wall like horny teenagers there for a long while before they simultaneously realized that pushing the button wasn't working while the power was out.

"The power—" she gasped.

"It's two floors up—" Frank panted.

Frank seemed perfectly willing to lift her back up into his arms and carry her up those stairs. He picked her up and staggered a little because she wasn't that light and he was busy kissing her, besides the fact that he'd been hopping around on one leg for so long.

"Our fort," Anita suggested instead. "It's closer." She was pretty sure that Frank would get her up those two stories without dropping her, but she wasn't sure that *she* would last that long, and she thought it would be more comfortable making love in a pile of tablecloths than it would in a stairwell landing.

Frank said something that might have been a dirty word, or the word *flock*.

"Yes, please," Anita said to either one.

Frank ran into one of the tables by the entrance to the ballroom and nearly dropped Anita. She only screamed a little when she felt herself falling, and Frank caught her at once.

"Sorry," she said. "I'm a screamer. Apparently." The split-second of fear only heightened her excitement.

Frank actually growled as he clutched her possessively. Anita hadn't thought that she'd ever want anyone to be possessive of her again, but this was nothing but delightful. "I love it when you scream," he promised. "Tell me what will make you."

"Oh, options," Anita purred. "Missionary, doggy style? Hold me down, let me ride you? Up against a wall? Sixty-nine? Can we try them all?"

He nearly dropped her again, because he'd gotten them to the fort itself then and Anita wasn't sure how he got over the sideways table, but he finally laid her down in the pile of tablecloths at last and bent to kiss her, hard.

Frank slowed to undress her, and then suddenly paused. "There are condoms in the penthouse," he said between gritted teeth. "I should get one."

"I'm on the pill," Anita said, honestly touched that he'd think of it. "I know that I'm impulsive, so I try to make up for that with common sense."

"You are so amazing," Frank said, and Anita could not have disbelieved him if she had tried. "You are so smart and funny and unexpected and beautiful."

"I should always stop one sentence earlier," she said sheepishly.

"Never stop one sentence earlier," Frank said firmly. "I want to know your every last sentence forever."

# CHAPTER 21

*F*rank was not sure if Anita had been serious about the positions she listed or not, but he was determined to try them all, particularly once he'd gotten her shirt off and freed her breasts from her bra.

They were stupendous breasts. They were round in all the right places, with hard little nipples and tiny freckles over the top where sunlight might hit them in a low-cut shirt.

Even his flamingo was stunned by them. *Breasts...*

Frank might have stayed there the rest of the night, kissing every inch of them, marveling at the way they moved and how they felt when he squeezed them, but Anita was working on getting his shirt off, and her hands on his skin were making him aware of all the other things that he wanted to do with her.

He helped her shuck off his shirt and her breasts against his chest when they kissed again were so perfectly soft and firm and intoxicating that for a while they just sort of rubbed against each other happily while their tongues were busy.

Then her hands were at the button of his jeans and he swiftly drew them both back up to their feet so he could figure out how to get her out of her pants. He forgot about shoes until he got that far, then had to backtrack in order to get them off her feet, both laughing.

Sometimes sex was an awful lot of knowing what went where but not really being sure how to get it there, fumbling together in hunger but not really graceful or comfortable.

Making love to Anita was something else entirely. They were good together from the very start, matched in urgency and readiness, completely compatible and hyper-aware of every touch and reaction. There were no layers of expectation, no wondering if they'd be able to talk afterwards, no awkward surprises. They laughed and kissed and explored each other, gauging reactions and readiness, and needed very few words of direction.

A few whispered *theres* and a couple of *mores* and a hissed *yessssss* and he was buried inside of her where he knew that he belonged, and she was so hot and so tight and so wet that he had to think fixedly about imported titanium screws and machine tolerance to ride out her wave of pleasure and not take his own.

They only got through three of the positions she'd listed, first very safe and vanilla on a bed of curtains, then her on top, with those gorgeous breasts in glorious motion above him. She was as enthusiastic about gratification—his and hers—as she was about everything else she did, and her face, eyes closed in pleasure, mouth parted, was like a painting in the sunset light.

Finally, Frank had her bent over one of the tables on a folded tablecloth, her ass in his hands every bit as alluring as her breasts, her soft cries not quite proving that she was a screamer, but definitely expressing her appreciation. His world narrowed to her sounds, to the feel of being sheathed in her, to her heat, and he lost his last shred of self-control and let himself fall in a glory of release that he'd never imagined.

He wasn't entirely quiet himself, at the end, and they collapsed together and listened to the sounds of their pleasure fade in the echoes to just their panting breath.

"Good thing Harriet didn't stick around," Anita giggled.

She was shivering. The heat was still out, and the hall had

continued to get colder. The sun was nearly gone, but Frank could see a wisp of her breath in what was left of the light.

He pulled one of the drapes out from underneath them and flung it over top of them. Unfortunately, this knocked over the box of cupcakes that was still perched on one of the tipped-over tables. The lid popped open and one of them rolled right on top of Anita.

"Let me get that," Frank said nobly, picking up the cupcake and bending to lick the frosting off of her belly. It was one of the yellow cupcakes and tasted like lemon with a hint of mint. "Yum."

Anita was looking at him avidly. "Yum is right," she said, staring at him. "How'd I luck out with a bird like you?"

Frank kissed her and then laughed when Anita licked a smudge of frosting from his nose.

"You're my mate," he said contentedly.

"Crikey," Anita teased. Then her face turned suddenly serious. "Oh, Harriet might have been onto something!" she said, sitting up so fast that she nearly cracked Frank in the face. "Er, sorry."

"What was Harriet onto?" he wanted to know.

"The vinegar sprinkle! I could make a sour lemon cupcake! A cheek-sucking lemon drop! Not much, of course not as much as she would have used to ruin them, but I could totally market it as a specialty. Oh, and maybe a red hot cinnamon! People love challenging food! I could label the box 'Cupcakes that make you sweat!'" She considered. "Okay, maybe not that. You can help me come up with something better."

"I can't wait," Frank said happily.

Anita sobered. "I suppose we should talk about that, actually."

"Cupcakes that make you sweat?"

She smiled like she was trying not to. "About what happens next. Where do we go from here?"

"The penthouse has blankets. I have a sweater you can wear if you're cold."

"I mean…after this." She wasn't trying not to smile now, her mouth wide and happy in her darling face. "Where would we live? Do you have a mansion or something? I'm not sure my apartment allows flamingos."

"I don't need much," Frank promised. "A yard with some lawn and maybe a wading pool. Flamingos are actually quite resilient. We can stand in boiling or freezing water, drink saltwater, handle acids and toxins. We're like cockroaches; we'll outlast just about every-thing you throw at us."

Anita giggled helplessly. "Be serious," she said.

"Do I have to?" Frank said. He felt giddy.

Part of it was the afterglow of the greatest sex of his life, but most of it was that he'd found the woman who made him happier than he'd ever imagined possible…and she was willing to be his. "Maybe I can buy this place and we can live here in this table fort. One of those back conference rooms would make a fine nursery."

"It does have a lot of happy memories," Anita agreed. "Screaming in the bathroom. That time we snubbed Victoria Hennings."

"That time I was in an aerial battle with a trespassing owl," Frank added.

"Did I win the flamingo sculpture?" Anita wanted to know. "I don't think the bidding ever came to an end."

"I'll give it to you," Frank promised. "As a wedding gift."

"It's kind of big," she said, looking across the ballroom at the stage thoughtfully.

Frank snorted. "'That's what she said!'"

They giggled and cuddled together under one of the velvet drapes that didn't have cupcake frosting on it. It was so delicious to have her in his arms, just skin against skin against velvet. They had it tented over their heads, like they were having the greatest sleep-over ever.

"Did you mean that?" Anita asked.

"I've always thought that I was quite reasonably endowed," Frank said. "You certainly didn't *sound* disappointed."

"I meant about a wedding," Anita said shyly.

Frank hesitated and his flamingo froze. *Flock?*

"I love you, Anita," he said honestly. "But we don't have to rush into anything you don't want. You can move in with me; I've got a flat downtown with a guest room that can be yours and we can live in dirty sin. Or you can keep your apartment if you like. Or we can rent something in between. I'm not worried about time, or cost, or judgmental relatives, or gossip columns. I only care that you're happy and feel safe and know that I love you. If you want me to prove it with a ring, I will."

He couldn't really see Anita under the dark drapery, but he could feel her snuggle closer and give a great sigh of contentment.

*Snuggle!* his flamingo said happily.

After a moment, Anita lifted her head, knocking it into his chin the way she had when she woke up. "Er, sorry. Still graceless."

"Still Frank," he replied.

She giggled. "You are. You are perfectly Frank. And I love you, I think, and I'm not quite ready for wedding bells but I wouldn't say no to a ring."

"I'll make you one!" Frank declared. "Do you want a clockwork ring with a tiny little pink diamond flamingo in it?"

*Flock!*

There was no way that he could resist kissing her then, cradling her into his arms and leaning her back so that he could feel all of her against all of him.

A sudden pop drove them back up to upright. "Did you hear someone?" Anita asked, her arms tighter around him now.

Frank eased the curtain-tent back and squinted into unexpected brightness. "The power is back on!"

The sounds of lights and ventilation were loud after the post-storm silence, and Frank felt a little lost and off balance. He and Anita got to their feet. Neither of them had a stitch of clothing on and Anita's reflection in the window was like a curvy little goddess. She was shivering. "I bet the elevator works now," she suggested hopefully.

Frank thought that this was a great plan. "It might take a little while, but I bet there will be warm water soon, and we can have hot showers and airplane nuts in my penthouse."

"'Airplane nuts, you say?'" Anita had slipped back into her snotty voice. She stooped to gather up her clothing. "'I say, Frank

Wilson, you do throw a very fine all-day charity event and sleepover.'"

"The sleepover part is the best part," he promised.

"As long as there are blankets on that bed," Anita said, shivering in earnest now.

"I will keep you warm," Frank promised. "For the rest of my life, I will keep you warm." He grabbed one of the tablecloths to swirl around them and helped her vault over the tipped-over table.

*Snuggle*! his flamingo yodeled, as they hurried for the elevator, which obediently came at their command this time. The hallways were very bright and different now that they were lit again, but the timing was good, because it was almost full dark outside.

"'I suggest that you escort me to the penthouse, Mr. Wilson,'" Anita commanded as the elevator doors opened for them.

"'I shall do exactly that, Miss Townsend,'" Frank said.

*Flock! Flock! Flock!* his flamingo cried in joy.

# EPILOGUE

*H*arriet landed on her balcony, shifted, and limped to the sliding door she'd left unlocked. She had to wade through a rather shocking amount of snow and wrench on the door much harder than usual, because ice had formed at all the edges.

She wrestled it shut again, and snow fell in all over the carpet and started to melt.

Harriet was too tired and sore to deal with it and she kicked off her silver shoes and went to the bathroom to start a well-deserved bath. At least her apartment had power, though the blinking light above the kitchen stove suggested it had been out.

Frank had gotten a good strike with his beak at her leg while they were fighting, and Anita had just about crushed her in that last tackle. Harriet probably would have made a better showing in the battle if she hadn't foolishly strained her wing flying to a useless *canceled* charity event.

That stupid bubbly baker and her ridiculous flamingo billionaire beau.

She didn't suppose that it was really their fault that her grand plan had failed because of the unexpected snowstorm. They were pretty cute…and so *clueless*. They had bought into her 'sabotage the cupcakes' story without a single doubt or hesitation.

Anita had even *hugged* her.

The bathroom was starting to steam as Harriet wriggled out of her fancy dress, hanging it with the other high end frocks that she'd accumulated. She paused to run her fingers down a velvet black gown.

It was an impressive collection for a simple baker.

But it was perfectly in character for a jewel thief.

Harriet returned to the bathroom to pile her hair up onto her head and check the temperature of the water. The tub was half full.

Oh, Harriet had certainly intended to ruin Anita's cupcakes, and she hadn't feigned *all* of her sympathy once they'd actually met and her rival baker proved to be a ridiculous rube. A ridiculous rube with a sense of humor and whimsy that Harriet found herself reluctantly *liking*. And it wasn't really Anita's fault that she made better cupcakes and had an actual business plan that involved selling them.

Harriet's bakeries were just a front for the money that she made stealing jewels and art, the perfect, innocent excuse for laundering the cash from her crimes and heists. Her cupcakes were mediocre and she knew it, but if sales fell off too obviously, her cover was blown.

The Wet and Wild Charity Gala and Auction was a chance for the city's fanciest, frocked-up fellows to come out showing off their wealth and good fortune by wearing it around their necks and at their wrists and ears as they pledged pittances to worthy causes.

Harriet had planned to arrive early and hide until the event was under way, then mingle as one of the guests, carefully relieving them of a choice selection of the easiest pieces to fence. She was very talented at evaluating risk and reward, and she had a half dozen acts in her pocket.

*Oh, you've lost an earring, let me help you find it!* and *That's such a lovely necklace, tell me all about it* while she lifted their bracelets or gently released diamonds from their settings. She made sure that her brilliant red hair (a temporary dye over her more usual strawberry blonde that would wash out in a few days) was more memorable than her face, and she was an expert at deflection.

If they recalled her with suspicion when they eventually discovered their loss, there was nothing to trace back to her. She wasn't on the guest list, and Patty Cakes hadn't even gotten the contract for the event!

Tainting Anita's cupcakes would have acted as a diversion, a topic of conversation, and taken her pseudo-rival out of the picture, all in one neat package.

Once she'd forced a little more charity than they had in mind, she'd be off on the wing with her prizes, and richer by a lot.

Instead, she'd had to witness the world's most awkward courtship and come away completely empty-handed.

Harriet liked things hot or cold. Drinking water should be a degree from freezing and bath water should be a degree from boiling alive. That was the bath she stepped into now, hissing a little as she slipped gingerly down into it until she was completely covered up to her chin.

Slowly, her tense body began to relax and Harriet wadded a washcloth up to lean her head against.

She had a great life and a thrilling career. She had no reason to be jealous of someone like Anita, who was silly and boring. So what if Frank was a well-built billionaire who'd known at once that she was his mate?

Harriet hadn't intended to eavesdrop, but an owl's hearing was almost as keen as their eyesight and it had been hard to miss their exuberant exchanges in the quiet hall.

It bothered her exactly how much she longed for the kind of connection that she'd witnessed. She was tough and independent... and she came home to a house that was echoing empty.

Was it possible that there was someone out there who could fill that emptiness? Someone for *her*?

She blew impatient ripples on the surface of the water.

*Who?* her owl asked wistfully.

*Who* indeed.

# A SNEAK PREVIEW OF GNOME
# SWEET GNOME...

Tobias knew that people often wondered if he wasn't just joking about being a gnome because of his height. At five foot and no spare change, he was usually the shortest person in the room, and the shortest man by far.

He let them think that he was just saying it for a laugh, using the easy quips to break the ice and make sure that no one thought he took his own stature too seriously. He wasn't ashamed of his height, and he used other people's reactions to it as a measuring stick of character. Women who knew what they wanted would want him, and other men usually betrayed their own insecurities by realizing that he was everything that they wished they were.

But his gnome heritage was no joke at all, and that meant dutifully grooming every morning.

Tobias stared at his shaggy reflection. Every morning, his eyebrows needed to be clipped close to the skin. They looked thin when he was done with them in the morning, and by noon they were ordinary eyebrows. By evening, they were bushy and unkempt again. He usually maintained a beard, cutting a few inches off of it every morning, because it was easier than explaining why his five-o'clock shadow was a rug that few men could grow at all.

He kept his hair long, fine, and blonde like his Scandinavian ancestors, and trimmed it frequently to just past his shoulders. When he shaved it off altogether, he was barely bald for a day, sprouting to a buzzcut by that night. In a few days, he was scruffy, and in a week, he was in "get a job, hippy!" territory. He had grown it to his waist briefly in college, but it had been unruly at that length, so he preferred it somewhat tamed.

Fortunately, it was only the hair on his head that was so super-charged; the rest of his body had a decent dusting of curly hair, but it didn't tend to be quite so *take-over-the-world* as the follicles in his face.

There was a handsome face beneath the hair, Tobias knew, and sometimes he shaved clean just because he liked the effect it had on people of both sexes.

Today…Tobias fingered his beard. It was on the long side right now, and Frank had been making noises about having him play a Christmas elf at the rescheduled charity gala that evening.

"Now that it's so late in the year anyway, we should lean into the season," the flamingo shifter had said.

"Candy cane cupcakes!" his new mate, Anita, exclaimed in joy. "And gingerbread!"

Tobias liked Anita, in small doses. She was pretty intense and excitable, and Frank was absolutely swept away by her, going along with every crazy plan that she came up with. Fortunately, her inter-ference seemed to be limited to refreshments, and Tobias was relieved that she seemed to have very little interest in Frank's busi-ness management or in his money at all.

Tobias told himself that he wasn't jealous. He was a gnome of the noblest lineage, fabulously wealthy, devastatingly handsome, and brilliant to boot. What did he care if his best friend had a new favorite person?

He'd known about shifter mates, but he hadn't really believed in them until he saw how Frank looked at Anita, like she was the other half of his soul. Tobias knew what infatuation was, and he was skilled in reading people; this wasn't empty attraction or passing fancy. Frank was head-over-heels for the curly-haired baker, absolutely smitten, to the bottom of his big, pink, flamingo heart.

Tobias didn't need that. He didn't want to be anchored to a single person like that, attached at the hip to just one woman. It wasn't like he was lonely or unfulfilled. He picked up the heavy-duty trimmer (he had a dozen of them, and went through them like most people went through flossers) and frowned at his reflection. This gala would attract the most important people in the city, and he was one of them. He had an image to maintain.

Sometimes, he feared that image was all that he had.

Continue the story in Gnome Sweet Gnome...

# FROM ELVA'S DESK...

I am so grateful that you picked up this collection. Whether you're a brand new reader, or doing a re-read, I get to keep writing my whimsical and wacky ideas because you pick my books up! I hope that you enjoyed this glimpse at all of my many worlds, and that they've given you a happy escape and a little joy.

I would love a review if you enjoyed this set (I read all my reviews!), and please feel free to reach out at any time to elvaher self@elvabirch.com. Sign up to my mailing list for updates and sales, or join my friendly Reader's Retreat on Facebook!

Love recklessly,
Elva Birch

# MORE BY ELVA BIRCH

Get a free Shifting Sands Resort short story, Not Kitten Around, at my webpage!

Want some more extra short stories, including a Shifting Sands Resort ménage? Join my mailing list for sneak previews, extras, bonus stories, and more, or join my Reader's Retreat on Facebook!

~

**A Day Care for Shifters**: A hot new full-length series about adorable shifter kids and their struggling single parents in a town full of mystery and surprise. Start the series with Wolf's Instinct, when Addison comes to Nickel City to take a job at a very special day care and finds a family to belong to. A gentle ice-cream-straight-from-the-container escape. Sweet and sizzling!

~

**The Royal Dragons of Alaska**: A fascinating alternate world where Alaska is ruled by secret dragon shifters. Adventure, romance, and humor! Reluctant royalty, relentless enemies...dogs, camping, and magic! Start with The Dragon Prince of Alaska.

~

**Suddenly Shifters**: A hilarious series of novellas, serials, and shorts set in the small town of Anders Canyon, where something (in the water?) is making ordinary citizens turn into shifters. Start with Something in the Water!

~

**Birch Hearts**: An enchanting collection of short stories and novellas. Unconstrained by theme or setting, each short read has romance, magic, and heart, with a satisfying conclusion. And always, the impossible and irresistible. Start with a sampler plate in Prompted 2 for fourteen pieces of sweet-to-sizzling flash fiction, or dive in with the novella, Better Half. Breakup is a free story!

# WRITING AS ZOE CHANT

**Shifting Sands Resort**: A complete ten-book series - plus two collections of shorts. This is a thrilling shifter romance set at a tropical island resort. Each book stands alone but connects into a great mystery with a thrilling conclusion. Start with Tropical Tiger Spy or dive in to the Omnibus edition, with all of the novels, short stories, and novellas in my preferred reading order! This series crosses over with Fire and Rescue Shifters and Shifter Kingdom.

∾

**Fae Shifter Knights**: A complete four-book fantasy portal romp, with cute pets and swoon-worthy knights stuck in a world of wonders like refrigerators and ham sandwiches. Start with Dragon of Glass!

∾

**Green Valley Shifters**: A sweet, small town series with single dads, secret shifters, sweet kids, and spinsters. Low-peril and steamy!

Standalone books where you can revisit your favorite characters. Start with Dancing Barefoot!

~

**Virtue Shifters**: Sexy and funny, each book set in the little town of Virtue promises a heartwarming story, a touch of fate, and a little bit of adventure. This series crosses over with Green Valley Shifters! Start with Timber Wolf!

# BEHIND THE SCENES

## What is Patreon?

*Patreon is a site where readers and fans can support creators with monthly subscriptions.*

At my Patreon, I have tiers with early rough drafts of my books, flash fiction, coloring pages, signed and sketched paperbacks, exclusive swag, original artwork, photographs…and so much more! Every month is a little different, and there is a price for every budget. Patreon allows me to do projects that aren't very commercial and makes my income stream a little less unpredictable. It also gives me a place to connect with my fans!

Come find out what's going on behind the scenes and keep me creating at Patreon! patreon.com/ellenmillion